THE
RIGHT HAND
OF GOD

BOOKS BY GILBERT MORRIS

Through a Glass Darkly

THE HOUSE OF WINSLOW SERIES

1. *The Honorable Imposter*
2. *The Captive Bride*
3. *The Indentured Heart*
4. *The Gentle Rebel*
5. *The Saintly Buccaneer*
6. *The Holy Warrior*
7. *The Reluctant Bridegroom*
8. *The Last Confederate*
9. *The Dixie Widow*
10. *The Wounded Yankee*
11. *The Union Belle*
12. *The Final Adversary*
13. *The Crossed Sabres*
14. *The Valiant Gunman*
15. *The Gallant Outlaw*
16. *The Jeweled Spur*
17. *The Yukon Queen*
18. *The Rough Rider*
19. *The Iron Lady*
20. *The Silver Star*
21. *The Shadow Portrait*
22. *The White Hunter*
23. *The Flying Cavalier*

THE LIBERTY BELL

1. *Sound the Trumpet*
2. *Song in a Strange Land*
3. *Tread Upon the Lion*
4. *Arrow of the Almighty*
5. *Wind From the Wilderness*
6. *The Right Hand of God*

CHENEY DUVALL, M.D.
(with Lynn Morris)

1. *The Stars for a Light*
2. *Shadow of the Mountains*
3. *A City Not Forsaken*
4. *Toward the Sunrising*
5. *Secret Place of Thunder*
6. *In the Twilight, in the Evening*
7. *Island of the Innocent*

THE SPIRIT OF APPALACHIA
(with Aaron McCarver)

1. *Over the Misty Mountains*
2. *Beyond the Quiet Hills*
3. *Among the King's Soldiers*
4. *Beneath the Mockingbird's Wings*

TIME NAVIGATORS
(for Young Teens)

1. *Dangerous Voyage*
2. *Vanishing Clues*
3. *Race Against Time*

THE RIGHT HAND OF GOD

GILBERT MORRIS

BETHANY HOUSE PUBLISHERS

MINNEAPOLIS, MINNESOTA 55438

The Right Hand of God
Copyright © 1999
Gilbert Morris

Cover illustration by Chris Ellison
Cover design by the Lookout Design Group

Published by Bethany House Publishers
A Ministry of Bethany Fellowship International
11400 Hampshire Avenue South
Minneapolis, Minnesota 55438
www.bethanyhouse.com

Printed in the United States of America by
Bethany Press International, Minneapolis, Minnesota 55438

Library of Congress Cataloging-in-Publication Data

Morris, Gilbert.
    The right hand of God / by Gilbert Morris.
        p. cm. — (The Liberty Bell series ; bk. 6)

    ISBN 1–55661–570–1
    1. United States—History—Revolution, 1775–1783 Fiction.
2. United States—History—Revolution, 1775–1783—Participation,
German Fiction. 3. Hessian mercenaries Fiction. I. Title. II. Series:
Morris, Gilbert. Liberty Bell ; bk. 6
PS3563.O8742 R54   1999

                                                                99–6388
                                                                CIP

To Lucile Montgomery—

a lady after my own heart!
Full of grace and truth—
and one of the most entertaining human beings
I've ever known.

GILBERT MORRIS spent ten years as a pastor before becoming Professor of English at Ouachita Baptist University in Arkansas and earning a Ph.D. at the University of Arkansas. During the summers of 1984 and 1985, he did postgraduate work at the University of London. A prolific writer, he has had over twenty-five scholarly articles and two hundred poems published in various periodicals, and over the past years, he has had more than seventy novels published. His family includes three grown children, and he and his wife live in Alabama.

CONTENTS

PART FOUR
The Soldier
March–July 1778

THE LIBERTY BELL

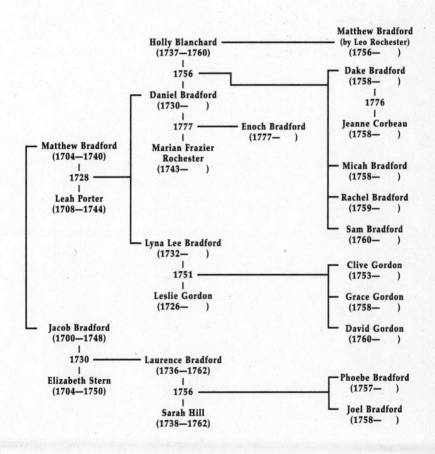

Matthew Bradford
(by Leo Rochester)
(1756—   )

Holly Blanchard
(1737—1760)

1756

Dake Bradford
(1758—   )

1776

Jeanne Corbeau
(1758—   )

Daniel Bradford
(1730—   )

1777 —— Enoch Bradford
(1777—   )

Marian Frazier
Rochester
(1743—   )

Micah Bradford
(1758—   )

Rachel Bradford
(1759—   )

Sam Bradford
(1760—   )

Matthew Bradford
(1704—1740)

1728

Leah Porter
(1708—1744)

Lyna Lee Bradford
(1732—   )

1751

Leslie Gordon
(1726—   )

Clive Gordon
(1753—   )

Grace Gordon
(1758—   )

David Gordon
(1760—   )

Jacob Bradford
(1700—1748)

1730 —— Laurence Bradford
(1736—1762)

1756

Sarah Hill
(1738—1762)

Elizabeth Stern
(1704—1750)

Phoebe Bradford
(1757—   )

Joel Bradford
(1758—   )

PART ONE

THE HESSIAN

May–November 1777

1

A Bitter Choice

JACOB STEINER HAD NEVER BEEN HAPPIER in his entire life! The marble-paneled music chamber in the palace of the Prussian capital of Berlin resounded with the strains of Boccherini's String Quartet in C Major. The ensemble, of which Jacob was a member, was seated in small giltwood chairs with crimson velvet upholstery, and there was a mounting crescendo as they neared the end of the final movement. The fingers of Jacob's left hand rose and fell swiftly on the strings of the violin, while with his right, he drew the bow skillfully, bringing forth exquisite sound from the instrument.

It was the most rewarding moment of his life and one toward which he had plotted with desperate intensity for years. None of the Steiners had ever been anything but farmers, and Jacob's father, Franz, had bitterly opposed his son's tenacious insistence on becoming a musician. A sudden thought swept through Jacob's mind as they reached the penultimate crescendo and the room swelled with the sounds of the instruments. *I've had to fight almost every day of my life to get to this hour.* An overwhelming sense of triumph filled him, for he knew now that his battle was won. His music teacher, Hans Conreid, had told him with glowing eyes, "Your future is made, my son. Once you have played in the capital under the maestro, your true value will be appreciated. You will never have to plow another field as long as you live!"

Jacob's eyes swept across the audience, spread throughout the large, magnificently furnished room. The women's gowns made flashes of blazing color—crimson, emerald green, sky blue—all the colors of the rainbow. The men were more sedately dressed in dark clothing. Even as he watched, he saw the approval in the eyes of the minister of cultural affairs, Paul Van Dow. Van Dow was a tall man with tremendous influence in the Prussian court and a fervent lover of music. Jacob had never met him, of course, but he had heard of Van Dow's interest in young musicians and offered up a prayer, *Oh, God, let me find favor in his sight!*

Finally the piece ended on a deep, vibrating chord, and the room exploded with the applause and delighted cries of the audience. Jacob's heart was beating fast as he lowered his violin and, at a sign from the maestro, arose with the other musicians. As they had practiced, they bowed simultaneously to the distinguished audience. The applause continued to rise, and finally the maestro whispered, "We will do the Haydn for our final number."

It was a piece that Jacob particularly loved, and he threw himself into his playing, as he always did, with gusto and a vehement spirit. His teacher had rebuked him often, saying, "You must mind your manners, Jacob, and do not be so rough with your instrument. She is like a loving wife, my son, and will respond most warmly if you treat her with the utmost tenderness."

Music to Jacob was indeed a lifelong passion, a relationship not unlike the bond a man feels to the woman he loves. His life was consumed by his love for it. At the age of six, he had first picked up a violin that belonged to his uncle and had somehow sensed from that moment that music was his destiny. His mother, Maria, had encouraged his gift, procuring the services of an able music teacher and overseeing the boy's daily practice times. By the time he had reached adolescence, he could play so excellently that he was always invited to join the musicals in the villages of Hesse-Cassel. He had become quite well known in the region, and some had even linked his name with the great musicians Haydn and Handel.

None of this, however, had influenced his father, Franz, who had said with typical German stubbornness, "My son is to be a farmer, not a fiddle master!"

Now as Jacob rose and watched the distinguished audience file out, he thought, *Surely, Father won't object now.* He heard his name called and turned to see the maestro standing before him. He was a towering, corpulent man with brilliant blue eyes that seemed to flash when he was conducting.

"Fine! You played very well tonight, Steiner."

"Thank you, maestro. You are most kind."

"I could see that Van Dow was impressed. I will mention your name, and perhaps he will want to meet you. He's very fond of encouraging the best of the young German musicians."

"I would be most grateful, sir," Jacob said, and his heart beat faster at the thought of what might come as a result of this concert.

"Keep yourself available."

For two days Jacob stayed in Berlin, anxiously awaiting word from the maestro. In the end he was disappointed, for he did not have an audience with Van Dow, who was called away on official business. Jacob spent most of his time either practicing or wandering the streets of Berlin. It was May of 1777, and spring had come to the Prussian capital in a riotous blaze of colors. The streets were lined with flowers, and the trees put forth their buds in a profligate fashion. Jacob had never been to Berlin before and was stunned at the size of the city. His own village of Pelsen in Hesse-Cassel could have fit in one city block.

As he walked along the broad boulevards listening to the sounds of the great city, breathing in its aromas, and sensing the excitement, he said under his breath, "If I could come here and play in the symphony, I would ask nothing else of God." He stopped to buy two apples from a vendor, munching on them as he continued on his way. They were good, but not as good as the ones that were in the Steiner orchard. Jacob soon found himself in the shop district of Berlin. He counted out the little money he had saved and took the rest of the afternoon spending his small store on gifts for his family. For his mother, Maria, he bought a brilliantly colored scarf. For his younger sister, Anna, he argued and bartered for over an hour and finally succeeded in buying a blouse in her favorite shade of bright blue. Hilda, his sixteen-year-old sister, was also fond of bright colors, but for her he decided on a pair of tiny gold earrings. His father's gift was more difficult. He searched the bookstores and finally found a book on raising a better strain of chickens. *Not a very romantic gift, but then, Father's not very romantic. He's more interested in chickens than he is in his son's ambitions*, he thought with just a trace of bitterness.

A few days later he ran into the maestro, who, with regret, informed Jacob, "I do not think that Van Dow will be back for some time."

"Do you think I can secure a post in the symphony, maestro?" Jacob held his breath as he watched the older man frown. He knew it was the maestro's decision to choose among all the young German musicians and recommend which ones would become apprenticed, and there were many who would give anything to obtain such a post. Young Jacob felt as though his life hung in the balance as he waited for the answer. He swallowed down the rising fear that he would never achieve his goal. At the age of twenty-six he was very tall, six feet two, with a lean but muscular build, hardened by years of hard work and farming. The maestro studied the face of this handsome young man with light blond

15

hair, the color of straw in the fields in harvesttime, and piercing blue eyes. There was a Nordic appearance about Jacob Steiner, with his strong jaw, broad forehead, and skin so fair that he burned crimson at the first rays of summer.

The maestro finally said, "I will be able to tell you something more in two weeks. Go home, Steiner, and wait. I will do my best for you." A broad smile suddenly creased the musician's face. "You are my own choice—and my choices are usually respected."

Relief washed through Steiner like a flood, and he expelled his breath. "Thank you, sir! Thank you so much! I will be waiting for your letter." He shook hands warmly with the man who held his future and then returned to his boardinghouse. It was still early in the morning, and there was no point in paying for his room for another day. He carefully packed his meager belongings in a worn canvas case, then even more carefully packed his violin in the lined leather case that he had made himself and left his room. He had only enough money for passage on the coach for home.

Later that day he was seated inside watching the countryside roll by. He had no eye for the fat cattle that lined the roadside, nor the blossoming orchards riotous in white and pink bloom. His thoughts were all on the letter that would come soon, asking him to return and become a professional musician. As the coach rattled over the road, raising great plumes of dust behind it, Jacob's jaw tightened. "Father can't say no to this. He just can't!"

The coach stopped at almost every village, it seemed, so the progress was slow. Jacob grew sleepy late that afternoon and wedged himself against the side of the coach. Placing his head against the leather side, he dozed off. He was semiconscious as the coach stopped to let people off and enter, and finally a loud voice woke him from his fitful sleep.

"*Ja*, it is settled. He's going to do it."

Jacob opened his eyes to see a small, prosperous-appearing man sitting directly across from him. He had a set of obviously false teeth that flashed and glittered and a huge gold chain big enough to anchor a ship. When he pulled out his watch, it was the largest one Jacob had ever seen. As Jacob listened he discovered the man's name was Ridel. His companion sitting beside him was named Streuben. Streuben was as large as his companion was small. He was corpulent, with huge jowls that quivered as the coach rattled over stones and dropped into potholes. He also was dressed in an expensive-looking suit. Jacob listened as the two talked about politics. Actually politics appealed very little to Jacob Steiner, for he found the issues confusing. German-speaking peoples were loosely governed by nearly three hundred sovereignties scattered all over the territory. Some were no bigger than a township, but each had its own little court army, and the smaller ones were ruled over by threadbare princes who had little in the way of national treasure but pride. The great city of Berlin was the capital of the kingdom of Prussia, but Jacob felt no allegiance to the Prussian king. All German sovereignties, large and small, were under the banner of the Holy Roman Empire, but the emperor seemed to Jacob to have little to do with the day-to-day lives of those he supposedly governed.

Franz Steiner often rebuked Jacob for taking so little interest, saying, "You are wrong, Jacob. What the emperor decides *does* affect the way we live. You must pay more attention." Jacob, however, could not fathom how his paying attention would have any influence at all on the emperor, or upon the local ruler, or "landgrave," of Hesse-Cassel. As far as Jacob could fathom, the man's only accomplishment in life was fathering children—more than one hundred, it was rumored, in and out of wedlock. The present landgrave was a descendant of a seventeenth-century landgrave who had conceived the bright idea of renting out his army to the highest bidder. The soldier-renting business became popular, and many of the small sovereignties looked upon it as a respectable occupation. The problem was that men were sold into service like cattle, not hired of their own free will. It was an abominable system and one political idea that Jacob Steiner hated vehemently. Now as the two men began to talk of this very subject, Jacob opened his eyes and listened more carefully.

"I tell you it's a foul, obscene system!" the small man said. "You know it, Streuben. You just won't admit it. Why, in the War of the Austrian Succession, George II hired six thousand Hessians, and they did battle against a like number of their own countrymen. Tell me, where's the sense in that?"

"I don't say it makes sense," Streuben shrugged, causing the fat to ripple down his cheeks. "I only say that we're a poor country and we have to take what we can get."

"Nonsense!" Ridel snorted. "It's an immoral thing! It's making slaves of our own citizens!"

"They're not slaves."

"Not slaves! Of course they're slaves! Suppose someone forced you into an army and made you fight against France or some other nation. You'd have no say, would you?"

"Well, perhaps not, but that's the way things are," Streuben said.

Ridel squirmed in his seat, and his eyes suddenly met those of Jacob

Steiner. "Well, young man," he said. "What do you think about all this?"

"Me, sir?"

"Yes. How old are you?"

"I'm twenty-six, sir."

"How would you feel about it if you were forced to serve in an army?"

"I wouldn't like it, sir."

"There! You see? No one would like it," Ridel said triumphantly. He leaned forward and began to lecture Jacob Steiner, hoping, perhaps, to find a more receptive audience for his views. "Did you know that George III of England submitted a bid of seven pounds each for twenty thousand soldiers to Catherine the Great of Russia?"

"No, sir. I didn't know that."

"Well, he did. And what's more she said no. Do you know what that means? The fact that the English king cannot get soldiers from Russia?"

"Why no, sir, I don't."

"It means he'll be coming over here to hire his mercenaries to do his filthy business."

Streuben asked, "Who is England fighting now? France or Spain?"

"Why, neither. Don't you ever read the papers? They're having a rebellion over in America. King George III has sent the largest army he's ever raised to fight his own colonists. They call themselves Americans."

"Indeed! Well, that'll be the end of that."

"I'd not be so sure!" Ridel snapped. "But that's their business. My business as a German is to see to it that our own citizens are not involved in these foreign wars. We need our men here to work the farms. If we send them all over to be killed by the Americans, who will do the plowing?"

For some time Jacob listened as the two argued about politics. Finally the coach arrived at Pelsen. Jacob scrambled out holding his violin case, then turned to catch the canvas bag the driver carelessly tossed down to him. He walked through the single large street in the village, speaking to the people he had known all of his life. The farm was located two miles out of town, and by the time he arrived, darkness was beginning to close in. The farm itself was set back off the road about a quarter of a mile, and it warmed his heart to see the yellow square of light that marked the windows of the house. As he drew nearer, he was greeted by two large shepherd dogs that leaped upon him, barking and trying to lick his face. "Down, Brutus! Down, Prince!" he said but leaned over to give them a rough caress. "You're glad to see me, are you? Well, I'm glad to see you, too. You'll have to be more respectful now. I'm a famous musician." Laughing, he moved toward the door, which opened and was filled with the large form of his father.

"Oh, it's you, Jacob," Franz Steiner said. "You're late."

It was as good a greeting as Jacob had expected, for his father could never hide his displeasure with Jacob's choice of profession. "Yes, I'm late, but I have good news."

"Jacob!" Maria Steiner rushed out. She was a tall woman with large bones and a face that was durable rather than beautiful. As a matter of fact, Jacob's own rough features had been his inheritance from his mother. She threw her arms around him, and he hugged her, pulling her off her feet. "I'm so glad you're back, son," she said. "Come in. I'll have something on the table for you."

"Did you bring us anything?" Anna Steiner had come out and was pulling at Jacob. At the age of thirteen, she had the beginnings of beauty.

Her sister, Hilda, soon joined her but rebuked Anna. "You shouldn't be asking for presents."

"Jacob doesn't mind, do you?"

Anna was Jacob's favorite, and he laughed as he picked her up. "I have a little something," he said.

"Come in. You must be starved," Maria said. She pulled at Jacob, and soon he was seated at the table with a bowl of steaming potato soup and a large slice of dark homemade bread. He ate hungrily, for he had been able to afford only the most meager of meals while he was gone. He listened as Anna prattled on, telling of what she had done while he was away, and finally at the end of the meal, he opened his traveling bag and passed out the presents he had brought. Jacob saw that he had chosen well for his mother. She smiled as she put the colorful scarf over her head and tied a knot. When she turned to him, her blue eyes were filled with approval.

"You shouldn't have spent your money on us," she said, shaking her head.

"Oh, these are beautiful!" Hilda said. She was fastening the gold earrings and turned her head for his approval. "How do they look?"

"You look like a princess." Jacob smiled.

Anna had gone off at once to try on her blouse. She came back and turned around, preening for all to see. "How do I look?" she demanded.

"Like a young woman should look," Jacob said. "Beautiful indeed."

He turned to his father, who was sitting in his chair reading the new book on improving the breeding of chickens. He saw his father's thick fingers turn the pages as he peered at the print. They all waited for some response. Finally Franz Steiner looked up and said grudgingly, "Ja, this is a good book. I have heard of it but could not afford it. How much did it cost?"

It was typical that his father should have asked that. He was a strong man but worn down by years of struggling against poverty. Jews were not accepted by most people, and Jacob's parents had known what it was to be persecuted for their faith. Franz himself never attended religious services, but Maria's father had been a rabbi in Russia, where he had died in a hateful massacre of his Jewish village. Maria herself had barely escaped with her life. She had immigrated to Germany, where she had married Franz, despite the fact that he called himself an atheist. It was Maria who kept the children aware of their Jewish heritage and had stirred a faith in Jehovah God in all of their hearts.

After opening Jacob's presents, the family sat around the room that served as a kitchen, dining room, and living area. There was one bedroom in the back and two upstairs under the steep, slanting roof. Anna and Hilda shared one, while Jacob slept in the other.

Jacob was tired from his journey and he went to bed early, as did the others. Being farmers, the Steiners usually went to bed as early as possible and rose before daybreak to attend to the morning chores.

Before climbing into bed, Jacob stood at the window staring out at the stars overhead. He had learned from the schoolmaster to identify some of the constellations, and he quickly found the Big Dipper. The handle of it pointed down to the brightest star in the sky, which he knew was called Arcturus. Below that the second brightest star he viewed was called Spica. He loved looking at the stars, and by using the cup of the Big Dipper, he found the constellation Leo and tried to see in it the figure of the lion. Finally he knelt beside his bed, as he had done every night since his mother had taught him to do so, and said, "Oh, God, I thank you for a safe journey. I pray you will soften my father's heart. Let him agree to allow me to follow my heart and become a musician!"

🔔   🔔   🔔

The two weeks that followed were agony for Jacob Steiner, for he could not put the matter of the letter out of his mind. He had told his father of the maestro's offer, but Franz Steiner had immediately narrowed his eyes. "You will not be a musician. You will be a farmer."

Arguments had not availed and the situation had grown tense. Franz had purchased a new flock of chickens, and Jacob spent his days building hen houses for them. He looked down often at his hands, which were hard from years of manual labor, and knew that every time he drove a stake in the ground or nailed a board he was taking away some of the sensitivity and flexibility that enabled him to play.

Once his mother said, "Try not to hate your father. He cannot understand music. To him it is frivolous."

"I know, Mama," Jacob said quietly. "But if I get the offer, you understand I will have to go. It's my life. I can't stay here raising chickens. There's nothing wrong with that, but somehow I know I've got to do something else."

By the end of the second week, Jacob was almost in despair. He had great confidence in the maestro, but the final decision was not in his hands. "At least he will write and tell me I have not been invited to join the symphony," he said as he came in late one evening after a day's hard work. When he stepped into the house, he saw his father standing beside the table with an odd look in his eyes. He knew his father was not a man to worry or given to fears. There was something in his attitude that caused Jacob to ask, "What is it, Father?"

The girls were apparently up in their room, and Maria came over to stand beside her husband. She looked up at him, and when he did not answer, she whispered, "Herr Lieberman was burned out today. The house and all the barns. They have nothing left."

A chill went over Jacob. There was no need for his mother to explain. They all knew who had done this to their Jewish neighbors. The warnings had gone out to all of the Jews in their small farming community, but the Steiners had brushed such threats off as the rantings of young hotheads out to cause trouble. After all, the Steiners were no different from their German neighbors. They were simple farmers trying to eke out a living. They did not even look Jewish but displayed the light complexion and blue eyes typical of northern Europeans. They could not understand why others feared their Jewish ancestry so much. Jacob had never experienced any real persecution himself, but he had heard his mother tell of the terror of it in Russia. There had always been an anti-Semitic atmosphere in Hesse-Cassel, but it was relatively mild. Now when he saw the fear in his father's eyes, Jacob asked, "What does this mean for us, Father?"

Franz shook his head. "It could mean death."

"No, it cannot mean that!" Maria said. "They are just trying to drive us out. At the worst we would have to leave here."

"Where would we go? Everything we own is here." Franz Steiner's voice trembled as he looked at his wife in growing disbelief at the enormity of this news.

Jacob blurted out, "Yes, Mama is right, Father. Maybe we could simply sell the farm and go somewhere else."

But Franz Steiner was a stubborn man. Pulling himself to his full height, his voice once again steady and strong, he said, "No, I will never leave here. They will have to kill me first."

🔔　　🔔　　🔔

Six days after the Steiners had heard about the torching of the Lieberman farm, Jacob was returning home from the village carrying a load of supplies. He saw horses and soldiers drawn up in front of his house, and a terrible dread shot through him. He felt tempted to simply turn and run, but there was no place to flee. As he advanced, the six soldiers outside, dressed in crimson uniforms and carrying muskets, looked at him without much interest. They did not speak, nor did Jacob speak to them. He stepped inside and saw a short, fat lieutenant standing in the center of the room. He examined Jacob callously.

"Is this your son?"

Maria came over at once to stand beside Jacob and faced the officer. "Yes."

"You are now conscripted into the Prussian army. You will leave with us now."

Jacob could not believe what he was hearing. He stammered, "Why . . . what does this—"

"You cannot take him," Maria cried. "He is not a soldier."

The lieutenant grinned cynically. "He is now, woman! If you have anything to bring with you," he said carelessly, "then now is the time to get it."

"Please, you cannot take my son," Franz said.

The lieutenant's eyes were cold and almost the color of pewter. His mouth tightened, and he said, "Frederick II has agreed to provide twelve thousand soldiers. Your son will be one of them. There is no point in discussing it."

"I won't go!" Jacob said loudly.

The lieutenant fixed his eyes on Jacob. His voice lowered to a threat. "You will go or else your family will be deported. Your mother comes from Russia. They will all be sent back there to live."

Jacob knew how hard it would be for his family if they had to give up their livelihood here and try to survive in Russia. They would be penniless. He looked at his parents, and everything in him cried out to say no. He looked over at his sisters and thought of them suffering the horrors of poverty.

A silence fell over the room, and Jacob Steiner knew with a leaden feeling that he had a bitter choice. He looked at his parents and said, "I will have to go."

"Make your farewells quickly!" the lieutenant snapped. "We'll wait outside."

Maria came over weeping and held on to her son. Over her shoulder Jacob saw his father standing there, bitterness etched on his face. "You see," he said, "there's no God. If there were, He would not let this happen."

Anna and Hilda had come, and they also clung to Jacob. Jacob was stunned like a man who had fallen from a far height and struck the ground with great force. The only life he knew was over. He had heard of the horrors of being a soldier from those few who had come back, and his heart was overwhelmed with despair.

Maria Steiner was a woman of strength, and now she whispered in his ear, "God will take care of you. You will be safe."

Ten minutes later Jacob was stumbling along in front of the six soldiers with the lieutenant in front of him. In one brief moment, his dream to become a musician had been dashed to pieces. He thought, *The letter will probably come this week, but I won't be here. I will never have what I want most in all the world.*

The sound of the soldiers' measured pace on the cobblestones as they marched down the center of the street was like a funeral dirge to Jacob Steiner. He was aware that many were looking at him. Some jeered, and one voice cried out, "Now, Jew, see how you like shedding your blood for the emperor."

2

Death in a Far Field

MISERY SUCH AS HE HAD NEVER KNOWN had descended upon Jacob Steiner. He had never been farther than ten miles from his home except for his one trip to Berlin. His world had been the farm, the fields, the streams, and the low ridges that grew into great mountains in the far distance. Now to be snatched from all of that and thrown into a mercenary life that he could not understand and could hardly bear had taken the heart out of him.

It had all started when he had been herded with eleven other young men from the village into a camp designed, it seemed to him, to break one's spirit. Not all of them were young. One man was over forty and had cried piteously, stumbling all the way to the camp. The sergeant had repeatedly struck the man with a baton, but it made no difference. He seemed not even to feel it. His name was Leo Schmidt. He was not a healthy man, but the lieutenant had jeered, "He'll do enough to fill a trench with cannon fodder, my boys. Cannon fodder."

Since Leo was the one man who seemed at least as miserable as he was, Jacob drew near to him. "Bear up, Leo," he said. "We'll survive this and come back home."

"No. We'll die in America. We'll never see our home again," Schmidt moaned.

"Quiet in the ranks there!" Lieutenant Hart came along and slashed out with his quirt. It struck Jacob across the back of the neck and he flinched. He looked up at the officer, anger in his eyes. But Hart only laughed. "Well, I'm glad to see you have some spirit in you. What's your name?"

"Jacob Steiner."

"Jacob Steiner, *sir!*" Another flick of the whip caught Jacob across the face, and he reeled backward.

25

"Stand in line!" Hart said. "Bring these men along! They're loitering."

That day's march was a nightmare. They camped outside and were fed only a small bowl of rice with a few crusts of bread. All night long the wind howled, and there was no cover, so Jacob crouched and hugged himself. Though fortunately it was June, Jacob thought bitterly, *It would all be the same, even if it were in the dead of winter.*

The next day they reached a training camp where they were put under the command of a sergeant named Mosel. "More recruits for you, Mosel," Lieutenant Hart said. "See that they shape up."

"I hear we will be leaving soon. They're loading the ships already. There won't be much time to train them, sir."

"Do the best you can, Sergeant."

"Yes, sir."

The army that Jacob was thrown into was, perhaps, typical of the armies of the day. The officers came from the aristocracy, but the enlisted men came from the lowest dregs of society. Many of them turned out to be criminals faced with a choice of jail or service with the Hessian forces.

They all had one thing in common, Jacob soon found out, and that was misery. It became his daily companion. The uniform that at first had pleased some of the men soon became a nightmare. It was splendid to look at but miserably uncomfortable, especially in hot weather. The scarlet coat, the white belt, the white britches, the knee-high gaiters, and the cocked hat all had to be brushed and piped constantly. He also had to clean his weapons thoroughly, so that the few days before setting sail were filled with grinding labor. When he was not working on his uniform, he was subjected to the brutal discipline of how to load and fire his musket or how to form ranks. He and his fellow soldiers were also forced to learn the drumbeat patterns that would signal the various commands of the officers.

Military discipline is only possible by the threat of punishment, and the Hessian system was severely cruel. The lash was the most common, and Jacob saw one man suffer five hundred lashes across his back with a cat-o'-nine-tails for insulting an officer. So many men had their backs scarred and bloodied in the British army that they were called "lobsterbacks."

It was like being in a prison camp. No man could leave, no man could speak unless he was given permission, and the slightest infraction was punished with a rigid cruelty that made Jacob shudder.

The brief training included carrying enormous loads while wearing heavy, uncomfortable clothing. Sometimes the packs weighed up to one hundred and twenty-five pounds, and some of the men collapsed under them. The weight of their packs came from clothing, cleaning equipment, blankets, the fifth part of a tent, a haversack filled with rations, a canteen, a box of sixty cartridges, a short sword, a bayonet, and a musket.

The musket was a joke. It was called the "Brown Bess," referring back to Queen Elizabeth. Sergeant Mosel, during the drill, said, "You can kill a man at three hundred yards with this." But this proved to be a fallacy. A ball from a Brown Bess fell harmlessly to the ground at no more than one hundred fifty feet. In addition to this, it was practically of no use when the wind was blowing, for the wind would blow the powder out of the pan or would whip the flash out of the touch hole into a man's face or eyes—or the rain could wash away the powder. It was enormously uncomfortable to handle, at five feet long and weighing fourteen pounds. It fired a round leaded ball weighing about an ounce, and during the brief time of training, Jacob learned the twelve movements necessary to load and fire. It was slow and painstaking, and Mosel insisted a good marksman could fire five times a minute. Jacob knew this was a lie and so did the others who had been sucked into the net of the Hessian army.

Day after day he would fire his Brown Bess. It was not worth much for fire power, but it was used basically as a platform for a bayonet. The volley was designed to frighten the enemy, and then the bayonet charge would be ordered by the officers. The sergeant drilled them over and over again to scream at the top of their lungs. "You will frighten them!" he said. "You will see their backs, and a bayonet in the back is as good as a bullet in the brain!"

And so the training went on. The food was terrible, the fear of the battle was a constant pressure on Jacob's mind, and at night he found himself wanting to weep for his lost home. He bit his lip, but he heard others crying, including Leo Schmidt, who cried constantly.

����������☣ ☣ ☣

The crossing of the Atlantic was even more of a nightmare for the ill-prepared troops. The ship was an old one that wallowed in the waves, throwing its passengers wildly to one side, even during the mildest of breezes.

Jacob had been crammed belowdecks, and the stench of unwashed bodies, waste matter, and the bilge itself was enough to sicken him. He wedged himself against the curving side, and Leo Schmidt settled down beside him. Schmidt had eaten practically nothing for weeks, and his shrunken flesh clung to his bones.

"You've got to eat something, Leo," Jacob said. "Here, I saved a bit of the bread from breakfast this morning."

"Not hungry."

"You'll die if you don't eat."

"Better to die now than to go through what's coming."

A day later Jacob agreed with Leo. Half the men became seasick and vomited over themselves and the floor. The fetid stench of waste and vomit was overwhelming. Jacob himself became seasick and could do no more than lie with his head against the rotten wood of the hull.

Day after day the voyage dragged on, and all of the men suffered. Fever broke out among them, but there was no doctor on board. With no treatment or medicine, six men died before the ship landed. It was reported to the soldiers cramped into their miserable prison below the waterline that those who died had been tossed overboard without ceremony.

Finally, word came that their sea voyage was over. "Get your gear together!" Mosel had appeared holding a lantern. "We're here. Time now for you to fight."

Jacob struggled to stand. He was so weak he could hardly walk. He reached down and pulled at Leo, whispering, "Come along. We'll be better now."

Leo had ceased to talk. The two of them stumbled out, blinded by the bright sunlight, and were pushed by Sergeant Mosel into a small boat that ferried them to shore.

As soon as the bow of the boat crunched against the sandy beach, they were commanded to get out into the waist-deep cold water. Mosel herded them like animals to a temporary camp that had been established by the German officers. As they stood there shivering miserably, sick and unhappy, Lieutenant Hart came over to inspect them. His eyes were dull, for he himself had been sick on the voyage. "A sorry-looking group of men, Mosel. You must see to it that their condition improves. Why, they couldn't defeat the inhabitants of a nunnery!"

Mosel gritted his teeth. It was unfair, but he knew better than to answer back. "Yes, sir. A few days ashore, some good food, and we'll have them ready for anything the rebels throw at us."

"See to it, then," Hart said.

"Come along," Mosel ordered the recruits. Turning, he trudged off, and soon they came in sight of a tent city. Mosel assigned ten men to every tent.

When Jacob pulled the flap back and went inside, he was relieved to see that at least there were some blankets. Shivering, he stripped off his wet clothes and put on dry ones. He had to force Leo to do the same thing. When they and the rest of the troop met outside in the sunshine, they found a good meal waiting for them.

"This is rebel beef," Sergeant Mosel grinned. "But it's good." He saw to it that the men ate heartily of beef and fresh bread, and then said, "We will rest here for a few days. We must be ready to meet the call when our commander gives it."

𝕋   𝕋   𝕋

The call was not long in coming—only two weeks. During that time Jacob had regained most of his strength, but Leo had not. Jacob was in despair, for he saw that Leo had given up. "You've got to have faith, man," he urged one Thursday morning.

"Faith in what?"

"Why, faith in God."

"You still believe in God after all this?"

"Yes, I do."

"Then you're a fool."

Jacob bit his lip. He could understand the man's anger, for he felt more than a trace of the same. During the voyage, when he had been so sick he wanted to die, he had clung to some remnant of hope. Now that things were better, he had made one great determination. "I'm not going to die in this country. I'm going back to Berlin, and I'm going to become a musician."

Just the very idea of a future put some iron into Jacob Steiner's spirit. He managed to rise up, go through the drill, and make such a good impression that even Sergeant Mosel was pleased. "You are a good soldier, Steiner. Keep it up and you will be a corporal."

Nothing was further from Jacob's desires than to be any kind of non-commissioned officer. Nevertheless, he had learned to keep his own counsel. "Very well, Sergeant. I will do my best." He asked cautiously, "Do you think we will be in a battle soon?"

Mosel looked around and saw no officers standing close. "I'm certain of it. I've learned to smell these things, and the men are not yet in good shape. But we'll have to give a good account of ourselves."

Later that night when he was sitting in front of the fire outside the tent made from fence rails, Jacob urged Leo to eat more. "Mosel says there's going to be a battle," he said. "You need to be strong. We may have to march a long way to even get there."

29

"I don't care."

"Leo, don't you believe in God at all?" Jacob asked quietly.

Leo shook his head. "No."

"Did you ever have any faith?"

For a moment Leo Schmidt was silent. The fire flickered. It sent up small clouds of fiery sparks, and the voice of some men singing far down the line could be heard. It was a quiet, peaceful night, with a myriad of stars overhead. Leo looked up and said quietly, "I had faith once, Jacob. But how can I believe when all of this has come upon me? I've been torn away from my family and I know I'm going to die. How could a good God let things like this happen?"

Jacob leaned forward and stared into the flames. The high planes of his face were cast in shadow so that his features stood out sharply. Throughout the long months together, he had shared his faith with Leo—had explained his Jewish heritage and why he believed as he did. Leo's question now brought him up short. He remembered his own father questioning how a merciful God could let so much suffering happen in the world. Privately, he wondered if he himself still truly believed in God. But he chose not to voice those doubts to his friend. "I suppose, Leo, that everybody who thinks at all has asked that question, but I have read the Scriptures so many times. It says that God is merciful, that He loves His people."

"His people. You mean the Jews, like you?"

Jacob considered the question carefully before answering. "We like to consider ourselves the chosen people, Leo. But no people has ever suffered more than the Jews. If you know your history, you know that. We've been slaughtered time and time again, but a remnant has always risen to pass on our heritage. That's one of the great miracles of God—and one of the reasons I believe in God. You know that no other people has ever survived as we have. We've been scattered all over the earth, and we're still a people."

"Not much of a people. You're probably going to die just like I am."

"If I die, it will be believing in God," Jacob said confidently, as much to convince himself as his friend. "But I'm believing that God's going to bring us through it."

The two men talked quietly, and finally Leo said, "I try to pray, Jacob, but it's hard."

"I know, my friend." Jacob reached over and put his hand on Schmidt's shoulder. "Don't give up. God will get us out of this."

The next day a rattling of drumbeats awoke the men. They crawled out of their bedrolls, knowing at once that something was happening.

30

Lieutenant Mosel shouted, "All get dressed. We're marching in an hour. Be sure you eat breakfast and fill your canteens. It's going to be a long march."

It *was* a long march, and some of the men fell by the wayside. After three days of such marching, it was a ragged crew that pulled up before a low-lying mountain ridge. Some were even brought in later by wagon. They were lined up, and a Hessian officer on a mottled gray horse rode back and forth in front of them, studying them. Finally he drew the horse up and said, "You are German soldiers. We will bring honor to our regiment. Over that ridge lies the enemy. It is our duty as soldiers to see that they are defeated. Your officers will be with you. Your sergeants and corporals are ready. Do not fear, the Americans will run when they see the sun shining on your bayonets. They are cowards and traitors to their country."

The speech went on for some time, but Jacob did not hear most of it. He was wondering what would happen when they crossed that ridge. He had never fired a shot in anger and had no thought of ever doing so, but soon he knew he would have to perform such an act.

The drums finally rolled and the regiment moved out. They wound through deep valleys that sloped up into high ridges on each side. Finally they emerged through a V-shape that led out into open country.

"I never saw so many woods. Look, it goes on forever," Jacob whispered.

When Leo did not answer, Jacob turned to see that his friend looked pale. "This is my last day on earth, Jacob. Pray that God will be merciful to me."

Jacob did not have time to answer, for they were quickly ordered into a double time. Soon Sergeant Mosel said, "Form a skirmish line. You, Steiner, will anchor the right of the line."

"You stay behind," Jacob whispered to Leo. "The skirmishers, they say, are in the most dangerous place."

But Leo was ordered to stand beside Jacob in the line. His face was pale as death, and sweat poured down his features, blinding him so that he wiped his eyes constantly with his sleeve.

They had not gone far before they heard the sound of gunfire, faint poppings in the distance. *It sounds like sticks breaking,* Jacob thought.

"There's the battle, boys," Mosel said. "It'll be hot enough pretty soon. We'll give 'em the bayonet."

The line advanced as the firing grew heavier. They had to cross a wide field about one hundred feet wide, and when they were halfway across, Jacob heard a grunt. As he turned to his right, he saw a man fall,

31

clawing at the dust. When the man rolled over, Jacob saw that his face was covered with crimson blood. It spurted from his throat and was redder than he would have believed.

"Move on!" Mosel said. "You can't help him! Charge with bayonets!"

There was no choice then, and the line moved forward with their bayonets. Jacob could see the muzzles of the enemy, although he saw no men. They were hidden in the trees. The exploding muzzles of the Americans winked like fireflies, and up and down the line he heard the screams of the wounded and the cries of the officers urging them forward into battle.

This is suicide! Jacob thought wildly. *We've got to turn back!* But no order came, and he knew that if he tried to run, he would be shot down or killed by the swords of one of the officers. *If I can make it into the trees*, he thought, *I'll find some shelter.*

His breath was coming in great gasps, and sweat poured down into his eyes so that he could not see. The heavy pack cut into his shoulders, and Jacob simply carried the clumsy rifle; there was no thought of killing anyone. He simply wanted to make it to the shelter of the trees.

Finally he reached the deep shade and turned to see Leo staggering across the field. He was moving from side to side, and his mouth was open as if he were gasping for air. Suddenly he stopped, stood up straight, and with a small cry fell over backward, his rifle dropping to the ground. He spread his arms out like a cross. Dumping his rifle, Jacob slipped off his pack and ran to where he lay. He lifted the man's head up and said, "Leo, are you shot?"

Leo's eyes were open, but there was no life in them. They were glazed, and there was a limpness in his body that told Jacob his friend was dead. He saw blood begin to seep from the shrunken chest right over the heart.

"Good-bye, old friend. I pray that things will be easier for you now." Jacob laid his head down and turned to rush back into the shelter of the woods. He heard the shouts of his officers, and to his shock, he heard them saying, "Retreat! Retreat!"

I've got to get my pack and my rifle, he thought. It was only a few steps away, so he dashed into the woods. He reached down to pick them up, and suddenly right before him appeared two men. They were not wearing uniforms but were dressed in common clothing. Yet each had a rifle trained on him.

"Never mind the rifle," one of them said. He was a tall, lanky man with bad teeth and a pair of close-set gray eyes. He lifted his rifle and grinned at his friend. "One more dead Hessian won't matter, will it, Simms?"

"Nah, shoot his head off."

The bore of the musket seemed to enlarge as Jacob stared into it. *So this is death*, he thought. Curiously, he felt no fear. He knew it would all be over in a moment, and that his dream of becoming a musician and of returning home was never to be. He wondered if he would feel pain as he stared directly into the muzzle.

"Well, he's got courage. I'll say that," the tall man said. He lowered the rifle and said, "Come on. You don't speak English, do you?"

Jacob almost answered. He had learned English quite well in the village school in Pelsen and understood what they were saying. But even at that moment he was thinking, *If they don't know I understand English, they'll talk more freely in front of me.* So he merely stood there staring at them.

"Nah, they only speak that German talk. Come on. Let's take him back to camp."

"Get his bag first. Maybe he's got something to eat in there."

The two soldiers rifled through Jacob's pack, and picked up his musket, and then one of them prodded at him with the bayonet. "Get along there, Hessian! Your good days are over. You're going to the prison camp."

Jacob's first thought was, *At least I will live. If I survived this battle, I will survive the prison. God was surely with me.* His thoughts, however, soon turned to Leo Schmidt, who lay cold and still back in the field, his sightless eyes staring up into the sky. Sorrow washed over him, and he asked within his own spirit, *God, why did he have to die so far from home?*

3

A Midnight Intruder

THE COLD FINGERS OF A FRIGID NOVEMBER WIND rattled the windows of Rachel Bradford's room. The winter of 1777 was arriving early, sweeping in almost overnight, driving away the last vestiges of a beautiful fall, and laying an icy hand over Boston. The glass windows were frosted, and from cracks around the frame the frigid air entered, lowering the temperature of the room until a tiny skim of ice had formed over the blue basin that sat on the washstand across from Rachel's bed.

Rachel was a sound sleeper, but the cold brought her out of a deep slumber and into that semiconscious state when one is uncomfortable but not enough so to do anything about it. She had not put on enough covers, and now she snuggled down under the sheet and single blanket. The feather bed mounded up around her, but still she could not drop off to sleep again.

Restlessly she hugged herself and tried to burrow deeper, but even as she did, she heard a noise. At first she thought it was simply the huge oak tree that dipped its branches down during windy weather to scratch at the pane. The tree was bare now, and sleepily Rachel thought, *It's like bony fingers scratching at the window—or more like a skeleton trying to get in*. She often had fanciful thoughts like this. Now, however, she realized that what she heard was not a branch being raked across a pane. As she became more alert and pulled her head out from under the covers, she could discern faint voices outside. Since she was on the second floor, it had to be someone on the ground below her window.

Probably just someone passing by, she thought sleepily. For a moment she began to drift off, but then the sounds became louder. "What is that?" she muttered, wide awake again. "It must be after midnight." With firm resolution she threw the covers back, and as the cold struck her, she shivered and groped in the darkness for her slippers. She found them, put them on, and then moved a few feet to her left where a Seth Thomas pendulum clock ticked slowly on the shelf. She loved the sound of it. The rhythmic accents put her to sleep at night, and somehow it still gave her a sense of security as it had since she was a little girl. Now as she leaned forward, the bright, silvery moonlight flooded through the window and lit up the face of the clock.

"Two-thirty!" she whispered. "Who could be on the streets at this time of the morning?"

Turning, she made her way to the window, but it was frosted with a silver opaque coating, and she could see little. As she stood there, for a moment she thought she had imagined the noises, but then they came again—the rattling sounds of someone moving somewhere below. Carefully she reached out and tugged at the window. It was frozen in place. Muttering under her breath, she strained, and finally, with an abruptness that caught her off guard, the window shot upward, causing her to stagger back for a moment. Despite being dressed in a long-sleeve woolen nightgown, she shivered as the cold night air struck her.

Thrusting her head out of the window, Rachel scanned the ground below. The house sat well back from the street, farther than most houses in Boston. It was an old structure, built in the style of a farmhouse, but the city had crept in on it, and now it was surrounded on both sides by houses that hugged the cobblestone street.

Quickly she looked up and down the street and saw no carts, wagons, or even pedestrians, which was not unusual. Boston did not begin stirring until five-thirty or so. Still there was a slight noise to her left. Turning her head, she saw with a start two shadowy figures moving out of the carriage house that was hidden from the street by a tall hedge. She thought for a moment, *Maybe it's Dake or Micah.* But then she realized they would have no business out in this cobwebby hour of the morning. She could not make out the figures, for they were in the shadows, but she saw that they were carrying a ladder and were headed straight for the side of the house. If they had been talking loudly and cheerfully, she would not have been so suspicious, but there was a stealthiness about them, and she heard one of them say in a savage, muffled voice, "Be quiet! You'll wake everybody up."

Instantly Rachel reacted. She waited only long enough to see them begin to raise the ladder so that it was directly under her window, then she turned away, breathing rapidly. "Burglars!" she said. She left the room, her feet padding on the bare floor. Turning to her left down the broad hall, she went to the door next to hers and knocked on it.

"Who is it? Who's there?"

"It's me, Dake. Get up!"

Rachel heard the rustle of bedcovers and the scuffle of bare feet on the floor. The door opened and her brother Dake loomed before her in the shadowy darkness.

"What's going on?" he asked huskily.

Even in the dim light she could see that under his mussed straw-colored hair his eyes were alert.

"It's burglars, Dake. Somebody's putting a ladder up to my window."

Dake instantly stiffened. He turned and whispered, "Rachel, you stay where you are." He limped heavily across the room. He had taken a bad wound at the Battle of Brandywine and was still unable to walk except with great effort. He stood there for one moment, then said, "The pistols are all downstairs."

"You won't have time. They're climbing up right now."

"What's going on?"

Rachel turned to see Micah Bradford, Dake's twin brother, who had come from his room down the hall. He had thrown on a pair of pants with his nightshirt tucked inside.

"It's burglars," Rachel whispered. "They're coming up a ladder at my window."

"Come on," Dake said. "We don't have time to get the pistols. They're not loaded anyhow. Grab a stick or something. We'll take them from below."

"Maybe we can jerk the ladder out from under them," Micah murmured.

As the two brothers hurried down the hall, they passed a young woman who had emerged from the attic stairway that led down to the second floor. She asked Rachel, "What's going on?"

"Someone's trying to break into the house, Keturah."

Keturah Burns had had a hard life and was more accustomed to things like this than Rachel. Her mother had been no more than a camp follower. Micah had rescued her from a life that was leading straight toward that same profession. She was not tall, no more than five four, and now her eyes grew large as she said, "Are Micah and Dake going to shoot them?"

"I don't think so. Come on. Let's go to my room and watch."

The two ducked into Rachel's room. They crossed to the open window and peered out.

"One of them's coming up. He's almost here," Rachel whispered. She stepped back from the window and said, "We've got to get out of here. They might be armed."

Keturah, however, did not move. Her eyes glowed with excitement. She was not afraid, for she had seen too much in her brief sixteen years to be frightened by a burglar. Quickly she looked for a weapon but saw nothing.

A stubbornness arose in her and she doubled up her fists, but she knew she would be defenseless against a strong man.

Then she had a thought. Reaching under the bed, she pulled out the large ceramic "thunder mug" that was a necessary part of every bedroom in the Colonies. She felt its heft with some satisfaction.

Moving back toward the window, she held her breath as a head appeared. She could not see the face, for the intruder had his back to the moon. Keturah waited until he had thrown one leg over the windowsill and then with all of her might swung the thunder mug. It caught the unsuspecting burglar right on the top of the head. The ceramic pot smashed into bits with a resounding crash, the pieces tinkling onto the floor.

The intruder grunted but was knocked backward by the force of the blow. Keturah saw his hands brush by the window facing, and then he tumbled out of sight.

Rachel leaned out the window and exclaimed, "They're having a fight down there! Come on. Maybe we can help."

The two women rushed out of the room and down the stairs. Keturah snatched up a walking stick from the umbrella stand by the front door, and the two stepped out into the cold.

The sight of Dake struggling with one of the burglars held them suddenly still. Dake had evidently gotten in one blow, for the man was staggering backward. He was trying to say something, but Dake struck out and his fist caught the intruder squarely in the mouth and drove him to the ground.

Meanwhile, the burglar who had fallen from the window was trying to get up, but Micah kept a firm grip on him. Dake now leaped on the man who was struggling to get to his feet, slipped behind him, and threw his steely forearm across his throat.

"Let's drag them inside. We'll tie them up until we can get the sheriff," Dake said.

The two women moved back as Dake forced his prisoner toward the house, and Micah jerked the other one up and dragged him forcefully.

Rachel turned and went before them. Quickly she picked up the candle that was always left burning on the table just inside the hall. As she approached the men, she heard a familiar voice.

"Let go of me, Micah. I think I'm killed. . . !"

Micah had twisted the arm of his opponent behind his back. Now he suddenly blinked with surprise and released him. "Sam!" he exclaimed. "What are you doing here—and who's that with you?"

"It's Jubal. Turn him loose, Dake!" Sam gasped.

Rachel lifted the light as Dake jerked the hat off the other man and exposed the square face of Jubal Morrison. Blood was running down his chin from a split lip, and it was obvious he was going to have a black eye. He took a deep breath and then nodded as he gasped, "Good evening, Miss Rachel. We just came by for a little visit."

"Jubal Morrison! What in the world are you doing breaking into our house?"

"It was Sam's idea," Jubal said, rolling his blue-gray eyes in Sam's direction. A scar beside his left eye gave Jubal a permanent squint, making him appear even more annoyed with his friend. He was six feet tall and weighed nearly one-ninety, which was somewhat larger than Dake, who had now dropped his hands in disgust.

"It's a wonder you didn't get shot, Jubal," Dake growled. Then he turned to Sam. "And you, too! What kind of a tomfool thing do you call this, Sam Bradford?"

Sam reached up and touched his head painfully. He looked at the blood that stained his fingers and winced. "You busted my head! Who hit me?"

"I did," Keturah said proudly. "We thought you were a burglar."

Sam, who had romantic notions toward Keturah, glared at her, forgetting that for the moment. "You could have killed me," he said. "What did you hit me with?"

Keturah began to laugh. "A thunder mug."

"A thunder mug!" Sam spat out. His face wrinkled up in a wry expression of distaste. "Why did you do a thing like that?" He spoke with some difficulty, for his fall from the window had landed him flat on his back, knocking the breath clean out of him. When Micah had jumped him, he had not even been able to fight back.

Looking the two "burglars" over, Rachel said, "Sam, your head is split wide open. Jubal, you've got blood on your face. We'll have to clean you up, then patch up this cut."

They all went into the kitchen, where Rachel lit two lamps, giving her more light to work on the two culprits. She moved close to Jubal and said, "Let me see your lip. It's split."

Jubal flinched when she touched his head and glanced at Dake. He was no longer angry; indeed, by now the whole thing seemed amusing. "I'm all right, but next time I'll get another helper when I decide to break into a house."

"Why in the world were you breaking into the house, Sam?" Micah demanded. He loved this younger brother of his, who, at the age of seventeen, had a gift for all sorts of mischief.

"Why, me and Jubal were just taking the *Defiant* on a midnight cruise. We wanted to see if we could handle her in the dark and try out our new lighting system." The *Defiant* was a small craft classed as a spider catcher. It was designed to be navigated by a small crew with a mounted cannon in the front. It also had a sail and could capture English merchant vessels that ventured too close to shore.

"I told you, you should have stayed with me tonight. It was too late to come back," Jubal Morrison said. He reached up and touched his eye gingerly and winced. "That's quite a punch you got there, Dake."

"You're lucky you didn't get worse," Micah grunted. "I don't expect Sam to show much sense, but you're a grown man, Jubal."

"It was my fault," Sam said. "The doors were all locked, and I left my key on the ship. I thought it would be easy just to climb in a window."

"Why were you climbing in *my* window?" Rachel demanded.

Sam glared at her. "Don't you remember? You told me you were going to spend the night over at Abigail's house."

"That's right. I did," Rachel said.

Keturah said, "Come here, Sam. Sit on this stool. I want to look at your head."

"I guess the rest of us might as well go to bed," Dake growled, then he suddenly remembered. "Jeanne doesn't know any of this."

As Dake turned and left the room to return to his wife, Micah gave a despairing shake of his head toward Sam. "Sam, are you ever going to grow up?"

"If I don't get killed first, I will," Sam said defiantly. He had auburn hair and striking blue eyes and was not as tall or as strongly built as his brothers. Now he perched on the stool and watched Keturah, who proceeded to find a basin and fill it with water from a pitcher.

She dipped a cloth in the bowl and said, "First I've got to wash this blood out of your hair."

"Ow! Will you be careful!"

"Don't be such a baby," Keturah said. She pulled his head forward and mopped at the blood, saying calmly, "You're going to have a scar there."

"It'll be good for him," Rachel said. "Maybe if he gets enough scars and bumps and broken bones, he'll learn to come in a house the right way. Come over here, Jubal. Let me take a look at you."

Jubal obediently sat down, and Rachel began to examine him. "Open your mouth," she said. Rachel studied the results of Dake's blow and said, "You're going to have a fat lip."

"I already have, and this eye's going to be a pain."

"Let me get you a piece of cold steak to put on it. That'll keep the swelling down." She moved quickly. "I'll have to go to the smoke-house."

"I'll go with you," Jubal said. "A burglar might get you. A real one."

The two left the room, and Sam squirmed on the seat as Keturah continued to sponge away the blood. "This ought to have some stitches in it, but Dr. Morgan's out of town."

"I don't want anybody sewing my head up!"

"You're just a baby. Maybe I'll do it myself. I'm a good seamstress."

Sam shook his head, which was a mistake. "Oh!" he said. "That hurts."

Keturah continued to wash the blood that seeped from the cut. "I don't know any way to put a bandage on this in the middle of all your hair," she said. "Here. Let me just hold this cold cloth on it until the blood clots."

Sam was not adverse to that. Keturah had changed a lot since Micah had first brought her home. She had become almost like one of the family, since her mother had died and she had no kin. Now as her face was just a few inches from Sam's, he studied the large blue eyes, almost startling in color. They were widely spaced and deep set. She had thick, dark lashes and arched black brows and a nose that turned up slightly. She was, indeed, an attractive young woman. He reached out suddenly and touched the cleft in her chin. "How did you do that?" he said. "Cut it with an ax?"

"I was born with it, silly!" she said. "I hate it, too."

"I think it's pretty."

Keturah snatched his hand away with her free hand. "Be still!" she said. "I'm trying to get you patched together."

"Keturah, why couldn't you have hit me with something besides a thunder mug? That's downright humiliating!"

Keturah's lips turned upward in a most attractive smile. "It was all I could find," she said. Then she grew more compassionate. "Does it hurt much, Sam?"

"Enough. But if you'll hold that cloth there, I think I'll be better.

Maybe you'd better hold my hand. I think I'm feeling faint."

Keturah knew Sam very well. "Keep your hands to yourself!" she said sharply; then she began to laugh. "It was so funny when you fell backward out the window. It's a wonder you didn't break your neck."

"What if I'd landed on my head? I might have killed myself."

"You were born to hang, Sam Bradford. Now, you be still or I'll leave you to bleed all over the kitchen floor."

While Keturah continued to work on Sam in the kitchen, outside in the smokehouse, Jubal watched Rachel take a knife and trim a small chunk of a meat from a side of beef that was hanging there.

"Here, put this on your eye," she said, handing him the meat. "Maybe I'd better tie it there. Come back in the house." She led Jubal into the house, and they went into the supply room that was just off of the kitchen. She found a piece of cloth and, reaching up, said, "Be still now. Let me tie this."

Jubal was standing directly in front of her. She had to reach up behind his head, so she half leaned against him. The touch of her firm figure against him gave him a roguish thought. He said, "You'd make a good doctor." He could smell the lilac perfume she always wore and now was more conscious of her loveliness than he had ever been. He had become acquainted with her through Sam, with whom he had formed a partnership to build the *Defiant*, but he had been too busy to give much thought to romance. Now, however, with her arms around his neck as she tied the knot, he was tempted to reach out and put his arms around her slender waist and pull her forward. The impulse was strong, but he knew Rachel Bradford would resent such a thing. "Sorry to be such a bother," he said.

Rachel had finished tying the knot. Suddenly aware that she was almost embracing Jubal, her face flushed slightly. "It's all right," she said, stepping back quickly. "Sam's always getting into mischief, and he usually takes someone down with him. When we were younger, it was always me."

"You love your brothers very much, don't you, Rachel?"

"We're a close family. Dake and Micah are a little older, but Sam and I are so close to the same age that we grew up together."

"I was never very close to Stephen. He's my only brother, but he's so different from me," Jubal said.

"I've never met him. What's he like?"

"Well, he's a poet, for one thing. I couldn't write a poem if my life depended on it."

"He's opposed to the revolution, isn't he?"

"Yes. But I'm surprised that Grace is going to marry him. He's not the kind of fellow I'd have picked for her." A thought came to him, and he said, "You know. We're almost kinfolk."

Stephen Morrison was marrying into the Bradford family. Grace Gordon, his fiancée, was the daughter of Lyna Lee Bradford Gordon, Rachel's aunt and her father Daniel's only sister.

"We don't get along too well," Jubal sighed. "Actually we divided our inheritance. He'll be moving to South Carolina with his new bride."

"I think it's sad the way our families are split up. I just love the Gordons. My aunt is a lovely woman."

"This revolution has split up lots of families."

The two stood there talking for several moments, then Jubal said regretfully, "I'd better get along. You need to get back to bed."

"Oh, it's too late for that. Why don't you just stay over? We'll fix breakfast."

"You mean now?"

Rachel suddenly laughed. "All this adventure has made me hungry, and as for Sam, he's always ready to eat. Suppose we fix up some battered eggs and ham. I'll even make some biscuits."

"Lady, you have won my heart." Jubal smiled at her, and despite the squint in his left eye, he was a very handsome young man.

The breakfast turned out to be a popular idea, with everyone in the house finally joining in. Jeanne, Dake's wife, was expecting their first child, and her cheeks were glowing with health as she joined the impromptu meal.

It was a good time for Jubal Morrison. He had few friends in Boston, and as the dawn finally arrived, he was escorted to the door by Rachel. He said, "This has been a good night for me." He had removed the meat from his eye, and it was almost swollen shut. He touched it and said, "I'd take a black eye anytime for a breakfast like that."

Rachel Bradford had decided that she liked Jubal Morrison a great deal. Impulsively, she said, "Come by after church Sunday for dinner. I'll show you some real cooking."

Quickly Jubal nodded. "That's a kind heart speaking. A bachelor never turns down a free meal. Good night, Miss Rachel."

"Good night, Jubal. Sleep well."

As Rachel turned away, she shut the door and leaned against it. Keturah came to stand beside her. "He's a good-looking fellow, isn't he?"

"Yes, he is." She turned to Keturah and smiled. "Is Sam mad at you?"

"Oh no. I babied him, so he's all right."

"He is kind of a baby, but someday he's going to grow up and be a real man just like his pa."

The two stood there quietly, and then finally Keturah sighed. "It's too late to go to bed. We may as well get to work."

"I asked Jubal to Sunday dinner after church. We'll have to fix something special."

"Is he courting you, Rachel?"

"Oh no. Nothing like that."

Keturah, however, smiled. "Better be careful. A good-looking fellow like that has probably had lots of experience with women. No doubt he knows how to get around a girl."

Rachel laughed. "Get on with you, Keturah Burns."

As Rachel returned to her room, thoughts of Jubal Morrison came back to her. *He is fine looking. What would I do if he did come courting?* She laughed aloud and said, "Behave yourself, Rachel Bradford! You're always dreaming up things that will never happen."

4

A Fine Brace of Suitors

THE DAWN OF THE SABBATH DAY had somehow inspired Rachel Bradford to wear a more elaborate outfit than was her habit. She donned a dark green silk caraco and skirt with apple green edgings and a flounce. Just briefly she peered at herself in the small mirror in her bedroom and then moved downstairs and left the house. The other inhabitants were all sleeping, for Rachel had told them the night before that they would have to see to themselves. "I'm going to have breakfast with Papa in the morning," she had said.

The skies overhead were blue-gray, and a chill hung in the air. Fall had come with a sharp bound, and now she pulled her woolen coat with the marten fur collar more closely under her chin. She liked cold weather, however, and exuberantly drew in deep breaths of the air. Few were stirring at that early hour on Sunday morning, and she had decided to drive the carriage to her father's house. It took only a few moments to hook up the light vehicle, and patting the horse on its nose, she whispered, "Time to go to church, Sally."

Getting into the carriage, she urged the mare forward and soon was driving along the deserted streets. After her father's marriage to Marian Rochester, he had felt it necessary to live at the large house that her late husband, Sir Leo Rochester, had left. Marian's father had been ill and had depended upon Daniel Bradford a great deal. The two men had been in business together for several years. Mr. Frazier had since passed away, but Daniel had decided to stay in the Frazier home as his own was a bit crowded. As Rachel drove along at a rapid

45

pace, she thought with satisfaction of how happy her father was with his new life.

She smiled, a slight dimple appearing in her right cheek. *It's like a love story in a novel, my father and Marian,* she thought. Quickly she reminisced on how Daniel Bradford had come to this country as an indentured servant to Sir Leo Rochester. He had fallen in love with Marian Frazier, a woman above his social station, but being a man of honor, he had never pursued her in a dishonorable way. She had married Sir Rochester, much to her later regret. At the death of Sir Leo, Marian and Daniel had decided to forego the long courtship customary in Boston. They had married quickly and now were as happy as any newlyweds. The only disappointment, Rachel knew, was that Marian had never been able to have a child.

"Well, that's taken care of now," Rachel said with satisfaction. Indeed, Enoch had come into the lives of the Bradfords very unexpectedly. His parents, Ezra and Leah Tyrone, had both died, and with joy Marian Bradford had said to her husband, "God has told me that this is the son I never had."

The thought pleased Rachel. At the age of eighteen, she was a young woman who was rather easily pleased—though at times her temper could sometimes leap out uncontrolled. As she pulled up to her father's house outside of Boston, she nodded with satisfaction. "Papa's going to be fine. He's got a good wife and now a new baby."

The Georgian-style house was set back off the road. The clapboards were painted salmon with green trim, and the two stories had a hipped roof with balustrades across the top deck. A red chimney rose on each end of the house, and pilasters flanked the entryway with pedimented dormers. The five windows across the second story and three on the first floor lent balance and symmetry to the structure.

Getting out of the carriage, Rachel tied Sally to the hitching rail, patted her nose, then walked up the steps to the house. Before she could reach the top step, the door opened and she was met by her stepmother, who greeted her with a warm hug. "Come in out of this cold weather. You must be frozen."

"I like it, Marian. I wish it were like this all year."

Marian tugged her by the arm and said, "Come along. You can take care of Enoch while I fix breakfast."

Marian Bradford, at the age of thirty-four, was an extremely attractive woman. She was very tall with dark auburn hair and green eyes, well set and widely spaced. She had a heart-shaped face and a complexion that was the envy of many younger women. Leading

Rachel into the kitchen, she went at once to the cradle by the fireplace along the back wall. "Enoch, we have company. This is your sister, Rachel."

Pride showed in Marian's eyes as she held the baby in her arms. She had given up hope of ever having a child of her own, but in just a few weeks this one had become the joy of her heart. "Isn't he precious?" she whispered.

"Let me hold him," Rachel said. She took the baby and held him in the crook of her left arm. Enoch looked up at her and she touched his cheeks. "Smile for me," Rachel said. But to her amazement he suddenly pouted and let out a mournful cry.

"I'm not doing too well with him. Why don't you let me cook breakfast and you take care of Enoch?"

"Oh, he'll quiet down. Let me rock him a little bit," Marian said. Sitting down in the oak rocker, she began to rock and at once Enoch stopped his yowling. "Just wants his mother," she said with satisfaction.

"You've already got breakfast started."

"Phoebe has. Clive's here with us and he's a big eater."

"Father likes Clive a great deal, doesn't he?"

"Very much indeed. He's very proud of him, too."

Clive Gordon was the son of Daniel Bradford's only sister, Lyna Lee Gordon. He had fallen in love with Katherine Yancy, a young woman who lived in Boston. Katherine and Rachel were the best of friends, and it was only recently that Katherine had come to say that Clive had decided not to join the British army as a surgeon.

"Has he made up his mind what he's going to do?" Rachel asked Marian.

"He's talking to your father about it a great deal. I think he'll settle here in Boston. He doesn't want to go back to England. He's too much in love with Katherine for that."

"Well, Boston can always use another good doctor."

Enoch soon fell asleep, and after putting him down carefully, Marian came to help Phoebe Bradford and Rachel, who were cooking a large breakfast. Phoebe was Daniel's young cousin from England who was now staying with them. Soon they were taking to the table a platter of scrambled eggs, a rasher of bacon covered with a white linen cloth, a huge bowl of mush, freshly churned butter, a jug of cream, and a pitcher of fresh milk. This was followed by golden brown biscuits that filled the kitchen with a delicious aroma. As Rachel was setting a pot of honey on the table, her father came in. She turned to him and said, "How is it you always know when food's on the table? You never missed a meal in your life, Papa."

Daniel Bradford had always secretly favored this tall daughter of his. He came to her at once and hugged her. He was forty-seven now but still weighed one hundred eighty-five pounds, which filled his six-foot, one-inch frame with solid muscle. He had wheat-colored hair and hazel eyes, with a fair complexion that burned easily. His face was thin. He had high cheekbones and a broad forehead, a cleft chin, and a scar on the bridge of his nose received from some early encounter. "That's because you're such a good cook."

Daniel moved around to take a seat just as Clive Gordon entered. He was wearing a snuff-colored velvet coat, knee britches, and a waist-coat. He wore buff silk stockings and a pair of leather shoes with silver buckles. A white cravat completed his attire. His hair was tied back in a simple fashion and he was pleased to see Rachel. "Good morning, Rachel," he said.

"Good morning, Clive." Rachel gave him a quick look. He was very tall, over six three, and lean, weighing no more than one hundred ninety-five. He had the long, sensitive hands that she always thought a doctor should have. His hair was reddish and his eyes were as blue as cornflowers.

"Sit down and let's eat. I'm starved," Daniel said.

When they were all seated, Daniel bowed his head and said, "Lord, we thank thee for this food, for every bounty that has come into our lives. We thank thee especially for this child, Enoch, and we once again dedicate him to you and to you alone. In Jesus' name. Amen."

"Amen," Clive said. "How does it feel to have a little one in diapers again, Daniel?"

"I don't mind a bit," Daniel said. "I'm enjoying my new son as much as I did my first crop. I intend to spoil him until he can't see straight."

"That you will not!" Marian said quickly. "We're giving him to God, and God doesn't need any more spoiled people. He's got plenty of those as it is."

"I think she was looking in my direction when she said that, wasn't she?" Daniel grinned. He reached over and squeezed Rachel's hand. "You look pretty enough to pose for a picture. Got a new dress?"

"No. Not really."

"I have an idea why she's all dressed up," Daniel said. He shoveled a huge spoonful of eggs into his mouth and mumbled, "We've got a new minister."

"Oh, Papa, don't talk foolish!"

"Is the new minister a candidate for marriage?" Clive asked. He was layering a biscuit with butter and took a bite of it before completing the question with a twinkle in his eye. "And is your daughter suitable to be the wife of a minister?"

"Yes to the first. No to the second," Daniel said. "She's got too quick a temper."

"Daniel, stop picking on Rachel," Marian jumped in. "She has a sweet temperament. Much better than yours."

"You see! Everything I say she pulls apart. No peace in this house. None at all."

Daniel Bradford's warm look and quick smile toward his wife modified the tenor of his words. Clive, who was watching this exchange carefully, glanced across and met Rachel's eyes. The two smiled. They were both tremendously pleased with the success of her father's second marriage.

The breakfast continued only a short time before Clive asked about the new pastor. "What happened to Reverend Carrington? I remember him. I've always thought he was an outstanding man."

"Fine pastor and a fine man," Daniel nodded, "but he felt God leading him to join the army as a chaplain. He's with General Washington now."

"I admire his spirit," Clive said. "Who is his replacement?"

"Reverend Josiah Grierson," Daniel replied. "We're fortunate to have him during Reverend Carrington's absence."

"A good preacher, is he?" Phoebe asked.

"Yes. I've heard him several times. An excellent scholar, too."

Rachel's eyes revealed a flash of humor. "Well, if I'm to set my cap for the new pastor, I need to know more about him. Tell me what sort of women he likes. Shall I be shy and demure, or would he appreciate a more outgoing type?"

Daniel knew his leg was being pulled. He had always enjoyed being teased by his witty daughter, and now he threw himself into the spirit of the conversation. "Why, daughter, anything to get you off my hands. I'll tell you the truth. Reverend Grierson is a real catch. He was married once to a very wealthy woman, but she died. He's a widower."

"There you are, Rachel." Marian smiled across the table, her eyes bright with merriment. "You don't have to break in a brand-new husband. Here's one already trained."

"Exactly right," Clive put in. "I'd hate to think what a chore Katherine's going to have breaking me in as a husband. You'd better take advantage of this man, Rachel. He sounds like a bargain to me."

"I suppose he's creaking with age and has lost all of his hair."

"Not at all. Not at all," Daniel denied, shaking his head firmly. "He's a well set-up man. Not tall but strongly built. He's a great friend of Micah's, you know."

"Well, I'll have to interrogate Micah, but it sounds like he's exactly the sort of man that half the widows in Boston would like to catch," Rachel said. "No. I think I'll have to deny Reverend Grierson. It would be tiresome living with a minister. I'd have to be good all the time instead of just when I'm in public."

Daniel laughed suddenly, the sound of his deep voice filling the room. "I never particularly noticed you being good in private *or* in public. I must have been away the day that happened."

The breakfast was a merry time for all, and when it was over the party started for church. When they arrived at the front of the large white-framed building with the towering steeple, they found a larger crowd than usual had gathered.

"Everyone wants to get a look at the new preacher," Daniel said as he helped Marian down. She was carrying the baby in her arms, and he said, "Let me hold him." Taking the child, he walked up the steps, followed by Clive, Rachel, and Phoebe. After greeting a number of friends, they found themselves a place close to the back. "I think we'd better sit close to the door, Marian," Daniel said. "Your son here might throw a fit."

"My son, indeed! Any bad habits he'll get from you, Daniel Bradford!"

"Come along," Clive grinned at Rachel. "Let's get down as close as we can to the front. If you're going husband hunting, you need to get the best shot you can. Right up close."

Phoebe grinned and said, "You just want to go sit by Katherine."

Phoebe and Rachel accompanied Clive, and the three found seats only five rows back from the front next to Katherine Yancy. They saw Micah, along with Sam, Keturah, Dake, and Jeanne, seated in the second row.

The service began almost at once with a time of singing, and during the third hymn, two of the members of the board of the church walked in accompanied by a stranger. Rachel knew this would be Reverend Grierson and studied him carefully. She had enjoyed being teased but now was surprised to see that the man was far more handsome than she had imagined. As Daniel had said, he was not tall, being slightly below average height, but was strongly built. He had dark brown hair and heavy eyebrows of the same color, which shaded deep-set gray eyes, wide spaced and very penetrating. His face was square and strong, and he had the chiseled lines of a man who was firm in all of his ways. As he looked out over the congregation, Rachel was impressed with his demeanor. Daniel had not mentioned his age, but she guessed that he was somewhere in his mid-thirties. He took his seat and began singing with the congregation until finally Lloyd Statler introduced him. The introduction was rather flowery and full of accolades for the new pastor, and from time to time Rachel noticed that Grierson did not seem to care for that.

Finally, when he stood up, he looked over the congregation and said in a clear voice, "Thank you for that kind introduction, Brother Statler. I found myself looking around from time to time to see who the paragon was that was going to speak, since it obviously could not be myself."

He has a sense of humor at least, Rachel thought. And she discovered that he was at ease in the pulpit. *He must be a little nervous, though. It's like a bride coming into her husband's house. He doesn't know any of us, yet he seems very self-assured.*

The sermon was excellent. Grierson preached from the Ninetieth Psalm, the psalm written by Moses. He centered his thoughts on the first verse, which was, "Lord, thou hast been our dwelling place in all generations."

The sermon stressed the fact that human dwellings may change. We may move across the sea, but if God is our home, that does not matter. He had a warm, rich baritone voice, and Rachel had the feeling that he had but to lift it to rattle the windows. He did not do so, however, but modulated his tones.

When the service was over, Micah came to her at once, his face smiling. "What did you think of him, sister?"

"I think very highly of him. He's an excellent preacher."

"I've always thought he was one of the finest I've ever heard. Come along. I'd like for you to meet him."

Rachel glanced at Clive, who was standing beside her. He winked at her, but she shook her head to put off any teasing he might utter.

She followed her brother up to where Reverend Grierson was standing. Micah said at once, "Josiah, I'd like for you to meet my sister, Rachel."

51

"I'm happy to meet you, Miss Bradford. Micah's told me so much about you."

"The pleasure is mine, sir. And might I tell you how much I enjoyed your sermon. It was most moving, and I will look forward to your ministry."

"You're very kind." Josiah Grierson was youthful in appearance, and when he smiled he seemed even younger. "I fear sometimes I'm too strong with my preaching, and I've asked Micah to tone me down. At least with a warning. Perhaps I might ask the same of you."

"I don't think that would be wise. As a matter of fact, we hear very few sermons these days. Why don't you preach one sometime called 'Turn or Burn'?"

Reverend Grierson found that amusing. "That's a wonderful title! When you hear it, you don't even need to hear the sermon."

Micah said quickly, "If you're not busy this afternoon, Josiah, come home and take dinner with us. I'd be glad for you to get to know our family better."

Grierson's eyes went at once to Rachel. He hesitated only for a second, then nodded. "Nothing would give me greater pleasure."

As the family filed out, Rachel found Sam standing beside Jubal Morrison. "I'm glad you asked Jubal home to dinner, Rachel," he announced. "We've got to talk about the plans for the next raid."

"Do you plan to climb up and break in through the window, Sam?" Rachel smiled at Jubal, and he immediately grinned sheepishly.

He touched his eye that had been injured and said, "I think I'd prefer to go in through the front door, Sam, if you don't mind. Will you ride home with us, Rachel? We've got plenty of room."

"Yes. That would be nice, Jubal."

As Jubal helped her into the carriage, then climbed up to sit down beside her, he asked, "What did you think of the new preacher?"

"Very fine sermon. Did you think so?"

"I'm not much of an authority on sermons or preachers."

"You'll know more about him soon. He's taking lunch with us today."

Sam nudged Rachel in the side with an elbow. "Watch out for him. He's a good-looking fellow, and you know how these preachers are. Micah tells me he's not married."

"Oh, be quiet, Sam!" Rachel said.

The meal proved to be successful. Keturah and Jeanne had prepared quite a feast, including roasted venison and a platter of roasted goose basted with butter. This was accompanied by spinach baked in cream and butter, a specialty of Jeanne's, and boiled potatoes in sweet cream sauce. Fresh buttermilk biscuits were arranged on a tray, and at the end came a delicate peach flummery served with dark-roasted coffee.

The meal was a lively one, and Reverend Grierson, while not dominating the conversation, proved to be a welcome guest indeed. He seemed particularly interested in the family and had learned the history of Dake and Jeanne and even something of Keturah's painful past.

"It was kind of you to take pity on an old bachelor," Grierson said finally. "I get very tired of my own cooking."

"I'll say amen to that, Reverend," Jubal said quickly. He was wearing a suit made of fine wool with a waistcoat edged with a dark brown brocade. His white linen shirt had ruffles down the front and at the wrist. He was a strong man, and the snug-fitting britches that came below the knee and the white silk stockings covering the lower part of his legs revealed his muscular development.

After the meal was over, Jubal came to Rachel and looked across the room where Micah and the minister were in some deep discussion. "How do you like the new minister, Rachel? Does he take your fancy?"

Instantly Rachel knew that someone had revealed the teasing that had gone on by her father. She saw the mischief in Jubal Morrison's eyes and did not mind. She had always found Jubal an amiable man, and now she said, "An old spinster such as myself can't afford to pass up any opportunities, Jubal. Reverend Grierson seems to have all the qualifications. He has money, I understand, and all of his own teeth, so it seems, and as my father told me, he's been broken in as a husband." She tapped her chin thoughtfully, her eyes mocking, and said, "Yes. I suppose I shall have to put my name on the list."

"The competition will be keen. There must be a church full of candidates for such a paragon of goodness."

"Well, faint heart never won fair husband," Rachel smiled.

Jubal shifted his weight. "I've been a little lax, Rachel, but I've been meaning to tell you for some time how much I admire you."

Rachel was surprised. Her eyes opened wide, and then she laughed aloud. "Don't tell me you've decided to become a suitor, too! Why, Jubal, that's downright ludicrous!"

"What's ludicrous about it?" Jubal demanded. "I've always thought you were an attractive woman, but I've been too busy building the *Defiant* with Sam."

"Oh, so now you have some free time on your hands and you'd like to come courting?"

Jubal suddenly saw the fun in Rachel's eyes. "Laugh if you will," he grinned, "but anytime I can't beat out a preacher with a woman, I'll take my sign down."

The afternoon turned out to be quite a long one. It was quite obvious that both Grierson and Jubal Morrison were setting their attentions on Rachel. Keturah watched all of this develop and finally whispered to Jeanne, "Look at those two. They act like a couple of raw schoolboys."

"It's funny, isn't it? I've wondered why Rachel never seemed interested in any of the fellows who tried to court her."

"Well, those two are certainly interested in her," Keturah grinned. "It looks like they've started an endurance contest. I think you'll have to get Dake to throw them both out of the house."

Indeed, it almost came to that. Finally the two men, both of them highly intelligent and discerning, quickly recognized in the other a stubborn spirit. They sat for hours in the drawing room with Rachel and whoever else cared to come, but finally Sam came in and said, "Come on, Jubal. We've got to change the setting on the guns on the *Defiant*."

Reluctantly Jubal got to his feet, nodded to the family, and said, "Well, I've enjoyed the meal tremendously." He turned to Reverend Grierson and said, "Perhaps you'd like to come along and see the ship Sam and I have put together."

"Thank you, Mr. Morrison, but it will have to be some other time. I would be most interested, though." Grierson was standing over by the window talking with Rachel, and a small smile turned up the corners of his lips. "I will see you in church, no doubt."

After Jubal had left, Grierson turned to Rachel and said, "A fine fellow. Have you known him long?"

"Not too long. He's a great friend of Sam's. His brother is going to marry into our family in New York."

"I've heard from Micah and from others of your gift for singing, Miss Rachel. I would like to depend on you to help with the music at church, and also with the school I would like to start for the unfortunate children of the town who have no help."

"Why, I'd be glad to do what I can, Reverend."

"Please, not 'Reverend.' When we're alone, Josiah sounds much better to me."

"Very well—Josiah."

Soon after this Grierson took his leave. Micah came over to Rachel, his face beaming. "What did you think of him? Isn't he the finest fellow you ever saw?"

"I like him very much indeed."

"He said he was going to ask you to help with some of the church work."

"Yes, he did."

"It will be good to have Josiah here. He's a good friend." A thought struck Micah, and he said innocently, "He's not married, you know. He's a widower."

Rachel glanced at her brother sharply to see if he was set for more teasing. All sincerity was in his face, and she said, "Now, don't you start, Micah. Father's already been teasing me about the minister, and so is Clive. I don't need that kind of complication."

"Complication? What sort of complication?"

"Well, for one thing he's older than I am."

"Common thing for a man to marry a woman younger than himself."

"I'm sure it is, but I would make a terrible pastor's wife. I'm far too rambunctious." She reached up, pulled his head down, and kissed him on the cheek. "Give up your matchmaking. It was a good joke for Father and Clive, but it's all over."

🛠   🛠   🛠

Two weeks later Rachel thought about what she had said to Micah. *It's all over.* "I was wrong about that," she muttered as she prepared to leave the house. The weather had turned even colder, so she put on a new coat made of blue velvet. Tying it at the neck and just below the bosom, she snatched up a fur muff after fastening a silk bonnet on her head. As she went out the door, Keturah met her.

"Which one are you going to see? Jubal or the preacher?"

"Keturah, don't tease me about those two. They're driving me crazy."

"Well, they're quite a brace of suitors. Two handsome men chasing around after you. I would think you'd like it."

Irritation swept across Rachel. "They're making fools out of themselves."

"That's what men do when it comes to women. Didn't you know that?"

"Well, I don't want them making fools of themselves over me. They come and sit for hours staring at each other. Don't they know how ridiculous they look?"

"I think they're rather sweet. Jubal got a late start. I think he feels like he's challenged. He told me that if he couldn't beat a preacher out for a woman's favor, he'd quit courting."

"Oh, I know. He told me the same thing." Rachel tied her bonnet ribbon tighter and shook her head. "They don't have time for such things, and I don't either."

Keturah leaned against the door and studied Rachel more carefully. She herself was an attractive young woman of sixteen. Sam was wildly in love with her, or professed to be, but she did not seem to be interested in him. She had thick lashes over arched black brows and a slightly turned-up nose. She was not tall but had an attractive figure. "I think you ought to just enjoy it. Everybody's talking about it, you know."

"I know it!" Rachel said with exasperation. "Everybody's making jokes about the preacher and Jubal camping on our doorstep. I told Micah to hint around that it's not seemly."

"What did Micah say?"

"Oh, Micah's blind as a bat! He's thinking so much about getting married to Sarah, he can't think of anything else. Anyway, I'm going over to see Father."

Leaving the house, Rachel made her way to her father's home. As soon as she entered, she found Phoebe Bradford in the kitchen. While Phoebe was her cousin, of sorts, she was becoming a good friend. She and her brother, Joel, had been brought over from England by her father. Joel had not known he had other relatives but had been pleased to discover that he did. Joel was nineteen and Phoebe one year older. Joel had joined General Washington's army, and Phoebe had stayed to help keep house for Marian. She was a tall, shapely girl, short waisted, with ash blond hair and extremely dark blue eyes. "What do you hear from Joel, Phoebe?"

"I got a letter from him this week. Here, let me read it to you." Pulling the letter out of her pocket, Phoebe read:

Dear Sister,

I hope this finds you well. We have been in action at a place called Germantown. I was attached to General Greene's division, and we attacked the town from four different avenues. Unfortunately, the timing was off and we did not all arrive at the proper time. So we did not win the battle. Nevertheless, we showed ourselves strong and gave the lobsterbacks quite a time of it.

I hope you are well. I hear often from Heather, and we look

forward to the day we will be married. I am so glad you have a good place to stay during this war. When it is over we will be together again. I know you will love Heather and accept her as a sister, and she is very anxious to meet you.

There was much more to this, and Rachel listened as Phoebe read about Heather in glowing terms. When the letter finally ended, Rachel said, "I'm glad that Joel has found a good woman."

"I think she is, from all that he tells me. I'm anxious to meet her. I worry about him being in the war, though. It's so dangerous."

"I know. Micah's going back in, and Dake says he'll go back too as soon as his leg is healed."

At that point Marian entered carrying Enoch, and that, of course, stopped all other talk.

As usual, Rachel took over the baby, playing with him and enjoying his antics. She was holding him on her lap when he doubled up his fist and hit himself firmly in the eye. He began to cry and Rachel laughed. "Don't cry, and don't hit yourself in the face, Enoch!"

Daniel had not gone to the foundry, and as the women played with Enoch, he and Clive were having a rather serious conversation in his study. Clive said soberly, "I want to marry Katherine, Daniel, but I'm not sure that it would be wise in a war. The future's so uncertain."

Daniel Bradford was standing over the fireplace poking at the logs. He watched the sparks fly upward in a myriad of golden dots of fire, then shrugged his broad shoulders as he turned back to face his guest. "It's always that way, Clive. The Scriptures say our days are as a shadow. No man knows what a day will bring forth. If we waited for a safe time, nobody would ever do anything." He went over and sat down behind his desk and then asked abruptly, "What are you going to do, Clive?"

Clive Gordon had been leaning his long figure against the door. Now he straightened up and shook his head. "I thought about it a lot, Uncle Daniel, and I've decided what I want to do. I don't know what my parents will think, but I want to join General Washington's army as a surgeon."

"I thought it might come to that," Daniel said quietly. "Have you told your parents?"

"No. Not yet. I'll have to do it by letter. I am not too welcome back in the British line." He laughed and said, "When I pulled Joel away from the squad that held him as a prisoner, it sullied my reputation." He referred to his rescue of Joel Bradford and Heather Reed. Joel had been serving as a secret agent for General Washington and had been captured. It had been Clive who had managed their escape. He grinned ruefully now, saying, "I think there's a reward out for me. They don't take kindly to their own who turn against them."

"Well, we don't either."

"I suppose not. It's all in how you look at it. In any case, I'm going to join the army." He came over and sat down across from Daniel and said, "How does it look to you, Uncle? The situation as a whole?"

Daniel's face clouded. "It doesn't look good at all. General Washington is all that's holding the army together, but he's lost almost every battle."

Surprise washed across Clive's face. "You don't say?"

"Yes. He lost at Long Island, then again at Harlem Heights. He got whipped at White Plains, and more recently at Brandywine, and just this month in Germantown. The only battles he's really won have been at Trenton and at Princeton, and they were both small skirmishes."

"I don't understand it. If a British general lost that many battles, he'd be out on his ear in a minute."

"That's because war is different in Europe. Over here it doesn't matter who holds the territory. In Europe, once a capital is taken, the war is over. But look at this. The British held Boston, they still hold New York, they took Philadelphia, but they haven't taken Washington's army. We're a young country and it's easy to move our legislature. The Continental Congress simply packs a bag and they go somewhere else."

"Then you think we'll win?"

"I think we will, and I'm glad to hear that you've thrown your lot in with us, Clive. Would you like for me to speak to General Washington, or at least write you a recommendation?"

"I'd like that very much, sir."

"Well, God knows we need good surgeons. I don't know what the general's going to do during the winter. General Howe has gone back to Philadelphia. He'll winter there, but our poor fellows have no place to go. They'll have to build huts, I suppose, and stay out in a winter camp."

"I'm determined to do it, sir. Katherine and I have agreed. I'm going to write to my parents, and I'd appreciate it if you would write to my mother and my father."

"I'll do that. Your father will be understanding, I think."

"I think he will. He's never been in favor of this revolution. He thinks it's been a mistake from the beginning, but he does his duty as soldiers must."

"Very well," Daniel nodded. "I may be doing myself a favor. I think Micah will be back with the general as a chaplain, and Dake talks of going back, although he's not fit yet. In any case, you can take care of our family while you're caring for the soldiers of the general."

5

DEVIL-KILLER

SAM BRADFORD RUBBED HIS HAND lovingly over the cannon that protruded from the bow of the *Defiant*. It was a six-pounder, which simply meant it threw a six-pound cannonball. Most of the other "spider catchers"—the name given to the small boats used by budding privateers—threw only a four-pound ball. Sam and Jubal Morrison had worked hard to build the *Defiant* larger and heavier so that they could carry a heavier cannon. Now as Sam stood there, the wind blowing his auburn hair about, he ignored the cold weather and cast his eyes in admiration down the craft that had come to occupy so much of his thoughts. Indeed, ever since he had joined Jubal in the project to build a craft that would take English merchantmen captive, he had thought of little else.

Now he looked down the length of the *Defiant*. At forty feet, she was longer than most, which averaged only thirty. She weighed ten tons and could accommodate ten rowers, who now sat at their benches laughing and joking with one another. All of them were armed with pistols; muskets were stored in cases along the side and could be reached easily when needed.

Jubal came down between the rowers and checked the furled sail. He stood before Sam and grinned. "Well, are you ready for your first raid, Sam?"

"It's going to be great, Jubal," Sam beamed. He took a deep breath of air, expelled it, and struck his friend on the chest with a sharp blow. "With this little devil-killer, we'll be rich by the time we get back to shore."

Jubal Morrison returned Sam's grin. Though the scar beside his left eye caused a permanent squint, he looked as excited as Sam. At the age of twenty-five, he had become hardened through work and had an adventurous spirit that had led him into this dangerous occupation. "If we run into a British man-of-war, you'll think differently."

"Oh, Jubal, you know we can duck into the harbors where they can't come. Don't worry."

This, indeed, was the entire theory behind the spider catchers. No one knew exactly where the name had come from, but everyone called them that. The plan was that the merchant ships that had to come close into shore to find harbor would be easy prey. The spider catchers, mounting a single cannon, could dart out, head them off, and capture them easily. If they gave any problem, they could hole the hull with a few well-aimed cannonballs. In addition to the cannon, Jubal and Sam had mounted a swivel gun, loaded with small shot that could sweep a deck as effectively as twenty muskets. It was quickly loaded, easily aimed, and once in range of a merchantman, no crew on a deck could stand against it.

"You've got the balls all ready, Sam?"

Giving Jubal a look of scorn, Sam said, "What do you take me for? They're as smooth as marbles." He leaned down and picked up one of the six-pound shot and admired it. "Look at that. It'll pierce the side of any merchant that comes our way."

"If you can hit her," Jubal suggested with mischief in his eyes. Actually he was very proud of Sam, who was a mechanical genius of sorts. It had been Sam who had installed the cannon and had drilled them in, and it had been Sam's idea to add the swivel gun in the stern. By throwing the *Defiant* at right angles to their prey, the deck could be raked quickly and the men could pepper any defense with their muskets.

"Sometimes I think we're both crazy, Sam," Jubal said. "And my brother is convinced of it."

"He'll think differently when we waltz back with a prize." He glanced over toward his left where there were two other spider catchers getting ready. "I wish we didn't have to share it all with them."

Jubal and Sam had argued over the method of operation. Jubal had insisted that they join forces with two other privateers. "We can surround a vessel that way, Sam," he had explained. "Then they can't get away."

"But we'd have to share the prize with them," Sam had argued. "I want it all for ourselves."

Now Sam shrugged and looked displeased. "They're not as sharp as the *Defiant*," he said.

"No, but they've got a cannon, and they've got good captains, too." He thought of the captains named Roberts and Felman and their conversation just prior to launching. "We're all set. Roberts and Felman will follow us."

"I guess you're kind of an admiral, then," Sam laughed. "Admiral Jubal Morrison. What are your orders, Admiral?"

"I guess we're ready to pull out. We'll follow the coastline down to Mackey's Point. That'll be a good place for a fat merchantman to try to sneak through." Mackey's Point was, indeed, widely used by merchant ships. Ships that came this way had to go between two sets of reefs. The small spider catchers could lie behind a jetty built of rocks and could scoot out and capture anything that passed by.

"All right, men. We're ready to go." A cheer went up at Jubal's words.

Sam nodded and said, "I'll be ready. I'll check all the boarding weapons, Jubal, while we're on the way."

"That's a good idea."

Sam went around checking the weapons, which included boarding axes, boat hooks, and, for each man, a flintlock blunderbuss—a short musket that could be loaded with small shot.

He checked to see that each man had a cutlass by his side and spoke a friendly word to each of them. They were all local men, and they had worked together to perfect their maneuvering ability. All of them were strongly built, and although some did not have the best reputation in the world, Sam and Jubal were convinced they were tough enough to handle anything that might come their way.

The boats moved out as the men rowed, and there was a good spirit among them as they followed the coastline. The three boats were close enough so that the men could sing a chantey, their voices rising on the cold air.

> A Yankee ship came down the river;
> Blow, boys, blow.
> And all her sails, they shone like silver;
> Blow, my bully boys, blow.

As the coastline slid by, Sam sat beside his cannon, until finally late in the afternoon they pulled into the small cove that would serve as a hiding place. Once they were safely out of sight, he broke out the rations—cold beef with mustard, fresh bread that Rachel had baked, and small jars of pickles and peaches.

The men were not yet through with their meal when suddenly Jubal, who had been keeping watch on a small jetty, yelled, "Here it comes! A merchantman!"

As Jubal scrambled back down the steep rocks and flung himself into the boat, Sam began to load the cannon. They never carried it loaded, of course, but now it was time for action. Taking one of the balls, he picked up a wooden shot gauge and carefully tried the cannon. If a ball was too small, it lost most of the force; if it was too large, it would not go into the mouth of the cannon. This was merely to cover his nervousness, for he knew his weapon well. Pulling out a bag of powder, he rammed it down with the rammer, then dropped a ball in. As soon as he had done this, he rammed a wadding down to keep the ball from rolling out as it shifted. The cannon was mounted on wheels, else it would tear the boat apart. When it was fired it rolled backward, being brought up short.

"Got your quick match, Sam?" Jubal yelled.

"Ready, Captain." Taking a gunner's pick, a sharp piece of stiff wire with a circle on one end, he held it over the touch hole. When the time came to fire, he would ram the pick into the hole, then touch the match to it. He checked his rammer and his sponger. After every shot he would have to dip the sponge into the water and ram it down the mouth of the cannon to clear all the foulness from the muzzle, and also to be sure there were no sparks left. Otherwise, an explosion might occur when he rammed the next powder bag down.

Every man was quiet now, but they rowed powerfully. Standing on the stern, Jubal could see the muscles of the men roll over their shoulders, their powerful forearms pulling on the oars. They had tested the *Defiant* again and again, and he felt a surge of pride at how well she had performed. Now they would see some real action. Though the breeze was slight, he called out, "Simpkins, drop the sail!"

"Aye, sir!" Simpkins, a tall, lanky man, jumped up and lowered the lateen sail. Its triangular shape immediately caught what little wind there was.

Jubal could feel the ship pick up speed and he grinned. "We got her, boys!" He looked over at the other captains, Roberts and Felman. "You take her on the stern, Roberts. You on the bow, Felman. I'll take her broadside."

"Right you are!" the captains answered.

"They've spotted us!" Sam yelled, for he had seen activity on the deck of the merchantman. Sam was disappointed at its small size, for he had wanted to take a large one for their first prize. *Still,* he thought, *it'll be easier to take her. She probably doesn't have a crew of over ten, if that many.* He stood beside the cannon, and when they came close, he turned and hollered, "Captain, can I put a shot over her bow?"

"Yes. They may give up without a fight if they see what we are doing," Jubal called back.

Sam eagerly sighted the gun. They were moving through the water at right angles to the merchantman, so there was no question of swiveling the cannon from one side to the other. The only question was the height. He had practiced this time and time again by shooting at a cask, and now he felt confident. He sighted carefully, then plunged the gunner's pick down into the touch hole. Quickly he reached down and picked up the linstock that held the slow match. It was smoking and he saw the spark was good. Blowing on it, he reached forward and said, "Here you go! Our first shot from the *Defiant*!" He rammed the slow match down, the spark hit the powder, and the cannon exploded, throwing it backward on its platform. It was caught up by the heavy ropes, and Sam, who had stood back to keep from getting harmed, thought he saw a black streak going over the mast of the merchant ship. "We almost hit him," he said. And then he yelled, "Look! She's stopping. She's running up her colors."

Sure enough, the others saw that the merchant, surrounded fore and aft and being attacked by cannon, simply ran up her colors as a sign of surrender.

Five minutes later Sam and Jubal were on board the merchant ship called the *Amy*. Her captain was a sullen man. He was part owner of the ship and now it was lost, and he himself would be lucky to escape without a prison sentence.

Sam and Jubal, accompanied by Roberts and Felman, went below to check the cargo. They were both excited, especially Sam, who rummaged around quickly, saying, "Looks like it's mostly hardware."

"Always a market for that," Roberts said. He grinned broadly and slapped Sam on the shoulder. "I reckon we're some privateers, eh, Sam?"

"They won't all be this easy," Felman said. "Some of these merchantmen have good gunners right out of His Majesty's navy. We were lucky this time."

But Sam was euphoric. He could see a whole string of prizes coming their way soon, and now he went over and clapped Jubal on the shoulder. "We're on our way to being rich and famous. How does it feel?"

Jubal Morrison envied Sam's youth, although he himself was only twenty-five. Sam seemed like an overgrown boy, which, in fact, he was. "I'm glad nobody got hurt. What are you going to do with your share of the booty?"

"I'm going to buy myself whatever I want."

"We'd better be saving for our new ship," Jubal said. "You know, I'd like to have a real ship sometime, Sam. Maybe a sloop. Then we could go anywhere. Wouldn't have to stick to the shoreline."

Sam had not thought this far ahead, but his fertile imagination instantly took fire. "That's right! That's what we'll get, a sloop. How much do they cost?"

"More than I've got, but we'll see. That would be something, wouldn't it? To go cruising for weeks at a time. Well, we might take ten prizes and send them home with prize crews."

Sam was silent for once in his life. A new vision had come to him, and his eyes glowed as he said, "Do you think we can do it, Jubal?"

"Men have done it before."

🔔　　🔔　　🔔

Josiah Grierson had become quite familiar with the large parlor of the Bradford house. It contained a harpsichord, and he had made it a point to come often so that he and Rachel could practice the music for the services. He himself had a rich baritone voice, and with her contralto, they made a fine duet. They had just finished singing "A Mighty Fortress Is Our God," one of his favorites.

"That was fine, Rachel," he said. "I think we might try that one next Sabbath day."

Rachel looked up from the harpsichord. She had enjoyed Josiah's visits as she had enjoyed his preaching. Now looking at his strong figure as he stood, one hand resting lightly on the polished grain of the harpsichord, she smiled up at him, saying, "It's a little bit heavy for me. I like Mr. Watts' music much more."

"Very well," Josiah said with a smile. "Suppose we try this one." He arranged the music before her, and soon they were singing one of Isaac Watts' hymns:

> O God, our help in ages past,
> Our hope for years to come,
> Our shelter from the stormy blast,
> And our eternal home!
>
> Under the shadow of thy throne
> Still may we dwell secure;
> Sufficient is thine arm alone,
> And our defense is sure.

Before the hills in order stood,
Or earth received her frame,
From everlasting thou art God,
To endless years the same.

As the last notes died away, Rachel was suddenly shocked by the touch she felt on her shoulder. Quickly she glanced, seeing that Josiah had laid his hand there and was beaming down at her. It was the first time he had ever shown any sort of intimacy, and she hardly knew how to respond.

"You have a beautiful voice, Rachel," Josiah said. "I've rarely heard a better one."

"Was your wife a good singer?"

Grierson's eyes grew cloudy and he removed his hand. "No. Actually she was not. She played beautifully on the harpsichord, though. Just as you do."

Rachel was relieved that the moment was broken. She had learned that Josiah Grierson had been deeply in love with his first wife. She had died in childbirth a year after their wedding, and he had been grieving ever since. He himself did not speak of her, but Micah had told Rachel that they had apparently enjoyed a perfect marriage.

The two were quiet for a moment. Rachel rose and said, "Shall we have tea?"

"That would be very nice."

Rachel set about making the tea, and they sat down together at the dining room table. As they drank their tea, she studied the minister's face. It was a strong face, rather square; the best feature was his deep-set gray eyes. She had discovered that Josiah was a rather complex man. Sometimes he was so quiet and withdrawn that he seemed almost angry, but there was a witty streak in him, and he was excellent company, able to suit himself to any group. Now as she studied him, she was surprised when he turned to her.

"I have something I would like to talk to you about, Rachel."

For one moment Rachel panicked. It sounded very much as though he was about to propose. She knew he was fond of her, although he had never expressed more than his admiration of her character and faithfulness to the church. *What will I do if he proposes?* she thought, and utter confusion came over her. "Why . . . what is it, Josiah?"

"I've been thinking of starting an orphanage, but I hesitate to take on such a task without much preparation." Grierson sipped at his tea and then put his eyes on her and smiled. "I've been wondering if you would be willing to help me."

"Why, of course I'll do anything I can, and my father would be more than glad to help. He's often spoken of such a thing."

"That will be most helpful. I will have to engage many of the businessmen in order to raise the funds." He sat there silently for a while and then shook his shoulders with some sort of impatience. "I sometimes get involved with too many activities."

"That's natural for a minister, isn't it?"

"For good ones I think it is, but there's such a thing as being too busy." He grinned at her suddenly and said, "Do you know the busiest chicken in the whole chicken yard?"

"Why, no. Which one?"

"The one that's just had his head cut off."

This struck Rachel as being very funny indeed. She had seen chickens with their necks wrung that continued to run about and flop with great activity.

"It doesn't last long," she said, "but it's exciting while it's going on."

"Perhaps it's not the best analogy," Josiah said, shaking his head. "But I've seen many ministers wear themselves out trying to do too much. I fear that's a fault of mine. I'm never satisfied doing nothing."

Rachel continued to speak of the possibilities, saying, "There will be no problem getting orphans. There are plenty of them right here in Boston and others in the outlying country. Some of them suffer pitifully."

"You have a kind heart, Rachel." Leaning forward, Grierson hesitated, then asked, "I'm surprised that you've not married. Why is that? You must have had plenty of suitors."

"Why, I'm not sure," Rachel said. It was a question she had been asked before, and as she felt the pressure of his eyes on her, she sipped her tea nervously. "I just haven't found the man yet that I want to share my life with."

"But you're not opposed to marriage."

"Oh, certainly not! I'm just opposed to bad marriages."

"Very wise, I'm sure." He hesitated again and the silence seemed to thicken. From outside the window came the cries of some children playing at a snowball fight, and the ticking of a clock on the mantel filled the quiet room. "I have rather rigid ideas on marriage," Josiah said. He looked up and added, "I think it sounds very romantic, but you may be surprised."

"I'd like to hear your ideas."

"Would you, indeed? Well, I think that marriages are ordained by God." A slight smiled tugged at the corners of his lips, and he said, "Of course, I'm a Calvinist. I think everything is ordained by God."

"I've always had trouble with that doctrine, Josiah. Do you think we have no free will at all?"

"Of course we do. I was being facetious. I do think God has plans for our lives. We may get out of God's plans at times, but His plans are always good."

"Well, I agree with you. The Scripture certainly teaches that."

Interest flickered in the minister's eyes, and he put his hands together and stared at them for a moment. Then he lifted them and said, "Do you think that there's one man whom God has ordained for you to marry? That all other men would be outside of His will?"

The question took Rachel by surprise. She said, "I'm not sure I ever thought it through. I, of course, want to marry within the will of God, and that means I would never marry an unbeliever. I wouldn't marry a man I couldn't grow to love, but there are many men I could probably care for who are firm Christians." She was intrigued by the question. "Are you saying that I've got to find that *one* man whom God has decided I'm to marry?"

"That's my theory."

"But how am I to do that?" Rachel smiled. She found this conversation stimulating. "There are probably a thousand eligible bachelors right here in Boston, not to speak of the rest of the world. How would I find the very one God wants for me?"

Grierson saw that she was half amused by his theory. He laughed slightly, saying, "My theory doesn't always hold up, but I know God cares for us, and at times we see in the Scripture how carefully He planned things. For example, when the famine was coming to the family of Jacob, He saw to it that Joseph went down to Egypt as a prisoner. And when the famine came, Joseph was there to save his family. That was the hand of God moving in every circumstance. Could He not move in the same way in smaller things? Say, in our choice of a husband or a wife?"

"Is that why you've never remarried, Josiah?"

The question brought a flush to Grierson's pale face. He seemed unable to frame an answer. Finally, he said, "I believe that is exactly why. I had a very happy marriage, Rachel. There was no question that Martha was exactly the woman God had for me. And, of course, as all people who suffer loss must wonder, I, too, wonder endlessly why she was taken. But there's no answer to that, is there?"

"Would you marry again if you found a woman to whom you felt God had brought you?"

Whatever Josiah Grierson's answer might have been, Rachel was not to know. At that moment the door slammed and she shook her head. "I know that sound. It's Sam. He comes in like a wild bull."

"Rachel!—Rachel!" Sam burst through the door quickly, followed by Jubal. "We did it! We took a prize!"

"Oh, Sam, I'm so happy for you!" Rachel beamed. She went over and gave him a hug and then hesitated for a moment. Putting out her hand, she said, "And, Captain Morrison, I congratulate you. Sit down and tell us all about it."

"It wasn't much," Jubal said. "Just a sorry old merchantman. Sam here put a shot over her bow, and she gave up like a whipped cur."

"Will it be very profitable?" Rachel said.

"Loaded down with hardware all the way from England. We'll be able to sell it for a neat profit," Jubal said. He looked over then and said, "Good day, Reverend Grierson."

"I congratulate you, sir. A victory. Your first, I believe."

"The first but not the last!" Sam exclaimed. "We're going to get us a sloop, and then we're going to cruise all over. We can take the biggest merchant ship afloat."

"Whoa, Sam," Jubal laughed. "You go too fast."

"Sam always does," Rachel smiled. "Sit down. I made a fresh cake this morning. Or would you rather stay and take dinner with us?"

The question seemed innocent enough, but it turned out to be another endurance contest. Jubal did stay. Sam left. And the Reverend Grierson fastened himself firmly in his chair.

Rachel saw at once what was happening. The two men eyed each other cautiously, and she thought, *Oh no, they're here for another siege!*

♯   ♯   ♯

The continued attentions of Jubal Morrison and Reverend Josiah Grierson had become tedious to Rachel Bradford. She also had to endure teasing from Keturah and Jeanne, who found the whole thing extremely amusing. When her father had come and asked her to spend some time at his house, she was tremendously relieved.

"I've got to go with Clive to General Washington's camp, and I need someone to stay with Marian. Our housekeeper's away, and it's more work than Phoebe can take care of alone."

"I'll be happy to come," Rachel had said. "How long would you like for me to stay?"

"As long as you like. I always like having you around, daughter. You know that." Suddenly Bradford's eyes had gleamed. "Perhaps you could invite your suitors to come and spend some time with you over there. I hear they are both like hounds on the trail." He had laughed at her and then hugged her. "Have them or anyone else you please. I'll hate to lose you, but it will come sooner or later."

Daniel related this to Clive as the two made their way to Washington's camp. It was a difficult journey, for the weather had turned foul. A mixture of sleet and rain fell from time to time, and Daniel was glad he had brought the covered buggy. They had drawn the leather aprons along the side, covered their feet with another, and rigged a sheltering sheet in front of them so that Daniel could drive without being overly exposed to the weather.

"I think it's rather amusing that Rachel's being courted by Morrison and the minister," Daniel said.

"I heard a little about that," Clive grinned. "Which do you favor, Daniel?"

"They are both good men, I think. Jubal is a little young and hasn't made his way yet. I admire Josiah Grierson. He's a fine preacher." He thought for a while, and the wind whistled as they moved along. "Reverend Grierson is thirty-five, somewhat older than Rachel."

"That's not uncommon. I've heard he has money."

"Yes. He was married to a very wealthy woman. From what I understand he was very attached to her."

"When did she die?"

"It's been nearly ten years now."

"I wonder why he hasn't remarried. Perhaps he was so much in love with his first wife he couldn't think of marrying another woman."

"That's possible."

"What about Sam and this vessel of his?"

"You know, I think that really may amount to something. Sam's all afire to get a bigger ship. They've made only one raid, and now he sees himself as the buccaneer of the high seas."

"That's Sam, isn't it? He's always been a bit that way, hasn't he?"

"Yes. He's full of life. I'm very proud of him."

The two talked on and finally were stopped by a sentry, who called out, "Halt!"

As the soldier came forward, Daniel said, "My name is Daniel Bradford. I have a pass here to see General Washington." He waited until the half-frozen sentry examined the pass that he carried at all times.

"Go along. Camp is over to your left," the sentry said.

It took some time to get to the camp itself, which was a miserable collection of tents offering little shelter from the bitter cold.

"The general will have to do better than this," Daniel said, disturbed by the sight of the ragged soldiers huddled around the small, smoky fires they had managed to ignite from the damp wood.

"It is pretty bad," Clive agreed.

The two men had some difficulty getting to see the commanding officer, but finally they were admitted into a house that had been commandeered for headquarters. As they entered, the tall man behind the desk stood and said quickly, "Daniel Bradford, I'm happy to see you, sir."

"I'm glad to see you, General Washington. May I present my nephew, Clive Gordon."

"I'm happy to see you, Mr. Gordon. Your nephew, you say?"

"Yes. He's the son of my sister, Lyna Lee Gordon. Her husband is an officer in the British army."

This brought a look of surprise to Washington's gray eyes. "Indeed! Well, we welcome you anyway. We may be enemies on the field."

"No, sir. We will not be enemies," Clive said. He was as tall as Washington himself, though not as heavy. Hesitating for a moment, he said, "My father's opposed to this war, as I am myself. I left New York under rather stringent conditions."

"Indeed! I think there's a price on my nephew's head." Daniel grinned and went on to explain how Clive had rescued an American spy from the clutches of the secret service. "I don't think it would be safe for him to go back to New York at the moment. In any case, he is a fine physician."

"Well, Dr. Gordon. What are your plans?"

"I would like to enlist, sir, if you would have me."

Washington beamed. "Indeed we will! We need all the help we can get. I am afraid we can offer you little in the way of monetary reward." A shadow swept across the tall man's face. "As a matter of fact, our men are going to have a hard time this winter. Any medical help will be greatly appreciated."

"My mind's made up, General."

"You're determined to take the other side in opposition to your family?"

"Yes, sir. I believe in this country, and I do not believe England is just."

"We all feel that way, Dr. Gordon. Here, sit down. I'll have something brought in to eat. You must be tired from your journey. I'll send for one of our medical officers. You'll like him, I'm sure. He has a rather odd name. Dr. Albigence Waldo."

Indeed, when Dr. Waldo came he seemed a strange individual.

Washington, after introducing them, said with a small smile, "Dr. Waldo is not only a surgeon. He is a wit, an amateur musician, an artist, an orator, and a faithful diarist."

Dr. Waldo, at twenty-seven years of age, had the pale look of a chronically ill person. He shook his head at the general's compliments. "I can claim no excellence in any of those, but I do welcome you, Dr. Gordon."

"Perhaps you two gentlemen would like to enjoy a meal together. I have my duties," Washington said. "You must excuse me."

"General, I would like to see another relative of mine, Private Joel Bradford," Daniel said.

"Yes. We've heard of that young man."

"That's the young man I managed to help, General," Clive said. "Is he doing well as a soldier?"

"Actually he was of great value in the secret service as an agent. But he is a fine soldier. I'll have my sergeant take you to him, Mr. Bradford."

"Thank you, General."

"And we will have a meal together tonight, of course. We'll have more time to talk then. I'm still hoping that your family will produce many a musket to win this revolution."

Daniel was escorted by the sergeant through the maze of tents and saw Joel Bradford almost at once. "Joel!" he said and moved forward quickly to shake the young man's hand. "A little airish out here."

Joel Bradford had a great admiration for Daniel. He was a tall young man but very thin with blue-gray eyes, a lean face, and a prominent nose. He had become a secret agent for Washington through a set of peculiar circumstances, and now he greeted Daniel very cheerfully. "I'm glad to see you, sir. Very glad. How is Phoebe?" he asked.

"Your sister is fine. Here, I brought you some food."

Daniel shifted the bag from his shoulder, and Joel snatched at it almost greedily. Looking inside, Joel said, "Oh, sir, this will be most welcome! Here, fellows, look what my cousin has brought."

Daniel felt pity for the ragged men who gathered around. He sat down as they began to snatch at the food and gulp it down hungrily like a flock of starving seagulls.

"Things are quite bad, Joel."

"They will be all right soon," Joel said. "I've heard a few rumors, and we'll be moving somewhere to make winter camp."

"Where will you be going? You haven't heard that, I suppose?"

"The rumor is a place called Valley Forge."

"I hope there's nice warm quarters there."

"I don't know, sir. We'll wait there until spring. We'll train all winter, and when we come out, we'll be a better army. You'll see, sir. We'll whip the English come spring!"

6

ESCAPE?

A YELLOW RAY OF LIGHT came through a crack between the logs, breaking the murky darkness. It served only to illuminate the shivering bundles that could scarcely be recognized as men. Jacob pulled himself up painfully and coughed with such violence that pain tore around his ribs, causing him to shut his eyes against the agony of it. For a time he sat there struggling to contain the racking cough that had come to plague him since his capture. One of his feet was sticking out from the threadbare, filthy blanket that served as his mattress and covering, and the rags that he had tied around his foot had come loose. Even his foot looked blue and was certainly swollen, but the cold had so numbed it that there was no feeling left. Bending over carefully, he drew his foot up and wound the dirty scraps of rags around it and then tucked it under. He leaned back, his head against the rough logs, and sighed deeply. The sigh was a companion to the sighing of the wind that came through the chinks in the logs that made up the prison hut where he had lain for months, and the stench, which had overpowered him at first, had so deadened his senses that he was no longer conscious of the waste and unwashed bodies and the ever present smell of sickness that surrounded him.

The hut itself was not large—fifteen feet wide and twenty feet long. There were others like it strewn along the foothills of the mountains nestled along the banks of the Delaware. It was a low, marshy ground, and during the late summer, mosquitoes and other insects had swarmed through, thickly covering Jacob and his fellow prisoners. The miasma of the swampy country had brought fever, and Jacob had grown accustomed to helping pull out the stiff bodies of those who had not survived so that their guards could throw them into a shallow grave. Death had become his constant companion, and only by sheer strength of will had he been able to keep faith that one day this cruel existence would be only a terrible memory.

During the summer, and even the fall, life had been bearable. But now in November the snows packed the huts to a depth of two feet, and the cold was a numbing force that seemed to freeze not only the half-naked prisoners but the mind as well. Hours would pass by, and Jacob would hear nothing but the coughing and groans of the other prisoners, while he himself would remain perfectly still, his mind a blank. Sometimes he would dream of home, of the warm fields and the harvest that would spring forth in his native land. At other times he would dream of being in the large room with a crackling fireplace sending out waves of heat and sparks swirling up the chimney. But these dreams always ended when he awoke half frozen and starved.

"All right, you baby eaters. Come and get your rations."

The door to the hut opened and the full light fell across Jacob's eyes. He blinked owlishly, then painfully drew his blanket back and got to his feet. He found himself weak and staggered across to where the guard, a thin, older man whose name was Ezekiel, stood waiting for the prisoners to make their way to him.

He grinned, saying, "My old uncle used to tell me that it wasn't good for men to eat too much. Bad for the digestion. So, I may have to take some of this back. What do you think, baby eater?"

Jacob still had not let it be known that he was able to understand English. He let no recognition flicker in his eye but came to stand before the man the other guards called Zeke and nodded. He had brought his wooden plate and said, *"Danke."*

"Danke, is it? Why can't you speak English!" Zeke growled. He dipped into the pot he held in his left hand with a pewter spoon and slopped some of the contents onto Jacob's wooden plate. "There, don't eat too much now. Bad for your health."

As the others came for their daily rations, Jacob turned and stood, for his bones ached from sitting on the hard, frozen ground. He pulled the wooden spoon from his pocket and began to eat the revolting mess that had been plopped on his plate. It contained some sort of fish and other contents he could not identify. He would never have eaten such a thing had he any choice, but now he knew that to stay alive he must somehow force it down. He ate slowly, watching as the guard stood there leaning against the door. He had formed a habit of talking to the prisoners, even though he believed none of them spoke English.

"Well, all of you got good, healthy appetites, I see. There's nothing better for a man than to spend a few days not doing any work, but me and the sergeant finally got the permission for some of you to get out and do a little something to earn your keep." His eyes ran over the skeletal forms of the prisoners and he snorted. "Ain't none of you fit to do no work much, but you could do something. Any volunteers?"

Jacob almost spoke up, but he managed to restrain himself. He waited until the private said, "All right. You there." He pointed at Jacob and then at another man. "Come along."

Escape was never far from the minds of any of the men, but no one had ever managed it, as far as Jacob knew. Several had been shot while trying. Jacob now followed the gesture of the private and stepped forward.

"Put your coats on, you two," he growled. "Follow me."

Jacob glanced quickly at the other man, whose name was Claus Donniz. Claus came from a part of Prussia far from Jacob's home in Hesse-Cassel. He spoke no English whatsoever. The two of them had more than once discussed the possibility of escape. Now Jacob pulled his coat together, grateful that they had allowed him to keep it, and the two men followed the sergeant outside. The bright sunlight blinded them, and they stumbled along on numb feet as they were led to a tree that had been felled. A two-man saw lay beside it.

"Get busy and cut that in two!" the sergeant ordered, gesturing with his arms to show the men what he wanted them to do. "It'll give you an appetite for supper." He laughed, showing rotten teeth, and then pulled a small bottle out of his pocket and took a long drink of it. "Do a good job," he said, "and I'll give you a bit of this."

Jacob and Claus picked up the saw and began to work. Claus had been a prisoner for only two weeks and still had some strength. Jacob was weakened by long months of inactivity and bad food. He clung to the saw and whispered beneath his breath, "We must do well, Claus."

"Ja, it's our only chance to escape." Donniz was a very short man, thick-bodied, and with cold blue eyes. He pulled steadily on the saw, doing the bulk of the work.

The two worked for two hours, and the guard came back accompanied by a sergeant. "Well, Sarge, they're good for something."

"Good for being shot. That's what they're good for." Sergeant Hawkins was a small man bundled up to his ears with a heavy woolen coat. He wore a pair of thick boots and stood in the snow shivering. "How many can make the move without dying on us, Zeke?"

"Don't know." Zeke stamped on his feet to warm them and then glanced at the two critically. "Well, that one there's pretty fresh, but this one's pretty scrawny. Got a bad cough, too. Don't reckon he'll make it."

Jacob listened avidly, although appearing not to understand a word of their conversation. He pulled on the saw, and the wheeze and whine of it as it cut through the wood broke the stillness of the air.

"I'll be glad to get out of this. I want to get home for a while," Zeke complained.

"So do I. No job for a soldier watching a bunch of prisoners." He pulled something out of his pocket and studied it. "It appears to me we got over two hundred to move."

"Where are we taking them?"

"There's an old abandoned factory just outside of Boston. It ain't much, but it'll be better than this. But gettin' them there is the trick. We'll have to march 'em until they drop, and if they drop, they die."

"Let 'em die, I say," Zeke said callously. "If I had my way, we'd just shoot 'em all now and be done with it."

"We'll be pulling out tomorrow morning. Either of these two speak English?"

"No. I don't reckon. Hey, you speak English?"

Both men turned and looked at the sergeant. Claus understood the question vaguely. *"Nein. Ich kann nicht englisch sprechen."*

"You blasted baby eater!" Sergeant Hawkins growled. "I'll get the supply wagons ready and we'll pull out at dawn."

"Some of them will try to escape."

"Good. Shoot 'em. Be less mouths to feed."

Jacob said nothing until he was back in the hut. As soon as the guards left, he spoke up. "We're being transferred."

"Where?" Donniz demanded.

"He said a place called Boston."

"That's over on the coast," Donniz said quickly. "If we get away near there, we maybe could sneak aboard a ship going back to Europe."

That did not sound very likely to Jacob, but he also had the hope of escape on his mind. "It'll be our only chance, Claus," he murmured. "Once they get us in a town and lock us in a prison, we'll never get out alive."

"We'll have to make our break somewhere between here and this Boston place," Claus nodded. "It'll have to be at night."

"Ja. We will make our try," Jacob whispered. "I will not survive in that place. It will probably be as bad as this one."

🔔   🔔   🔔

The journey from the Delaware Valley to Boston was a nightmare. The guards had not been wrong, for several men had already given up and died on the way. Two others had tried to escape and had been promptly shot. They had not been buried but were simply abandoned, their eyes staring blankly up at the sky.

Jacob and Donniz spoke quietly between themselves. "It must not be a mass break. Just the two of us," Donniz growled.

Jacob was so ill he could barely answer. He nodded wearily and said, "We'll both be killed. There's little chance, Claus."

"There's as good a chance as any."

"For you maybe. You're still strong, but I couldn't run a hundred yards."

"I'll take care of you," Claus said. "It's just the two of us."

One night Jacob heard two of the guards talking. One of them said, "Well, it'll be Boston tomorrow. I'll be glad to get out of this terrible cold."

"Probably day after tomorrow. These Germans can't walk over ten miles a day."

"Let 'em drop. I want to get where there's a nice warm fire, some whiskey, and some women."

At supper that night, which consisted of several chunks of bread and a bowl of lumpy rice washed down by water, Jacob said, "Tonight, Claus. We'll be in Boston tomorrow. We'll have to take our chance, whatever it is. May God be with us."

"I'm not trusting in God. I'm trusting in us. We can do it, though," Claus said. "They'll be marching straight in. They may not even miss us if we can get away without being seen."

The men were kept in a clearing near a roaring fire that had been built up. There were over forty men in their unit, watched by three guards. It was a dark night, for which Jacob and Claus were grateful. They lay close together, alert with their nerves tingling. Even Jacob seemed to grow stronger at the thought of escape.

Once, Claus started to move, but Jacob said, "Wait. That guard always drinks himself to sleep."

Claus looked over to where the guard was seated on a log, his musket butt on the ground. He had no bayonet, and he lifted a bottle from time to time. Soon he was swaying back and forth mumbling to himself, and finally he became quiet and slumped over.

"Now," Claus whispered. "We will crawl."

Jacob nodded as Claus began to wiggle across the ground. The other prisoners, exhausted by the trip, lay like corpses with their heads under their meager blankets. As Jacob followed, every sound he made seemed to be as loud as thunder. The remaining two guards were down at the other end of the encampment. Jacob could hear their voices, but when he peered cautiously into the night, he could see only their silhouettes by the light of their fire and knew they could not see him. On and on he crawled away from the fire. Finally the two men reached the edge of the trees. Jacob stood up and Claus followed suit. They stood there, and Jacob said, "Which way, Claus?"

"Any place away from here. We'll go find a farmhouse and hide in the barn."

To Jacob that was not much of a plan, but he had nothing better to offer. The two men stumbled on through the darkness. Their faces were scratched by low limbs and briars, but they forged on for hours, it seemed. Finally Jacob collapsed, his feeble strength gone.

"Come," Claus said and reached down and put his arms around Jacob. He pulled him to his feet. "We have to hide ourselves somewhere."

"I can't make it, Claus. Save yourself."

"No. The two of us. We will be all right."

Claus was a strong man, but soon he was gasping from the effort of half carrying Jacob. As they came out into a field, he said, "There's a road over there." Together, they struggled over to the road, then stood staring down it. At this hour there was no one on it, but both men knew that by daylight they had to find a place to hide.

"We will go until we find a farmhouse," Claus said.

The two men staggered along for half an hour until Jacob, who was practically unconscious, felt Claus stop and utter an oath. "A patrol. Come. They have seen us."

Jacob opened his eyes enough to see a small group of horsemen, perhaps six men. He heard a call and then the horses came toward them.

"Run!" Claus said. He tried to help Jacob, but he stumbled and Jacob fell to the ground.

"Save yourself, Claus. We'll split here. You go that way," Jacob said.

He got up and started to run, when a blow struck him in the back. He stumbled forward but, in the darkness, fell over a ditch he had not seen. It was a deep ditch filled with frigid water, and the shock of it seemed to freeze him to the very core. He was barely aware of the sound of the horses' hooves beating on the frozen road, and then he heard shots.

"That got him! Where's the other one?"

"Over there somewhere. I think I put a ball in him."

Jacob backed up against the edge of the ditch. The dry, dead grass hung over the side, and he pulled himself up under it with only his head above water. He heard the sound of voices and men as they faded, then came back. Finally he heard one say, "Maybe there was only one."

"No. There were two. The other one got away. We'll have to put out the word. We'll catch him come daybreak."

Jacob waited until the sound of the horses' hooves faded, then using the last of his strength, he pulled himself out. The wind cut through him like a knife and his teeth chattered.

"Got to get out of the wind," he muttered. He staggered forward, aware that he could be seen but knowing that he would die if he did not get warm. He did not know how far he had traveled along that road, but finally he saw a dark shape off to the side. He staggered toward it and soon realized it was a house. There were no lights, but around the back he saw a barn. With the last of his strength he reached it, thankful that there were no dogs. Slipping inside the barn, he groped until he found a ladder. Moving like a dead man, he climbed into the loft and, with the last of his strength, burrowed under the mound of straw. The pain from the musket ball in his back washed over him now like waves of fire. He lay there half conscious, shivering, and finally fell into a semi-coma. His last conscious thought was, *God help me—only you can!*

7

THE ENEMY

RACHEL WAS HAPPY at her father's house. Her days were filled with the activities that occupied most women of her day. With the absence of Mrs. Williams, the housekeeper, she and Phoebe Bradford found themselves occupied from early until late. The estate was a large one and Marian had offered to hire more help, but both Phoebe and Rachel were accustomed to being busy. So the two of them threw themselves into the work of keeping the household going.

The young women were busily engaged in making butter one Wednesday morning. The gardener had milked the cow that was kept mostly for Enoch's benefit, but Daniel Bradford also loved fresh milk. Rachel strained the milk into a pot and stirred it for half an hour and then left it for a time. Afterward she sat there churning and finally washed the butter in flour water, then salted it and beat it well. Carefully she formed it into a wedge the thickness of three fingers; then she tried it out on fresh-baked bread that Phoebe had grown quite expert at making. Phoebe had also cooked up some peas porridge, a favorite of everyone in the household.

"You make the best peas porridge, Phoebe," Rachel said as she layered a slice of the bread with fresh butter and bit into it. "I've got to have your recipe."

"Why, I don't think there is any. I've never seen one!" Phoebe exclaimed.

"That's what good cooks always say. Seems like the best ones don't have anything written down. They just add a pinch of this and a pinch of that." Actually peas porridge was rather simple to make. One simply took a quart of green peas, boiled them in water with dried mint and a little fat, then added some beaten pepper and a piece of butter rolled in

83

flour. All that was left was to stir it, let it boil, and finally add two quarts of milk and serve it.

"I'll be glad when Mr. Bradford gets back. I'm anxious to hear how Joel is doing."

"You two are very close, aren't you?"

"Yes, we are. We grew up together, and we had to take care of each other, for the most part. I'm worried about him now that he's in the army. It's so dangerous."

"I know what you mean. I'm always worried about Dake and Micah."

"But Micah's a chaplain, isn't he? He won't be fighting."

"When the fighting starts, I don't think that will matter. A musket ball will hit anybody that gets in its way."

"That would be awful. Is your brother Dake's foot any better?"

"Oh, it's much better, but I'm afraid he'll always have a limp."

"He was lucky to keep his foot, from what I understand."

"Yes, he was. If Clive hadn't come along and rescued him out of the hands of the British, I think he would have lost it."

The two women sat down at the table, and Phoebe smiled as she heard the sound of Marian Bradford's voice singing to the baby. "She loves that child like I never saw, doesn't she?"

"Well, she's waited a long time for a baby."

"She loves him as if he was her own."

"Well, he is her own, Phoebe."

"I guess that's right, isn't it? He'll sure get good care. There's no doubt about that." She listened as the words came from the nursery:

> Eeny, meeny, miney, mo,
> Catch a tiger by the toe.
> If he hollers let him go,
> Eeny, meeny, miney, mo.

"I said that when I was a baby in England. It was the first thing I ever learned."

"Did you ever hear this one?" Rachel asked.

> Eena, meena, mono, mi,
> Panalona bona stry,
> Eewee, fowlsneck,
> Hallibone, crackabone, ten and eleven,
> O-u-t spells out, and out goes you.

"I never heard that one."

"It's a little counting game we used to play when I was growing up. I remember that."

The two women sat there, and finally Phoebe gave a calculating glance toward Rachel. "What are you going to do with those two men who are courting you?"

"I'm not going to do anything with them."

"They'll pester you to death. Why, they've been here three nights in a row."

"I know. I wish they'd take turns. They sit there glaring at each other, and if I pay one bit of attention to one more than I do the other, why a storm cloud comes up."

Phoebe laughed and sliced a piece of the fresh bread. She buttered it, opened a pot of blackberry jam, and spread it on top. "I'm going to get fat as a pig if I don't stop eating so much." She chewed thoughtfully for a moment, then said, "I wish I had two handsome men chasing after me."

At that moment Marian came in carrying Enoch. She was wearing a bright maroon dress with a high neck and long sleeves trimmed in off-white lace. On top of her dress she wore a crisp white apron that tied in the back and came down almost to the edge of her long skirt. She looked radiant. "Here, take this fat slug," she grinned. "He's breaking my arm." She surrendered the infant to Phoebe and sat down and sniffed. "Oh, fresh bread! Why didn't you call me?"

As Marian helped herself to fresh bread and butter and jam, Phoebe said, "I was just telling Rachel that I wish I had two good-looking young men chasing after me."

"Well, I don't have two good-looking *young* men. The pastor's not young. He's thirty-five."

Marian shot a glance at her and made a mock frown. "He's practically tripping over his beard. He's one year older than I am."

"Oh, I didn't mean *you* were old, Marian!" Rachel cried quickly. Then she saw the laughter in the eyes of the other women. "Well, anyway, I always thought it would be nice to be pursued by a string of suitors, but it's not really all that wonderful."

"You think either one of them will ask you to marry him?"

"I hope not."

"Wouldn't you have either one of them?" Marian asked. "The minister has money."

"But Jubal's more fun," Phoebe said.

"You can't live on fun, Phoebe," Marian admonished. She turned to face her stepdaughter. "I rather admire Reverend Grierson, Rachel."

"Why, so do I. But you can't marry everyone you admire."

Phoebe laughed and said, "Too bad you can't have as many husbands as you choose."

"That's right," Rachel rejoined. "I may marry them both. Then I'll have one for every day and one for Sunday."

"Oh, don't be silly. Marriage is a serious thing."

"It doesn't have to be. I've seen how much fun you have with your husband. You and Papa have a good time. He's always teasing you and you tease him right back."

"I don't think it'd be proper to tease a minister, would it?" Phoebe asked. "It doesn't seem so, anyway."

The same thought had occurred to Rachel, although she did not say so. "I don't want to talk about it anymore. I'm going out to see if there are any fresh eggs. Those pullets haven't been laying like they should."

"Maybe you ought to do with them what Queen Elizabeth once said she did with an admiral."

"What was that?"

"She did away with him! She said it was a good thing to execute an admiral every now and then just as an example to the rest."

Rachel laughed. "I may just wring one of their necks. That'll give the rest of my suitors something to think about."

She went to the door, put on her blue wool cloak, and pulled a woolen bonnet over her head. She then walked out to the barn, where most of the chickens were roosting in the cold weather. She had had Sam build them some nesting boxes, and now she picked up a basket and went down the row checking them. When she reached the end, she said with exasperation, "Only three eggs from fifteen chickens! I think I will wring a neck or two!" One of the white chickens walked by clucking and then was joined by the others. "Don't come clucking at me," Rachel said. "I'm going to wring your necks if you don't start laying better! What's the matter with you silly chickens?"

She went back to the house and told Phoebe, "Only three eggs from fifteen chickens."

"That's not many, is it?" Phoebe said. She was holding the baby on her knee, joggling him up and down. "Maybe we ought to get more chickens."

"I suppose so." Rachel went about her duties that day, but the thought kept coming back to her, *Why do chickens stop laying?* She had asked their handyman, Sam Marshall, and he had simply grunted, "Don't know. Sometimes they lay; sometimes they don't."

"But they were laying up to twenty eggs a day just a while back."

"Can't say, Miss Rachel."

Rachel took the afternoon off and went to visit Abigail Howland, a friend of hers. Abigail was a young woman of twenty who lived with her mother in the home of her aunt, Esther Denham. Esther had invited Abigail and her sister-in-law, who was in bad health, to stay with her. This was a good thing because the Howlands had nothing since the death of Saul Howland, Abigail's father. They had lost everything in Boston when the Americans had retaken it. It was only the charity of Esther Denham that offered them shelter at all.

"Why, come in, Rachel," Abigail Howland greeted her. She had an oval face, bright hazel eyes, and brown hair. She was a very attractive young woman and had been quite a man chaser before becoming a Christian. She had also fallen in love with Daniel's oldest son, Matthew Bradford.

"How is your mother?" Rachel asked as she took off her coat and hung it up. "Is she any better?"

"Not much, and now Aunt Esther is sick as well. Seems like half the people I know are sick. I'm sorry you won't get to see them. They're both sleeping."

"Oh, that's all right. I just wanted to bring you some of this bread. Phoebe always makes enough for a regiment."

"Oh, that's wonderful! She makes the best bread."

"I would've brought you some eggs, but the chickens have stopped laying."

"Well, we have plenty. Ours are laying a lot these days. I can give you some," Abigail said eagerly.

"We can use them."

"Has Daniel come back yet from General Washington's camp?"

"No. He had some other things to do. I don't know what. It had something to do with the army." She looked over and said cautiously, "He got a letter from Matthew this week."

"Oh, really." The reply was rather strained. Abigail could not bring herself to say much about her love for Matthew Bradford. She had deceived him shamefully in the past, and when he had found out, although he had been very much in love with her, he turned away bitterly, refusing to have anything to do with her. "I hope he's well," she said finally.

"He's still trying to decide whether or not to change his name."

"That's rather strange, isn't it? For a man to change his name."

The matter of Matthew's name was important. He was actually not Daniel Bradford's blood son. Daniel had married Holly Blanchard, Matthew's mother, when she was carrying him, and he had only later discovered that the baby's father was Sir Leo Rochester. Before Sir Leo's recent death, he had been urging Matthew to take his own name, for he had no sons to carry on the Rochester name.

"What do you think he will do, Rachel?"

"Who knows what he'll do? Matthew's always been different."

"Did you notice that much when you were growing up?"

"Oh yes. Dake and Micah were so different from Matthew."

"Yes. Matthew's the image of Leo, isn't he?"

"Yes, he is. I hate to see him do it. I'll always think of him as my brother. Nothing can change that."

"I understand he's doing very well with his painting."

"Oh yes. He said in his letter he had sold three canvases for a considerable sum."

Abigail shook her head. "I hope he does well."

Rachel got up and went over to sit down beside her friend. Putting her arm around her, she said, "You still love him, don't you?"

"Yes, I do."

"Then don't give up. God can do wonderful things."

Tears filled Abigail Howland's eyes. "I led such an awful life before I was saved. I can't ever really put it behind me."

"You mustn't dwell on those things. God says He puts all of our sins as far as the east is from the west, as deep as the deepest sea."

"Still it's hard not to think of the things I did."

"They're all washed clean by the blood of Jesus," Rachel said firmly. "Now, you put it out of your mind."

"I'll try," Abigail said. She wiped her eyes and tried to smile. "Come along and I'll give you some of the gingerbread I made this morning. . . ."

🔔   🔔   🔔

"Well, they're both here again." Phoebe was peering into a kettle. The steam from the soup came up and she savored it. "I don't know if we have enough to feed them or not. Both of them eat like horses."

"We'll have enough, but they're going to have to start bringing their lunch if they're going to shove their feet under this table all the time," Rachel said grimly as she moved back out into the ornate dining room. It was a large room with wall-to-wall dark green carpet, and bold green walls with gold diamond wallpaper. A green marble fireplace almost covered one wall, and above the mantel was an elegant gilt-edged mirror and a series of Chinese paintings. She walked over to where the mahogany table was draped with a fine white cloth and put down the bowl, saying, "I think this is about all."

"It looks like it ought to do us," Jubal said cheerfully.

Indeed it was a fine meal. A large venison roast had been cooked over the fire and was now placed on a large platter. The women had sliced it into thick, juicy slabs that sent up their own aroma. A pie tin contained a large beefsteak pie with a flaky crust that had been made the day before. It was served cold. Bowls of sweet potatoes covered with slices of tart apples and green beans in a cream sauce decorated the table with their bright colors. They served freshly baked bread with thick butter and preserves and mugs filled with steaming hot tea.

"I'm going to have to buy larger clothes if I keep on eating like this," Jubal said. He looked across the table and said, "Do you find yourself happy in your new charge, Reverend?"

"Perhaps we'll ask the blessing first and then I'll answer your question."

"Oh, I beg your pardon. We rough sailors sometimes forget the niceties of life," Jubal said, a mocking light in his eyes.

Grierson locked eyes with Jubal Morrison. The two looked almost as if they were ready to run at each other and lower their heads like fighting goats.

Rachel glanced across at Marian, who was trying to contain a smile. They waited and finally Grierson pronounced a rather crusty blessing, not at all in his usual eloquent style.

"Have you taken any more prizes, Jubal?" Marian asked.

"No. No success yet. Sam is chomping at the bit."

"He's a rather brilliant young man, isn't he?" Marian said. "Did you know he built me a bathtub and piped hot water to it? And on the second floor, too. It's a marvelous invention."

"How does the water heat?" Grierson inquired. He was not really interested, but he felt he must show some attention to his hostess. He had come to admire the Bradford family very much indeed, and found Marian Bradford a most attractive and charming woman. He listened as she described Sam's invention and then said, "He seems to be a very fine young man. I know you're proud of your brother, aren't you, Rachel?"

"Oh, Sam can be a pain," Rachel smiled. "He's always into something. But he has a good heart."

The meal went on for some time, and after it was over, the men were led into the larger of the two parlors. There Rachel played on the harpsichord, Marian sang, Enoch was brought in to be admired, which he duly was, and the evening moved along quite well.

But by ten o'clock Rachel whispered to Phoebe, who had come to bring another pot of tea, "Aren't they ever going to go home?"

"Why don't you tell them to?"

"It's not my house," Rachel said grimly, "or I would."

Finally Jubal won the contest. He simply sat there until Reverend Grierson sighed and said, "It is rather late. I think I should go."

"We will be happy to see you anytime, Reverend," Marian said. "I'll show you to the door." She winked at Rachel as she said this, knowing that was not at all Reverend Grierson's plan.

When the two were gone, Jubal grinned broadly. "I thought he'd never leave, didn't you?"

"He did stay a long time. It is rather late, Jubal."

Jubal had been standing at the fireplace. He came over, put out his hands, and lifted her up. She was taken by surprise, and he suddenly put his arms around her and kissed her.

It was done so quickly that Rachel was taken aback. She had been kissed before and actually was not angry. But when he tried to kiss her again, she put her hands on his chest and said, "That's enough of that, Jubal Morrison."

"You don't need a preacher for a husband. It would be boring."

"I don't need a pirate either!"

Jubal smiled and cocked one eyebrow. He was a forceful man, totally masculine and quite attractive in a rugged fashion. He took her hand, and though she tried to pull it away, he kissed it and said, "You're going to think a lot more of me in the future than you do now, Rachel."

"Oh, do you think so?"

"Yes indeed, I do."

"You're very egotistical."

Jubal smiled. "That's the way we pirates are." He said, "I'll go now. I just wanted to see how long that preacher would sit there. Very thoughtless fellow keeping you up this late. Good night, Rachel."

Rachel saw him to the door, and when she closed it, she smiled. She liked Jubal Morrison very much and his kiss had been exciting to her. She shook her head and scolded herself. "That's enough of that! I don't need a preacher *or* a pirate!"

🔔   🔔   🔔

Perhaps it was the business of the chickens not laying well that triggered it all, but Rachel also discovered that other things were missing out of the smokehouse. She remembered specifically that she had hung several smoked chickens up, five to be exact. They were some of Daniel's favorite dishes, and she had stood stock-still one Thursday afternoon when she came in and saw that there were only four. *Perhaps Phoebe took one in for supper tonight*, she thought. She went into the house and inquired, but Phoebe denied any knowledge of it.

That's odd, Rachel thought. Her mind worked quickly and she concluded, *Someone's stealing*. At once she knew she had to do something. *It has to be at night*, she thought. *I'll wait up for them. Whoever it is has got to be stopped.*

🕆   🕆   🕆

Everyone in the house had gone to bed when Rachel quietly stepped out of the back door. She held in her hand a pistol she had primed and loaded herself. Her father and her brothers had given her good instruction on firearms, and this particular pistol was a favorite of her father's. She had loaded and fired it many times under his direction. Now, wearing a dark blue cloak, bonnet, and a pair of heavy gloves, she moved out onto the back porch. The skies were filled with stars and she could see clearly by their light. The moon also was half full, so there would be no question that she could see anyone.

She took her position in a straight-back cane chair, ignoring the cold. "They've got to come sometime," she said grimly. "When they do, I'll be here."

She waited until almost midnight, and it was so cold she could not bear it. "I'll have to go get more clothes," she muttered. She stood, but even as she did, a shadowy figure suddenly appeared. She could not see clearly, for the barn was some fifty yards from the house and shaded by a large elm tree. Still it was human, not an animal. Catching her breath, she froze and watched.

It was a man, she could see that much, and he slipped into the smokehouse. He was gone for only a few minutes, and then he was out again with something in his hand.

Rachel moved off the porch, keeping her eyes fixed on him. She walked as soundlessly as she could over the frozen snow, careful not to slip and lose her balance. She saw him go into a small barn that had been abandoned some time ago. It was used now only for storing the second buggy and was packed with belongings too good to be thrown away but not good enough to keep. She had gone there only once with Marian, looking for several items for the house.

Reaching the door, she slipped inside and waited for her eyes to adjust. It was dark, but some light filtered through the gaping cracks in the clapboards. When her eyes adjusted, she lifted the pistol and moved forward. The floor was covered with straw that had filtered down from above, and there was a musty smell. She saw no one, but then a sound overhead caught her attention.

He's upstairs, she thought. *I'll have to climb the stairway.* Moving to the stairs, she began going up. She knew they probably squeaked, so she placed each foot on a tread, lowering her weight slowly. The fourth one she stepped on squeaked despite this, and she caught her breath and stood there in the darkness waiting. She could hear it then, the sound of heavy breathing. Carefully she advanced until her head cleared the opening. It was much easier to see here, for the loft opening let in the rays of the moon. She looked around quickly and there he was, a man. She could not see his face. He was wearing some sort of a coat and a floppy hat that came down over his ears. He was gnawing on the chicken that he had taken, and anger flared through her. Not knowing whether he had a weapon or not, she suddenly mounted the remaining treads and threw the pistol down on the man, saying, "Don't move or I'll shoot you!"

The man suddenly looked up at her. He dropped the chicken on the floor and then began to get to his feet.

"You stay right there or I'll shoot!" Rachel warned. He seemed not to hear, however, and she noticed he pulled himself up painfully, using the wall as a brace. She took a step closer and said, "You stand right there."

"I will not—harm you."

The words were in a whisper, and she knew from his speech that he was a foreigner.

"Who are you? What are you doing here?"

The man lifted his face, and she saw it then as the moonlight fell on it. He had not shaved recently and his eyes were dark hallows. He tried to stand straighter, then he tried to speak, but somehow he could not.

The man took one step forward and Rachel leveled the pistol. "I'll kill you if you don't stay where you are," she whispered.

He was very tall, she saw, and she saw also that his coat was some kind of uniform. "You're an escaped prisoner of war, aren't you?"

"Yes. I am a prisoner."

The words came haltingly, and then he started to collapse. His knees folded and he fell face forward full-length on the straw. He did not attempt to break his fall, and there was a looseness in him that a man could not fake. His arms fell out and his face was pressed against the moldy straw.

Rachel stood there half frightened. She didn't know what to do. "Get up!" she said. "I'm not joking! I'll shoot you." The figure was absolutely motionless. Rachel moved closer and, reaching over, pushed at him with the muzzle of the pistol, but he did not move even then. "Are you hurt?" she whispered. No answer. Carefully Rachel reached out and grabbed his shoulder. Shaking him, she said, "What's wrong with you?" And then she saw the bloodstain that covered the upper part of his back. She touched it and found it stiff with dried blood, but his fall had evidently opened the wound, for she could see a small crimson stain forming. She touched it and whispered, "Blood. He's been shot."

The silence filled the loft completely. The only sound was the hoarse breathing of the man who lay facedown before her. Taking a deep breath, Rachel pulled at his shoulder and rolled him over loosely. His eyes were closed, but his mouth was open, and she could hear the raw sound of his breathing.

As she crouched there in the darkness, Rachel Bradford was confused. She knew this man was an enemy soldier. He sounded German to her by the few words she had heard, perhaps one of the hated Hessians. But as she looked at the face, she saw no brutality there. Indeed, all she saw was a wounded man, perhaps dying. He did not move, and for one moment the breathing stopped and her heart leaped. "Oh no, he's dead," she whispered.

But then his labored breathing began again. "What can I do?" As always, Rachel Bradford prayed when she was uncertain. "Oh, Lord," she said, "this man is an enemy of mine." She waited, praying silently, then added, "But he is not your enemy, Lord. What can I do?"

An owl noiselessly sailed by the opening. The shadow fell across the wounded man's face and then vanished. Rachel leaned forward and put her hand on his forehead. *He's burning up with fever*, she thought. And again she felt confusion. She had heard of the Hessians, who were called "baby eaters." Rumor had it that they did eat children. She thought that was foolish, but she had heard of their cruelty and how viciously they attacked. The man that lay before her, however, was totally helpless. *As helpless as Enoch*, she thought. His hat had fallen off, revealing fine blond hair. Once again she touched his forehead. "He'll die with fever. But what can I do? I'll have to turn him in."

The man suddenly moaned and cried out something that sounded like "mother."

She leaned forward, "What did you say?"

"Meine Mutter. . . "

"He's calling for his mother—just like a little boy." Rachel crouched there in the darkness and then slowly laid the pistol down. She knelt beside the wounded man and somehow knew that he had been put into her path. She did not know why, nor for what reason, but she prayed earnestly, "Oh, God, if you want me to help this man, you will have to help me!"

PART TWO

THE PATIENT

November–December 1777

8

An Unusual Patient

A TEARING PAIN IN HIS SIDE brought him out of the deep darkness. The smell of moldy hay came to him, but then a different odor, one he could not identify, struck his senses. Breathing shallowly, he lay there as consciousness came creeping back and confusion drove his thoughts into a maelstrom for a time. His face was blistering, it seemed, with the heat, and indeed his whole body radiated as if it were a furnace. His clothes were soaked with sweat, and fragments of the stale-smelling hay made him want to claw at his skin.

Slowly he opened his eyes and knew something was different. The loft was a gloomy place even during the height of day, but the sunlight was falling down in slanting bars through cracks in the warping boards. Now, however, he was aware that to his right was a soft yellow glow, and turning his eyes, he blinked. Squinting, he peered between half-shut lids to see a woman standing there.

Memory came rushing back over him, not clearly but in changing patterns. He remembered the terrible strain of climbing up the stairs, and he remembered this same woman who had appeared with a pistol in one hand. She was watching him now, and by the amber light, he saw that her broad mouth was drawn into a thin line and her expression held something of anger. She had a heart-shaped face and deep-set eyes, either light blue or light green, and in his delirium he could do nothing but lie there and stare up at her.

Rachel paused, filled with confusion. The soldier lay there looking up at her, as helpless as a sick kitten. There was no danger in him, she saw, so she took the gun off cock and placed it on the rough floorboards. Moving closer, she leaned over and studied the face of the wounded man.

His hair was light blond, and beneath the slitted eyelids she could

97

see eyes of a peculiar light blue color. He had a strong jaw and a broad forehead; if he were cleaned up he would have been a handsome man indeed.

"Can you hear me?" she asked finally. She had to lean forward to catch the whisper.

"Yes. I can . . . hear you."

The voice was very weak, and Rachel carefully placed the lantern on an empty wooden crate. It shed light over the countenance of the man, and without considering what she was doing, she leaned forward and put her hand on his forehead. *He's burning up with fever*, she thought.

Even as she kept her hand there, his eyes closed and his body seemed to go limp. For a moment Rachel was afraid that he had died, but putting her hand on his chest, she felt it rise and fall in a shallow fashion. Her eyes were becoming more accustomed now to the feeble light, and she saw that the entire right side of his shirt was crusted with dried blood. Touching it with her palm, she found that there was still a wetness there. "He's bleeding," she murmured aloud. She bit her lip and considered going for help but for some reason could not bring herself to do it.

Determination came to her then, and she rose and picked up the lantern. Moving quickly, she went back to the house, poured fresh water into a bucket, and found some old but clean white sheets and a basin. Leaving the house, she entered the barn, looking around fearfully to see if anyone was watching. She felt guilty for all of this, but still the thought of the wounded man who was perhaps dying pulled at her like a strong magnet. Climbing the stairs, she laid out her supplies and then unbuttoned the uniform shirt. When she pulled it away, the dried blood had caused it to adhere to the wound, and the soldier moaned slightly and opened his eyes.

"You'll have to be still," she said. "I've got to look at your side."

As she laid the shirt back, she noted the leanness of the man, and the thought came involuntarily, *He's half starved!* Moving the lantern closer, she saw that a bullet had pierced his side. It had made a great tear along the ribs, where it had entered. As she reached underneath him, she felt the exit wound, which was puffy and still seeping blood. Carefully she washed the gaping wound in the side, cleaning away the blood, and then did the same for the smaller wound in the back. She tore the sheet into long strips and formed a compress, but then she saw that she could not apply the bandage while he was lying down.

"You'll have to sit up," she said. She did not know if he understood her, for he did not open his eyes. Still, when she pulled at him, he came upright to a sitting position. Awkwardly she placed the compress over the worst wound on his side, then reaching around, she began to wind long strips to hold it in place. The other compress she had more difficulty inserting, but finally she had bound up the wound and tied the strips. She looked up to see the soldier's blue eyes peering at her.

"*Danke schön,*" he whispered.

Rachel said brusquely, "Now, let me see the head." She saw that something had torn a ragged gash along the side of his head and that it was filled with the dust from the old straw. "I'll have to wash that out," she said. She did not look at him, but dipping a cloth into the basin, she began to wash the wound. The blood in the hair was dried, so she held it there until it was soaked. Once he swayed and would have fallen back. Putting her arm around behind his back, she said, "You'll have to sit up."

"Ja," he whispered. "I will."

Finally the blood and dirt were washed away, and Rachel quickly wound a white strip all the way around the head and tied it off neatly. "Now," she said, "you can lie back." She was afraid that in his weakness he would fall back and injure himself again, so putting one arm under him and the other around his neck, she helped him ease back down.

She straightened up then and pulled a small crate around and sat down on it.

"I thank you," he said.

"Are you thirsty?"

"Ja. Very . . . thirsty."

Rachel poured fresh water from the basin into the cup. "You should have drunk this while you were sitting up."

"I can sit up again. I feel better now."

Rachel watched as he drank thirstily, and then he did not offer to lie down again. "You've got a bad fever," she said. "I'm no doctor, but I know that you need one."

"They will send me back to the prison," he said quietly. "I would rather die here than do that."

"You can't stay here," Rachel said quickly.

"What will you do with me, then? Turn me in to the authorities?"

"You're an enemy soldier. I'll have to notify the army." She expected him to protest, but he did not. It was as if he had given up all hope of anything good happening. The fever had dulled his eyes, and the only sign that he gave at the impact of her word was a tightening of his lips. He sat there immobile.

Finally he said, "I thank you, madam, for your care. You have been ... good ..."

The words trailed off and he swayed alarmingly from side to side. He started to fall backward and Rachel dropped the cup and managed to catch him. She eased him down, her hand under his head, and then paused for a moment. He was a very tall man, well over six feet, and she could tell that ordinarily he was strong. But just now he was like a hurt child. It somehow touched her that he had not begged her for mercy, and she had the impression that he was not the kind who would beg anyone. Slowly she stood to her feet and picked up the lantern. She paused for a long moment in the silence of the loft looking down on his face, wondering what sort of man he was. *In any case,* she thought, *he's my enemy.* That did not seem to give her the release she sought. Reason told her to go at once and notify the army that an enemy soldier was taking refuge in their barn. For some reason she could not do this, and as she turned and moved down the steps, she thought, *I'll have to think about it. If he goes back to the prison, he'll die. I don't want to be responsible for that.*

When she reached the house, no one was stirring. She undressed and went to bed, but for a long time she thought about the lean face of the Hessian.

🔔   🔔   🔔

As Rachel put the final touches to her hair, her eyes went to the calendar that hung on the wall. She noted the date: November the twenty-sixth of the year 1777. As with most people, she mentally subtracted the years and months that had passed since the revolution had begun. It seemed much longer than two and a half years when the British had fired on the farmers who had gathered on the green at Lexington. Everything in life seemed to have revolved around that one incident, and now as she moved across the room, she wondered if it would ever end. She glanced at herself in the small mirror and was satisfied that she looked well enough dressed for church. She was wearing a taffeta mantelet, a pale green color, crossed in front and tied in the back. Her skirt was of a darker hue of green, and she picked up a velvet pelisse and slipped into it. The room was cold, and she knew that the church itself would be cold, so she grabbed a fur muff, then pulled a silk bonnet on over her red hair. Quickly she left the room and found Marian and Phoebe downstairs. Marian was holding Enoch, who was muffled up so that only his eyes were visible.

"You're starting Enoch's churchgoing early, Marian," Rachel smiled.

100

Actually her mind was on the wounded soldier out in the barn, but she knew she had to carry on her regular affairs. She had hardly slept, falling into a fitful sleep for a time and then waking up, puzzling over what to do about him.

"Yes. He may grow up to be a minister," Marian said, smiling proudly at her baby. "Come along now. Caesar's got the carriage out."

The three women went outside, and Caesar, the huge black coachman, assisted each of them. When Rachel put her hand in his, it gave her an odd feeling, for his hand practically swallowed hers. "Thank you, Caesar," she said as she stepped up.

"You're welcome, Miss Rachel. You look mighty fine today."

"Thank you, Caesar. You look fine yourself." Caesar was wearing a suit that Marian had had specially made for his huge frame. He was six inches over six feet and weighed close to two hundred seventy pounds. He wore a brown watch coat over a single-breasted coat and beneath this a blue-and-white-striped vest. His leather britches were forced down into heavy black jackboots, and his cocked crimson hat was of the style worn by fashionable gentlemen.

"Don't be late, Caesar," Marian called out as he got up into the box, his great weight pulling the carriage over in an alarming fashion. "No, ma'am," he said. "We'll be there in plenty of time."

As they turned along the street, the wheels of the landau rumbling over the cobblestones, Rachel listened as the other two women talked. She herself was not at all certain that she should have come to church. *Perhaps I ought to have stayed and seen to the man. His fever was so high. People have died with high fevers like that.*

They arrived at the church, and as Rachel stepped out, she glanced at the massive structure with its heavily buttressed walls, pointed arches, and window tracery. It was a survival of Gothic architecture, and there was no other building exactly like it in all of Boston.

"I'll wait until after the service is over, Mrs. Bradford."

"You can go on up in the balcony and hear the sermon," Marian smiled.

"All right, ma'am. I'll do that."

The women hurried inside and were indeed a little late. Despite the extremely cold weather the church was practically full. Mr. Patrick Dennison, one of the leaders of the church, came at once with a smile. "Come this way, ladies. There's room right down over here close to the stove."

The three sat down and at once Enoch began to cry. Marian quickly fished out a rounded glass bottle and stuck the cloth nipple into his mouth, which ceased the crying immediately.

Up on the platform Reverend Josiah Grierson sat up straighter. Rachel saw with embarrassment that his eyes were fixed on her.

Phoebe nudged her, saying, "That preacher can't keep his eyes off you, Rachel."

"Hush, Phoebe! Don't talk nonsense!"

Unfortunately, Phoebe was not the only one who noticed the minister's attention as it focused on Rachel. As the song service continued, Grierson, although singing in a clear baritone voice with the congregation, obviously had his eyes on Rachel Bradford.

Marian took all of this in and smiled but knew better than to say anything to Rachel. She and Daniel had talked about the possibilities of a match, but Marian had said, "No one knows what a woman will do about choosing a man."

Daniel had laughed. "You never said a truer word, but I admire your judgment, wife."

Now as the service continued and Grierson rose to preach, Rachel found herself wondering what it would be like to be married to a minister. Church had been her entire life. She had not known a time when she had not been involved. Her father was a leader of the church, and there was never a question of "Shall we go to church today?" That was settled forever and, like the laws of the Medes and the Persians, was unchangeable—at least for the Bradfords.

The sermon was excellent, but then Reverend Grierson had already proven that he was an outstanding preacher of the Word. Taking over the leadership of the church had been a challenge for him, for the congregation was deeply committed to the Reverend Asa Carrington, who had been their minister for years. However, the younger man had proven himself to be not only an exemplary preacher but a fine pastor as well.

Finally the sermon was over, and as the women moved toward the door, they found Reverend Grierson waiting to shake hands with each of them.

"A fine sermon, sir," Marian said.

"Thank you, indeed, Mrs. Bradford."

"If you have no other obligations, would you care to take dinner with us?"

"You ask a bachelor that?" Reverend Grierson smiled. "Just name the time."

"Give us an hour. It won't be ornate."

"It will be excellent, I'm sure. You may depend on my being prompt."

Rachel shook hands with the minister as he said these last words, and his hands closed on hers in a manner somewhat more intimate than was usual. "I will look forward to seeing you, Miss Rachel."

"Certainly." Rachel pulled her hand away and moved outside at once.

Sam Bradford had been in line behind the women. He had heard the exchange and quickly turned and dug his elbow into Jubal Morrison's ribs. "Well, we can't let that preacher get ahead of you now, can we, Jubal?"

Morrison was wearing a simple suit, dark blue britches, and white stockings. He wore a gray cloth coat and a matching waistcoat, and instead of a wig, his hair was drawn back and tied with black ribbons. "I don't see what it does to us. We didn't get any invitation."

"You leave that to me, Jubal. What's the good of having a stepmother if you can't get a meal out of her every once in a while?"

Sam stepped outside and caught up with the group who were being helped into the carriage. "Hello, Mother dear," Sam grinned. "Why don't you take mercy on me and feed me today."

"Why, we've invited the minister," Marian said, but she had a weakness for Sam. "All right. Come along."

"And I'd like to bring Jubal." The irrepressible Sam turned his face away from Marian and winked broadly at Rachel, grinning at her discomfiture.

"Oh, of course, bring him along, too," Marian said.

When they were in the landau, she said, "Will it be uncomfortable for you, Rachel, with your two suitors?"

"Yes it will!" Rachel said crossly. "And you knew that when you asked them!"

"Oh, now don't be upset, Rachel. I feel sorry for bachelors like Mr. Morrison and Reverend Grierson. They're going to ruin their stomachs with their bachelor cooking."

The three arrived at home and immediately set about putting a meal together. Rachel looked more than once at the barn and wondered how long it would be before she could get back to see how the Hessian was. It surprised her that she had thought so much about him, but then nothing like this had ever happened to her before.

Finally the meal was prepared and the gentlemen, all three of them, arrived. "You'll have to take what we could put together," Marian smiled.

"Aw, you don't know how to cook anything bad," Sam said. "Just lead us to it."

"Come on. It's all ready." They gathered into the dining room, where the large walnut table was already set. The women had prepared sausage in peas porridge and potato pie. They had added artichoke bottoms baked in rich pies with dried currants, raisins, and dates. There was also cheese and a bowl of potted fish.

"Why, this is a meal fit for a king!" Jubal Morrison smiled.

"Certainly! It's even fit for two sea captains and a preacher," Sam said. "You don't eat like this every day, do you, Reverend?"

"Indeed I do not, Samuel," Josiah said.

"Would you ask the blessing, Reverend?" Marian said.

After the blessing Sam led the way. He filled his plate and ate so voraciously that Rachel reached over and slapped his hand once. "Sam, you eat like you haven't had a bite in weeks! You were taught better manners than that!"

"You fellows see how bossy she is?" Sam grinned. "Be careful what you're letting yourself in for."

Rachel flushed and Reverend Josiah Grierson looked embarrassed, but not so Jubal Morrison. He leaned back and studied Rachel with mischief flickering in his deep-set eyes. "I think I'd be willing to be bossed a little bit if the woman was beautiful enough and could cook like this."

Phoebe, who had gone to get more bread from the kitchen, heard this and giggled.

Rachel looked up and said, "Phoebe, stop your simpering and set the bread down!"

"Yes, ma'am!" Phoebe went into the servants' back room, where she had set a plate for Caesar. The huge black man sat carefully on a kitchen stool and ate rather daintily for one his size. He grinned at Phoebe, saying, "The preacher and the captain are really after Miss Rachel, ain't they?"

"Yes, they are. It's funny, isn't it?"

"Which one d'ya think will win?"

"I don't know. If it were me, I'd take Mr. Morrison. He's so fine looking and lots of fun."

Back in the dining room, Morrison was enjoying his meal. He was extra polite to the Reverend Grierson, however. Finally, when the meal was over, Sam said, "You know what I'm going to do in exchange for this fine meal?"

"What?" Marian asked, knowing that Sam was up to mischief.

"I'm going to take you ladies for a voyage on the *Defiant*."

"Not me," Marian said.

"Well, you then, sis." He grinned broadly, saying, "You'd make a fine lady pirate."

Rachel's mind was elsewhere. "Don't be foolish, Sam."

"Well, that puts us in a bind," Morrison said. He leaned forward and studied Rachel thoughtfully, then his eyes moved to the minister. "You can give her a good sermon to pay for your meal, but if Miss Rachel won't come out on our boat, I don't know how we'll pay her back."

"I'm not becoming a lady pirate! You can bet on that, Jubal Morrison!"

Her sharpness caught the attention of everyone, and Rachel knew it. She was glad the meal was over and began at once to help Phoebe clear the table. She was aware that both Jubal and Josiah were in for another of their matches, trying to see who could outstay the other, so she said to Marian, "I think I'll go upstairs and lie down. I'm rather tired."

Marian said, "Oh, I'm sorry, dear. Maybe you'll feel better later."

She turned her eyes on the suitors and said, "I'm sorry that we won't be able to entertain you. I have to take care of Enoch."

Jubal Morrison said at once, "I think we're being thrown out, but I don't mind that after a meal like this. I'm very grateful to you, Mrs. Bradford."

"Certainly. Certainly," Grierson said. That he was disappointed was obvious, but he made the best of it.

The two men left together, and when they were outside, Jubal said, "Why don't you give up, Pastor?"

Grierson turned at once. "Give up? What do you mean?"

"Well, I mean we've been courting Miss Rachel now for some time, and it's obvious that she favors me."

"Not obvious to me!"

"It's not? Well, I think everyone would tell you that most women are drawn to romantic captains rather than to ministers."

Josiah gritted his teeth. Ordinarily he would have liked Jubal Morrison, but in truth he was not used to being crossed. He had been pursued by many women, for a bachelor minister in a church was fair game. Now, however, humor came to his aid. "May the best man win," he said.

"Why, thank you. I'm glad to hear you accept your defeat with such grace," Jubal grinned. He put out his hand and said, "I admire you, sir. You're a fine preacher. I hope you won't take my unseasonable levity amiss."

"No. Not at all."

"Well then, the contest will continue at length another time. Good day, sir."

"Good day, Jubal."

⚓   ⚓   ⚓

The night fell early during the winters, and by seven o'clock most of the household had retired. Rachel had waited impatiently and finally she dressed warmly, pulled on her wool coat, and stopped at the kitchen long enough to put together a light supper of hot soup and fresh bread for her patient. Outside, she sensed that snow was coming. The frigid air foretold it, and she had a way of guessing the weather rather well. She kept the lantern hooded until she stepped inside the barn, then removing it, she moved up the stairs carefully. As soon as she stepped out on the rough floor, she held the lantern high and saw at once that the Hessian was much worse. His face was flushed, and she could distinctly hear his teeth chattering. Quickly setting down the lantern, she moved over to him and put her hand on his forehead. He flung his arm over, striking her across the chest, but was obviously totally in a delirium.

"That fever's got to come down," Rachel muttered. She bit her lip and then said, "He needs more blankets. We've got to sweat this fever off or he'll die."

Moving at once down the stairs she started toward the door, but as soon as she stepped out, she caught her breath, for there a dark, shadowy shape, huge and frightening, stood before her.

"Miss Rachel, is that you?"

"Caesar!" Rachel gasped. "What are you doing here?"

"I saw you leave the house, ma'am, and I thought something might be wrong."

Rachel could not think clearly for a moment. Finally, she knew that somehow she would have to have help, and the huge black man was highly intelligent and had a special regard for her. "Caesar, I've got something to tell you."

"You mean about the man up in the loft?"

"You know about him?"

"Yes, ma'am. I seen you come out before, and after you left I went up and took a look around. He's hurt mighty bad, ain't he?"

"Yes, he is. He's very sick, Caesar. I've got to go get some blankets."

"You want me to go stay with him, ma'am?"

"Yes. I think so—and, Caesar—" Rachel hesitated for a moment, then stepped closer and looked up into his dark face. "No one must know about this."

"Yes, ma'am, if that's what you want. I'll just go sit with him."

Rachel hurried to the house, returning soon with an armload of blankets. She moved up the stairs, where she at once piled them over him. "There's nothing else we can do except hope that he doesn't die. I've never seen such a high fever."

"He mighty bad, ma'am. Who is he?"

"He's a Hessian."

"A Hessian? What's that, Miss Rachel?"

"A German soldier fighting against our men."

"Is that a fact?" The black face of Caesar turned toward the mountain of blankets. He leaned forward and studied the soldier's face. "He don't look like a bad man."

"I don't know what he is. He's the enemy but . . . " She hesitated, then said, "If we turn him in now, Caesar, they'll send him to a prison camp and he'll die."

Caesar shrugged his massive shoulders pragmatically. "I reckon then we'd better get him well before we do that, Miss Rachel."

Caesar's ready willingness to help took a load off of Rachel's shoulders. She knew now that she would not have to bear the burden alone. "Thank you, Caesar. I know I can trust you."

"Yes, ma'am. I reckon you can do that."

T   T   T

When Jacob came out of the delirium, he found himself soaked with sweat and stared up with shock at a huge black man who was bending over him. He blinked his eyes and tried to speak, but found that his lips were dry as paper. His tongue seemed raspy, and as he tried to sit up, he found that he was weaker than he had ever been in his life.

"Here, you better let me help you, Mr. Soldier." A powerful arm straightened Jacob up, and then there was the sound of water being poured into a cup. "Here, you're bound to be dyin' for a drink."

"Thank you," Jacob rasped and fumbled at the cup. He drank so eagerly that some of it ran down his face.

"Ain't no hurry. We got plenty of water. Your fever's done gone now. Me and Miss Rachel thought you was gonna die."

Jacob drank more slowly then. The cold water was delicious, and he found himself becoming more alert. "Who are you?" he whispered.

"My name's Caesar. I'm the coachman for the Bradford family. Miss Rachel, she's gone, but she'll be back soon. I reckon you'll be gettin' hungry now that your fever's done broke. And, as the Book says, consider the fowls of the air. They sow not, neither do they reap, yet your heavenly Father feedeth them."

"What's that from?" Jacob asked.

"Why, from the Bible, sir. You don't know that?"

"I know the Old Testament."

"No. I reckon this is from the other part."

"You read, then."

"Oh no, sah, I don't read. But I hears people and I remembers. Seems like I got a mighty good memory for a Scripture." The white teeth gleamed as Caesar added, "Some people say too good. Seem like I don't never forget nothin'."

"Who is Miss Rachel?"

"Miss Rachel Bradford. Her daddy's a very important man, Mr. Daniel Bradford. He's my master."

"You mean he owns you? You're a slave?"

"No, sah! I's a free man. Done bought and paid for. Mr. Bradford paid for me and he gave me my papers, so I'm as free as you are."

Jacob Steiner smiled briefly. "A lot more free than I am, Caesar."

"Now, don't you worry, sah. The Bible says give not thought for the morrow, for thou knowest not what a day may bring forth."

Jacob pulled himself up against the wall and studied the kindly face of the massive man who sat cross-legged on the floor. "You know that I'm an enemy soldier?"

"Miss Rachel told me, but she says you'll die if you go to prison."

"She might be right. I nearly died while I was there."

"You was in prison?"

"Yes. I escaped."

"Well, the Book says the Lawd done set the prisoners free, so I guess that means you."

Jacob smiled, and then he heard the sound of footsteps. Both men turned to watch as Rachel came in with a covered dish.

"How is he, Caesar?"

"He done fine, ma'am. Fever's broke."

"I'll sit with him for a while. You can go if you want to."

"I don't mind staying if you want me, Miss Rachel."

"Suit yourself, Caesar."

Rachel turned to the wounded man and said, "Are you hungry?"

"Yes, I am."

"I brought some soup. How long has it been since you've had anything to eat?"

"I can't really remember. I stole some things from your storage shed, some potatoes."

Rachel suddenly laughed. "You're not a very good thief."

"I never had much practice."

Rachel removed the pewter top from the dish and handed him a large bowl. "Here. Be careful, it's hot. Don't burn yourself, and here's some fresh bread."

"It's potato soup. *Sieht sehr gut aus!* My mother made it often. My favorite kind." He looked at the two, and then said, "My mother would have asked a blessing on this, so I ask the blessing now in the name of Almighty God to fall upon you for your kindness to an enemy."

Rachel was shocked. "Your mother's a Christian?"

"Oh no. We are Jewish."

Rachel blinked with surprise, not knowing what to say. "Well, eat your soup."

Jacob found that he was ravenous, so he ate most of the soup along with the bread. Finally he leaned back and said quietly, "That was the best meal I ever had in my life."

Rachel had pulled one of the boxes up, and now she said, "You understand that as soon as you're well enough to endure prison, we'll have to turn you in."

"I understand that very well."

"You speak very good English. Why is that?"

"I had a good teacher. He spent much time in America."

"He knows some of the Bible, Miss Rachel," Caesar spoke up. "The old part."

"The Old Testament?" Rachel asked, lifting her eyebrows.

"Yes. We read it in Yiddish."

"Yiddish? What's that?"

"It's . . . more or less Jewish." He looked up and smiled. "My favorite verse is in the book of Exodus, when Moses asked God to show him His glory. My mother always loved that part of the Scripture," Jacob murmured. He looked up, and somehow he appeared very young by the light of the lantern.

"I don't believe I know that part," Rachel said.

"I remember it," Caesar spoke up suddenly. And then he quoted, " 'And he said, I beseech thee, show me thy glory. And he said, I will make all my goodness pass before thee, and I will proclaim the name of the Lord before thee.' " He grinned with pride. "I remember that from what the Reverend Carrington preached one time before he left."

"That's right," Jacob murmured. "And then the Scripture says, 'And the Lord descended in the cloud and stood with him there, and proclaimed the name of the Lord. And the Lord passed by before him, and proclaimed, The Lord, the Lord God, merciful and gracious, longsuffering, and abundant in goodness and truth.' " He spoke the words reverently and very quietly.

Rachel exchanged a quick glance with Caesar. "It's a beautiful verse," she said.

"My mother's favorite, as I said."

Rachel suddenly could not bear to face the man any longer. She reached out and said rather brusquely, "I'll bring you some more to eat tomorrow. You ought to be warm with all these covers. Good night."

"Good night, Miss Rachel," Jacob Steiner said. He watched as she left and then turned to meet Caesar's gaze. "I've put her in a hard position," he said quietly.

"Don't you worry about Miss Rachel." And then he grinned broadly and quoted again. " 'Who can find a virtuous woman? For her price is far above rubies. The heart of her husband doth faithfully trust in her, so that he shall have no need of spoil. She will do him good and not evil all the days of her life.' "

"Her husband's a fortunate man," Jacob murmured.

"Oh, she ain't got no husband. Not yet. She's lookin' around right now." He saw that the German was getting sleepy. "You go to sleep now. You need all the rest you can get."

"All right. Good night, Caesar—and thank you for your help."

Caesar nodded and moved across the room, his massive weight making the boards creak. He descended the ladder and then stood at the door of the barn for a moment and shook his head. "Lord, you do things I don't understand sometimes, but I reckon I'll have to ask you to help that poor man upstairs. He's all alone in a foreign country and he's hurt, so he needs you. And in the name of Jesus I beg you, do in him what you done me. Just save him from his sins and put his feet on the high way. Amen and amen!"

9

HUSBAND AND WIFE

THE WEDDING DAY OF GRACE GORDON and Stephen Morrison had arrived, and the families were gathered at St. Andrew's Episcopal Church. The bride and groom made a most attractive couple. Stephen was waiting at the front of the church with his best man, David, the bride's brother. He looked as nervous as a bridegroom should look, and as his parents studied his face, both of them were breathing a prayer that he would be the husband Grace needed and would love forever.

As Grace stood in the foyer, ready to walk to the front of the church, she felt her heart beating faster. A myriad of pleasant memories came to mind, and she smiled. She had, as all young women do, looked forward to this moment for a large part of her life. Even as a very young girl she had dreamed of being a wife and a mother. She had watched her parents all her life and had formed her opinion of what a husband and a wife should be by their loving actions. Even when she was a small child, she had noticed the affection they had shown to each other. The parents of her friends, she had observed, were usually not so overt about their feelings. But her father would often stop, with a look in his eye that she had quickly learned to identify, and would go over and put his arms around her mother and kiss her. Her mother, of course, had always returned these caresses. It had been a lesson Grace had learned not from her elders but from observing a happy marriage as it was played out before her all the days of her youth.

Now as she started to walk down the aisle, she met the gaze of her friends and her neighbors, most of whom she had known only since the family had moved to New York. Her father, as an officer in the Royal Forces of His Majesty King George, had been unable to stand the strain of being alone. He was a family man to the bone, and so he had brought the whole family with him. Unlike many officers who took the expedition to conquer the Colonies as a mandate to live as loosely as they pleased, Leslie Gordon centered his life around his God, his family, and his life as a soldier. Now as she met her father's eyes, Grace smiled but could not miss the anxious light in them. *He hates to lose me*, she thought. *But all fathers give their daughters away at some time.* Her glance shifted to her mother, and she was somewhat disconcerted to see the same odd look in her mother's eyes. *Mother's troubled, too, but I love Stephen and he loves me.*

Now her eyes lifted as she was stepping up to where Father Jones, the young priest who had been such a comfort to her family in difficult times, smiled at her with reassurance. He was a slight young man with hazel eyes and a broad, generous mouth. Standing beside him was her brother David. Quickly Grace searched her brother's expression to see if he had the same anxious look as her parents. But David was difficult to read. He was a lean young man of seventeen with crisply curled dark brown hair and widely spaced brown eyes. His face was square and deeply tanned. Now as Stephen stepped forward and turned to face Father Jones, Grace was thinking, *I'm losing David in some way. We've been so close, and we can never be that close again.* She stole a glance at Stephen, who was not looking at her but had his gaze fixed on Father Jones. The thought that rose in her was simply, *Well, Stephen, you'll be all I have now. I'm leaving everything I've ever known for you.*

It was not the first time the thought had come to Grace, and she forced herself to concentrate on the words that Father Jones was intoning. These were words she had heard many times when her friends had gotten married, but now they had a special meaning for her: "Dearly beloved, we are gathered together in the sight of God and in the face of this company to unite this man and this woman in holy matrimony. . . ."

⚜   ⚜   ⚜

"I don't know what I'm going to do without you," Lyna Gordon said. She was standing beside Grace in the kitchen and had turned to her, making this statement in a rather constrained voice. The two had come into the kitchen to bring the coffee and tea cakes into the dining room to serve as a dessert. It was the last regular meal that Grace would have with her parents now that she was married.

Grace forced herself to smile, saying, "Oh, Mother, please don't be sad! I want everything to be happy today. I know you'll miss me, and I'll miss you, too, but you had to leave your parents' house, too."

"It was different with me. I really didn't have any home life, but don't let me talk like this," Lyna said. The two women stood for one moment, and then Lyna reached forward and pulled Grace into her arms. "I'm sorry. I'm happy for you, Grace, and I know you're going to have a wonderful life."

Clinging to her mother for a moment, Grace felt like a very young girl—indeed, she felt like a child. She had always been able to come to her mother with anything, no matter how serious the problem. Since her engagement to Stephen, however, there had been a slight barrier between the two. Nothing perceptible to her mother she hoped, but there had been times when Grace had experienced some tiny fear that perhaps she was making a mistake. She told herself it was just the feelings of a young woman who was facing an unknown experience. She felt much like a voyager getting on a ship that was sailing out to unknown waters where dangerous shoals and menacing storms awaited. The feeling came to her now as she clung to her mother, but with a fierce resolution she shoved it out of her mind. Giving her mother a squeeze, she stepped back and said, "You just wait! When I give you your first grandbaby, you'll feel different about all this."

"May your first child be a masculine one. That's what your father said, isn't it?"

"Yes. He wants a grandson to juggle on his knee. Come along. Let's go in. We have to leave. The coach leaves in an hour and we just have time for dessert."

When the two women entered the dining room, Leslie Gordon looked up with obvious affection at his daughter. "Well, you won't have me to keep you in line from now on, daughter. I shudder to think of what will become of you!" He turned and smiled at his new son-in-law. "You'll have to be careful with this one, Stephen. She takes a great deal of attention. As a matter of fact, I think I have a peach-tree switch somewhere that you ought to take with you in case of emergencies."

Stephen Morrison was startled at this. He had little sense of humor, and only when he saw the others grinning at Gordon's remark did he realize that the tall soldier was joking. "I hardly think that will be necessary, sir," he said. He put his gaze on Grace and said, "She'll have a hard enough time living with me. I'm afraid I'll be the one who gives problems."

"Nonsense, Stephen," David said. "Do as Father says. Whip her regularly and don't let her get accustomed to anything like frivolity. No more new dresses. She's got enough to do her the rest of her life."

Grace was passing behind David's chair. She reached out and thumped him on the head sharply. "You're the one who needs the switch, David Gordon! Father, I trust you'll stop pampering this one."

113

"Indeed I will," Leslie Gordon said and assumed a frown. "Well, David, you heard what your sister said."

Lyna sat down, and to her it was a sad time. She listened to the light talk and was able to join in with some of it, but all the time she felt a hollow sensation inside her.

Finally the meal was over, and Stephen said, "We must leave, dear."

"Yes, Stephen. I think all our things are in the coach."

"I'm glad you're going by ship to South Carolina," Leslie Gordon nodded. "That would be a tiring and dangerous trip overland. What time does the ship leave?"

"Within two hours," Stephen said. He went over and shook hands with his father-in-law. "I'll do my best to make her happy, sir."

"I'm sure you will, Stephen."

Lyna came forward. Instead of shaking hands she put her arms around Stephen. She felt his own arms go around her, but his embrace felt awkward and stiff. She had often noticed that he was not a man who showed affection easily. Still, she smiled into his eyes, saying, "We're giving you our treasure, Stephen. I know you'll treasure her as we do."

"Indeed I will, ma'am—indeed I will!"

David came forward, shook hands with his brother-in-law, then gave Grace a kiss on the cheek. "Sister, don't forget to write."

"You're the one not to forget." Grace was very close to tears, but she blinked them back. "All of you. I love you very much." She could say no more but turned and left. She was followed by Stephen, who helped her up into the coach, then climbed in after her. He spoke to the coachman, and as the horses lurched forward, giving the passengers a jolt, Grace leaned out and took one last look at her parents. Her throat was tight, but she made herself smile gaily and said, "Good-bye," then the horses sprang into a fast pace, turned the corner, and she lost sight of them.

🔔   🔔   🔔

The motion of the ship was the first thing that startled Grace. She came out of a sleep with a start, opened her eyes, and glanced wildly around the cabin. It was no more than eight by ten, with only room for two bunks, an upper and a lower, and a small desk. She was in the lower bunk, and as she thought of the previous night when Stephen had come to her on the narrow bunk, a flush rose up her neck, and she closed her eyes as if someone could see.

Lying there she listened to the creaking of the timbers of the ship

114

and could hear the faint voice of one of the sailors calling something up on deck. The ship rolled and she was happy that she was not seasick. She had not feared that, but Stephen had been apprehensive for himself.

Snuggling under the warm covers on the narrow bunk, she stretched and yawned, thinking about last night. She arched her back and opened her eyes suddenly. "It wasn't what I expected," she murmured, "but I think Stephen surely knows that I love him." A tiny smile touched the corners of her mouth. "I certainly showed him enough affection."

Now she felt complete and satisfied. The only thing that troubled her was that Stephen had said little and had not even told her that he loved her, except in a very strained and artificial way.

Cautiously, she reached up and touched the underside of the bunk, no more than two feet above her head. She playfully tapped on the wooden underframe and lay waiting expectantly. But there was no response. Throwing the covers back, she shuddered with the cold and stood up and stared directly into the face of her new husband. "Stephen, get up. It's time to begin a new life."

Stephen Morrison came groggily awake and muttered, "What? What's that?" He was confused, and when he saw Grace's face not ten inches from his, he started. "What—!"

"It's me. Your new wife."

Stephen blinked and came awake abruptly. He glanced down at the thin white nightgown that revealed Grace's figure plainly, and he seemed embarrassed. "Why don't you get back into bed while I get dressed," he said.

"All right, dear," she said. She plumped into the bed again, pulled the covers over her, and as Stephen climbed down, she lay there waiting for the roll of the ship. She turned her eyes toward Stephen, who was scrambling into his clothes in a furtive way, and his eyes met hers. She could see by the light of the lamp that he was highly embarrassed.

"All right. I'll go see about getting us some breakfast while you get dressed, Grace."

"All right," Grace agreed, puzzled by her new husband's nervousness. She put on a pair of white flannel drawers and a chemise, slipped on a heavy white petticoat, and then a brown woolen dress that buttoned down the front and had long sleeves and a full skirt. On top of this she pulled on a heavy dark blue velvet coat and grabbed the matching bonnet. She left the cabin and walked along the deck of the ship. The captain of the *Mary Ann* was a thick-bodied, white-whiskered man with a head of hair to match. As she approached him, Grace smiled. "Good morning, Captain Minton."

"Good morning to you, ma'am." He stopped and his eyes beamed merrily. "You've got a new name today, I understand."

"That's right."

"Well, may the Lord give you a happy marriage."

"Are you married, Captain?"

"Twenty-nine years with the same woman, and I've enjoyed every second of it."

This pleased Grace exceedingly. She said, "I hope that my husband will be able to say that."

"A pretty thing like you, ma'am? Indeed, he would need to be keel-hauled if he said anything else! Now, you come along with me. We'll give you a breakfast you won't soon forget."

Stephen was waiting for her, and he came over at once and said, "A fine breakfast Captain Minton has provided."

Minton sat down next to the first officer, a tall, dour individual named Blake. "Mr. Blake, we have newlyweds this morning." He introduced the pair, and Blake made the usual congratulations, although not with much fervor.

The breakfast was lovely and the day went well for Grace. She loved the sea, and she spent much of the time walking around the deck, taking care to stay out of the way of the sailors. One of them, a young man who reminded her of her brother, David, was bashful but she drew him out. Among other things, she discovered that he had a sweetheart, and she gave him some advice. "You be sweet to her, Robert," she admonished. "Women need to be told sweet things."

"Indeed, ma'am, I'll do my best, but I'm not very good with words. Does your husband say such things to you?"

The innocent question of the young man caught Grace off guard. "As much as he will. He's a poet, you know."

"No, ma'am, I didn't know. Well, then he ought to be able to say lots of flowery things and make up verses for you." The young boy's face was lit with respect. "You've done well to marry a poet. Maybe I could get him to write me some verses for Millie."

"I'll ask him, Robert."

She went at once to Stephen and related the incident. "He's such a nice young man, Stephen, and he's almost inarticulate. He wants you to write him a little verse or two for his sweetheart."

"Why, I can't do that!"

"Why not?" Grace looked genuinely surprised. "He's not asking for an epic—*Paradise Lost*, or anything like that."

Stephen's face assumed a mulish expression. "You don't understand,

116

dear. I have to wait for inspiration."

"Well, couldn't you get a little inspiration from things you've done in the past?"

"I'm afraid not. He'll just have to find another poet."

"But it would be so kind if you would help Robert out. Please, dear, do it for me."

Stephen Morrison looked at Grace and saw the winsome expression. Finally he shrugged. "Well, I'll do my best, but I can't promise much."

"Oh, thank you, Stephen! I'm sure Millie won't expect much, and it will mean so much to Robert."

Late in the afternoon the sea grew somewhat rougher, and by nightfall the weather had worsened. When Grace and Stephen got ready for bed, the ship was rising and falling with alarming motion.

Ignoring the tossing of the ship, Grace changed into her silk nightgown, which had been a gift from David. She remembered his impish grin when she had held it up and how he had winked at her. "That ought to fetch him, sis," he had chortled.

There was no privacy in the small cabin, but as Grace removed her clothes and pulled the nightgown over her head, she could not help noticing that Stephen kept his gaze fixed on his book. He had taken a seat at the small desk and had begun reading at once. Grace slipped into bed and lay there for a time. The ship continued its incessant rolling, and finally she asked tentatively, "Stephen. . . ?"

"Yes, Grace?"

"Aren't you coming to bed?"

"I . . . I think I'll read a little. You've had a tiring day. You see if you can't go to sleep." He seemed embarrassed by the inadequacies of his own reply and could not meet her eyes. "It'll be a tiring journey. Good night, Grace."

Grace lay there stiffly. She felt rejected and could not imagine why. She closed her eyes and tried to sleep, but there was a small unhappiness in her, and she thought, *When we get off this ship and in our own place it will be different. Perhaps he doesn't feel well from the rocking of the ship.* She cast one glance at her husband, who sat there reading by the amber light of the lamp, and then closed her eyes. Time went by slowly and she wrestled with her feelings. She felt a sadness come upon her, for it was not the honeymoon she had thought she would have. She felt tears rising and fiercely blinked her eyes. *I can't let this trouble me,* she thought. *It will be all right when we get in our own home. . . .*

David Gordon looked over the pile of bank notes that had accumulated in front of him but let his face show nothing. Although he had mobile features and usually expressed what was in his heart by those features, when he gambled, it was entirely different. To the great displeasure of his parents, he had become an expert gambler. This was not a career they would have chosen for him. Indeed, it was not a career he would have chosen for himself, but he found he was good at it, and little by little he fell more deeply into it. The more money he made, the less inclined he was to pursue an honest profession. He had discovered that whatever was that combination of skill, intellect, intuition, and plain luck that makes gamblers successful, he had been gifted with it. He usually thought of the term "gift" as something God gave a man, and more than once he had said to himself scornfully, "God didn't give you this ability to take other men's money. Be honest with yourself. You're little more than a highwayman."

Now displeased, although he was the big winner at the table, he said, "Well, if you gentlemen are satisfied, I suppose I must go."

"You're too lucky, Gordon." The speaker was a big, burly man, a New York merchant. His face was flushed and he was on the verge of saying more than that. Then he seemed to reconsider. His firm did business with His Majesty's army, and he knew the father of this young man could ruin him if he so chose. He shook his head and said, "Sorry, Gordon, but blast my eyes you *are* lucky!"

David had been waiting for the insult, wondering if he would take it up and make a duel out of it. He had never gone out with a man, but he knew that his father had. He also knew that his parents were adamantly opposed to dueling. "It's a stupid way to behave," his father said. "When I was a young man, I was filled with all sorts of notions about honor, but now I think it's stupidity."

David picked up his winnings, stuffed them into his pocket, and made his way through the tavern. He stopped abruptly when his eyes fixed on a thick, burly man of middle age with a short, brown, curly beard and a mass of curls to match. "Jan!" he said. He moved over and shook hands with the individual. "Jan Vandermeer, I haven't seen you in a long time."

"Ja, it has been a long time." He studied David and said, "I watch you play. You never lose, eh?"

"Oh, I lose sometimes, but I usually make it up sooner or later," he said with a gleam in his eye, for he was fond of Jan Vandermeer.

Vandermeer was a struggling artist and had some connection with the Gordon family, at least with the Bradford side of it. He was a good friend of Matthew Bradford, who was a fine artist himself and whose reputation was growing. Jan had kept Joel Bradford in his rooms while Joel was in New York.

"Have you eaten yet, Jan?"

"Not in several days. Nothing good, that is."

"Come along. We'll perform the ancient art of gluttony."

"Ja, that will be *gut.*"

Thirty minutes later the two were ensconced in the Black Swan Inn, and the proprietor, a skinny man with an eye patch and a few gaps in his teeth, brought them their meal. It consisted of kidney pie, a leg of lamb, fresh bread, assorted cheeses, and tall mugs of dark ale.

Jan said, "Vill you ask the blessing, or vill I?"

"Why, you're not even a Christian, Jan."

"Neither are you, but I vill be someday."

"How do you know that?"

"Because I'm a seeker, and one day God will reveal himself to me and I will give myself to Him."

David found this theology rather amusing and at the same time liked it. "I think that's my case exactly. I've never seen better Christians than my parents. I don't know why I've run away from God for so long."

"Ve vill stop running one day because God vill catch us."

Jan was stuffing his mouth. He waved his knife around in an almost dangerous fashion. "Ja, God vill catch us. He is on our trail. One day He'll bring us to bay and then ve'll be His. Then ve vill die and go to heaven and be happy forever."

David laughed out loud. He liked this young man very much. "Have you heard from Joel?"

"Ja. He is in the army with General Washington. He fooled me pretty good, that young man." Joel Bradford was a cousin of Daniel Bradford. He and his sister, Phoebe, had been brought from England to serve at Daniel's behest. Joel had wanted to join the Continental Army, but the head of the secret service had persuaded him he could do much better for his newly adopted country by serving as a spy, especially since he had a relative who was a member of His Majesty's army. "He's a fine young man, that Joel. A great actor."

"I hope he doesn't get killed in the army. I like him very much."

"Yes. What about your cousin Matthew?"

"I haven't heard from him for a long time, but Mother hears from Uncle Daniel that he's been out of the country."

"Ja, this time I think he went to Italy. He's coming back. He wrote me last month."

"Is he a good artist, Jan?"

"He could be the best—except for me, of course!" Jan Vandermeer grinned.

"Well, of course, no one is better than Jan Vandermeer. You remember my sister, Grace?"

"Do I remember her? Did you ever know me to forget a pretty woman?"

"No. I never have. Well, she got married last week."

"Oh, to the young man she was with when I had supper with you some weeks ago?"

"Yes. Stephen Morrison. He owns property in South Carolina. I hated to see her leave. We're very close, Grace and I."

"He seemed like a nice fellow."

"He is. Honest and has property. All of that—"

Seeing David Gordon's hesitation, Vandermeer said, "What is the problem? You don't like him?"

"It's just that he doesn't seem like the kind of man Grace would be happy with. I mean she's always fiery and impulsive and always fun, and Stephen is . . . well, he's a—"

"He's a dullard. I saw that at once. Why did your sister marry him?"

"Who knows about things like that? In any case, they're married now. They'll have to make the best of it."

"What about you? Are you going to get married?"

"Have to find a wife first."

"What are you going to do with your life? Be a gambler?"

The question troubled David. "I don't know," he said. "Of course I don't want to be a gambler, not a professional one. As a matter of fact, I'd be better off if I'd quit, but Father doesn't make much as an officer, and I paid for most of my education through my ill-gotten gains."

"Too bad you can't paint."

"Well, I can't. I don't seem to have any talents, except taking men's money away."

"A good vay to get yourself hanged or shot," Vandermeer said cheerfully. "Come along. I vill take you and show you my latest masterpiece!"

🏵   🏵   🏵

David stood with his back against the wall watching his father cross swords with Maurice Stapleton, the drill instructor for the regiment. He admired his father, who had always been an expert swordsman. Stapleton, of course, was far more skilled, since he had devoted all of his energy to that particular art. David smiled cynically as he saw that the drill instructor was careful to let his father win a bout.

"Very well! Very well indeed, Colonel."

"I'm not used to being called colonel. My promotion seems to have left me unchanged, except for a title and a bit more money."

"Everyone is happy that you have been promoted. You're very popular with the men."

Leslie Gordon handed the foil back to Stapleton. "That usually means a lack-sorry officer."

"Not with you, sir. Not with you." Stapleton turned and his eyes met David's. "Will you try a turn, sir?"

"Yes. Let's see if you've lost any skills, son."

David shrugged. He liked fencing, and the thought came to him, *Gambling and fencing. I should have lived a couple hundred years ago. I could have been a very romantic figure in Queen Elizabeth's court.* He took the protective vest his father wore and allowed him to strap it on, then placed the guard over his face. He moved forward and assumed the standard position, and Stapleton, one foot advanced, moved forward. Stapleton engaged, and David parried.

"Very good! Very good indeed, sir! You haven't lost your skill!" Stapleton cried out.

The two moved around the floor of the large room filled with the sounds of other swords clashing and men talking. Within a few minutes, the contest became quite heated. David did not have Stapleton's years of experience, but he had the quickest hand and eye any drill instructor had ever seen. The foils clashed and made streaks of light as the two men advanced and retreated. Leslie Gordon stood back watching with pride, knowing that Stapleton was putting out every effort. Few men could hold Maurice off like that. Finally Maurice did manage to touch David's vest with his point, but he was out of breath.

"Well, sir—you have improved! If you would practice, I would have . . . no chance with you at all, sir."

"Very good, David. Good, Maurice. Thursday at the same time."

"Yes, Colonel, and congratulations on your promotion."

The two men left the academy, which was nothing more than an old barn that had been once used to stable the animals of the wealthier patrons of New York. "Let's walk home," Leslie said.

"Yes, sir. It's cold, isn't it?"

"I like cold weather." Leslie looked up at the gray sky and shook his head. "There's snow coming. Going to be a hard winter."

"What about General Washington?"

"He's holed up somewhere out there in a place called Valley Forge. I don't see how he holds that crew together. They're better soldiers than we gave them credit for." A grimace crossed his features. "I'd hate to try to hold our men together if they were starving and dressed in rags. They'd desert to a man."

"How does he do it, Father?"

"There's something in him. I can't explain it. Some men have that. Men will follow them through any peril, and George Washington is one of those men. He's not the greatest strategist in the world, but he has absolutely no fear and loves his country."

The two walked on speaking of the war, and finally Leslie said, "I'm worried about Grace."

Quickly David glanced at his father. "What do you mean, sir?"

"It's what she doesn't say in her letters that concerns me. She does her best, but I can tell she's not happy."

David hesitated. He also had received two letters from Grace, and beneath the superficial happiness she expressed and her contentment with the house and the large plantation, he could tell her marriage was not all she had dreamed and hoped for. "She's not the same," he said. "I worry about her, too."

Leslie gave his son a quick look and said heavily, "David, she's not happy. Why is that, do you suppose?" He knew this son of his had quick intuition and discernment.

David shook his head. "He's not man enough for her, sir. He never was!"

⚜   ⚜   ⚜

It was one week to the day after this conversation that Lyna Lee said at the supper table, "Leslie, would you mind if I left you to your own cooking and your own devices for a while?"

Both Leslie and David were surprised. "Why, were you thinking of going back to England for a visit?"

"No. There's nobody I want to see there. But I would like to go see Daniel. It's been so long since we've had any time together."

"I think that's an excellent idea. Nothing's going on this winter. When would you go?"

"As soon as you think best."

"Well, tomorrow. The next day. Whenever I can make the arrangements."

Lyna suddenly turned her eyes on David. "I wish you'd go with me, son. It would do you good to be around your uncle some."

David blinked with surprise. "Why, of course, Mother, if that's what you want." He hesitated, then said, "As a matter of fact, I'd like it. I could get to know my new aunt, Miss Marian, better."

"And your cousins," Leslie nodded. "When this war is over we won't have this terrible thing hanging over us." He spoke of the fact that while he and his family were for the king, and because of his position, he had to carry out his duty. In his heart he knew that the Crown would never win this revolution. He had seen the indomitable spirit of the Colonists and the sorry spirit of his own soldiers. From his years of experience in the army, he knew that men who believe in a cause will win it if there's any chance at all.

Lyna at once brightened up. She had been lonesome for Grace, and the idea of a change had pleased her. "We'll go tomorrow, then, if you can make the arrangements."

It was two days before Leslie could do so. Lyna worried over the cost of the trip, but Gordon laughed at her. "It's only money," he said, kissing Lyna before she got into the coach. "You have a good time. Don't forget to write me every day."

"I will, dear." Lyna pulled his head down and kissed him. "You behave yourself now. You're too handsome a man to leave around these man-hungry army wives."

David grinned at that, and as his father turned to him, he said, "I'll write to you too, sir."

Leslie nodded. "Just be careful."

"Be careful? In what way?"

"Well, you're the son of a colonel in His Majesty's army. I hear in Boston they're very alert about spies. Don't get yourself hanged for one."

David shook his head and laughed. "Not me. I'm no hero. Goodbye, Father." He got into the coach beside his mother, and his father kissed Lyna through the window, then stepped back.

"All right, Jackson. Take them to Boston."

10

"You Were Made to Be Loved"

"LOOK, MARIAN—it's snowing."

Rachel stood at the window of the parlor and watched as the flakes drifted downward.

"They're as big as shillings," she said. "I've never seen such large snowflakes."

Across the room sitting in a rocking chair, Marian looked up to where Rachel was standing. "I love the snow," she said. "There's something so peaceful about it. I don't think there's a quieter time on earth than when you're outside and the snow is falling. It seems to muffle all other sounds." She looked down at Enoch, and even as she did, the baby began to cry. His face was red, and the sound of his crying seemed to fill the large room. Marian held him up, put him on her shoulder, and patted his back. "There now, baby. Don't cry."

Turning from the window, Rachel came over to look down at the two. "Is he sick, do you think?"

"I don't know. He's been so fussy lately. I hope it's just the colic."

"I wish we had some of the syrup that Father dosed us with."

"What kind of remedy was it?"

"I don't know. It was something he made up himself. If he were here, we'd ask him. But we haven't used any of it in years. You know how Father is. He's always experimenting on people with medicine."

"I don't want him experimenting on Enoch!" Marian's lips grew tight, and a worried expression crossed her eyes. She patted Enoch's back firmly, but it did not seem to help. The sound of his cries grew

125

more shrill, and finally Marian said, "I wish you'd go down and ask Dr. Hollins to come by."

"All right, I will, but it'll do no good to go now. He never makes his house calls until after he's seen the patients who can come in."

Rachel sat down and picked up her sewing again. Her mind was not on it, however. All she'd been able to think about for the past few days was the German man in the barn. Now that he was getting better, she had learned that his name was Jacob Steiner. She was only half listening to Marian when suddenly she heard her say, "Well, you haven't heard a word I've said, Rachel."

"Oh, I guess I'm just mind gathering. What was it, Marian?"

Enoch had finally drifted off to sleep, a fitful rest, and Marian held him closely, patting his back. "I asked you which one of your two suitors you favor."

"Oh, them!"

"Most young women would be flattered to have two eligible bachelors chasing around after them."

" 'Chasing around' is about right!" Rachel snapped peevishly. "I haven't given either one of them any encouragement."

"Has either one of them kissed you?" Marian had her eyes fixed on Rachel's face and saw the telltale flush of guilt. She giggled and said, "I see they have. Was it Jubal or the minister?"

"I declare, Marian! You're getting to be a gossipy woman. I never thought I'd see the day."

"All women are interested in romances, and after all, you're my daughter now. Why shouldn't I be interested?" She studied Rachel's face for a moment and said, "Have you thought about what it would be like to be the wife of a minister?"

Reluctantly Rachel nodded. "It would be difficult," she said slowly. "It would be like living in a fishbowl. Everybody in town keeps their eyes on the preacher and his wife. They get judged for everything they do. It's not fair."

"I suppose it'll always be like that," Marian nodded. "I don't think I could handle it very well. It's hard enough to be a wife with all the problems that come up without having to contend with that."

For a while the two women sat quietly. The clock on the mantelpiece broke the silence with its rhythmic tick-tock, and finally Rachel shook her head. "I'm not interested in getting married—at least not right now."

"Oh, come now! That's not true."

"Why would you say that?"

"Every woman's interested in getting married. What else is there for her to do? What else was she made for but to make a home and have children?"

"I wish I were a man!" Rachel spat the words out. "They can do so much. Have a career, travel, never have to ask anyone."

"Well, that's half true, but when a man marries he's not free."

"They're freer than women are!" Rachel argued.

Phoebe entered and said, "It's time to start thinking about dinner, Mrs. Bradford."

"Why don't we just have leftovers, Phoebe." She halted, then said, "Have you heard from Joel?"

"Yes, ma'am. He says he's happy, but that he misses the cooking."

"Food must be pretty scarce at that place. What's the name of it?" Rachel asked.

"Valley Forge," Marian said. "I'm not sure exactly where it is. I got a letter from Daniel. He's there for a while with the general. You know it's flattering that my husband would be so close to General Washington. So many would like to be."

"And so many would like to get rid of him," Rachel said sharply.

"They're envious. General Washington is the only one the men in the army would follow."

"Some of the other generals don't think so," Rachel said quickly. "There's talk of replacing him."

"There's always talk of that, but if it weren't for General Washington, the army would go home. It's only their loyalty to him that holds the men together. It makes them endure starvation and freezing weather. Some of them are even barefooted. No. It's only His Excellency that keeps the revolution alive. I shudder to think what would happen if he resigned or were killed in action."

Phoebe listened to the two women, then turned and went back into the kitchen.

"She's a sweet girl, isn't she, Marian?" Rachel said.

"Yes, she is, and her brother is a fine young man. I'm glad Daniel brought them over from England."

Rachel did not speak for a time. She was only too glad to have her mind taken off of the problem of the wounded German. She was a strange girl in many ways. Beautiful, indeed, but her mind had a habit of taking strange quirks, and she often said things that no "self-respecting" woman would ever utter. Daniel had often been somewhat shocked by her blunt questions and pointed remarks. Now one of them came out almost without volition. "Marian, what's marriage like?"

"What's it like? What do you mean, Rachel?"

"I mean the intimate side of it."

Marian stared at her stepdaughter with astonishment. Her eyes flew open and she shook her head, uttering a rueful laugh. "I declare, Rachel! If you are not the awfulest thing! What a question to ask!"

"Well, there are only two ways to learn about things like that," Rachel said peevishly. "Either have an experience or ask someone about it. I'm sure you wouldn't approve of the former."

"Certainly I would not!" Marian snapped. She thought for a moment and saw that Rachel's eyes were fastened on her firmly. Her mind went back to her girlhood. She had been highly attracted to Daniel Bradford, but at the time he was only a groomsman for Sir Leo Rochester. She had chosen Leo against her heart, and the resulting years had been painful, knowing she was in love with one man and married to another. But she also remembered that just before her marriage she had been terribly worried about her wedding night. She had no experience, and aside from having heard a few remarks, she had no teaching, no training. Marian Bradford was above all things an honest woman, and now she knew what she must do.

"Rachel, when I was around your age and about to be married, I had the same fears as you do. I expect all virtuous young women do, so I'll try to help you. It's embarrassing to talk of these things, perhaps, but I'm going to be honest with you so when you marry, at least you'll know something." She began to speak, and as she watched Rachel's eyes, which were anxious, she knew that she was doing the right thing. She explained the aspects of intimacy candidly, and when she was finished, Rachel got up and came over, putting her arms around her.

"Thank you, Mother," she said and turned and left the room.

A warm glow came over Marian Bradford then. It was the use of the word *Mother*. All of her adult life she had wanted children and had not been able to have them. Now God had given her Enoch, who was her own in every way but by blood, and that seemed a small thing now. But she thought of her relationship with Daniel's children and knew they had become hers as well as his. Tears came into her eyes, and she said, "Thank you, God. I was barren for so long, but now I have children!"

☙   ☙   ☙

Jacob was sitting down on one of the crates as Caesar came up the stairs. The big man had a bundle in one hand and a chair in the other, and he grinned, his teeth showing white against his ebony skin. "Miss

Rachel done washed all your clothes, Mr. Jacob. And I done fixed up an old chair for you."

"Well, thank you, Caesar." Jacob stood up at once rather carefully. He moved too quickly, and the sharp stabbing pain in his side nearly folded him over. His head still had a light bandage on it, but it was healing quickly. It did not give him the pain that his side did. "I wish I could do something to pay you back for all your trouble."

"No trouble at all, suh." Caesar unfolded the clothes. He had found an old chest downstairs and had brought it up the stairs. The weight was nothing to his powerful strength. Opening it, he arranged the clothes carefully and said, "I was a body servant for a while to a gentleman and learned how to take care of all of his garments." He held up a shirt and said, "The blood wouldn't all come out of this, but I thought you'd want to keep it anyhow."

Rachel had sent enough of Daniel's old clothing for Jacob to wear. Jacob was much thinner than Daniel Bradford, but at least the clothes were clean. The thought came to him once that if he were caught out of uniform, he would be shot as a spy.

Jacob reached over and took the shirt from Caesar. He examined the two holes, one in the front and one around to the back. "If it had been another inch to the right, it probably would have killed me," he said.

"Yes, suh. I think maybe it might, but as the Book says, you are of much more value than many sparrows."

Jacob was amused and impressed, as always, for it seemed that Caesar could not utter a sentence without tacking a verse on. He had spent a great deal of time with the black man reading to him from the Bible that Caesar treasured. Caesar could not read a word of it himself, but he pressed everyone he could into service by asking them to read it to him. The words seemed to stick in his mind as if they were glued there.

Jacob sat down again, leaned back against the rough boards, and studied Caesar. "You had a hard life as a slave, I suppose?"

"Yes, suh. It's always hard not being free. But the Book says stand fast in the liberty where with Christ has made you free."

"That must be from the New Testament, I think. I don't know it."

"Yes, suh. The New Book." Caesar had a habit of calling the Old and New Testaments "the Old Book" and "the New Book." He pulled the Bible out of his pocket and said, "This Bible means a lot to me and to you, too, don't it, suh?"

"The Old Testament does. That's all I know."

"I like the Psalms the best."

"They're very beautiful. I like them, too."

"You know what I like the best? Psalm one hundred and nineteen."

"That's the longest psalm in the Old Testament, isn't it?"

"Yes, suh, but I got it all down. Would you like to hear it?"

"Yes, I would."

Jacob leaned back. The deep bell-like tones of the ex-slave broke the silence of the loft. It was indeed a long psalm, one Jacob had always liked. He had never thought of anyone memorizing it, but as he opened the Bible, he saw that Caesar knew it word for word. When Caesar was finished, he said, "That's wonderful, Caesar. You have a marvelous memory."

"I wish I could read."

"Why, I'm sure you could."

"No, suh, I can't. There's something wrong with my eyes."

"I never noticed that you had trouble seeing."

"It ain't that. I can see far enough. It's just that . . . well, the words get all mixed up. Miss Marian done tried a hundred times and Mr. Daniel, too, but I just can't make them letters out."

"That's a shame, but at least if you keep on as you have been, you'll have the whole Bible."

"Yes, suh. That's what I intend to do before I die."

There was a warmth of companionship that came to Jacob Steiner as he talked to Caesar. The large man possessed a gentleness and a goodness that matched his tremendous strength and endurance, but there was also something that Jacob had rarely seen—a real love that did not come to many people. He had seen it in a few, mostly in his mother, but out of the simplicity of the man emanated a genuine love that Jacob envied. He sat there talking idly, grateful that he had someone, and finally he asked, "Tell me about the Bradfords, Caesar."

"Well, I guess I could talk all day and all night and next week, and I couldn't tell you about how good my folks are."

"They're your folks, are they?"

"Yes, suh. They treat me just like one of the family. I've never seen nothing like it. They all good people. Most families have some boys that are mean and some girls that are no count, but the Bradfords are solid gold."

"I'm glad to hear it," Jacob said.

"You can bet on it. They's good all the way to the bone!"

"Tell me about them. All of them."

For the next hour Caesar spoke of the Bradford family. He wound up by saying, ". . . and so Miss Marian could never have no babies, but then God brought this baby into their lives not long ago. His parents died, and the poor little fellow didn't have nobody. Miss Marian said God sent that baby to her after all these years, and so it's a sight to see how she loves that child. Of course she loves all the children—Mr. Daniel's children, that is."

"It's nice to see something come out right, isn't it? So many things don't work in this world." A slight tinge of bitterness was in Steiner's voice, and he looked down at the floor, silent and moody.

Caesar reached over and put his massive hand on Steiner's knee. "Don't you worry. You trust in the Lord God and in His Son, Jesus Christ, and it's all gonna come out all right."

"But I don't believe in Jesus. I'm a Jew."

"So was Jesus a Jew."

Nonplused, Jacob stared at the black man, and the simplicity of the expression prevented him from speaking. "True enough," he said. He could not explain the intricacies of theology to Caesar. He had known all his life the world had been divided into two camps—Christians in one and Jews in the other. He well knew the history of his people, how throughout the ages the Jews had suffered at the hands of some Christians. A bitterness had come to him, but now looking at the black face before him, he thought, *Now, he's a Christian, and for all his strength he's as gentle as a child.*

"Tell me about Miss Rachel," he said.

Humor shone from Caesar's dark eyes. "Well, she's about the prettiest young woman in Boston, I reckon. A little bit sharp sometimes, but she's got a good heart."

"I know that better than anyone, I suppose. Most women would have turned me in immediately."

"I reckon as how they would."

"Why hasn't she ever married?"

"Her papa says she's just too particular about men. Says she's too hard to please. But she's got two men after her now." Caesar went on to describe the competition between Jubal Morrison and the minister. "I don't know as how she likes either one of them enough to marry them, but it sure would be a sight if she married that preacher. She'd cause him a lot of grief."

"Why is that, Caesar?"

"She's just too outspoken. A preacher's wife has to learn to keep her mouth shut at times, don't you think?"

Jacob suddenly laughed. "I don't know much about preachers' wives, but I know that Rachel Bradford will never make it if keeping her mouth shut is a qualification."

The two talked for some time, and finally Caesar left. Jacob sat think-ing about the family and wondering how it was that out of all the places he might have wandered into, the Bradford household was probably the one safe place.

"It's enough to believe in Providence," he murmured. He had al-ready become bitter in his young life. But somehow the influence of the slave and the generosity of Rachel Bradford was beginning to change that.

☉   ☉   ☉

The muffled sound of footsteps awakened Jacob. He had been doz-ing on the cot that Caesar had brought up. The floor had grown hard and uncomfortable, especially on his side, but along with the cot, Cae-sar had brought a shuck mattress, so that he was able to sleep much more comfortably. Jacob sat up at once and came to his feet, moving carefully as Rachel's head appeared. He waited until she was standing before him carrying a large tray covered with a towel. *"Guten Morgen,"* he said. "I mean, good morning."

"Guten Morgen. Does that mean 'good morning' in German?"

"Yes. Here, let me help you with that." He took the tray from her and set it down on an upturned crate.

As he lifted the towel, she said, "German's such a rough-sounding language."

Jacob laughed. "Yes, it sounds like two cats fighting sometimes. At least that's what an Englishman told me once."

Rachel watched as he turned to her, obviously waiting for her to sit down. There was something almost courtly in the young man's behav-ior, an inborn gentility, that made her wonder if he came from an aris-tocratic family. She sat down, and as he took the cloth off of the tray of food, she was intrigued as he bowed his head and silently prayed. It was just a short prayer, but she had noticed that he never failed to pray before eating. She had no idea of what Jacob Steiner's spiritual condi-tion was. She knew only that he was a Jew. He began to eat eagerly the mutton and the fresh bread and seemed particularly to like the peas she had simmered long and flavored with onions and other spices. "Your appetite's coming back," she said. "That's good."

"Yes. I'm much better." He swallowed, then looked over and nod-ded. "All thanks to you, Miss Bradford."

Rachel had always had a peculiarity. She disliked intensely being thanked for anything. Her father had often told her that it was an in-verse form of pride. *"You like to give, but you rob people of the grace of thanking you."* Rachel had thought about that a great deal and now had reached the point where she could be a little more graceful. "You're very welcome, Mr. Steiner."

Jacob noticed that she always called him by his last name. Perhaps the familiarity of using a first name was asking too much. He always thought of her as Rachel but adhered strictly to Miss Bradford in speech.

After Jacob had eaten, Rachel said, "We've got to change those bandages."

"Yes. Of course. I hate to be such a burden."

"Don't be silly. I'd do the same for anyone."

"I believe that is true," Jacob said solemnly. "If you would do it for an enemy, you would certainly do it for a friend."

His answer caught at Rachel, and she sat still for a moment wondering about it. He was such a strange man! She had heard so many awful and horrible stories about the Hessians, even that they ate babies, which she knew was ridiculous. Still, there was evidence aplenty that as soldiers they were brutal. American troops were terrified of the Hessians with their long bayonets and their almost animalistic courage. She saw none of this, however, in Jacob Steiner. Putting this thought aside, she stood and filled the pewter basin with water. She soaked the bandage around his head with a cloth, and when she took it off, she gently moved his head and stared at the wound. "It's healing very well. I think after tomorrow we might try it without the bandage. For now we'll just put on another one."

Jacob was intensely aware of the pressure of the woman's hands on his head. She had strong hands, he knew, but they were gentle and it stirred strange emotions in him.

"Now the side."

Jacob stood up while Rachel unwound the bandage that wrapped all the way around his body. The wound had bled in the back and was stuck to the bandage. "I'll have to soak this off."

"Just give it a quick pull," Jacob said.

"No. It'd be too painful. It might make it worse. Here. Just stand still." She reached out, soaked the cloth, and then held it onto the outside of the bandage. In the silence Jacob noticed, over the odors of the dusty barn, the fragrance of her scent. He did not know what it was, but it was more feminine than anything he had ever experienced. Jacob had, as a matter of fact, little experience with women. Being a handsome man, he had exchanged a few kisses at dances, but music had been his life, and he had observed that men were often distracted from their real lives, their real work, by the frivolity of young women. Now in the murky darkness illuminated by the rays of pale sunlight coming through the cracks in the boards and by the single lantern that burned feebly, casting amber light over the loft, he was intensely aware of the femininity of Rachel Bradford.

Right then she looked up sharply and saw his eyes fixed upon her. She dropped her eyes and said hurriedly, "There. That ought to do it." She removed the bandage and put a salve on it that Marian had told her Daniel found useful on such things. Quickly she put the bandage on, but this involved reaching around Jacob so that she was practically hugging him. Her face flushed and she did not look up. When she had tied the bandage off, she stepped back a little too quickly.

"Would you sit down, Miss Bradford?"

"Oh, I must go."

"Please. Just for a few moments. There's something I have to say to you."

Rachel stared at Jacob, then nodded briefly. "All right, but only for a few minutes."

Jacob waited until Rachel sat down, then he pulled up a stool and seated himself. "It is hard for me to put into words what I feel, but I must try." He tried to smile, adding, "If you could speak German, I could say it much better. But I will do the best I can with my poor English."

"Your English isn't poor. It's better than most people's around here. I've wondered about it."

"My teacher was a scholar and he had a ruler. Every time I made a mistake in grammar or pronunciation he would slap me on the knuckles." Jacob held up his hands and smiled fondly. "I had bloody knuckles for several years, but I'm grateful now." He dropped his hands and then bit his lip for a moment. "What I must say is very simple really. I have been wondering why you would do such a good thing for one who is an enemy. I don't think I will ever understand it, but I must tell you how very much my heart is thankful. No one has ever done such a good thing for me, not in all of my life. I wish I could say better, but my heart says, Miss Bradford, thank you from the very depths."

The man's simple eloquence moved Rachel greatly. Once again she was impressed with his gentleness, and the first impulse that rose in her was to simply brush off his words. But she remembered her father's teaching that receiving thanks was also a grace, so she sat quietly for a moment. He did not speak or move either. Taking a deep breath, she nodded. "You're very welcome, Jacob." It was the first time she had used his first name, and she did not even notice it. The intimacy of the moment was strong upon her, and she did not see the flicker in his eyes at this unaccustomed breach. "I'm very sorry that you have been wounded. I could not sentence a man to death, even—as you put it— an enemy. I believe you would have died in a prison camp."

"Most certainly I would."

Rachel saw with relief that Jacob was not going to burden her with more thanks. "Tell me about yourself. How did you come to be in the army? Why did you enlist?"

"I did not enlist," Jacob said.

"You didn't?" Rachel was surprised. "But how did you get in the army?"

"It is a long story. Well, perhaps not. It is short but unhappy." He related the circumstances of how he became a soldier in the Prussian army. His voice was moderate and he showed little sign of anger but a great deal of grief. When he had finished, he spread his hands and said, "I never chose to come. None of us did. We were forced into the army. All of my fellow soldiers would have gone home instantly if they had had any opportunity at all."

"I didn't know it was like that," Rachel said. "What about your family?"

"I do not know. They do not know about me. They probably think I'm dead."

An impulse came to Rachel. "Suppose I were to write to them and tell them that you were well."

"You would do that?"

"It would take a long time for a letter to get to Europe, but if you will write it, I will see that it gets posted."

"That would mean so very much to my mother and to my family. But I have no paper, no ink, and no pen."

"I'll bring some when I return."

"You're very kind. My mother would thank you if she could." He hesitated and then said, "My mother would like you very much, Miss Bradford. And I think you would like her."

"Tell me about your family."

Rachel sat quietly listening as Jacob told about his home and his family. The more he spoke, the more she felt that she knew this man.

Finally Jacob gave her a startled look and grinned sheepishly. "I've become as talkative as a magpie," he cried. "Forgive me, Miss Bradford."

"No need for forgiveness. I was very interested."

Jacob hesitated, then said, "Caesar has been telling me about your family. You are very fortunate."

"Indeed I am. I have a fine family."

"And I understand you are to be married soon."

"Did Caesar say that?"

Hearing the asperity in the woman's voice, Jacob held up his hand. "No. He merely said that you were being courted by two fine men."

"I suppose that's true enough."

Jacob cocked his head to one side, studying her features. He had long been impressed with the beauty of this woman, and now he saw some of the sharpness Caesar had spoken of. "You do not like either one of them?"

"I like both of them, but you don't marry someone because you like him."

"So how will you decide?"

Suddenly Rachel laughed. It was the first time Jacob had heard her laugh, and it was a delightful sound. "What is funny?" he asked.

"Someone asked me that and I told them I'd marry *both* of them. One for Sunday and one for the rest of the week. That way I could be good one day a week and be as bad as I pleased the rest of the time."

Jacob chuckled. "That would be one way, but I doubt that you will do that."

"No. I was just being silly."

The two sat there and Rachel was obviously thinking hard, her mind far away. "Which one will you take, then?"

"I think I'll just be a maiden lady. An old maid. I don't know what you call one of those in your country."

"I know what you mean, but you will never do that."

"I won't be a maiden lady? Why not?"

Jacob put his gaze full on her. He had very direct blue eyes that seemed to burn right into whatever he looked at. "You will never be an old maid because you were made, Miss Bradford, to be loved. You cannot live without love."

Rachel was utterly speechless. She stared at Jacob Steiner, his words seeming to imprint themselves on her mind. She knew that she would never forget them. It was one of those moments of truth. Now as she sat stone-still in the silence staring into the blue eyes of the man who called himself her enemy, she knew he had spoken a truth that she needed to hear. *You were made to be loved. You cannot live without love.*

In a flustered fashion she rose and began gathering up the dishes.

She left quickly, murmuring hardly a word, and Jacob stood staring after her.

"That touched her," he said. "How strange! Doesn't she know how lovely she is and that she has to have love? I could see it in her as plain as day."

11

THE MESSIAH

LYNA PULLED HERSELF CLOSER, huddled under the thick woolen blanket she had brought for the journey. Ever since she and David had left New York, the weather had turned foul, a combination of sleet and freezing rain, alternating with thick-bodied weights of snow that had inundated the countryside. Twice the horses had been stopped by the drifts of snow that covered the road. They had taken shelter wherever they could, mostly in houses along the way. Only two other passengers rode in the coach, for the bitter weather was too much for most to travel.

"My fingers are numb, Mother. I've never seen such bitter weather." David Gordon had on thick gloves, but still the cold and the inactivity had stiffened his limbs. He reached over and pulled the blanket around his mother, tucking her in, and grinned at her. "Your face is blue," he said. "A most attractive color, I must say."

Lyna smiled wanly. The trip had tired her, and she murmured, "I wonder if we should have tried it in this weather."

"Cheer up. Can't get any worse." Then his lips twisted with a grimace. "That's what I said yesterday, wasn't it? And sure enough, it *is* worse!" He slumped back in the coach, looking outside at the dead landscape. Everything was either white or a dead grayish brown. At times it was rather attractive with the hills and the mountains covered with soft, rounded layers of snow, but now the rain mixed with freezing sleet was blowing so hard that he could not see more than twenty-five feet away. "I don't see how the driver's making it." He suddenly opened the door and yelled against the freezing blast that rocked the coach. "How much farther?"

"Lights of Boston right up ahead."

Slamming the door and shuddering with the bitter cold, David nodded and managed a smile. "We're all right now. It'll be good to get a warm bed without any livestock in it."

"Yes. And some hot food!" Lyna said, encouraged by the news. She sat up and pulled back the leather curtain but could see very little among the swirling flakes of snow. Closing the drapes, she turned to David and said, "It'll be good for you to be with your relatives."

"I'm looking forward to it. I haven't seen them in so long. I don't know them very well."

She sat there braced against the cold, rocking from side to side with the swaying of the coach. Finally she turned to him and said, "David, what are you going to do with yourself?"

Startled by the abrupt question, David turned and saw that his mother's face was very serious. It was pinched with cold, but her blue eyes were bright and alert. "Do with myself? You mean while we're here in Boston?"

"No. I mean with your life."

Suddenly David could not meet his mother's level gaze. He dropped his eyes and chewed on his lower lip thoughtfully. Outside he heard the voice of the driver muffled by the wind, urging the tired horses onward. Finally he shrugged and struck his fists together several times in an effort to beat some warmth into them. "I suppose you and Father have talked about it quite a bit."

"Of course we have. We want you to do well, but it seems as though you have no—direction."

David shook his head with a short gesture of despair. "I don't know, Mother," he said. "Seems I'm not good at anything but gambling and fencing."

"You can't build a life on that unless you intend to be one of those horrible roughs that grow old before their time hanging around taverns."

Distaste was evident in Lyna's voice, which did not surprise David in the least. He looked at her, noting that her fine features were as firm and attractive as they had always been. He had friends whose parents were not so admirable, and he had been grateful for his father and mother, their steadfast love for each other, their fairness and consideration for David and for Clive and Grace. Forced to say something, he said, "I suppose I'll decide someday."

Lyna did not answer, but her silence spoke louder than any words she might have uttered. Reaching over, she put her own mittened hand over his and squeezed it. "You have such gifts. You are so talented, you could be anything you wanted to be, David."

"I guess that's just it. I don't know what I want to be. I hate to plunge into a profession unless I'm sure, Mother."

"Your father and I are praying that you'll be sure."

David did not answer and was glad when a few moments later the coach lurched to a halt, and the driver's voice cried out, "Boston! I thought we'd never make it!"

David opened the door and almost fell when he came to the ground. His feet were numb, and he reached out to take his mother's hand to help her down. "Be careful," he said. "I'm frozen from the waist down."

Lyna was also numbed by the cold. She stamped her feet until a semblance of feeling returned and then looked around. The streets seemed to be empty except for a few hearty citizens who were braving the cold. "We'll have to get a carriage, I guess, and find Daniel's house."

"Get over here, Mother, under some shelter. I'll go see if I can find someone to help us hire a carriage."

Finding a carriage for hire proved to be difficult. Lyna sat alone for fifteen minutes until finally David came back, his eyebrows white with snow and his teeth chattering. "I can't find anybody. We may have to take a room in an inn somewhere while we thaw out."

"That'll be all right, David," Lyna said. "Anything to get in out of this cold!"

At that moment an officer, leaving a group of what appeared to be militia, came marching down the street past where Lyna and David were hunched up against the cold blast of the wind. He turned and called out, "Halt! Sergeant, give them men some close-order drills." Then turning, he marched stiffly over toward David and Lyna. He was a small young man, barely out of his twenties, with a pinched blue face and a pair of eyes set somewhat too close together. His uniform was a patched-together affair, and his large tricorn hat came down over his eyebrows. He peered out from under it and pulled himself up to attention. "You just got off the coach?"

"Why, yes we did, sir," David said quickly.

"What's your business in Boston? Where are you from? Do you have any papers?"

The questions were delivered in a high-pitched, rapid-fire fashion. He was evidently a young man who was not sure of himself and so tried to cover up those feelings with a gruff, harsh manner. It did not go well with his skinny frame and his thin, plain face. He had a pair of muddy brown eyes and did not relax as he continued to fire questions at them. David attempted to answer, saying, "We've just arrived from New York, Lieutenant—"

"New York! New York! That's a hotbed of loyalists! I suppose you're loyalists yourselves," he sneered.

"We are plain citizens on a visit to relatives, sir," David said. He was growing angry with the young man, but he kept a firm hold on his temper, remembering his father's admonition.

Lyna suddenly stood up and put her hand on David's arm. She knew he had a temper that could flare up quickly, and now she said, "Lieutenant, we are looking for my brother's house. If you please—"

But the young man interrupted brusquely. "I'll take you to headquarters. You'll have to give account of your presence here."

"What are you talking about?" David demanded.

"How do I know you're not a spy?" the young man said coldly. "You'll have a chance to defend yourself."

This infuriated David. "Why, you incompetent—" He stopped from saying what he truly thought of the man. "We're just plain, ordinary citizens! You have no right to hold us!"

"Sergeant!" The lieutenant stepped back quickly, seeing the fiery light in the young man's face. "Arrest these people! We're taking them in for questioning."

Lyna attempted to protest, but the lieutenant would not listen. The sergeant was a tall, comely-looking man with only a uniform coat that marked him as a militiaman. He grinned and said, "What will we do with them, Lieutenant?"

"Take them to headquarters."

At that very moment two figures emerged out of the swirling wind, and Lyna was astonished to hear her name called. "Aunt Lyna, what in the world are you doing out here in this weather?"

Lyna turned and Sam Bradford came to her at once. He was wearing a heavy coat, a beaver hat down over his ears, and thick mittens. He came and put his arm around her and kissed her on the cheek. "We've been expecting you for two days now."

"We got held up in the snowstorm, Sam," Lyna said.

"Well, come on. We've got a coach around here. We'll take you home. Oh, you know Jubal Morrison?"

Jubal stepped forward, took Lyna's hand, and bent over it. "Yes, indeed. Mrs. Gordon and I have met. As a matter of fact, we are relatives. I suppose I'm a step-son-in-law now that my brother married your daughter, Grace."

The lieutenant blustered. "Stand away there! These people are under arrest!"

"For what?" Sam demanded, turning and stepping forward until his face was no more than a few inches from the lieutenant's. Though even younger, Sam was taller and looked rather husky. In addition, Jubal Morrison loomed largely in the lieutenant's gaze.

"Suspicion, that's what for!"

"Suspicion of what?" Jubal Morrison said ominously. "Come on, Lieutenant. Make your charge or be on your way."

"They might be spies. They're from New York."

"Why, you tin soldier! This is my aunt, Mrs. Leslie Gordon. This is her son David." Sam turned and glared with indignation. "Be on your way, soldier."

"They're under arrest, I tell you!"

Jubal said, "That's right. You go ahead and arrest them. You'll find that you'll be arresting the sister of one of General Washington's dearest friends, Mr. Daniel Bradford. I'll be interested to know how you'd look in a private's uniform, because that's what you'll be if you offend one of the relatives of His Excellency's closest friends."

A sudden silence fell upon the lieutenant. He swallowed twice and then three times trying to find words and then made a noise that sounded like half a cough. "Well . . . " he said and then turned around and walked stiffly off.

"Thanks for your gracious apology, Lieutenant," David said. He turned and laughed at Sam and Jubal. "Just in time to rescue the perishing," he said.

"Come along, Aunt Lyna. We've got rooms ready for you at Father's house."

"I'll be so glad to see him, Sam," Lyna said as they hurried along through the wind.

"Well, actually, Father's not here right now."

"Not here? Where is he?"

"He's with the army. With General Washington. But we're expecting him back soon. We'll entertain you royally. Don't you worry. Come on now. Let's get out of all this."

🛡   🛡   🛡

"Still snowing," David said as he came away from the window. He had entered the dining room but had gone at once to peer out of the mullioned windows. Now as he came back, he took in the dining room and was pleased. He had been told that this was the house of Daniel's wife's family. Daniel and Marian had moved in when her father had taken quite ill. After Mr. Frazier died, Daniel simply had stayed on, leaving the original home he had lived in while the children were grow-

143

ing up for Rachel, Dake, Micah, Sam, and for Matthew when he chose to visit.

The long table was occupied by all of the Bradfords except for Daniel and Matthew, who was in Europe studying painting. David studied the faces of the twins, Dake and Micah, both strong, sturdy men. Dake still had a pronounced limp, for he had taken a bullet in a battle fighting for General Washington. Beside Dake sat his wife, Jeanne. *A beauty indeed,* David thought. *Hair as black as night, beautifully shaped eyes, and showing under her gown the signs of her pregnancy.* Micah's fiancée, Sarah Dennison, was also an attractive woman. A light shone in her eyes that was pleasing, and she turned often to smile at her husband-to-be. *A happy couple,* David thought.

His eyes went then to Phoebe, the distant relative of Daniel and the sister of Joel. Phoebe was helping with the serving, for she was, indeed, a servant, but Marian had insisted that this was a family gathering, and she had been placed beside David, knowing that the two of them had a bond in Phoebe's brother, Joel. David had become quite fond of Joel during that young man's stay in New York.

But the guest that took David's eye was Keturah Burns. He had met her briefly and wondered about her connection with the family. He had discovered her story simply by asking Phoebe before dinner about the young woman. Phoebe had said, "Her mother was an unfortunate woman. She followed General Washington's army." This meant, David knew, that she had been a common woman. "Micah found her when she was nearly dead and brought her home."

"A very romantic story. I suppose she fell dearly in love with Micah as they do in romances."

"I think she did, but she's over it now."

"Sam's in love with Keturah. Look at him. He's mooning like a sick cat."

The meal was excellent, and included roasted venison with a sugared and spiced sauce, fried chicken, baked spinach with cream and butter, boiled potatoes in a milk and butter sauce, freshly baked sponge biscuits, and for dessert, peach flummery. During the meal David turned to Keturah, who was seated directly across from him next to Sam. He saw that Keturah was interested in him at once.

"So your father's in the British army?" Keturah asked.

"Yes, he is. He's just been promoted to colonel."

"The rest of your kinfolk are in the revolutionary army," Keturah said.

"Unfortunately our family has divided loyalties. But, Miss Burns, I must tell you that none of our family is sympathetic to the war."

"Why is your father fighting in it, then?"

"He's a soldier. Soldiers have to obey when the command comes."

"He could quit, couldn't he?"

David liked Keturah's forthright manner. She was an attractive young woman with dark brown hair and large, startling light blue eyes. He glanced at his mother and winked. "Why didn't you tell Father to do that?"

"He's been a soldier all of his life, Miss Burns. Faithful and loyal to his command and to his country. Sometimes soldiers get orders that are displeasing to them—sometimes they even think they're wrong—but he swore an oath to be loyal to the king and to his country."

Keturah studied the face of Lyna Lee Gordon. She could see some of the similarities between her and her brother, Daniel. She liked Daniel Bradford very much indeed, and she trusted his sons, though she had not trusted any men most of her life. She smiled suddenly and the smile made her very attractive—at least to David.

"Well, tell me about yourself, Miss Burns. Do you like it here in Boston?"

"Oh yes. Very much."

"I suppose you have a great many young men knocking on your door. I expect Sam there has appointed himself your guardian, sort of a father figure."

"Father figure!" Sam exploded. "I'm not old enough to be her father!"

"It's just a figure of speech, Sam. I'm sorry."

Keturah suddenly laughed. "I couldn't depend on Sam. He's always out in that boat of his with Jubal Morrison."

"You just wait. Jubal and I are going to capture enough English merchants that it'll make us both very rich. You'll see."

Sarah Dennison took little part in the conversation, for she was a quiet young woman. As the dinner progressed, she leaned over to Micah and said, "I think your British cousin is very taken with Keturah."

"She's a pretty young woman."

"Look at Sam. He's not going to be happy if David furnishes a little competition."

Micah looked over at the trio in question and smiled. "I think you're right," he said. "Sam is the jealous type, anyway. He's been infatuated with so many young women that I can't keep up with it. When Keturah came she had some sort of feeling for me—because I saved her life," he said hastily.

"Yes, I know, and you were glad when she became interested in Sam."

"I think it's the other way around. I think Sam's interested in her. I can't tell about Keturah. She's had such a hard time, it's difficult to say."

Sam Bradford did not find the dinner as much pleasure as he had anticipated. He kept his eye on Keturah, but she kept her eyes on David Gordon. Gordon was a handsome young man, highly educated, attractive, witty, and Sam saw that Keturah was drawn to him. "Why in the world did Aunt Lyna have to bring him?" Sam muttered.

"What did you say, Sam?" Marian asked.

"Oh, nothing, Mother. I was just mumbling to myself." After the dinner was over, when they moved into the drawing room, he made it a point to outmaneuver David Gordon. Planting himself firmly beside Keturah, he cast a look of triumph at his cousin. His forced grin told David that Sam Bradford was defending his territory.

🔔   🔔   🔔

Rachel had been very quiet. So much so, indeed, that at some point during the time that followed the evening meal David asked Phoebe, "Is Miss Rachel always so quiet?"

Phoebe bit her lip. "No. As a matter of fact, she's one of the most lively young women I've ever met."

"She's hardly said a word all evening."

Phoebe hesitated, then said in a conspiratorial tone, "She may be worried about which man she's going to marry."

"Oh, she has a choice?"

"Yes, indeed! The minister, Reverend Josiah Grierson, is courting her."

"Oh, she's to be a preacher's wife, then."

"I don't know, and I don't think she does either. I believe that Mr. Morrison, whom you met this afternoon, is interested in Miss Rachel, too."

"Fine-looking man. As I understand it, he's going to be some kind of a pirate."

Phoebe giggled. "That's what Miss Rachel says. She's either going to marry a preacher or a pirate."

"Which would you choose?"

"Oh, I could never marry a preacher."

"So it would have to be the pirate."

"I suppose so." She asked curiously, "What's his brother like? The one who married your sister."

"Stephen? Well, I haven't known Jubal long, but he's not at all like his brother. Stephen's a poet, you know, and very much of a strict businessman. He's rather formal."

Phoebe studied David's face. "You don't like him, do you?"

"It's not that," David said hastily. "He's a good man, and I'm sure he'll make Grace a fine husband. He's just not quite the romantic type I would have expected Grace to marry."

"Well, Mr. Jubal Morrison's romantic enough. He looks like he just stepped out of the pages of a romance novel, doesn't he?"

"I suppose so. Look, I believe Miss Rachel's going to play."

"Oh yes. You've never heard playing like hers."

Indeed Phoebe spoke the truth. David was himself a rather indifferent musician. His mother had been disappointed that he had not pursued his studies. Now he was more of an admirer of good music than a performer. As Rachel Bradford played, he leaned back, studying her with pleasure. *Not only a beauty but talented, too. That preacher—or that pirate—better get busy. If she weren't my own cousin, I'd pursue her myself. She is a beautiful young woman.*

Rachel had tried to avoid playing, for she was not in the mood. Her mind was elsewhere, but at the insistence of everyone in the room, she went over and sat down and began to play. For a time she played the old Christmas songs and the others joined in. Finally when they were all almost hoarse, David asked, "Miss Rachel?"

"Yes, cousin?"

"Do you know any of Handel's work?"

"Yes, indeed. He's my favorite."

"It might be good this Christmas season to hear my favorite Christmas piece."

"You mean the 'Hallelujah Chorus' from *The Messiah*?"

"Yes, indeed."

"I'll do my best, although it's difficult to get the power and majesty in that piece on a little harpsichord like this."

As Rachel played, the magnificent music of Handel filled the house. At one point they all stood. It had been told that when the king had first heard this particular segment of *The Messiah*, he had stood to his feet in admiration and acknowledgment of Handel's genius. The rest of the audience had stood with the king. Since then, the world over, whenever the "Hallelujah Chorus" had been played, men and women and young people had stood in tribute to the magnificence of the piece.

After finishing the music, Rachel rose and said, "That's enough for me. We want to hear about Uncle Leslie and about Grace's wedding."

🛡   🛡   🛡

As always, Jacob Steiner was standing when Rachel climbed up the stairs in the barn. She had waited until long after midnight, when all the house was still, to come. Even Caesar had gone to bed, so now she came bringing the usual basketful of food. "I salvaged as much as I could for you, Jacob," she said.

Jacob realized she had come to use his first name with ease, and now he bowed in the German fashion and then took the basket. "Thank you. It's kind of you to stay up so late for a poor soldier."

"Sit down and eat. I can't stay long."

Jacob sat down and uncovered the food in the basket. "It looks wonderful. I'm getting fat."

Rachel studied his lean form. "You'll never be fat," she announced. "You're not the kind of man that gets that way."

"That's true. In my family all the men are tall and thin. Skinny as rake handles, my mother says."

"That's better than being fat as a lard tub."

"I suppose it is," Jacob smiled. He sat down and picked up a piece of chicken but did not begin to eat. His eyes grew dreamy, and finally Rachel said, "What's wrong?"

With a start Jacob blinked his eyes, came to himself, and said, "Oh, nothing is wrong, Miss Rachel." He also had dared to use her first name, always prefaced by "Miss," of course, and now he smiled gently. "I heard the music. It was very faint, but I went downstairs and stood at the door to listen."

"You shouldn't have done that! You might hurt your side."

"It would be worth it. Who was the musician?"

Rachel shrugged. "I was playing the harpsichord."

"Indeed! I must congratulate you. You play magnificently!"

"Well, thank you, Jacob."

"I especially liked the piece by Handel."

"Oh, *The Messiah*! Of course you would know that, Handel being a countryman of yours. Do you play?"

Jacob did not answer for a moment, and finally he nodded. "I play . . . a little."

"The harpsichord?"

"No, not that."

"What do you play, then?"

"The violin . . . a little."

"Is that so? I suppose you miss it."

"I had one in camp. I played for the soldiers, and they seemed to like it."

"My father has a fiddle. I don't know where he got it. I think it belonged to one of the soldiers he fought with when he was with General Washington at Monongahela years ago. He tried to learn, but he said he was too old. I'd bring it to you, but if anyone heard you playing, you'd be found out."

Jacob said eagerly, "If you would just bring me the violin without the bow. At least I could do the fingering."

"All right. Father wouldn't miss it. He hasn't looked at it for years. It probably isn't a very good violin, anyway."

Still Jacob flexed his fingers, which were indeed stiff. "It would be nice to feel the strings under my fingers again."

Rachel realized that the loft was freezing. "I wish there was some way for you to have a fire."

"I'm out of the weather, and I'm bundled up with all the warm clothing and the blankets you brought."

"Why don't you eat now."

"I will, and perhaps you will tell me about your party tonight."

Rachel did relate some of the incidents. She was surprised at how much Jacob knew about her family and discovered that what she had not told him, Caesar had. Finally she said, "I must go."

Instantly Jacob put the basket down and rose to his feet. She rose also and then on impulse put her hand out. He took it, and she said, "Christmas is coming. You'll be a long way from home."

"Perhaps in a prison by that time," Jacob said. He saw distress in her eyes and shook his head. "Do not be troubled. You must do what a loyal citizen would do, but I will never forget these days of how you have showed such kindness to a foreigner and one who is your enemy."

His hand was cold, as was hers, but she felt the lean strength of his fingers. He did not squeeze her hand but simply held it, pressing it lightly. She looked down at the fingers and saw that they were long and shapely. She tried to think of something to say, then finally whispered, "I don't think of you as an enemy, Jacob."

"That is good to know."

Impulsively Rachel squeezed his fingers and then asked a question that had been on her mind. "You liked *The Messiah*?"

"Very much."

"But it's about Jesus. You don't believe in Jesus."

149

A strange light crept into Jacob Steiner's eyes. "I do not know about this Jesus. We hear bad things from some of our people about how Christians have mistreated Jews. But I am not certain."

"Not all the followers of Jesus are perfect."

"Not all the Jews are perfect either, Miss Rachel."

"Would you let me tell you sometime what I think about Jesus Christ?"

Without hesitation Jacob said, "I would be most glad to hear anything from you, Miss Rachel Bradford."

Rachel drew a quick breath, then turned, but she paused halfway down and came back up several steps. "We will talk about this later, Jacob."

"Yes. Good night, and thank you again for all of your kindness."

Jacob did not sit down again but moved over to the small window at the end of the loft. He opened it and watched Rachel as she hurried back into the house. He often did this and wondered, *How long will it be before I'll be in a prison and unable to see her kind face again?* The thought saddened him, and he stood there for a long time ignoring the cold and gazing at the Bradford home.

12

A Gift to an Enemy

GREAT SWIRLING FLAKES enveloped Rachel as she forged her way through the icy wind that seemed to catch at her like fingers clawing at her eyes and almost blinding her. She felt a deep compassion for the soldiers at Valley Forge, knowing how miserable they must be living outside in such weather. Phoebe had received a letter from her brother, Joel, describing some of the hardships. Now, however, Rachel had no time to think of that. It was a hundred yards from the house to the old barn, and the force of the wind and the slick covering of icy snow gathering on the ground made it difficult to keep her balance. She carried a basket in one hand, a lantern in the other, and had a large sack looped around her neck by the drawstring. The sack dangled awkwardly in front of her, impeding her progress. The midnight sky was dark, covered with clouds, and there was no moon. The feeble light of the lantern she held cast a sickly glow that extended only a few feet.

The barn loomed out of the darkness. Gasping for breath, she set down the basket of food to open the door. She grabbed the handle but found that the door was stuck, frozen in place and barricaded by icy snow at the base of it. "Oh no. What will I do now!" she muttered through stiff lips. After putting down the lantern and carefully removing the sack from around her neck, she tried to yank the door open with both hands. When it wouldn't budge, she began to dig away the snow from around the base of the door. The wet snow soaked through her mittens, so that her fingers quickly became numb. She tried the door again and it gave six inches. "Not enough," she muttered, digging away more of the hard-packed snow. Finally, she got the door open a full twelve inches. She pushed her burdens through the narrow opening, then squeezed through herself. Straightening up, she replaced the sack around her neck, then picked up the lantern with her left hand and the basket with her right. Balancing them rather precariously, she mounted the steep stairs to the loft. Looking up, she saw the feeble light coming through the cracks in the floor overhead and knew that Jacob was awake. *He always is,* she thought as she cleared the landing and saw him standing there waiting as usual.

"It is very cold," he said quickly. "You should not have come out tonight in this weather."

"It's all right," she said. Her lips were numb, and her whole face felt stiff and unnatural, so that it was difficult to make the words. "I knew you'd be hungry."

"Here. Let me take that."

Jacob stepped up close to her, took the basket, then the lantern. He put the lantern on a shelf that Caesar had helped him fashion to keep his toilet articles, including a razor, soap, and brush, all of which Rachel had appropriated from her father's old things. He said quickly, "Please. Sit down. I wish I had a fire."

"I'm all right. I put on warm clothes."

Jacob waited until Rachel had seated herself in the single chair that Caesar had salvaged out of a pile of old furniture from the loft in the big house. He himself sat down on the cot and smiled at her. He was wearing a heavy overcoat that had once belonged to her father. It was buttoned up the front, and he said, "Your hands are wet. Here, put on these dry gloves."

"No. I'm fine," she said. She beat her hands together and felt the snow crystals on her eyelashes. Taking a handkerchief out of her inner pocket, she wiped her face. "The snow's beginning to come down hard."

"Yes. Colder than it is in Germany at times."

Something about his gaze made her uncomfortable and she quickly said, "Eat your food."

"Oh yes. I will." He took the basket, uncovered it, and took a deep breath, inhaling the fragrance. "Warm bread," he said softly. "I always think of home when I smell warm bread. My mother was always baking cakes, cookies, and bread." He picked up a leg of chicken that was still warm from where Rachel had kept it in the oven. "Good," he nodded. "Very good." He ate in a mannerly fashion, unlike what Rachel would have suspected of a rough German soldier, but then almost everything about this man surprised her. When he had finished, he thanked her again, his smile warm.

"I brought you a present," she said.

"A present?"

"Yes." She picked up the sack she had put beside her chair, opened the drawstring, and pulled out the violin she had found among her father's old belongings. She handed it to him and saw that he held it as if it were a precious jewel.

He pulled off his gloves, and again she saw the long, mobile fingers. He seemed to have forgotten her as he tucked the violin under his chin. He plucked one note, tightened the string, and quickly tuned the instrument. As Rachel watched, the fingers of his left hand flew faster over the strings than she could have believed possible. With his right hand he moved an imaginary bow, and it pleased her to see what great pleasure this simple instrument had brought to him.

Lowering the violin, he said, "You could not have brought anything that pleased me better."

Rachel extracted the bow and extended it with a warning, "You must not use this! If anyone heard violin music being played in this old barn, they would report it at once."

"No. I will not. Except for this." He smiled at her merrily, replaced the violin under his chin, then reversed the bow so that the wooden part lay on the strings. Once again the fingers of his hand flew like magic, but the only sound that came was a squeaky sound as the bow flew back and forth. "No more sound than a mouse, you see."

Rachel laughed. "I suppose that would be all right."

"Ja, and now I can practice."

She listened, aware that he was no ordinary musician. She had seen many violinists, and though she could not hear the music, she could see the certainty of his movement and the firmness of his touch. "What is that you're playing?" she asked.

"Oh, something I wrote myself."

"Oh, you write music! How wonderful! It's all I can do to play a little."

"No, you play more than a little. I'm no composer," he said. He put the violin on his lap, stroking it with his hands. He appeared to have forgotten the cold. "I cannot thank you enough. Your kindness is more than I have ever seen, except in my mother."

Rachel was pleased that he spoke so well of his mother. Evidently he had a deep love for her. She sensed a certain restraint in his remarks about his father, but now she said, "I have another gift for you."

"A gift?"

"Yes. Look under the napkin that is in the basket."

Jacob picked up the basket and reached out and removed the red-and-white-checkered napkin that padded the bottom. He stood staring at it for a moment, then reached down and pulled a square, black, leather-bound book from the basket. He held it up to the amber light of the lantern and read aloud, "Holy Bible."

"Yes. I promised you I'd bring you one. I know it gets lonely at times here without something to read."

Jacob ran his hands over the smooth leather, almost as he had the surface of the violin. He opened it and looked at the first page, reading aloud, "To my beloved daughter, Rachel. From her loving father, Daniel Bradford." He looked up startled, "Why, this is your own Bible!"

"Oh yes."

"I will be very careful with it," he said quickly. "I'll give it back to you before—" He almost said *Before I go to prison*, but instead he changed it to, "Before I leave."

"No. It's your Bible. I want you to have it."

"But it's from your father, a gift!"

"He would want you to have it, too."

Jacob felt his throat grow tight. He had grown accustomed to kindness from this woman, but of late the loneliness and the uncertainty of his future had brought a gloom into his heart. He had spent many hours trying not to think of what lay ahead of him. He had already suffered enough of prison life to know that it was nothing he wanted to endure again. He very much doubted if he could ever escape again, and he well knew the mortality rate of prisoners in the camps. He could say nothing, so instead he opened the Bible, looked down, and said, "I see you have written in it."

"I always mark a verse that means a great deal to me. Usually I put the date down."

Jacob held up the Bible and read a verse. " 'Wait on the Lord: be of good courage, and he shall strengthen thine heart.' Why, that's one of my favorites!" he exclaimed. "I memorized it in Hebrew, of course, when I was a little boy."

"That verse always encourages me to know that God is merciful and long-suffering. I need to be reminded of that often," she said wryly.

"I think I do, too," Jacob murmured. He was silent for a moment, then read the date written in the front of the Bible. "May 20, 1770. Why, you were just a girl!"

"I was eleven at the time."

"Do most girls read the Bible, especially the Old Testament, when they are only eleven years old?"

"I don't know, Jacob. I did because my father encouraged it. Besides, I've always found the Old Testament fascinating."

"I have never read the Bible in any language but Hebrew."

"Oh, it must be wonderful to read the Bible in the original language!" Rachel said. She leaned forward and locked her arms together, hugging herself against the cold. Her eyes were bright as she offered, "I'll try to find you a Hebrew Bible if you'd like. It might be difficult, though."

"No. I would like to read it like this in the English."

Rachel asked suddenly, "What is the Hebrew Bible like? You don't read from left to right, do you?"

"No. From right to left."

"That would be terribly confusing for me."

"It can be confusing at first, but you get used to it."

"Tell me something. What kind of a Bible did you have?"

"We didn't have a Bible exactly. It's hard to explain, Miss Rachel."

"I'd like to hear. What's your Bible like?"

"Well, I may sound like a lecturer, but it was like this." His eyes grew dreamy and he did indeed speak more like a professor in a schoolroom. "When the temple was destroyed in A.D. 70, the Jews were scattered all over the world. Many of them had nothing written down of their religion. All they had was what they called the 'Oral Torah,' which simply meant men had memorized portions of the Scripture. That was not satisfactory, and many felt that the traditions of our people were endangered. So the teachers took the Oral Torah and formed the 'Mishna.'"

"What does that mean, Jacob?"

"It means simply, 'to repeat.' But from the time it was written, arguments and discussions began to grow up around it, so these discussions were written down into what was called the 'Gemara,' the commentators' views of the Mishna. When the two were put together, the Mishna and the Gemara, that was called the 'Talmud,' which means simply 'teaching.'"

"How fascinating! But you've never seen a New Testament?"

"No. Never."

Moved by an impulse, Rachel arose and went over to sit on his cot beside him. "Here, let me show you." She had taken off her mittens to turn the pages of the Bible. Now as her hand touched his, she did not see the strange light that flickered in his eyes. He did not look at her but kept his eyes on the page. "This is the New Testament."

"Yes. The Gospel of Matthew. What does that mean, 'Gospel'?"

"It means 'good news.'"

Jacob smiled, very much aware of the touch of her hand. "I think I need that, this good news."

"We all do."

Looking down, he suddenly smiled. "You Christians must go back to the Jews for your roots. Look at all these names."

"Yes. That's the genealogy, the family tree of Jesus."

"They're all Jews!"

"Of course. Jesus was a Jew."

"I will start reading here tonight."

"No, don't start with Matthew. Start with the Gospel of John." She turned the pages and found it for him. "Here. It's my favorite book. It mentions a prophet named John the Baptist. He was preaching one day, and when he looked up and saw Jesus, he said, 'Behold the Lamb of God, which taketh away the sin of the world.'"

"The Lamb of God?" A startled look swept across Jacob's face. "What a strange thing to say."

Rachel saw that Jacob was staring at the Bible with a peculiar look. "What's wrong, Jacob?"

"It just struck me strange. I never knew that Jesus was called the Lamb of God." He glanced up at her and was silent for a moment, then nodded. "It's just that in all the studying of our history and our tradition, the lamb played such an important part among my people. It's impossible to read the Talmud without somehow coming to realize that the sacrifice is the center of our religion."

"Do your people still sacrifice lambs?"

"Oh no, nothing like that. But ever since the first Passover, the death of a lamb has been very real to every Jew."

For a moment Rachel sat there wondering what to say. Somehow she felt that God was putting something on her heart that Jacob Steiner needed to hear. She did not want to say anything that would offend his Jewish roots, but still she felt an urge to speak. "I'm not a Bible scholar, Jacob, but I heard a minister once speak about this. It was a marvelous sermon. He talked about all of the sacrifices, the hundreds and thousands and, perhaps, even millions of lambs and other animals that have died on Jewish altars throughout history, and then he said, 'But not all the blood of all those animals combined can wash away one sin. They were mere animals. It takes more than that to remove the guilt from a human soul.'"

Jacob listened with intense interest. "What else did he say? Do you remember?"

"He said that all of the lambs that died under the old Jewish law were saying, 'This is a symbol. It will not take away sin, but one day God will provide a lamb. When He does, all sin will be forgiven.' And that's what I think John the Baptist meant when he said, 'Behold the

Lamb of God.' You know what it's like to sacrifice a lamb, a real animal, but now God is furnishing His own Son as the Lamb, the one whose blood can really take away sins. And that's what Jesus did. He became, in effect, like the little lamb that was slain on the day of Passover. The lamb was innocent, had done nothing wrong, but somehow symbolically every Jewish family would place their guilt upon Him." Taking a deep breath, Rachel whispered, "At least that's what I've done, Jacob. I look on Jesus as the one who bore my sins." She hesitated, then said, "You know the fifty-third chapter of Isaiah. 'But he was wounded for our transgressions, he was bruised for our iniquities: the chastisement of our peace was upon him; and with his stripes we are healed.'"

"I know that almost by heart," Jacob blinked with surprise. He shook his head with bewilderment and said, "I can't understand how that could be, that a man dying two thousand years ago could have anything to do with my sins."

"Then let me remind you of another one of your Old Testament Scriptures," Rachel said quickly. "'Trust in the Lord with all thine heart; *and lean not unto thine own understanding.*'" She looked over at Jacob and saw that he was thinking deeply.

"It's very strange," Jacob said. "I've never thought of anything like this."

Suddenly Rachel understood, in that mysterious way that comes now and then, that it was time for her to leave. *It's like sowing seeds*, she thought as she stood up. *Just one little seed, but maybe it will take root in Jacob's heart.* Aloud she said, "I must go now."

At once he stood and watched as she put on her mittens. "I thank you very much," he said simply. "You have been so kind, as always."

Rachel felt heat coming into her face, and suddenly she pulled off one mitten and extended her hand. "I wish I could do more," she said, then she turned quickly and left.

She made her way slowly back toward the house, stumbling almost blindly against the biting wind. When she was almost to the back door, she heard a strange sound. Pausing and straightening up, she listened hard and discovered that it came from somewhere in the front along the road. *It sounds like a carriage, but who would be traveling in this kind of weather?* Curious, she made her way around the back of the house. When she turned the corner, she heard the sound of muffled horse hooves, which then stopped. Moving forward cautiously, she saw the bulky shadow of a carriage out in front of the house. "Who could be coming at this hour?" She moved forward again and saw the form of a man as he left the carriage and started down the front walk.

"Who's there?" she called out.

Immediately a voice came back. "It's me, Matthew. Who is this?"

Relief washed over Rachel and she came forward at once. "It's Rachel," she said. She came to stand before Matthew, who was bundled in heavy clothes so that he looked almost like a huge bear. "How did you manage to get out here at this time of night—and in this weather?" She set down her lantern and reached around her brother's massive bulk to give him a hug.

"It wasn't easy, believe me! There weren't any drivers out and about, but I managed to talk a man into renting his carriage to me—for a hefty fee, of course. My ship got in late and I thought I might as well try to get here rather than pay for a whole night in an inn. I'm pretty sick of inns anyway."

"Well, I'm so glad you made it before this storm got any worse. If this keeps up, the roads will quickly be impassable. Come inside and get warm."

"I'll put the horse up in the barn," Matthew said as he began to unhitch the animal.

Fear ran through Rachel as she thought of the barn where Jacob was hiding. Then she realized he meant the big barn where the horses and carriages were kept. "All right, but don't startle Caesar. He has a room out there. He might take you for a burglar."

"Caesar? Who's that?"

"A new stableman and carriage driver. Maybe I should go with you," she said.

The two went to the barn, and Rachel opened the door as Matthew led the horse inside. Caesar loomed out of the darkness and said in his deep voice, "Who's that!"

"It's all right, Caesar. This is my brother, Matthew. He has just arrived from Europe. Matthew, I'd like you to meet Caesar."

Matthew turned and his eyes widened at the size of the man who stood before him. "Well, no one's going to steal anything while you're here, Caesar." He tried to smile, but his face was numb from the cold.

"Will you rub the horse down and feed him, Caesar?"

"Yes, ma'am, I'll do that."

"Come along, Matthew."

Leaving the barn, she led Matthew into the kitchen, where the fireplace was still radiating hot coals. Quickly she stirred up the fire into a blaze and said, "I'll bet you're hungry."

"Yes. I could eat anything. The food on that boat was terrible."

"Come over and warm yourself by the fire while I fix something."

As Rachel prepared a meal, Matthew pulled off his coat and held his hands out over the blaze. The heat soaked through him, and he said, "That cabin I was in stayed wet all the way over from England. I feel like an icicle."

"You'll feel better with some hot food and a nice warm bed."

"Nobody knew I was coming. I hate to surprise you like this."

"Father's not here. He's with the army."

"You mean he joined Washington's forces?"

"Oh no, nothing like that. You know how General Washington's always been after Father to make cannons. Well, that's what he's doing for the cause. Dake has been working on it, too. You know how Father feels about General Washington."

Matthew leaned back in his chair. He was exhausted from his trip, and the warmth of the kitchen and the soft sound of Rachel's voice had a soporific effect. He drifted off and came to with a start as Rachel's hand touched his shoulders.

"What—what—!"

"Come on. Get something to eat."

"I nearly dropped off to sleep."

"*Nearly* dropped off!" Rachel laughed. "You've been sleeping for an hour. I didn't want to disturb you. I thought it would do you good. Here, sit up."

She had fixed a meal of fried ham and gravy, dressed eggs, fresh biscuits with apple butter, and hot black coffee.

"This is wonderful, Rachel. You always were a good cook."

Rachel sat down and held a cup of coffee between her hands, sipping it occasionally. "I've been staying here because Father was going to be gone, and the housekeeper, Mrs. Williams, had to leave. I thought I could help Marian and Phoebe out."

"How is Marian . . . and the baby?"

"They are both wonderful, and you'll love the baby, Matthew! Marian thinks she's the only woman in the world who has a baby. My, how she dotes on that child!"

Matthew took a bite of biscuit and chewed it thoughtfully. "Things do work out well sometimes, don't they?"

"What a strange thing to say."

Matthew shrugged his shoulders. "Well, most things don't, you know."

"You've become such a pessimist! Things have worked out well for you. You wanted to be an artist and now you're a famous artist, going to be rich, I suppose."

Matthew grinned slightly. "You always did look on the bright side of things, Rachel. I'm glad you're like that. I hope you always will be. Now, tell me about yourself. First, what were you doing out in the middle of the night—and in a snowstorm?" Matthew suddenly laughed aloud. "If I didn't know you better, I'd think you were out looking for your fellow somewhere. Come on, now. Confess."

"Oh, Matthew, don't be silly."

Matthew leaned back. He was very tired and it showed in his features. He was not a large man, being shorter and much less muscular than Dake and Micah. He had a sensitive face with brown hair and blue eyes, and there was a grace in his movements that was lacking in the other Bradford men. "All right, I guess that was silly. But still, it's after midnight. What *were* you doing?"

For one moment Rachel thought of unburdening herself concerning Jacob Steiner. For some time she had longed to talk to someone besides Caesar. She had the feeling that if her father were here, it would be easier, but to try to explain what she was doing for Jacob might prove difficult. For now she put Matthew off by saying, "Well, that'll give you something to wonder about. As a matter of fact, I do have two eligible bachelors vying for my hand."

As Rachel had hoped, her news caused Matthew to put aside the question of why she was out in the middle of the night.

"Well, may I offer you my congratulations and may your first child be a masculine one, as Father always says!"

"There's nothing to congratulate me about just yet! It's nothing like that."

"Tell me, then. Who are they? Do I know them?"

Rachel shrugged. "One of them is Jubal Morrison. You know, the brother of Stephen Morrison, the husband of our cousin Grace. The other is the pastor of the church, Reverend Josiah Grierson."

"And which do you favor, my dear sister?"

"They're about to drive me crazy, Matthew. I'm not interested in getting married in the least."

"Well, that makes one woman out of the half million or so that I have met who doesn't want to get married. Most of them have no other idea in the world."

"You have a very low opinion of women, haven't you, Matthew?"

"Have I? Well, I suppose so."

Rachel had a sudden impulse to reach out and shake him. His treatment of Abigail Howland was totally wrong, she thought. True enough, Abigail had deceived Matthew at one point, had indeed led an immoral life, but now she was totally different. But all she said was, "I know you have never forgiven Abigail, Matthew. I think you are headed for trouble there. She doesn't deserve the way you've treated her."

Instantly Matthew's face seemed to shut like a door being closed. He got up at once, saying, "I guess I'll go to bed."

"Oh, I forgot to tell you! Aunt Lyna and Cousin David are here for a visit. You can take the east room on the corner."

"It'll be good to see Aunt Lyna. How's David?"

"He's become very handsome." She smiled and said, "Sam's terribly jealous of David. You know his latest case of infatuation is with Keturah."

"How many cases does that make? He has as many brokenhearted romances as he does silly inventions."

"I know, but he's young."

"Yes, 'Grandma.' He's how much younger than you? A whole year?"

"Go along with you, Matthew!" She came over to him suddenly and put her hands behind his neck, pulling him forward. "I'm glad you're home, Matthew," she said quietly. "I've missed you."

"Why, what a nice thing to say!"

"Father should be home soon. He'll want to hear about your work, and so will all of us. You know what would be wonderful?"

"What?"

"If you could paint a picture of Aunt Lyna. She's so beautiful, and Father would love it, I'm sure."

"I will—and I'll paint one of him to give to her."

"That's sweet, Matthew. Now, off to bed with you. You need to rest up for the days ahead. I want to take my handsome artist brother around and tantalize all the unmarried maidens in Boston. You'll be besieged with offers."

"And I'm anxious to meet your minister and your sea captain. Perhaps I can find out if their intentions are honorable."

"Well, the minister's are, but I'm not entirely sure about Jubal's. He's pretty much a pirate."

"Pirate! Why do you call him that?"

"Because that's what he is. You remember, he and Sam have planned this out. They've already taken one prize, a British merchant ship. A small one. Sam thinks they're going to get terribly rich. He's already talking about getting a bigger boat so he can take bigger prizes. You know Sam."

Weariness came over Matthew then, and he said, "It's good to be home. I've missed you."

She followed him upstairs, both of them tiptoeing and walking softly, and when she went inside, she checked the bed and said, "I'll get the extra blankets over here in the chest." She got one out and, handing it to him, said, "Good night, Matthew."

Matthew took the blanket and looked at her fondly. "You thought you changed the subject, but I'm still wondering why you were out in the middle of the night."

"We all have our secrets, Matthew."

"I hope it was something shameful. Then I won't be the only black sheep in the family." He leaned forward and kissed her cheek. "Good night, sister."

13

A Brother Is for Hard Times

MATTHEW SAT DOWN at the table and surveyed the breakfast that was spread out before him. He looked up and smiled at his stepmother, a pleased expression on his face. "You're going to stuff me like a Thanksgiving goose, Marian," he said.

Marian, holding Enoch in the crook of her left arm, put him over her shoulder and tapped him on the back. An enormous burp filled the air, and everyone at the table laughed.

"My nephew's going to have good lungs," Lyna smiled.

"Yes," David said. "Maybe he'll become a shouting evangelist."

Matthew looked at his aunt and his cousin, thinking how handsome the entire Gordon family were. "It's good to see you again, Aunt Lyna. And you, David. I hope you and I can spend some time together."

"Nothing I'd like better."

"I don't think I'd trust these two out alone, Aunt Lyna," Rachel smiled. "Maybe you'd better send me along to keep them out of trouble."

David laughed aloud. "Yes, and you can bring your two suitors. With a preacher along we couldn't get into too much trouble."

"You look tired, Matthew, and you've lost weight." Marian examined her stepson with a critical eye. "I want you to stay here with us."

"I'd like that very much. When do you think Father will be back?"

"Soon, I hope," Marian nodded. "I'm lonesome when he's gone. Besides, he needs to be around to help me take care of this fat wad."

"How is he taking it," Matthew asked, "becoming a father at his advanced age?"

"Don't talk like that! He's the strongest man I know!"

"Only teasing, Marian. That is one fine baby you've got there. I hope he grows up to be the best of the Bradfords."

The compliment pleased Marian, and she said, "Phoebe, you may give Matthew another pancake for being so nice."

"How is Joel, Phoebe?" Matthew asked. He studied the young woman carefully, thinking how she had blossomed since he had first seen her. He had found Phoebe and Joel Bradford in poor condition, indeed, in England. With his father's help, he had managed to get them to the Colonies.

"Not as well as I'd like," Phoebe said. "They're having a terrible time at Valley Forge, starving and freezing."

Matthew examined her carefully, then he looked over at the Gordons. "I expect Uncle Leslie is thinking the war's about over."

"Not at all," Lyna said quickly. "He keeps telling General Howe that Washington will never give up."

"I imagine that doesn't make him very popular with the rest of the officers."

"No, but Leslie has always been one to speak his mind."

"What's it like in England?" David asked. "What do they say about the revolution?"

"Some of the best men over there, including William Pitt and Edmund Burke, speak out firmly against it. They say England can't win, and even if she did, it would be a hollow victory. But the king won't listen. He's got it in his mind to be a soldier of sorts, so he keeps feeding money and troops into this effort."

"Well," Lyna said with a trace of weariness, "I wish General Washington would win a great battle and the whole thing would be settled. Then the whole family would be together again."

"It doesn't look very likely," Matthew said. He shook his head and thought about the might of the imperial army of King George and of the few tattered and ill-equipped men struggling to survive a freezing winter. He said nothing more but changed the subject, and after that the talk went more easily.

🔔   🔔   🔔

Dr. Ian McClellan was a small, fair Scotsman resembling a terrier. His whiskers were not neat and sleek but bristled like gray wires, and his black eyes snapped from under beetling brows. "I dinna' like the look of it!" he said finally with a Scottish burr. "She's no so good as she was even yesterday."

"Can't you do something for her, Dr. McClellan?"

"The guid Lord can do something for her, but a poor doctor such as myself, we're not guid for much. Set a bone, pick out a bullet, sweat a fever, bleed a patient, but none of these will answer for Mrs. Denham."

The doctor looked at the two women who had waited for him to get the report of his examination of Abigail Howland's aunt, Mrs. Esther Denham. He knew that this was Mrs. Denham's house and that both Abigail and her mother were dependent upon the charity of the good lady. He had heard the rumors of Abigail's wayward youth and at first had felt hard toward the young woman. However, since Mrs. Denham had gotten ill, he had made several visits and now saw a gentle spirit in Abigail that had quite surprised him. He had put aside his prejudices, for he had seen how the young woman had devoted herself tirelessly to the care of Mrs. Denham. Her own mother, too, was ill much of the time. In effect, Abigail Howland was serving as a nurse for two invalids.

"What's wrong with her, Doctor?" Mrs. Howland asked. She was wearing a black dress and had a shawl wrapped around her shoulders. The cold winter had not done her any good, and now she sat in a rocking chair leaning toward the crackling fire for warmth.

"Pneumonia."

The single word sent a shock of fear through both of Dr. McClellan's listeners. They knew how deadly pneumonia could be even in a healthy person, and Esther Denham had been ill for some time.

"What can we do?" Abigail asked quietly.

"See that she eats as much as she will take, keep her warm and comfortable—and pray."

"We're already doing that," Abigail said quietly.

There was a spirit in this girl that McClellan liked. She had classic features, and her eyes reflected an inner serenity that was often lacking in young women. In the light of what he knew about her past, this pleased the doctor exceedingly. He was a fine Christian man himself, and it was encouraging to see that in the face of so much godlessness in the world, a beautiful young woman like this could manifest such a spirit. *She's a true handmaiden of the Lord,* he thought quickly, *and no matter what she's done in the past, I see the Lord Jesus reflected in her now.* Aloud he said, "I'll come back tomorrow."

"Thank you, Doctor. I'll show you to the door."

As soon as she had let McClellan out, Abigail returned to her mother. She paused, saying, "I'll fix your tea, Mother."

Mrs. Howland smiled at her daughter. "I believe that would be nice, but see to your aunt first."

Abigail moved out of the small parlor and went down the hall. Opening a door cautiously, she saw that her aunt was asleep. Closing the door quietly, she went to the kitchen, where she brewed tea, then arranged the cups and teapot on a silver service. Coming back to her mother, she poured the tea, saying, "There. Drink all of this, and I'll fix you a good lunch."

"I'm not really hungry, Abigail."

"Now, none of that! We can't have you getting sick."

Actually, Abigail was very concerned about her mother's frail health. She had gone downhill steadily since their trip from New York, where they had barely escaped with their lives. She could see the weakness in her mother's face but ignored this, saying cheerfully, "I'll fix anything you like. What will it be?"

"Oh, a chop would be good if we have any."

"Yes, we do. I'll fix it after we've had our tea."

Suddenly Mrs. Howland gave her daughter an anxious look. "I'm worried, Abigail."

"About Aunt Esther?"

"No, about us." The older woman bit her lip and her hands trembled. "What will happen to us if she dies, Abigail?"

"We don't want to talk about that," Abigail said quietly.

"But we have no place to go. No place at all."

Abigail had encountered this worry in her mother often. Her mother was a Christian, she felt, but there was little faith in her. Abigail had to work constantly to encourage her, and now she said cheerfully, "Well, let me repeat what Reverend Grierson said last week. 'We spend so much time agonizing over problems that never happen that we don't have strength to serve God acceptably in the now.'" She leaned forward and squeezed her mother's hand. "Today we're fine, Mother. We have a warm place to stay, we have food to eat, we're well, and there's hope for Esther that she'll make a full recovery. Let's just, right now, give thanks to God for that."

But her mother was in no mood for prayer at the present. She sipped her tea, then looked up, and with anxiety threading her tone, she said, "What about Seth Bounds? Have you thought of marrying him?"

"No, I haven't."

"But he likes you very much. He told me so the last time he was here. In effect, he asked for my permission to ask for your hand."

"I hope you didn't give it."

"I wanted to, but I know how . . . how firm you are."

Abigail Howland smiled and even laughed aloud. "*Firm* you call it? Most people call it stubborn!"

"Perhaps you do have some of that in you, but you must think of yourself, not of me. I won't be here forever. You're a young woman and you've turned down several good men. Mr. Bounds seems to be a kindly sort, and he's very well off, you know."

"Oh yes, I know. He brought me a list of his properties the last time he came."

"He did! Well, you see that shows how serious he is."

"Serious, but it isn't very romantic. He insisted on going over the list with me, and he had even listed how many silver teaspoons he had."

"How many did he have?"

"Oh, Mother, I don't know! In any case, I'll never marry Seth Bounds."

"But why not?"

"Because he is fifty years old."

"That's not so old."

"Not from your point of view, and I know many younger women marry older men. But that isn't really the reason."

"Well, what is the reason, then?"

"He has a house full of children—or perhaps I should say wild banshees. Four of them. Two of them are already into their teens and wild as they can be. I suppose they are good enough boys, but I'm not fitted to bring up a ready-made family. When you get right down to it, Mother, Seth Bounds isn't interested so much in a wife. He wants a nanny, a housekeeper, and a cook. I almost told him to hire three women, one for each of those jobs, but Seth is very miserly. He won't spend money like that. Not when he can get a wife who will do all three jobs for nothing."

That did not end the conversation, for though Mrs. Howland was rather feeble, she was always ready to argue this point. Abigail had learned, however, how to handle it. She simply smiled and waited until her mother had run down, then said, "Now I'll go fix your chop, and then we'll have a nice lunch."

🜛 🜛 🜛

". . . And this is my cousin Matthew," David said. "May I introduce Reverend Josiah Grierson."

Josiah had arrived at the Bradford estate rather unexpectedly. He had hoped to find Rachel alone, but instead he had been met by David Gordon, who had introduced him to Matthew, who now stood smiling at the preacher's disappointed look. "I'm sure you two will have a lot to talk about. You're both artists—a musician and a painter."

"And never the twain should meet," Matthew smiled. However, he bowed, saying, "I am happy to make your acquaintance, sir. My step-mother has sung your praises. She is very much impressed with your abilities to minister the gospel."

"Well, that's good to hear, and, of course, I have heard much of your fine work. You've just returned from the Continent, I understand?"

"Yes, I have, Pastor."

"I would like very much to see some of your work. I have no gift along that line myself," Josiah said, "but I enjoy good paintings very much."

"It will be my pleasure, although most of them are at my father's old house. If you would care to call there, I'd be happy to show you what I have done."

Actually Josiah much preferred to stay in the same house with Rachel. He found himself being more and more interested in this young woman, and although she had given him but scant encouragement, he was a man of tremendous self-confidence. He prided himself on always finishing what he started. Now he was concentrating on taking Jubal Morrison out of Rachel's mind. He was well aware that there was a ro-mantic flavor to Morrison that he himself lacked, but he comforted him-self in that he was financially secure and Morrison was not as deter-mined to marry.

David slipped out, leaving the two men to talk, and found Rachel putting her bonnet on. "I think it's the preacher's turn. The pirate slipped up. Usually they're like Siamese twins joined at the hip."

"Oh, David, you say the craziest things!"

"I don't see anything crazy about it. From what I hear, they're neck and neck. What does my fair cousin say?"

"I say I have to get out of the house." Leaving, Rachel moved into the parlor and greeted Josiah with a smile. "I must go on an errand, Pastor, but I'm sure these gentlemen will entertain you."

Disappointment swept across Josiah's face. "Perhaps it's something I could help you with."

"No. I'm just going to see a friend." Quickly, in order to avoid any protest, Rachel said, "Matthew, it's Mrs. Denham."

"Mrs. Denham is ill?"

"Yes. She speaks of you so often. She always says you saved her life."

Josiah picked up on this. "Saved her life? How did that come about?"

"It was when New York burned," Rachel said. "You remember, David?"

"I certainly do. It missed our place, but it destroyed lots of old houses."

"Yes. Mrs. Denham's house was one of them. It was Matthew here who carried her out of the house along with some of her possessions, and brought her to Boston. She has a house here, and it's very comfortable."

When Matthew hesitated, Rachel understood that he was thinking that if he went to see Esther Denham, he would also be forced to see Abigail Howland. Quickly she said, "It would mean so much to Mrs. Denham. From what I understand, she may not be with us much longer."

"Well, then, of course I will go," Matthew said instantly. "I will look forward to showing you my work, Reverend."

"And I will look forward to having you in our services."

"Yes. With all the saints in your congregation, you need at least one sinner to practice on." Matthew smiled and winked at David. "You entertain the pastor, David."

🛡   🛡   🛡

Abigail heard the knock at the door and moved at once to answer it. She had been cleaning and had on her oldest dress and had spent most of the night up with her aunt. Now as she opened the door, her lips formed a greeting when she saw Rachel Bradford, but then her eyes fell on the man beside her and she could not speak.

"Look who's with me! He's come to see your aunt," Rachel said quickly.

"Come in, please." Abigail dropped her eyes and stepped aside. She closed the door against the cold and said, "Will you have tea?"

"We can't stay long. But I told Matthew how much Mrs. Denham thinks of him."

"Indeed she does. Perhaps you'd like to visit with her, Mr. Bradford."

Matthew thought *Mr. Bradford* was rather formal, seeing as how at one time they'd been a couple. He felt it was for Rachel's sake, however, and nodded, saying stiffly, "If you would be so kind."

"If you'd care to wait, Rachel, we'll make tea."

"Oh, let me do it."

"Very well."

Abigail could not think of a single word to say as she led the way down the short hallway. As always in the presence of Matthew Brad-ford, she could only think of how she had betrayed him and how he harbored bitter feelings that he could barely conceal. Opening the door, she saw that her aunt was sitting up in bed. "Aunt Esther, I have a sur-prise for you."

Esther Denham was so frail that Matthew hardly recognized her. However, he was at her side at once, sat down, and took her hand, say-ing, "My dear Mrs. Denham, I'm so glad to see you again!"

Esther Denham's voice was very feeble, but she was alert enough to summon a smile. "My dear Matthew. How wonderful of you to come see me!"

"I'm sorry to hear you've been ill, but we'll hope that things will get better."

Esther Denham had a deep wisdom, and now she said quietly, "I will never leave this bed, Matthew."

The announcement stunned Matthew Bradford, and he shook his head, his lips forming a thin line. "Don't say that, Esther! You don't know it."

"I'm not complaining, Matthew. I've had such a good life. Actually, I'm rather tired. I would like to go home."

Matthew was unable to handle this situation gracefully. He was not a man of God himself, although he knew that there was a reality in the faith. He had seen enough of his father and of his brothers, Micah and Dake, and of his sister, Rachel, to understand that. He reached out and took her hand and sat there silently. Finally he said, "I'm glad to see you again."

"Tell me what you've been doing."

Abigail took the opportunity to leave and give them some privacy, and Matthew spoke for some time until he saw that her eyes were grow-ing heavy. "I'll come back tomorrow," he said gently. "I'll be here every day."

"So kind," Esther Denham said. She held on to his hand, putting her other one over it. "Matthew, I've never forgotten your kindness in New York."

"It was nothing."

"Yes, it was a great deal. But I want to tell you something." She seemed to be almost gasping for breath, and Matthew leaned forward. She spoke in a faint whisper, and as good as his hearing was, he almost missed it. "Abigail has been such a blessing." She seemed to struggle and fight for the weakness that washed over her. She looked up and her old eyes were clear. "She has changed. I know that she hurt you terribly, but she has repented and is now a fine handmaiden of the Lord."

Matthew could not answer, but he sensed the urgency of her plea. *She's asking me to forgive Abigail. Lord knows I've tried*, he thought almost bitterly. He squeezed her hand, and then in an uncommon gesture for him, he leaned forward and kissed her withered cheek. "I'll see you tomorrow. You go to sleep now."

As he went outside and made his way to the small parlor, he found the two women. He said, "She's asleep. She's very weak, isn't she?"

"Yes," Abigail said. "Dr. McClellan doesn't offer much hope."

"I told her I would come back tomorrow," he said. "I hope it won't be an inconvenience."

"Oh no. It would be very kind indeed," Abigail said. She felt she was speaking in a stilted fashion and watched as the two put on their coats and left. When the door closed, she leaned her back against it and said, "He'll never forgive me—not ever!"

🔔   🔔   🔔

Rachel emerged from the kitchen with a bowl of baked beans in her hands. She looked at the table blankly for a moment and then asked as she set the dish down, "Where did Matthew go? It's time to eat."

Lyna and David sat on one side of the table with Marian at the head. Matthew had been sitting on her right hand, but now Marian said, "Oh, he's all excited about the paintings he's going to do of his aunt and his father."

"I think it's a wonderful idea," Lyna said. "Not of me, but I would love to have a good portrait of Daniel. I have nothing at all like that."

"Nor does Daniel have one of you, but he'll be excited about the prospect," Marian said.

"Where is Matthew?" Lyna wondered.

"Why, he had an idea," Marian said. For once she was not holding Enoch but had entrusted him to Phoebe, who was rocking him to sleep in the nursery. "Do you remember the old lamp that belonged to your mother?"

"Why, yes, of course."

"Well, Daniel wanted some of his own things when he moved into this place, and the lamp was one of the things that he most treasured. I'm sorry to say he hasn't used it yet, but Matthew wants it in the picture."

"Where is it?" Rachel said sitting down.

"I packed some things up a few weeks ago, and without thinking, I

171

put the lamp with them." She said casually, "I had Caesar store them in the loft of the old barn."

Instantly Rachel felt a sense of paralysis. *In the old barn! He'll find Jacob!* Her first impulse was to get up and dash to the barn, but when she started to rise, Marian said, "Oh, don't bother yourself. I told him how to get there. He won't have any trouble."

Rachel could not think of a single remark. She could foresee what was going to happen easily enough. Matthew would find Jacob, and then he would come and inform the whole household of the situation. *I should have done something different,* she thought. Numbly she sat there forcing herself to eat, but her mind simply refused to function.

"Well, here is Matthew now," David said. "And it looks like he found the lamp."

Sure enough, Matthew entered with the lamp. "I found it," he said smiling. "Here it is." The lamp stood about twenty inches high, had a pewter base, a small glass oil globe, and a shade made out of heavy paper covered with dark red cloth and a short gold fringe hanging from the bottom edge. "It'll be just the thing to put beside Father while I do his painting. We've seen him a thousand times—haven't we, Rachel?—sitting there reading his Bible by the light of this old piece."

"Why, yes, we have," Rachel stammered. She was almost as shocked by Matthew's behavior as she had been a moment earlier when she had heard of his search for the lamp in the old barn. *How could it be?* she wondered. *He must have seen him!* she thought wildly.

Matthew, however, sat down and, putting the lamp carefully on the table, began to speak cheerfully. Rachel could hardly understand any of it, for her mind was racing in fervid confusion.

Finally the meal was over, and she began clearing the table. Marian took Lyna and David into the library to show them some souvenirs that had come to her from her first husband, the only good memories she had from her marriage to Sir Leo Rochester!

"I'll help carry the dishes out," Matthew said cheerfully. He picked up a bowl in each hand and Rachel did likewise.

When they were in the kitchen, she put the bowls down and turned to him. Rachel Bradford was a courageous girl and very direct. Something in her refused to be intimidated, and now she asked intently, "Did you have any difficulty finding the lamp?"

Matthew had put the dishes down, and now he turned to face Rachel. "No. Not a bit."

Rachel waited for him to say more, but he simply stood there. Finally she saw a flicker of something in his eyes and knew that she could not conceal her thoughts anymore. "You found him, didn't you?"

"As a matter of fact I did. I think he was expecting Caesar."

A silence fell over the room then, and Rachel's mind worked swiftly. Taking a deep breath, she said, "Come up to my room, Matthew. I have something to tell you."

Matthew suddenly grinned. "I imagine you do."

☙   ☙   ☙

As soon as Rachel ascended to the loft, Jacob knew instantly that something was different. "Your brother has told you, I see."

"Not directly. I don't think he would have said anything, but I knew he had to have discovered you."

"Yes. When I heard the footsteps, I thought it was Caesar bringing food." He shrugged his shoulders, saying, "It was quite a surprise for both of us."

"What did he say?"

"He just stood there looking at me for a moment and I at him, of course. I couldn't tell what he was thinking, but the thought that came to me was, *It's all over now.*"

"But he must have said *something.*"

"Of all things he said, 'I assume you are acquainted with my sister, Miss Bradford.' He was very polite, but there was humor in his eyes." He shook his head and there was a puzzled expression on his face. "He does not resemble you a great deal. I would never have known he was your brother."

Rachel hesitated. "Actually he's my half brother."

"Oh, I didn't know that."

"His mother was abandoned before he was born, and my father married her and gave him the Bradford name."

"A generous thing to do, indeed."

"My father's always been generous." Rachel was nervous and put the lamp down. She had come in the daylight for once, and the pale sunlight left broad beams on the floor.

"He did not seem angry," Jacob observed. "I'm surprised."

"If it had been one of my other brothers, it might have been different. They both are devoted to the cause. Matthew doesn't care about the revolution one way or another."

"That's very strange."

"Well, Matthew's a little strange. He recently discovered that his real father, Sir Leo Rochester, had left his lands and all of his estate to him— provided he would take the name of Rochester."

"That must be very nice."

"Not really. Matthew's terribly confused. He's been a Bradford all of his life, and now he's been asked to become something he's not."

"He was very poised. He didn't even ask what I was doing here. Of course, he saw my uniform, and he must have known from my accent. In any case, I thought it was only fair to tell him." He hesitated, then said, "I told him how kind you were and he said, 'That's like Rachel.'"

"He will never tell, Jacob. I talked to him. He was somewhat concerned, but he doesn't have the same reservations that some men have. He . . . he thought you were my beau, he said at first."

Jacob's eyes flew open with surprise. "He thought that!"

"That's . . . what he said."

"Well, that's nonsense! You disabused him of that notion."

"Oh, of course! I told him how badly wounded you were, and I was only helping until you were able to survive a prison camp."

"What did he say to that?"

"He said, 'You'll never be able to turn him in, Rachel. I can already tell.'"

Actually Matthew had shaken his head, disbelief in his eyes. He had said, "You'll never turn him in. You always brought sick kittens home, and I never knew you to turn one out."

"In any case, this has gone too far. I will leave as soon as it is safe," Jacob said.

The two of them were standing, Jacob with his back to the window, so that the strong sunlight fell on the face of Rachel Bradford. For some reason it seemed to Jacob that time had stopped—or slowed to an imperceptible pace. He was still weak from his ordeal, and his mind seemed to become filled with one thought—the beauty and grace of the woman who stood before him. Jacob Steiner was not a man who knew a great deal about women, but at that moment he was filled with a sense of admiration and gratitude toward Rachel Bradford. Scarcely conscious of what he was doing, he moved closer to her, reached out, and put his hands on her shoulders. When she looked up at him wide-eyed and startled, he could not speak. Perhaps if he could have uttered what was in his heart, he would not have kissed her. It was a simple gesture, one that was in a strange sense unpracticed and awkward on his part. Drawn by the richness of her beauty and her deep spirit, he savored the softness of her lips and was acutely conscious of her as she pressed against him.

As for Rachel—she was startled when Jacob put his hands on her and ordinarily would have reacted quickly. She had been kissed more than once, but the same unearthly atmosphere that had fallen over Jacob had the same effect on her. She closed her eyes, and as his lips touched hers she did not resist. His caress was firm and strong, not demanding, and she was stirred by his masculinity. For a long moment she stood there, her heart beating quickly.

Then she drew back and with a pale face murmured, "I guess we're entitled to one mistake, Jacob."

"I was impertinent," Jacob said quietly. "But I meant no harm."

"No, I'm sure of that." Rachel felt a weakness in her lower limbs and hastily turned and left the loft. As she entered the house, she was afraid that someone would see her state of confusion.

Fortunately, it was Matthew who encountered her. He had seen her coming and had stepped outside, and now he said, "What will you do now?"

Rachel stood there silently for a time, and when she turned, Matthew was somewhat shocked to see tears rising in her eyes. "I don't know, Matthew. I'm so . . . confused."

Matthew Bradford felt a strong compassion for this sister of his. They had actually been closer since he had discovered that Daniel was not his biological father. Now he reached out his arms and held her for a moment.

"Well, sister," he said quietly, "you care for this man. I can see that."

"No—no!"

Matthew did not argue. "So you're confused. My little sister—always calm, always in control! Well, perhaps you know what I feel now." He comforted her for a moment and then pulled away and held her at arm's length. "So now there are two Bradfords totally ill at ease in worlds they never made. Come, you'd better go to your room. You're not fit to meet anyone else."

He watched her as she made her way and grieved over the struggle he saw in her. "It can't come out well," he murmured. "My poor sister!"

PART THREE

—

ENTRANCE INTO THE KINGDOM

December 1777–March 1778

14

RACHEL'S SONG

CHRISTMAS DAY CAME TO BOSTON, bringing with it milder weather. On the twenty-fourth, two inches of snow were dumped on the earth by a benevolent sky. When the citizens arose, the sight delighted them. The crystal landscape reflected a pale yellow sun overhead, while not a cloud moved across a blue-gray sky. The temperatures began to rise shortly after dawn, so that by the time all the Bradfords were gathered together in the parlor, the fires had to be banked and the windows cracked open slightly to allow a breeze in.

"Well, if only Father were here—and Micah and Joel," Dake murmured as he sat on the brown horsehide couch, holding Enoch on his lap. "All this would be perfect, wouldn't it, Mother? I know you miss Father."

"I thought from his letters he was going to get to come," Marian answered, "but I suppose if every soldier went home, the general would have no army left." She looked down at the round face of Enoch, who was balanced on Dake's lap, then reaching out, she ran the tips of her fingers over his silky hair. Her caress brought a quick smile from Enoch and a toothless grin. He chortled and struck himself in the eye with his chubby fist. "He's trying to talk," Marian said proudly.

Dake grinned at the child and said, "I'll be glad when Jeanne gives me that son she promised me. I'm bound to make him a real playmate. Why, the first thing you know, we'll be out hunting together, then I'll get him a horse, a little pony maybe, and then—"

Laughing at his enthusiasm, Marian reached over and picked Enoch up. "Let me hold him. It's time for you to make a Christmas speech."

"Me?"

"Yes. You're the patriarch now that your father is gone. You're the

179

old man with the long white beard. Now, get up and let's hear something wonderful out of you."

Dake looked around the room uncertainly but then managed a grin. "I'm not much for speeches, but I'll do the best I can." Getting to his feet, he looked over the room toward the Christmas tree and said, "Time for presents." Looking at the pleased faces smiling back, he turned to Marian and winked at her. "There. How was that for a speech?"

"You can do better than that, Dake Bradford."

Dake bowed his head for a moment, then looked around at those who were scattered about the large parlor. A Christmas tree that brushed the top of the twelve-foot ceiling gave off the fragrance of evergreens. A star crowned the top, and Dake and the rest of the men had been putting candles on. They were burning merrily now, and Dake shifted his feet, saying, "Well, I can't make a speech like Father can, but I want to say that I'm grateful to God for our family. He has been gracious toward us, tenderhearted, long-suffering as always, and on this Christmas when we remember the birth of Jesus, I'd like to think that we've all given our hearts to Him and that nothing in this world is more important than serving Him." He looked around the room, studying the faces that were so dear to him, then added, "I guess I believe that every one of us is a miracle. I remember Father said last Christmas, 'I remember the day each one of you were born. I thought, when I looked into your faces, God, this is a miracle. There's no way that I can ever thank God enough for giving me children.'" He hesitated, then said, "Next year, God willing, we'll all be together." He grinned suddenly at Jeanne, who had been having a difficult week but was now in good spirits. "And I'm hoping Jeanne will cooperate and give Enoch a cousin to celebrate with. A *boy* cousin," he said loudly.

"Yes, let's get at the presents," Sam said loudly. "Enough speech-making, Dake." As he glanced over at Keturah, he felt pleasure at how surprised she was going to be at his gift. Leaning over, he said to Rachel, "You wait until you see what I got Keturah. She's going to love it!"

"What is it, Sam?"

"Just wait and see."

Sam purposely let the others open their gifts first, then slipped out of the room and came back carrying a large rectangular-shaped box with gaily wrapped paper. Everyone's eyes were on him as he went over toward where Keturah sat. She was looking particularly pretty that morning, wearing an emerald green velvet dress with a high neck and long sleeves. White lace adorned the bodice around the neck, the cuffs of the sleeves, and the bottom edge of the full skirt. When she looked up and saw the large box, she said, "Sam, you shouldn't have spent your money on me."

"It's Christmas, Keturah. Open it."

Everyone was taking this in, for it was obvious that Keturah was showing inclinations of being favorably impressed with David Gordon. He had a cosmopolitan air about him that she liked. Besides, he was witty and very mature for his years. He had taken her more than once for long walks and twice into town so that she could do some shopping.

Now Sam swelled up as the last of the paper came off, and Keturah lifted the lid off of the box. She sat staring at it.

Finally Matthew asked, "Well, what is it, Keturah?"

"I . . . I really don't know."

Sam stared at her. "You don't know! Well, let me show you." He came over and lifted out a large metal object. It looked like an oversized frying pan and had four sturdy legs that had been fastened on the bottom. The top had a grill of some sort.

"Is it a frying pan?" Keturah asked.

"A frying pan! Certainly not! What kind of an idiot would give a girl a frying pan for Christmas?"

"Well, what is it?" Dake demanded. "It looks like a frying pan to me."

"It's a foot warmer." Sam lifted the top off and held it up so that Keturah could see the deep mouth of the instrument. "Look, before you go to bed at night, you fill this up with hot coals. As hot as you can get 'em until they're nice and cherry red. Then put the top on it, and then you can take it to your bedroom and put it under the bed, right under your feet. Don't you see?"

"Oh," Keturah said. "I guess so. You mean it gives off heat and keeps your feet warm."

"Sure," Sam said. "That's why it's called a 'foot warmer.' "

"Well, thank you very much, Sam. I'm sure I will find it very useful."

Sam was crushed by Keturah's lack of response. "Well," he murmured, "I thought you'd like it."

"I have a little gift for you, too, Keturah." David had stepped forward, and reaching into his pocket, he drew forth a very small box. "No time to get it wrapped. I'm not good at wrapping things, anyhow."

Keturah's reaction was noticeably warmer. She smiled and took the small box, then when she opened it, she caught her breath sharply. "Oh, David!" she breathed. "It's beautiful!"

Everyone watched as she reached in and pulled out a fine gold necklace that suspended a locket with a large blue stone also set in gold.

"Here, let me help you fasten it. It's very fine work," David said. He stepped behind Keturah, who lifted her hair, and then reaching around, he put the necklace on, fastened it, and said, "Now find yourself a mirror."

"There's one right over here," Rachel said. She went over to the sideboard, picked up a ten-inch mirror, and came back and held it up.

Keturah looked into it and her eyes were large, her lips parted with joy. "Oh, it's the most beautiful necklace I've ever seen! Where did you get it?"

Actually David had won the necklace gambling, but he did not dare reveal that—especially on Christmas morning. "Oh, I just picked it up," he said. "I thought it would look nice on you, and so it does."

Dake Bradford was not watching Keturah. He was watching Sam's face, and it was as if a light had gone out. He leaned over and whispered to Rachel, "She'll have a hard time keeping her feet warm with that necklace."

Rachel leaned back and said, "Yes, and she'd have a hard time wearing that foot warmer around her neck at a party. Sam should have known better."

"I'm sure he was just thinking of her comfort."

"Women don't like to get things that are comfortable. They like to get pretty things. I'm going to have a talk with that brother of mine."

"Well, I think that might be a good idea. He looks like the sky just fell in on him. Do your best to cheer him up. I think he's going to need it."

🔔 🔔 🔔

The Christmas dinner had been fit for kings and queens, princesses and princes. The only trouble with it was that everyone was so satiated they could hardly move. Rachel helped the servants clean up, insisting that the rest of them go take a nap. As soon as she could, she went to her room and got a small package wrapped in red paper. Going back downstairs, she slipped her heavy coat on and her wool cap. Then she picked up the heavy basket of food and left the house. The snow had mostly melted away. As she made her way out to the old barn, she glanced over her shoulder with some apprehension, but she felt fairly safe. Everyone had been so sleepy that they had gone to take naps without much argument. She slipped inside the barn, mounted the stairs, and as soon as she was upstairs, she saw Jacob waiting for her. "Merry Christmas, Jacob," she said.

"I heard the singing, and your playing was very good."

"I wish you could have been inside with us."

"That would have created quite a sensation, I imagine. Come and sit down."

"This is second best. I've brought Christmas turkey and dressing and all the trimmings."

"It smells wonderful, but I can't eat with you here. I'll eat it later."

"But it's warm now."

"No, later. Tell me about the party."

Rachel sat down, still holding the package, and for a time she described the party. Once again, she was impressed at how interested Jacob was to hear all about her family. Finally she said awkwardly, "I don't expect you to give me anything, Jacob, but I have a present for you."

Jacob sat still for a moment, then reached out and took the red package. He held it for a moment and ran his hand over the wrapping. "A shame to waste such pretty paper. I will save it." He unwrapped it carefully and found a rougher brown paper underneath. Carefully he removed that also, and then his eyes flew open. "It's a book!"

"A very unusual book," Rachel smiled. "See if you like it."

"Why, it's in Hebrew!"

"Yes, it is. It was in a bookstore in the center of town. I don't know how it got there or how long it had been there. It's not bound very well, but the bookstore manager was Jewish himself, and he told me what the book is."

Jacob was already running his eyes over the page. "What is it about?"

"It's written by a man called Chaim Suddeth."

"A very Jewish name. I know many with the name Chaim." He read quickly, then asked again, "What is it about?"

"Why, it's about one of your people who grew up and left his faith."

"I'm afraid that happens pretty often."

"He became an atheist at first but later became a Christian."

"That must be very interesting," Jacob said as he looked at her.

For a time the room was silent. Jacob looked down at the book, then he started. "Oh, I'm so sorry! I didn't mean to ignore you, but it's been so long since I've read anything in Hebrew."

"Well, I know you get lonely here."

"Not anymore. Not with the Bible and now with this." He suddenly rose and put the book on the shelf, carefully folding the paper and putting it underneath. "Now," he said, "I have a present for you."

"Why, you couldn't have! You haven't gone anywhere to buy anything."

Jacob said, "I think you will like this one. Come."

He went down the stairs, helped her down, and went to the back door of the barn. He opened it, and she cried, "Where are you going?"

"Just over there to that group of trees."

"Someone might see us."

"On Christmas Day? No, I think not. You cannot see the house from this side of the barn, so they cannot see us. Come now," he said as he picked up the small sack.

"Are you carrying your violin?" she asked.

"Yes. Come and ask no questions."

Nervously Rachel followed Jacob. The snow was unbroken, clean and white and pure and softly rounded over the mounds that made up the field. Soon they had passed out of the open field into a grove of evergreens. The snow overhead was balanced precariously over the branches, and as they moved deeper into the woods, it became very quiet.

Finally Jacob came to an open space. "No chairs," he said, "but there's an old log to sit on. Here, let me brush the snow off."

She watched as he brushed the snow off and then motioned toward the trunk. "There. Sit down." As she sat he removed the violin and quickly ran the bow over it. "It's stayed in good tune. It's a good violin," he said.

And then Jacob Steiner began to play. Rachel had heard musicians before, but never one who could draw forth the deep sounds that underlay the composition or the high ones that seemed to rise to the heavens. It was not a fast tune, but she watched as he caressed the bow lovingly and a beautiful melody filled the clearing where they stood. He played with his eyes shut, his lips forming a pleasant smile, and she knew that this was what this man lived for.

Finally Jacob lowered the violin, and Rachel said, "You play so beautifully, Jacob. I never dreamed . . . What's the song?"

A smiled turned up the corners of Jacob's long lips. "It's called 'Rachel's Song.'"

Surprise came to Rachel then, and she said, "Is it about Rachel in the Bible? Is it one of Handel's pieces?"

Jacob Steiner was enjoying himself hugely. "No, it's not by Handel and it's not about Rachel in the Bible." He came over and sat down beside her. He held the violin lightly in his hands and turned to face her, pleasure in his eyes. "This song is about Rachel Bradford, and it's from Jacob Steiner."

Rachel could not believe it. "You *wrote* that song?"

"Yes. It's your Christmas present, Rachel."

Rachel had seldom been so moved. She could scarcely believe what he had done for her. "The melody is so beautiful," she said. "I've never heard anything like it." She put her hand on his and smiled. "Thank you, Jacob. It's the most beautiful Christmas present I've ever received."

The two sat there, and she made him play it three more times, each time loving it more. Finally she said, "I must get back." She rose to her feet, and then he put his hand out. She put her hand in his; he lifted it and kissed it.

"Rachel's song. I hope it is beautiful, for it is about a beautiful woman."

Rachel had the impulse to reach out and kiss him. Suddenly she swallowed and turned, saying, "Come. We must go back. But I'll remember this Christmas always. Will you write the music down so that I can learn it?"

"Certainly. Come, it has been the finest Christmas of my entire life. As a matter of fact—it's the *first* Christmas I've ever celebrated."

15

A Brand-New American

AT THE SAME TIME THAT Daniel Bradford's family was eating turkey and dressing, pumpkin pies, and fresh-baked breads, Daniel himself was sharing a bowl of venison soup from a black iron pot with his young relative Joel. Daniel had wished more than once that he had brought more food from home, for the army of General Washington was practically starving. Many of them had lived for weeks primarily on what they called "fire cakes." A fire cake was simply a patty made out of cold water and either flour or cornmeal, then placed on a flat board before a fire. It was almost indigestible, but for the Continental Army it had become a regular staple.

Now as Daniel looked away from the bowl of venison stew that smelled as good as anything in life, he glanced around at the raw huts that constituted the living quarters for the army. The men had cleared away all timber for firewood as far as the eye could see, so that now it had to be hauled in. Only the fresh-fallen snow that covered the ground kept the landscape from being ugly. He winked at Joel, who was finishing his bowl of stew, and said, "Enough is as good as a feast. Right, Joel?"

"Yes, sir. Exactly!"

Daniel scraped the wooden bowl with his hand-carved spoon, then licked the spoon carefully. He had not had enough, and now he said, "I wish we could be home for about thirty minutes. You and I could show them something about eating, couldn't we, lad?"

Joel Bradford was a good-looking young man with a shock of blond hair and blue-gray eyes. He was worn thin by the difficulties of the win-

187

ter camp. Hunger and hard duty had whittled all the men down, so that now Joel looked like all the rest, with hollowed eyes and sunken cheeks. Despite the trying circumstances, he had a good outlook and now grinned as he reached into his inner pocket. "Got a Christmas present for you, cousin." He pulled out two potatoes and Daniel's eyes brightened. "I've been saving them. You want to eat them raw or roast them in the fire?"

"Just give me your bayonet and I'll show you how to roast potatoes!"

Joel laughed and said, "That's what I thought." He took his musket, removed the bayonet, and pierced the two potatoes. Holding them over the fire, he turned them as the two men spoke about home.

"Have you regretted signing on with General Washington?" Daniel asked. "It's a hard life and a thankless one."

"Not for a minute. I wouldn't be anywhere else in the world."

"Good man! One day this will all be over; then you and I can get back to living again." He swept his hand with a broad gesture. "And all these good fellows—how I wish I had something to feed them all. Some of them don't even have shoes to wear." Some of the soldiers had nothing more than pieces of cloth to wrap around their feet. More than once Daniel had seen blood stains in the snow where men had cut their feet, but their feet were so numb they had not even felt it.

Finally the potatoes were done, and Daniel pulled his off the tip of the steel bayonet. He juggled it, pulled out his pocketknife, and opened it. As he did so a burst of hot steam came forth, and the smell was delicious.

"Here, we do have some salt," Joel said, searching around in his pack. He came up with a small salt cellar and salted Daniel's potato and then did the same for his own. The two men sat there eating slowly, savoring the white meat of the potato. Finally when they were finished, Joel winked. "Well, Father, at least we won't have to wash dishes, will we?"

Daniel gave a start. The voice was that of his son, Micah, and somehow Joel even managed to *look* like Micah as he said it.

"You *are* a mimic, Joel. A born actor."

"Well, acting's all right, but I don't want to do it for a living."

"I expect you'll marry and have a house full of children."

"I hope so."

"Have you heard from Heather lately?" Daniel spoke of Heather Reed, the young woman Joel had recently fallen in love with.

"Not in a month, but she said she'd wait for me—and she will."

"She's a very courageous girl. The two of you saved Dake's life. I'll never forget it, Joel. You nearly lost your own in doing it."

Joel thought back to the time when he had been a secret agent for General Washington. He had been instrumental in saving Dake's life, but now he brushed it aside. "I was glad to do it. You've done so much for Phoebe and me."

"Let's go for a walk. I'm tired of sitting," Daniel said as he stood up.

The two men began to move through the camp. They received greetings everywhere they went. Joel was a very popular soldier, and everyone knew that Daniel Bradford was a close friend of His Excellency, General Washington. They were about ready to return to their tent when suddenly a group of officers appeared, and Joel said, "It's His Excellency."

Indeed it was General George Washington with part of his staff, including the chief of artillery, General Henry Knox, and a small man with striking eyes.

"Ah, Daniel, out for your Christmas walk, I see."

"Yes, General. We've just had an excellent Christmas dinner. I trust you had the same."

Washington was a tall man with a face pitted by smallpox. He was not handsome, but there was a nobility in his features that attracted the attention of everyone wherever he went. He was one of those men who cannot avoid attention. He was known as a rather stern man, but Daniel had seen the other side of him, as he saw it now.

"Come along with us, Bradford. And this is your kinsman?"

"Yes. Sergeant Joel Bradford, Your Excellency," Daniel nodded.

"He's done good service. I wish we had ten thousand more just like you, Sergeant Bradford."

"Thank you, Your Excellency."

"Well, come along. We have a happy chore to perform."

Daniel and Joel fell into step slightly behind the rest of the staff. They moved between the huts until finally they came to one where George Washington paused and knocked on the door. It opened at once, and a very tall red-haired man stepped outside. "Why . . . General Washington," he gasped.

"Sergeant, I've come to meet the newest American. My staff and I would like to welcome him."

Nathan Winslow at once said, "Come in, Your Excellence—all of you, come in."

Daniel squeezed himself into a corner with Joel wedged in beside him. He smiled as the tall young soldier went to the cot and took a bundle from the young woman who lay there. The room was small, and now Washington's bulk and presence made it seem even smaller. The room was filled with an enraged cry right then.

"He ... was having his supper, sir," Nathan Winslow said apologetically.

Washington stood in the center of the room, his head almost brushing the shakes of the ceiling, and smiled at the young mother, Julie Winslow. "A fine boy, ma'am," he said. He glanced down at the child, whose face was red with rage, and put out a finger. The flailing hand of the infant encountered it, grabbed it, and suddenly the baby stopped crying.

"You have a way with babies, Your Excellency," General Nathaniel Greene said.

Washington raised his head at Greene's statement, then looked back at the baby, saying with a wistful look in his gray eyes, "I love children."

He said no more, but Daniel knew that it was the sorrow of Washington's life that he had no children of his own.

After the visit, Daniel had an opportunity to speak to Nathan Winslow. "I saw an old friend of yours not long ago, Mr. Winslow."

"Who was that, Mr. Bradford?"

"Abigail Howland." He saw something change in the face of the young man and said, "I wanted to talk to you about her."

"Yes, sir." Nathan Winslow's expression was noncommittal. He had been betrayed by Abigail Howland, and by his kinsman, Paul Winslow. "What is it, sir?"

"I know that Abigail has had a very—well, a difficult life. As a matter of fact, not a good life at all. But I'm happy to tell you that she's had a deep change in heart. My son Matthew knows her quite well." He did not add that the two had been in love; nor did he supply the information that Abigail had deceived Matthew at the behest of Sir Leo Rochester. He felt that was better left unsaid. Now he said quickly, "As I say, she's had a hard life that she could not have been proud of. But she's had a change of heart."

"Indeed?"

"Yes, she has. She has found the Lord Jesus as her Savior, and I believe if you met her now, you would see a very different young woman."

Nathan's blue eyes were fastened on those of Daniel Bradford. "I'm so glad to hear that," he said finally. "I know she's had an unhappy life, but if she has the Lord, all will be well for her." He hesitated, then said, "Your son Matthew, is he engaged to her?"

There was a silence and Daniel shook his head ruefully. "No. They are not. They have had difficulties, but I only wanted you to know that in case you ever have an opportunity, you might find it good to pray for her."

"I will indeed do that. Thank you very much, Mr. Bradford."

Nathan then introduced Daniel to a beautiful young woman named Charity Alden and a large man named Daniel Green, who was a Quaker who had joined the army. Daniel found the Quaker to be extremely likable.

Daniel stepped over to where Joel was waiting, and then the two made their way back to the tent. "I'll be leaving early in the morning, Joel. If you want to write letters, I'd be happy to take them for you."

"Yes, indeed! I'll have them ready for you." He thought a moment and said, "It's nice that they named the baby Christmas Winslow, born on Christmas Day and all."

"Yes it is, and I trust he'll be as good a man as his father and his grandfather."

☙   ☙   ☙

The trip had been hard, but now as Daniel pulled up his horse in front of the house, his chest heaved and he gave a great sigh of relief. "I'm glad to be home," he said aloud. The mare nodded her head as if she understood, and then he laughed and slipped out of the saddle. "Caesar, where are you, you rascal?"

Almost as he spoke, the huge form of Caesar appeared out of the barn. He came running, his face alight with a smile. "Mr. Bradford, you're back!"

"Yes, I am." Daniel reached up and clapped the massive shoulder of his servant. "I see you haven't been missing any meals."

"No, suh, I think *you* have. You look plum peaked, Mr. Bradford. You wait until Miss Marian starts stuffin' you. You're gonna be like a Christmas turkey."

"Any of that turkey left?"

"Not much, suh, but we got another one. I'll kill him if Miss Marian say so."

"I don't think that'll be necessary. There's probably enough left."

Daniel slapped the mare and said, "She's done well, Caesar. Rub her down and grain her."

"Yes, suh!"

Daniel moved up the steps eagerly. He opened the door and called out, "Wife, where are you? And where's that fat son of mine?"

He heard a cry and moved down the hall as Marian stepped out, holding Enoch in her arms. She ran to him, careful not to squeeze the baby. He put his arms around her and kissed her. Then he took Enoch and held him up, grinning at him. "I believe you've grown, son. I'm going to have to work extra hard to keep you filled."

"Come into the kitchen. You must be starved."

"Starved is about right. I could eat a skunk."

"Oh, don't be silly, dear! Come on now."

It was forty-five minutes later when Daniel pushed the plate away and shook his head regretfully. "If I eat another bite, I'll explode!" he said. "I haven't eaten like that in so long. I wish all those poor fellows at Valley Forge had a meal like this."

"Tell me about them. How is Joel, and did you see Micah?"

"I saw him right before I left. He had just arrived. Joel had lost weight, but everybody has. The army's lean, but it's an army. When spring comes they'll come out in fighting trend."

Marian sat there holding Enoch, who had dropped off to sleep, and listened as Daniel gave her the news. "I have a letter from Joel for you. It's in my saddlebag. Tell me about everything. How was Christmas?"

The fire crackled in the fireplace as Marian spoke softly. She noticed the lines of fatigue and hunger etched on her husband's face. He had always been a strong man, but he had lost so much weight that part of that strength had left him.

Finally, after she had finished, Daniel said, "It doesn't sound like Grace is doing well."

"Not according to what Lyna says. She's very worried about her. I don't think she ever felt that Stephen Morrison was the man for Grace to marry and David feels the same way."

"What about David? Do you like him?"

"Oh, he's a fine young man." A worried frown came to her, and she said, "He and Sam are going to have a fight."

"Fight! About what?"

"Oh, about Keturah. You know Sam's been stuck on her a long time."

"And Keturah likes David?"

"Well, he's someone different. She's a little fascinated by him. He is handsome and witty."

"Sounds like me."

"Oh, you! Don't be silly!"

"What about Rachel? She didn't marry that preacher, did she, while I was gone—or Jubal?"

"No. Of course not. She wouldn't do a thing like that."

"Well, is she interested in either one of them?"

Marian said slowly, "I'm not sure, Daniel. She's quieter than I've ever seen her. She goes all day sometimes without speaking a word, unless someone asks her a question. It's strange."

"She's either sick or in love, I guess."

"I somehow don't think she wants to marry either one of her suitors. As a matter of fact, they've about driven her crazy. She's ready to show both of them the door."

Daniel sat quietly, and then said, "Come over here, wife, and sit beside me. Put that child down. Your husband's home now. You can pay attention to him tomorrow."

Marian came over and sat down beside him. He took her in his arms and then held her closely. "I've missed you," he said huskily.

"Did you? I missed you, too."

The two sat there holding each other as the fire crackled and snapped in the fireplace. Finally Daniel said, "Let's go to bed."

"All right. I'll go put Enoch to bed."

"I won't be long," he said. He kissed her again, then grinned. "I have a few remarks to make to you. Some things we haven't talked over."

She saw the teasing in his fine eyes and laughed. "I bet I won't get much talk out of you, but I'll be waiting for you."

16

JACOB'S LADDER

"COME ON, KETURAH! I've got the horses hitched up."

Keturah had answered the door to her room and now stared at Sam standing before her. His eyes were bright with anticipation, and there was a broad smile on his lips. For a moment she thought, then said, "Come on where, Sam?"

Sam's countenance seemed to break apart. His smile was wiped away instantly, and he looked almost like a little boy for a moment. "Don't you remember? I told you I'd come by and take you for a sleigh ride this afternoon."

"I remember you said something about it, but that was two or three days ago."

"I know, but I've been working hard on the ship. We wanted to get as much work done as we could, Jubal and me. By the time spring comes, we're going to be ready to make our fortunes. Come on now. I want to get back before dark."

"Oh, I can't go, Sam," Keturah said. She hesitated momentarily, then said reluctantly, "I promised David that I'd go to the concert with him." When Sam stared at her blankly, she said, "You know. It's the concert they're having in the city hall in the auditorium. The band from over at Mayton."

A cloud seemed to sweep across Sam's features. He was a cheerful young man, but from time to time a trace of a serious temper would show itself. He liked David Gordon very well, but of late he had allowed a strong streak of jealousy to develop within him. "But you promised me! You can't break your promise!" he said harshly.

"I'm not breaking a promise! You said we'd go on a sleigh ride, but you didn't say when."

Irrationally Sam exploded, "Well, you haven't done anything but

195

run around with that fellow! Have you forgotten whose side he's on? Why, he's no better than an enemy soldier!"

"Oh, that's ridiculous, Sam! You know it's not true. David doesn't have an opinion on the revolution. If you'd listen to him, you would have noticed that. Anyway," she said, "I promised to go with him, and we're leaving in half an hour, so if you'll excuse me . . . "

Sam stared at Keturah, then grated between clenched teeth, "You're as fickle as the wind, Keturah Burns!" He turned and stomped out, slamming the door behind him. Anger seethed through him as he marched down the stairs with his feet striking the treads sharply. He beat on the banister with his fist and headed for the door.

If things had chanced somewhat differently, Sam might have gone off and allowed his jealousy to dissipate, but as he passed through the front door he saw David Gordon, who had evidently been out for a ride, coming across the snow. David looked up and, upon seeing Sam, replied cheerfully, "Hello, Sam. Looks like a good, clear day. No more snow, I hope."

The sight of David Gordon's cheerful face irritated Sam. He knew he was being silly. *I'm making a fool out of myself*, he thought as he walked over to David. With his brow furrowed, he said in an angry tone, "Gordon, I want you to stay away from Keturah!"

"What?"

Ignoring David's look of absolute amazement, Sam ran on heedlessly. "She doesn't need you, and I want you to stay away from her! She's my girl and that's that!"

Being an astute young man, David had already noticed Sam's jealousy. He had observed Keturah carefully and even questioned her tactfully. Though she liked Sam Bradford a great deal, her attachment to him was not strong. Once David had suggested that there might be something serious between the two. Keturah had merely laughed and said, "Oh, Sam, he's had a dozen crushes and he'll have a dozen more! All you have to do is ask Rachel or Dake. They'll tell you about it."

She had been so easy and light about the matter that David had put the thing aside. Now, however, David saw that Sam was fuming with real anger. He tried to smooth it over by saying, "Why, Sam, I'm just trying to show Keturah a good time every now and then."

"She doesn't need you to show her a good time and she's not going to that concert with you! Now, you go up and tell her that it's all off!"

David Gordon was even tempered, but there was a strain in him that always resisted being ordered about, especially by a cousin of approximately his own age. If Sam had come in a more reasonable mood and had requested him to refrain from seeing Keturah, he might have laughed and agreed. But as he stood there facing Sam, a stubbornness rose in him, and he said shortly, "You're making a fool out of yourself, Sam! I'm taking her to the concert because I promised her I would! Now get out of the way!"

David started to move around Sam, but Sam reached out and grabbed him by the coat. "You're not going up there!"

"Let go of me, Sam!"

"I'll let go of you as soon as you agree to do what I'm telling you." Sam gave David a sharp shove, and David reached out and struck Sam in the chest with his open hand. It sent Sam backward, and he yelled, "You can't shove me around! You may work this sort of thing in New York, but it won't do here!"

"Get out of the way, Sam! I'm tired of fooling with you!"

Sam suddenly struck out at David. David managed to turn, and the blow caught him high on the shoulder. Anger ran through David, and almost without thought, he struck Sam in the face.

That was all Sam Bradford needed. With a roar of rage he threw himself forward. He was a strong young man, with muscles hardened from working in his father's forge and on the ship. He struck David over the left eye with a hard left hand that drove David backward. Even as David was staggering back, Sam caught him in the mouth with another blow that jarred the teeth of that young man. Losing his footing, David fell flat on his back.

David never really was able to pull himself together. He had actually been in very few fistfights in his life, while Sam had grown up learning to fight his way. At one point, David thought, *If this were with a pistol or a sword, I'd have a chance.* But he had no opportunity to think more. Blows came at him from every direction, in the body, in the face, and three times he went down. Each time he got up grimly, but finally a tremendous right caught him square on the point of his chin. The sun seemed to go out and he lost consciousness, never feeling the blow when the back of his head struck the hard, frozen ground.

Sam stood panting and looking down at the bloodstained features of his cousin. Suddenly he felt a wave of regret and even remorse rising up in him. "Hey—David!" he muttered and started to move forward. But before he could reach the fallen young man, a form shot by him, and he saw Keturah fall on her knees.

"David!" she cried, and her hands fluttered over David Gordon's bloodied face. She reached under his head, pulled him up, and kneeling, she held him close as if he were a child. Her eyes were blazing as

197

she turned to face Sam. Anger flared out of her, and she cried bitterly, "Well, are you proud of yourself?"

"Aw—look, Keturah, I didn't mean—"

"Get out of here, you beast!"

"Beast?" Sam was staggered. He had never seen Keturah in such a state. He took a step forward and said, "I didn't really mean to hurt him."

"You liar! You did it on purpose! You're jealous! Get out of here! I don't want to see you again!"

Sam stood there for a moment, then said, "Look. He's all right. You see?"

Keturah twisted her head and saw that David's eyes were fluttering open. "Are you all right, David?" she whispered.

"World's sort of going around . . ."

"Here. Come on in the house and I'll clean you up."

Keturah helped David to his feet. She put her arm around his waist, and he put his arm around her shoulders. "Come on," she said. "You'll feel better after I get something on those cuts."

Sam stared at the two and saw that David was hugging Keturah. As they passed, David raised his head, and although his right eye was closing rapidly, his left was unscarred. He winked at Sam and grinned broadly. But then when Keturah said, "Are you all right?" he said in a quivering voice, "I don't feel very well."

Sam stood there thunderstruck. He knew there was nothing really wrong with David. He himself had taken quite a few trouncings in his life, and he knew that his cousin was laughing at him. He stood there for a while pacing back and forth, feeling like an utter fool, then straightened up. "Well, I guess I'll go apologize to him." Moving into the house, he saw that David had his head in Keturah's lap, stretched out on the long couch. She had gotten a basin of water and was tenderly pressing a cold cloth against his face.

"Ah, he's all right. He's just putting on," Sam blundered.

"Sam Bradford, why don't you go down to the tavern and brawl with some of the drunks down there! That's all you're good for!" Then she turned and said in a gentle voice, "That's all right, David. Just lie still and you'll feel better soon."

Staring at the pair, Sam Bradford could not speak a word. He had, indeed, very deep feelings for Keturah Burns, and the sight of David lying there, his head in her lap, with Keturah sponging his face, was almost more than he could bear. For a moment he stood there considering thrashing David again, but he knew that was the wrong thing to do. David turned over and again winked at him. "I think I'm feeling a little faint, Keturah."

A burning anger rose in Sam Bradford, but he knew he had been outsmarted. He turned and stamped out of the house, bumping into Dake, who was coming in from the barn.

"What's the matter with you, Sam? You look terrible."

Sam stared at Dake and said, "Why are women so silly?"

"Didn't know they were. What's the matter? Keturah giving you a hard time?" Suddenly Dake laughed. "You're not jealous of David, are you? I noticed he's been hanging around a lot."

Sam Bradford turned and stalked away without a word, whereupon Dake called out after him. "Don't give up, Sam! Just outlast him. He'll have to go home sooner or later." He laughed at the stiff set of his younger brother's shoulders and then said under his breath, "Eat your heart out, brother. I guess all of us did it. I remember a few times when I had the same problem."

♈   ♈   ♈

Hearing the sound of footsteps on the stairs leading to the loft, Jacob looked up and was not surprised to see the huge shoulders of Caesar as he appeared balancing a tray.

"Hello, Caesar."

"I brought you something to eat. You must be getting hungry."

It was late in the afternoon, and Jacob carefully closed the biography Rachel had given him for Christmas. He laid it down on the bunk, came to his feet, and took the tray. "Sit down and talk to me a while, Caesar. I guess it is a little bit lonesome up here."

Caesar took a seat and watched as Jacob removed the soft cloth covering the food, then began to eat. "I guess you was expecting Miss Rachel to come."

"Well, I hoped she would."

"But she ain't home, suh. She gone over to Mrs. Denham's."

"Who is Mrs. Denham?"

"Why, she's the aunt of a friend of Miss Rachel, Miss Abigail Howland." Caesar rambled on, and as usual, Jacob absorbed all he could about the life of the Bradfords. "I expect," Caesar said, "that Miss Rachel wants her brother Matthew to marry Miss Abigail, but from what I hear, that ain't likely to happen. They was close once, but they done sort of split up. I don't know all the particulars."

After Jacob had eaten, he sat on the bunk listening as Caesar continued on. The huge man loved to talk, and Jacob was lonely in his prison loft. Finally he asked, "Is something wrong with the lady you mentioned?"

"Mrs. Denham? Yes, suh, I fear she is not long for this world."

"She's sick?"

"Yes, suh. Been sick a long time now. But Miss Abigail sent word that she was passing, so Miss Rachel said she'd better go be with her friend. It's sometimes sad when your folks die."

Jacob did not answer and was silent for so long that Caesar finally asked, "Would it trouble you to die, Mr. Jacob?"

Quickly Jacob Steiner looked up. "Certainly!" he said with some surprise. "It would trouble anybody."

"Maybe so, but what I means is, are you ready to die?"

Jacob suddenly began to feel peculiar. He had had long talks with Caesar prior to this, and more than once Caesar had mentioned his own hope in Jesus Christ. Now Jacob sat there, the fading afternoon light making lines on the floor of the loft as they filtered through the cracks of the boards, and he felt alone. A sense of alienation and fear settled on him. He was a sensitive young man, and during his long months away from home, he had become more and more conscious of his own isolation. Perhaps this is why the kindness of Rachel Bradford had meant so much to him. It had come as light in a dark place or as food to a starving man. He looked up and saw Caesar watching him carefully and shrugged his shoulders. "I suppose we have to die whether we get ready for it or not."

"Oh yes, suh! 'It is appointed for a man once to die but after this the judgment.'"

"That's from the New Testament, isn't it?"

"Yes, suh, it is."

"Well, every man who has any imagination at all thinks about dying. It's something that comes to all of us."

"Yes, Mr. Jacob, it do, but for those who know the Lord it's different. You see, before I knew Jesus I was scared of dying, but now if it comes, all it mean is I'll be with Him and be walkin' the golden streets with Jesus. Yes, suh."

Jacob studied the round face that seemed to glow with happiness. "You really believe that, don't you, Jacob?"

"Yes, suh, I does. It say so in the Book. Over and over again Jesus says, 'If I go and prepare a place for you, I will come again, and receive you unto myself; that where I am, there ye may be also.' So I may live a day, or a year, or ten years, but sooner or later I'm going to be with my Jesus."

A sudden start of envy came to Jacob Steiner then. It touched him and he felt a tinge of anger, although he knew it was irrational. He bit his lip for a moment, then shook his head. "I'm glad you feel that way, but it isn't so easy for some of us."

"It's the same for everybody."

"What do you mean by that?"

"Why, I mean the Bible says that all have sinned and come short of the glory of God."

"Well, I believe that, at least. Even the Old Testament teaches that."

"It also says the wages of sin is death."

Jacob shrugged his shoulders. "I believe that, too," he said.

"And then the Bible says, 'For he hath made him to be sin for us, who knew no sin; that we might be made the righteousness of God in him.' I always liked that verse."

"But what does it mean? I don't understand it. How could a man be made sin?"

"The way the preacher explained it when he preached on that text is that all the sins that every man and every woman and all young folks ever committed was gathered up in one big heap. Then when Jesus was on the cross, God put them all on Him." Caesar nodded. "Just like that lamb we talked about. When the priest put his hands on him, you know what happened. All the sins went on the lamb. So that's what happened on the cross. When Jesus was hanging there, all the sins I ever done or ever would do, and you, Mr. Jacob, and everybody who ever lived was put on Him."

Jacob sat there silently. Somehow the simple words of this simple man had struck deep into an inner part of his being. He had read the story of the death of Jesus in the Gospels again and again. The words had been like a magnet drawing him, and now suddenly it seemed as if he could almost see that scene in his mind's eye. But to think of all the sins of the world being put on one man was too monstrous to contemplate. "I just don't understand it, Caesar," he mumbled.

Caesar then began to talk about Jesus, better than most who could read; the memory of the Scriptures that had been implanted in his keen mind just rolled off his lips. From verse to verse he moved, always stressing that Jesus was the Lamb of God that takes away the sins of the world. He quoted at least a dozen or more Scriptures, stressing that without shedding of blood, there is no remission of sin.

As Jacob sat listening, he knew that something was happening in his own heart. It was not altogether fear, and it was not altogether hope, but there were elements of both. He realized as he sat there that he was afraid to die. He had felt the power of the death of Jesus as he read it over and over again. Now a sense of longing began to grow in him. One voice inside of him was saying, "You're a Jew. You can't believe in Jesus." But something else was happening. The simple faith he had seen in Rachel Bradford and now in the face of the gentle giant who sat with the light of joy and contentment in his eyes was as strong as anything he had ever known in his life.

Finally Caesar said, "Suh, I believe you need to get ready to go to heaven."

Jacob nodded, murmuring softly, "I think you're right, Caesar. But how do I get there?"

"Don't you remember? There was a Jacob in the Bible who was alone one time. God came to him, and he saw a ladder that went up to heaven."

"I remember that. They used to tease me about it. Jacob's ladder. And there were angels going up and down."

"That's right. And what you need is to go up that ladder to where God is."

"But how does a man do that?"

"Jesus said, 'I am the way, the truth, and the life: no man cometh unto the Father, but by me.'" Suddenly Caesar leaned over and laid his massive hand on Jacob's knee. "He loves sinners. That's what they accused Him of, that He loved sinners. And that's what I was, and that's what you is. But you don't have to be."

Jacob was feeling as miserable as he had ever felt in his life. He sat there as Caesar spoke of salvation in Christ and finally was almost unaware when the huge man got up. He heard his voice saying, "All you need to do is what the Bible says. 'Whosoever shall call upon the name of the Lord shall be saved.'"

Jacob heard Caesar's footsteps as they faded away, but he did not move for a long time. As he sat there, the words of the Scripture that the black man had given him seemed to burn into his mind.

After a time he got up and began to pace the floor. His mind was filled with a confusion. He longed for peace. Something about Jesus Christ drew him, but his Jewish heritage rose like a mighty wall between him and the Gospel he had heard both Caesar and Rachel set forth.

The hours passed and Jacob Steiner still paced between two poles. For a time he would read the biography of the Jew who had found Christ and given everything to Him. He found it compelling, and he thought, *If one Jew can do it, then I can do it, too.*

He picked up the Bible and reread the story of the crucifixion. He threw himself on his bed, but he could not sleep for a long time. Finally he dozed off and dreamed of a ladder. It was made of gold and reached from earth to heaven. Looking up at the top, he saw a figure clothed in light, and He heard a voice saying, *Come unto me and I will give you rest.*

Jacob awoke with a start to discover tears coursing down his cheeks. He groaned, "I can't go on like this." He got onto his knees and tried to pray. For a long time he could not. His heart seemed to be as hard as stone, and he struggled with the idea of becoming that which his own people loathed. Finally, however, there came a breaking. It was like a frozen river beginning to break up in the spring, just a little at a time, one piece of ice slowly floating away from the main body. But then finally it was as if everything inside him poured loose and the deep river of Jacob's lonely heart began to flow. He started to weep and cried out, "Oh, Jesus, help me!"

17

ONE FOR THE KINGDOM

"MATTHEW. . . ? MATTHEW, are you awake?"

Out of a deep sleep, Matthew Bradford swam back to consciousness. He had slept poorly all night, and now he was confused. For a few moments he could not remember where he was. Finally the insistent voice broke through into the lower level of consciousness and with a start he sat bolt upright in the bed and stared into the murky darkness. Glancing at the window he saw that it was still pitch black outside, but the voice came again. "Matthew, wake up!"

Throwing back the cover and swinging his feet out to the floor, Matthew stood up and stumbled across the room. He fumbled for the door and opened it to see Rachel standing there. "What's wrong?" Matthew asked hoarsely. He cleared his throat and ran his hand through his hair trying to pull his thoughts together. "What's the matter?"

"It's Mrs. Denham—she's dying."

The bold statement seemed to strike Matthew down in his stomach. He had grown very fond of Esther Denham in a way he could not explain. The news should have come as no shock, for the doctor had said repeatedly there was no hope for Esther to recover. As he stood there, something in him rebelled, and at the same time a grief constricted his throat at the thought of losing a dear friend. "Are you sure, Rachel?"

"Yes. Abigail sent word that Esther wants to see you before she dies."

"All right. Let me get something on. I'll be right down."

Throwing on his clothes, Matthew moved quickly out of the room and down the stairs, where he found Rachel waiting.

"I had Caesar hitch the team," she said. "He'll drive us over."

"All right. I'm ready."

The two left the house, and Matthew noticed the shadowy outline

205

of the buggy and the massive shape of Caesar. He helped Rachel inside, then climbed in beside her. Rachel said, "Let's hurry, Caesar," and the covered buggy lurched forward as the horses leaned into their harness.

Matthew had not thought of the time, and now he asked, "What time is it? I didn't bring my watch."

"It must be about three o'clock."

Matthew did not respond. He sat there silently, Rachel beside him, until they reached the Denham house.

A few minutes later, Caesar said, "Whoa now! Whoa up!" and the carriage came to a halt. Matthew opened the door and stepped out without waiting for Caesar. As Caesar helped Rachel out, he said, "I'll wait for you, Miss Rachel, until you're ready."

"You may as well go back home, Caesar," Rachel said, steadying herself by leaning against Matthew. "We'll send for you when we're ready."

"Yes, ma'am."

Turning, Rachel moved across the darkened pathway toward the house. The cobblestones gave off a faint echo as they approached the door. Yellow light streamed out from the upstairs window and faintly from one downstairs. Rachel knocked. After they stood in the silence, she glanced up at Matthew. It was too dark to see his face, but she sensed this loss was hurting him, and it came as a surprise to her. She had known that he was fond of Esther Denham, but Matthew's total silence told her that he was taking it very hard.

The door swung open and Abigail stood there holding a lamp. "Come in," she said. She waited until they were inside the house and turned to them, saying quietly, "I'm glad you could come. I wasn't sure whether to send for you or not."

"Why, of course you should," Rachel said quickly. "How is she?"

"She's . . . barely hanging on." Abigail was wearing a simple woolen dress with a blue robe over it. The amber light of the lamp threw her face into relief so that her smooth features were clearly delineated.

As Matthew watched her, he cast a quick glance at her face. He saw the pain and suffering in her eyes, and he asked quietly, "Is she awake?"

"She comes out of it every once in a while, and twice she has asked for you. Come along. I'll take you to her."

Matthew and Rachel followed Abigail as she moved down the foyer and mounted the staircase. A silence filled the house, and when they got to the top of the landing and turned to the right, Matthew felt a numbness creeping over him. He was fully awake, but there was something about the presence of imminent death that gripped him like a cold fist. He entered the room after Abigail opened the door, then stepped aside. His eyes went to the face of Esther Denham lying on the bed by the wall. He did not know what he had expected, but without a word he moved over and sat down in the chair beside the bed. Her hands were outside the covers, and he reached out and held one of them in his own. There was still warmth and life there, and as he studied her face, he was shocked at the peace and serenity he saw. He had always associated death with something like terror, or at least fear, but Esther Denham's face was as calm and peaceful as any countenance he had ever seen. In a way she looked even better, for the pain was gone and the lines that had etched themselves deep into her flesh during her sickness now seemed to be smoothed out so that she looked much younger. Leaning forward, he whispered, "Esther, can you hear me?"

The eyes of the dying woman opened immediately and recognition came at once.

"Matthew—?"

"Yes. It's me, Esther." Matthew felt her hand tighten on his, and he squeezed it gently in both of his. "How do you feel?"

Esther's gaze was placid, and her lips turned upward in a smile. "I feel very well indeed, Matthew." She had almost no strength, and the coverlet over her chest barely moved. Her breathing was shallow, and he had to lean forward to catch her words. "It was . . . good of you to come, my boy."

Matthew could not answer. His throat was suddenly thick, and he found it difficult to breathe, much less speak. He could only sit there holding her hand, and that seemed to be enough. She closed her eyes for a time, and her breathing relaxed. She looked up and said, "I wanted to see you before I went home."

It was so simply said that for a moment Matthew did not even grasp the significance of her words. She could have said that when she was visiting at a friend's house and talked about returning home to her own house, but he knew she meant more than that. For Esther Denham, "going home" was a simple matter of leaving earth and going to heaven. She had talked with him a great deal about this, and at first it had made him uncomfortable. He had never liked to talk about death, but her matter-of-fact and even cheerful attitude had been a revelation to him. Now as he sat there holding the thin hand in his and listening to the faint breathing of the dying woman, his eyes suddenly lifted and met those of Abigail Howland, who had moved to the other side of the bed and stood there silently. He had been more bitter against this woman than any human being he had ever known. Her betrayal had eviscerated him, in a sense, so that he could not think of her without a burning anger. Now, however, he saw compassion and love and gentleness in her eyes. In that moment, he knew he had abused her, and shame swept through him. He did not say anything, but he saw and understood that Abigail knew something was changing—something cold and bleak and bitter had melted. She did not speak, but there was a flicker in her eyes and a relaxing of the sternness around her lips that Matthew saw instantly.

The minutes went on and Matthew sat without moving. Abigail left once, and he was aware that Rachel was in the room, but his whole mind and heart and attention were focused on the slight form of Esther Denham. As he sat there, Matthew found himself praying desperately, "God, don't let her go! Let her live!" It was the first time he had prayed, he realized, since his breakup with Abigail Howland. It was a cry of heartbreaking desperation. He had not known he cared so much for this old woman, but she had become very precious to him in a way he could not understand.

The minutes turned into hours, but Matthew was unaware of the passage of time. He had never been a patient young man, but the world and time itself seemed to have ceased for him. Finally he was surprised to see that Abigail had moved over to pull the drapes open. A faint trail of sunlight tinged to a faint crimson in the east was coloring the skies, and he realized it was dawn. He felt stiff from having sat so long in one position, but he ignored it. Still time went on. Once in a while Esther would speak a few words, but he saw that she was slipping away. Finally, after a great deal of time had passed, or so it seemed, he saw that Abigail and Rachel had left the room. He was alone, and at that moment Esther spoke.

"Matthew?"

"I'm here, Esther."

A long silence was punctuated by a deep sigh, and Esther's eyes fluttered. She opened them for one moment, and the hand that was in Matthew's tightened. "You must . . . forgive Abigail."

Matthew stiffened. He did not answer for a moment and thought, perhaps, that he had misunderstood. "What is it, Esther?"

Esther Denham was almost gone. She looked much like a woman who was fighting sleep, but now she opened her eyes and tried to lift herself up. Matthew put his arm around her and held her. "What is it, Esther? Tell me."

"I have loved you, Matthew," she said with labored breathing. She struggled for breath, then said, "You're like a son to me. Not just because you saved my life, but because God gave me a love for you." She spoke for a time about this love, and then she turned her head and looked into his eyes. "You must forgive, Matthew. You must or it will destroy you!"

At that moment Matthew knew exactly what she was talking about. The bitterness he had felt toward Abigail Howland had grown in him, and as he held the dying woman, he knew if he had ever heard truth in his life, he was hearing it now. A shadow came then, and he looked up to see Abigail, who had come to the other side of the bed.

Esther saw her, too, and with the last of her strength she held her hand. As Abigail took it, Esther whispered, "You have been a hand-maiden of the Lord to this old servant of God."

As strength ebbed from her, she closed her eyes, then smiling gently, she said, "Jesus is waiting."

She did not speak again, and Matthew felt the remaining strength leave her body. There was nothing sudden or abrupt about it. She simply became limp and her breathing stopped.

Abigail was holding her left hand, and she bent over it and kissed it and her tears fell. She said something, but Matthew did not hear it. She got up and bowed her head, her forehead resting on the withered hand she held.

Matthew did not move for a long time. He was as still as she. Finally he straightened up, replaced the hand on Esther Denham's still breast, and stood to his feet. He took a deep breath and saw that Rachel had kneeled beside Abigail. He looked at the two women, and grief came over him. He turned and left the room, closing the door quietly behind him. Going downstairs, he turned into the study where he had often waited while Abigail prepared Esther for his visit. He was still standing there some time later staring out the window blindly when he sensed a movement. He turned quickly and saw that it was Abigail. Neither of them spoke for a moment, and then Abigail came closer and said, "Thank you for coming, Matthew."

Matthew again found it difficult to speak. "She was one of the best women I've ever known, Abigail."

"Yes, she was. I'll miss her so much, but she was ready to go."

Matthew knew that Abigail had not heard Esther Denham's words regarding him and his bitterness. As he stood there the words seemed to echo, *You must forgive Abigail.* Esther had said this more than once, and now he knew that he had to say something. He did not reach out or move to make any gesture of affection as he might have done, but he simply said, "I have been harsh with you, Abigail. I'm sorry."

Abigail's eyes grew wide. It was the first time he had ever said anything in the way of remorse for his cruel behavior toward her. She did not answer for a moment, then she said, "I'm glad you have said that. Not for my sake, because I deserve whatever you might think of me. But I'm glad for your sake."

"I think Esther saw what my feelings were doing to me," Matthew said. "She asked me to . . . to forgive you, and I do."

A deep joy filled Abigail Howland then. She saw that what Matthew was saying was very real, but she sensed something in him that she could not read. *It's going to take a long time. Even now*, she thought, *for him to recover. We may never be anything to each other. I love him, but I may have hurt him so deeply that love can never return.* She said aloud, "You were a good friend. Your visits were the brightest thing in her life these last days."

Matthew dropped his head. He did not speak for a long time, then said briefly, "I'm glad I've done one thing right, at least." Then he turned and left the house without speaking again.

Abigail watched him go. A mixture of joy and grief was in her, joy that he had forgiven her, but grief that he had not yet worked through the deep problems that plagued his heart.

🛡   🛡   🛡

The late afternoon sun was painting the skies with the last few touches of color as Rachel wearily mounted the steps. She was not aware of time but knew that it must be nearly four o'clock, and she had not slept at all the previous night. She had stayed with Abigail and her mother after Esther had died, for she felt very deeply their need for companionship. Mrs. Howland had become very close to Esther Denham, since they were both older women, and she had been stricken with grief and unable to accept the death of her sister-in-law. While Abigail had taken care of the necessary arrangements, Rachel had sat with Mrs. Howland and done her best to comfort her.

Rachel had asked briefly about Matthew, for he had disappeared immediately following Esther's last moments, but Abigail had said merely, "I think he wanted to be alone. It's hit him very hard, Rachel."

Rachel sensed there was more to it than this, but she had not pressed Abigail for details. Finally, late in the afternoon, Abigail had insisted that Rachel should go home and rest. She had ridden home in a hired carriage, and now her legs seemed very weary as she paused at the top of the stairs. She heard her name suddenly called and turned to see Caesar, who was standing there with a strange smile on his face.

"Yes. What is it, Caesar?"

"Will you come with me, Miss Rachel?"

"Come with you? Come where?"

Caesar lowered his voice and jerked his head. "To the barn."

Alarm came to Rachel then and she came down the stairs. "What's wrong? Is there trouble?"

Caesar was smiling strangely, and Rachel could tell that he was excited to tell her something. His eyes were gleaming as he said, "Come along, Miss Rachel. You've got to see something."

Puzzled by Caesar's behavior, Rachel followed him. It was almost dark, and she was afraid someone would look out the window and see them going to the barn, but Caesar appeared to have no apprehensions. He went right to the barn and opened the door. When they were in the murky darkness of the barn, he touched her arm.

"You go on up and you talk to Mr. Jacob. He got a big surprise for you."

Seeing that Caesar had no intention of saying more, Rachel stared at him for a moment, then smiled. "All right, Caesar." She turned and made her way up, calling before she reached the top. "Jacob?" Then taking the last few steps, she saw that he had lit the lamp and was standing beside the cot. She came closer so she could read the expression on his face. "What is it? Caesar tells me something has happened."

Jacob did not speak for a moment. "Sit down please, Rachel." He waited until she sat down on a crate, then he too sat down across from her. "How is your friend? Is she still living? I heard she was very ill."

"Mrs. Denham died early this morning."

"I'm sorry to hear it."

Rachel took a deep breath and then expelled it. She looked down at her hands and then up at Jacob and said with confidence, "She died very easily. It was like she stepped from one room to the other. I've never seen anyone die before, but when I go, I hope I can go as gracefully as Mrs. Esther Denham."

Jacob's eyes never left her face. He seemed to be considering her words, and then he said, "I'm glad for her. It is always hard to lose someone, but I can see that you have accepted it."

"Yes. We've been expecting it, but I never expected it to be this easy. In her last breath she spoke of going home to be with Jesus."

A silence filled the loft and Rachel did not speak. She was intensely curious but waited until Jacob was ready to speak. When he looked up, she saw that there was something different about him.

Quietly, he said, "It's strange, but Caesar was here, and he asked me a startling question. He asked me, Rachel, if I was ready to die." He

211

moved his shoulders restlessly and ran his hand over his blond hair that caught the highlights of the lantern. "The question took me worse than a musket ball in the chest, worse than the wound I took. I couldn't stop thinking about it."

Rachel sat there listening intently as Jacob related his experience. She hardly dared to breathe. His voice was husky, and she could see tears rise to his eyes.

"So I fell on my knees and began to cry out to God."

Rachel felt then much more than she had felt at the death of Esther Denham. A wave of happiness and joy overwhelmed her. She had been happy to hear that friends had been converted before, but the deep emotions that came to her over this tall foreigner coming to faith, so far from his home, was unlike anything she had experienced. Deep within herself she knew she felt something for him that she did not feel for anybody else. She rose suddenly and came over and sat beside him. His shoulders were shaking slightly, and he was weeping. He was a strong man, she knew, not one given to weeping. She took his hand and held it silently and fought back her own tears. Finally she said, "What is it, Jacob?"

"I cannot stop thinking of Jesus on the cross—how He died for my sins. He was the Lamb that bore my sins. When I called on Him, Rachel, I could not see Him, nor hear His voice as I hear yours, but He was here in my heart. And He was speaking forgiveness to me for all my sins." He turned his face and looked toward her, and the tears ran unheeded down his cheeks. "Is this what it means to be a Christian?"

"Yes, Jacob. It's what it means to be saved, to have your sins forgiven. Oh, Jacob, I thank God that you have found Jesus Christ!" A thought came to her and she squeezed his hand, aware that her eyes were brimming over. "When Esther died, I thought this earth had lost one of God's dear people. But now, Jacob, it comes to me that you are here. God has taken one from this earth, but He's given another for the kingdom."

Jacob was hardly aware how hard he was squeezing Rachel's hand. He was still struggling with his emotions and finally removed a handkerchief and wiped his face. He looked at her and said, "I don't know what to say or what to think. Everything is different."

"God will lead you, Jacob."

And then Jacob Steiner straightened up. He looked at her and said, "I must leave this place, Rachel. I cannot stay. It's different."

Rachel did not answer. There was a firmness and a timbre in his voice that she had never heard before. She looked into his eyes and saw something that had been lacking before. She did not argue. "God will guide you. He's your shepherd now, Jacob," she whispered.

18

A Guest for Dinner

TAKING A DEEP SIGH, Daniel Bradford looked around the parlor and was pleased with everything. It was a comfortable parlor painted pea green with a gilded paper-mache border; crimson, green, and gold carpet; two floor-length windows covered with bright gold curtains that fell to the floor in heaps of luxurious fabric; a large, elaborately carved fireplace; and heavy mahogany furniture with silk damask upholstery, overstuffed and very comfortable.

However, it was not just the decor of the room that pleased him, but the fact that Master Enoch Bradford was sitting on his lap staring up at him owlishly out of bright blue eyes. Since his return from Valley Forge, Daniel had spent a great deal of his time with this latest addition to his family and had enjoyed every minute with his new son.

The sight of his wife, who sat across from him sewing one of the endless garments for her new son, brought great satisfaction to Bradford. Studying her face as she sewed, he saw a placid but almost ecstatic expression. He had known for years that her inability to have children had grieved her heart. He had tried in every way he could to make her understand that this in no way lessened his love for her, but now as he studied Marian's face, he saw a happiness and a joy that made her even more beautiful in his eyes than ever before.

Marian suddenly looked up and blinked with surprise. "Why are you staring at me?"

"I'm just thinking about how bad it's going to be."

"How bad what's going to be?" Marian asked.

"Being married to a grandmother," Daniel said solemnly. "I don't know if I can put up with that, wife. I may have to get rid of you and get me a young woman after Dake and Jeanne have their baby. Oh, I'll admit you've held up pretty well for an elderly lady, but—"

215

Marian jumped to her feet and ran over and grabbed Daniel by the hair. "Don't you forget! I'll be married to a grandfather. A crotchety old grandfather, I might add. If I catch you even looking at one of these young women—"

Daniel reached up, caught her hand, and held it easily. He had been a blacksmith for years and still possessed the strength of a young man. He suddenly pulled her hand down, turned it around, and kissed the palm. "I guess you do very well for an old lady. Now your cooking, that leaves something to be desired!"

Marian could never even pretend to be stern with Daniel. She laughed and said, "You crazy thing!" She leaned over and kissed him, then planted a kiss on Enoch's rosy cheek. "Isn't he beautiful?"

"Yes. Of all the babies I've ever seen, he's one of them," Daniel said solemnly.

"Oh, you!" Marian straightened up, and just as she did, Rachel entered the room. "Hello, Rachel."

Rachel did not answer, and both Daniel and Marian saw that her face was pale. Daniel said with concern, "What's wrong, daughter?"

"I . . . have to talk to you."

"Certainly. What is it?"

Rachel was wearing a necklace her father had given her for her sixteenth birthday. It was a simple necklace with a green stone that she treasured greatly. She now fumbled with it nervously, and swallowing hard, she said, "Would both of you sit down and give me a few minutes?"

Marian exchanged a troubled glance with Daniel, then said, "Why, of course, Rachel." She sat down and watched as Rachel suddenly disappeared. They heard the door slam, and she murmured, "What is that all about?"

"I have no idea, but it's not good news. I've never seen Rachel look so troubled." His own countenance fell into a frown, and he shook his head. "Seems like there's lots of trouble. Matthew's been going around lately looking terrible. I don't know what's wrong with him."

"He just hasn't found himself yet, dear. But he's doing better."

They sat there tensely, waiting for Rachel to return. Finally they heard the door open and shut. Marian whispered, "Someone's with her."

"Probably Dake."

"No. It's not Dake. He's gone to town."

When Rachel appeared in the door, Marian and Daniel straightened up instantly at the sight of the tall man who was beside her. Daniel's eyes narrowed, and he got to his feet at once. He waited, keeping his eyes fixed on the face of the young man. He was good at reading men. He had been doing it for years, but this young man was different. He was wearing the uniform of a soldier in His Majesty's forces. Daniel recognized the Hessian uniform jacket, as worn and patched as it was. He studied the face of the man, which was lean and artistic, even aristocratic.

"Father—Mother, I would like for you to meet Jacob Steiner. Jacob, these are my parents, Mr. and Mrs. Daniel Bradford."

Jacob bowed with a Continental gesture and then straightened up. His German accent came across at once to both Daniel and Marian. "I am happy to make your acquaintance, Mr. Bradford, and you, Mrs. Bradford."

"I am glad to meet you," Daniel said. "I see you are wearing a Hessian uniform. Is it Private Steiner?"

Jacob hesitated. "That is a rather complicated question, Mr. Bradford." He would have said more, but Rachel spoke up.

"Please sit down. Jacob, would you sit over there." She watched as Jacob took the chair and sat bolt upright. Rachel herself could not sit down but stood there nervously fingering the green stone in her necklace. "I don't know how to tell you how I came to meet Jacob except as simply as I can."

"Perhaps that would be best," Daniel said dryly. "It's not every day our daughter brings a soldier in His Majesty's Royal Hessian forces into our parlor."

"Be quiet, Daniel," Marian said impulsively. She saw how troubled Rachel was and put her hand on Daniel's arm. "Let Rachel tell it."

Rachel cleared her throat, looked down for a moment, then said, "Jacob was conscripted into the army. . . ."

Daniel listened carefully, sometimes watching Rachel's face but more often studying the countenance of the young man who sat stiffly across from him. His glance never wavered, and Daniel had a rather favorable opinion of him. He did not miss a word of Rachel's story, and finally he heard her say, "And so Jacob was converted mostly, I suppose, by Caesar's witness, and he . . . has something to say to you."

Catching Rachel's look, Jacob said, "First, I must thank you for your hospitality. I know," he smiled slightly, "it was not intentional, but if it had not been for your daughter, I would have died. I would never have survived outside a prison camp, and sending me back there would have been no different than sending me before a firing squad, so I owe Miss Rachel my life."

Daniel listened as the young man spoke, impressed at how well he expressed himself. More than once he glanced to see how Rachel was taking this and saw something in her eyes that was unusual. Whether it was concern or something else, he could not tell.

"What I have to tell you, sir, is this. Obviously I have been in the forces sent to fight against your country, but I can no longer do that."

"You mean you're leaving the English forces?"

"I cannot fight against you. It was not my choice in the beginning. Many of us were simply forced to come. I know that may sound like a feeble excuse, but it is very different in my country. My people are often rented out, more or less, to foreign nations to fight in wars that are no concern of ours. I think this is wrong, but it is the way it is."

"And what do you propose to do now, Mr. Steiner?"

"We heard rumors, my friends and I, when we got to this country that it was possible for a British soldier to leave that army and serve in the army of America."

Daniel nodded quickly. "That is true. As a matter of fact, there is one option offered to those who will take advantage of it. I'm not certain about the details, but I do know that under certain conditions those who leave the Royalist forces and enlist in the Continental Army will be given full pardon and free land."

"That is what I heard, sir, but I did not think it could be true."

Daniel was quiet for a moment. His eyes went to Marian, and she nodded with encouragement. "I take it, then, that you would like for me to help you?"

"I would like very much to be an American."

Daniel was forcibly struck by this simple statement. His eyes were steady on Jacob Steiner's, and he could see nothing there but simplicity and honesty.

"Can it be done, Father?" Rachel asked quickly.

"I believe so, but it will take a little time." Daniel stepped forward and put his hand out, and Jacob Steiner grasped it instantly. "I understand your feelings. When I was a boy in England, I had nothing. I could not believe there could be a place of freedom like this. God has been good to me, Mr. Steiner, and I rejoice that you have found Christ."

"I have never known a Jewish man or woman to become a Christian," Jacob said. He hesitated and then said, "It is all very new and very difficult, but I know something is different, and I want only two things now: to be an American and to be a Christian."

Marian looked over and saw the shining eyes of her stepdaughter. *There's something more than his becoming an American,* she thought. A slight alarm came to her. Still she said, "This may require a little tact, Daniel."

"Well, I never won any awards for my tactfulness," Daniel said, grinning ruefully. "What do you suggest?"

"Why don't we introduce Mr. Steiner to the family at dinner. Then they can hear the whole story from him—and from Rachel."

"A splendid idea. I'm glad I thought of it," Daniel smiled. He turned to Jacob, saying, "We invite you to join our family for dinner."

"But I have only these rags, sir."

"I'm sure the women can put something together, can't you, Rachel?"

"Oh yes, Father. I'll take care of that."

"Very well. You are invited to your first dinner outside of the barn and in the Bradford household. And welcome to America, Jacob Steiner."

🔔　　🔔　　🔔

"Will you please hold still, Jacob!"

Holding his hand up over his head, Jacob cast a look of despair at Rachel, who was pinning up an oversized waistcoat to make it fit around his lean body. "Be careful," he said. "You're going to stick those things in me. Anyway, I feel like a scarecrow."

"Why, you look fine," she said. "My parents will be suitably impressed." The decision to invite Jacob to dinner had meant that he needed a respectable outfit in which to meet Rachel's family. The pants were a plum color and had belonged to Matthew, as had the white stockings and the black shoes with silver buckles. The shoes were a bit small, but she had told Jacob that he could put up with them for one night. The shirt had belonged to her father. It had a white stock and frills at the sleeves, and the fact that it was too large did not show under the emerald green plaid waistcoat. The outer coat was one her father had worn in his youth and was not noticeably too large. Rachel glanced at the fine blond hair of Jacob, which she had plaited and tied with a leather thong in the back and knotted firmly. "You look very fine indeed!"

"I feel like an impostor!"

"Nonsense. My parents want you to come."

"Your family will never believe me. Especially your brother Dake. You've told me what a fierce patriot he is and how he despises all the Hessians."

"He'll believe you when you tell him the truth. Dake is stubborn, but he's not without compassion. Now, come. It's time to go down. We're late."

Reluctantly Jacob left the room and muttered, "I feel like I'm going before a firing squad."

"Nonsense. They'll like you very much."

As they left the landing and went down the long hallway, Jacob could hear the sounds of laughter and talking. *I wonder if they'll be laughing after they see me,* he thought.

Then he stepped into the room at Rachel's side, and at once the talking ceased. Every head turned toward him, every eye on him, and he heard Rachel saying quickly, "Father, perhaps you'd introduce our guest."

Daniel said quickly, "Of course. I'd like to introduce Mr. Jacob Steiner. Let me make you acquainted with my family." He went around naming off every name, and then said, "Sit down, both of you. The food will get cold."

Jacob sat down, feeling completely intimidated by everyone. He hardly even heard when Daniel Bradford asked a blessing. The food came and went on his plate; he ate mechanically, hardly tasting it. Several times people spoke to him, asking polite questions or making comments, and somehow he managed to give an answer. He knew they all were curious. When the meal was finally over, he saw Daniel Bradford nod to Rachel, who was very pale.

"I know you're all curious about our guest, Mr. Steiner," Rachel said in a clear voice. "I would be. So I want to tell you a story. Jacob Steiner is from Prussia. He was conscripted into the army by force and sent to America. . . ."

Jacob kept his eyes down for the most part, but as the story went on, he saw the reaction on the faces of the Bradfords. Especially he saw that Dake Bradford was staring at him coldly.

Finally Rachel said, "And so Jacob has been converted and is determined to become an American."

A silence fell over the room. Then Dake said abruptly and harshly, "How can a man change his loyalties? Is it as simple as changing one uniform for another?"

The antagonism in Dake Bradford was obvious. Jacob knew that hatred toward the Hessians was common enough among the Continental soldiers. Now he said quietly, "I am sure I would feel exactly as you do, Mr. Bradford, if I were in your place. I can only say that I have never known what freedom was. Our people do not have the choices that you have here. I might add that I did not come out of any loyalty to the king of England, for I had none and never have. None of the men who came with me from my homeland did. We were bought like cattle and forced to obey." He hesitated, then said, "I want to be an American, but I do not believe that such a privilege comes without cost. That is why I want to become a soldier and fight for this new country of yours. Then after I have proven myself, perhaps, Mr. Bradford, you will feel differently toward me."

Dake had not taken his eyes from the face of the German, and now suddenly his wife, Jeanne, reached over and put her hand over his. "That's what you've done, Dake. You wanted to be free, so you fought for it, and that's what this young man wants. Isn't it the same thing?"

Dake nodded slowly and the hostility left him. "I think it is. In any case, I'll give you every chance to prove it, Steiner."

"That is all I ask."

Rachel had been holding her breath. She knew that the opposition would come from Dake, but now that he had given in, she felt suddenly as if a great weight had been lifted.

       ⚑   ⚑   ⚑

"Now you must hear Jacob play!"

Everyone had gone to the drawing room, where, as soon as they were seated, Jacob had found it much easier to talk. He found it very simple to talk to Sam, who was full of curiosity and completely at ease. He also found it easy to talk to Keturah, who was not a member of the family. For a time Rachel had disappeared. Now as he looked up, he saw that she had brought the violin and the bow from its place in the barn. She was smiling and holding it out. He rose and took it, and at once something happened. As he tucked the violin under his chin, all awkwardness seemed to vanish.

Daniel noticed it immediately and whispered to Marian, "I hope the fellow plays well. I love good fiddle music."

And then Jacob said, "What shall I play, Miss Rachel?"

"Anything you choose."

Jacob nodded, then half closed his eyes. His fingers began to move on the strings, and a silence fell over the room. The music that he played was like nothing any of them had ever heard. Daniel was thinking, *I've heard good fiddle playing but nothing like this!*

The music filled the room. At times it was soft as a breeze in summer, and they leaned forward to catch it. Sometimes it rose in a crescendo almost like a howling storm, and at other times it was as easy and simple as the song of a child. But whatever he played was beautiful and flawless and without effort.

Finally Jacob stopped and said, "I have played too long, but one more I will play. It is called, 'Rachel's Song.'"

Daniel's eyes went to Rachel's face as the music began, and he saw something there that he had never seen before. Then his glance went to the countenance of Jacob Steiner. He looked at Marian and saw that she had seen the same thing.

Finally Jacob removed the bow and smiled with embarrassment. "I have not played for so long. I apologize for taking so much of your time."

"That's the greatest violin music I ever heard, Jake," Sam said. "Play some more."

"No. That is enough for now."

Daniel leaned over and whispered to Rachel, "He's a fine musician."

"It's all he wants to do. Doesn't he play magnificently?"

"Never heard anything like it."

Rachel went to Jacob then and said, "That was beautiful. Everyone loved your playing."

"I'm glad." He looked up then, for Dake had come to stand before him. "I thank you for your understanding, Mr. Bradford," Jacob said. "I know how hard it must be for you to accept one who has been an enemy."

Dake was not a man who showed his feelings, but the music had affected him. He wanted to say a great many things, but now he said, "If you can shoot as well as you can play the violin, General Washington will be glad to have you." Then he grinned and put his hand out. "And the men will like it, too. Be sure to take the violin when you go."

19

THE BOUNDARIES OF LOVE

"CAPTAIN LAYTON, I'd like to introduce you to Mr. Jacob Steiner."

Jacob had been walking with Rachel when Phoebe had come to say, "Mr. Bradford wants you in the library, sir."

Now as Jacob entered, he saw a short, heavyset man wearing the uniform of a captain in the Continental Army. He nodded instantly and half bowed. "Captain Layton, I'm pleased to meet you, sir."

Layton was a hard-faced man with direct gray eyes. He wasted no words but said, "I understand you served with the Hessian forces. Is that right?"

"Yes, sir. That is correct."

"Mr. Bradford has told me your story, but I would like to hear it from you."

"Certainly, Captain. I was among those men who were conscripted by force. . . ."

Captain Layton listened as Jacob spoke, and finally he said shortly, "We've had some of your fellow Hessians come over in the past. Some of them apparently joined only in order to desert. They fled to other parts of the country to avoid service." He waited for Jacob to reply, and when he did not, he said sharply, "I take it that's not your intention?"

"No, sir, it is not."

Captain Layton seemed pleased by his response. "Well, you don't toot your own horn, Steiner. I'll say that for you." He turned to say, "Daniel, I'm not certain about all this. We've not had much success with so-called 'converted' Hessians."

"I think this young man is different. I'm happy to vouch for him, Captain."

"Well, I will take him on your say-so, but you understand, Steiner"—here the captain turned and faced Jacob directly—"some of our men hate Hessians worse than they hate the devil himself."

"Yes, sir. I understand that very well."

"They will give you a hard time, and there's nothing I can do to protect you."

"I would not expect it, sir. All I want is a chance to prove myself."

"Well, in that case, and with Mr. Bradford's recommendation, you will be enlisted. You will return with me to Valley Forge. How long will it take you to get ready?"

"I'm ready now, Captain, as soon as I get a few things. Give me ten minutes."

This also pleased Layton, and he said after Jacob left, "Well, we'll see."

"Yes, we will. All he wants is a chance, Davis." Daniel grinned and said quietly, "I appreciate your giving it to him."

Jacob had gone at once to the barn to gather his few things together that had been collected, mostly by Rachel, and to take one last look around. He started to leave but heard footsteps; then Rachel appeared.

"Rachel, I was going to find you," he said quickly. "I have to go."

"I know. Father told me. You're going to Valley Forge with Captain Layton."

"Yes. I will be serving there."

"I have a letter here for my brother Micah." She handed him a small paper folded and added, "You'll like Micah. He's one of the chaplains there. I told him about your conversion. He'll be a help to you."

"I'll look forward to meeting him."

They stood there silently, and Jacob finally reached out and took her hand. It was soft and warm, and he held it tightly. "I cannot thank you enough for what you have done. My life is yours."

The words might have sounded pompous coming from someone else, but Rachel had learned that this man held no pretenses. Her heart was full of admiration, and yet at the same time there was an emptiness in her. "I will miss you, Jacob," she said softly.

"And I you." Suddenly Jacob leaned over and kissed her hand. Then he dropped it and for a moment was silent. "There are many things I would like to say to you, Rachel." His voice was quiet and there was a warmth in it. "But I have to be a soldier, and I have to prove myself, and so it is farewell—for a time."

"Good-bye, Jacob. Will you write?"

"Of course. And you will write to me?"

"Yes. And I will pray for you every day."

"That would be very nice, I think."

Jacob motioned to the stairs and Rachel moved down them. Carrying the small bundle, Jacob followed her. When they got outside, he saw Captain Layton waiting with an extra horse. When they walked over, Daniel said, "Give this mare to my son Micah."

"Yes, sir." Daniel put out his hand and Jacob took it. "Thank you for your confidence. I will not let you down."

"I'm sure you won't."

Daniel was aware that Rachel had come over to stand beside him. They watched as the two men mounted, and then Layton swung his horse around and left the yard at a gallop, followed by Jacob.

"Well, daughter," Daniel said slowly. "He'll have a hard time."

"Yes, I know. But God will take care of him."

Suddenly Daniel reached out, took her arm, and turned her around. "Do you care for this man?"

"Oh, Father, it would be impossible! Even if I did, we're so different. I would never fit into his world, and I'm not sure he can fit into mine. There are big boundaries between us."

Then Daniel Bradford said quietly, "Perhaps so, but love knows very few boundaries."

PART FOUR

———

THE SOLDIER

March–July 1778

20

GENERAL VON STEUBEN FINDS A MAN

"I SUPPOSE THIS DOESN'T LOOK like much after the British camp you were accustomed to, Steiner."

Jacob looked carefully at the camp with an eager eye. He had made the trip with Captain Layton from Boston to Valley Forge as quickly as possible. During that time Layton had grown more talkative, and Jacob had learned much about the revolution. He sensed that for some reason Layton trusted him much more than he had expected and attributed that trust to his recommendation by Daniel Bradford. Now as he looked over the camp that lay spread out before him, he said quickly, "I am not disappointed, Captain. I understand that General Washington has to make do with what he has."

Layton gave Jacob an approving look. "That about sums it up," he said.

The two had halted their horses and now looked out across the camp teeming with activity. The rough log huts that had been built to protect the army during the harsh winter were still standing, and the memory came back in a bitter fashion to Captain Layton. "It was a hard winter. I have no idea how many of our men died, but there were many. Some simply froze to death."

"In my country this would not have happened. They would have gone home."

"I think in any country in the world that would be true, Private Steiner. These men are not fighting for anything you can put your hand on. They're fighting for an ideal. Of course, many of them did go home, and we had only a skeleton crew. But when spring came they started

229

coming back. They come in every day from all over, from the Carolinas, Massachusetts, Georgia, Rhode Island. I'll be anxious to see what our force totals now. Come along."

Jacob kicked the flanks of his horse, and the two wound their way down around and between cabins that seemed deserted. Most of the men, he saw, were outside. As he glanced into the dark, gloomy interiors of the small huts, he was not surprised. The spring had brought with it a welcome relief from the bitter cold, and now the men were out in the sunshine. Some of them were washing clothes over a barrel with a fire under it. Others were cooking some kind of meal, and Layton smelled the air.

"That's meat cooking. I'm glad to see it. Many weeks around here the men had no meat at all."

As they rode along, Jacob saw many of the men making some effort at drilling. He did not say so, but it was a poor show. His own training had been rigorous, and he was accustomed to a close-order drill that had been sharpened almost to perfection by the Hessian drill masters. Most of the men, he saw, were halfhearted in their attempts, and even as they passed, one lanky soldier said, "Ah, Sarge, there ain't no sense in this. I don't need to do no about-face to shoot the lobsterbacks." He turned and walked away and was followed by several members of the squad, despite the admonition of the sergeant.

Captain Layton shot a quick glance at Jacob and made a hasty apology. "These men aren't like British soldiers. Some of them come from the militia, where there's no discipline at all. It takes a while to make soldiers out of them."

"I see they look rather fit, although lean as wolves," Jacob remarked.

"Those that made it through are tough, and we're expecting a big in-flow of men from the rest of the Colonies. We'll give General Howe something to think about this year," he said eagerly.

The two men wound around until finally they came to a house, and the captain suddenly said, "Look. There's General Washington."

Eagerly Jacob turned his eyes toward the small group that had exited from the white clapboard house. Somehow he knew instinctively that the tall man in the foreground was the general he had heard so much about. George Washington had become almost legendary, not for winning battles, for he had won few, but for keeping a discouraged army intact. No matter how many times he was defeated on the field, Washington had whatever it is that makes men follow. Now as they approached, Jacob, as was proper, pulled his horse up so that Captain Layton could go ahead. He slipped to the ground and took Captain Layton's lines without being asked.

"Why, thank you, Private," Layton said with approval.

"Hello, Layton. You're back sooner than I thought. Did you bring the papers from Boston?"

"Yes, sir. I have them right here." Layton turned to his horse and removed a saddlebag and handed them to a slight young man with violet eyes.

Alexander Hamilton nodded and murmured in a gentle voice, "Thank you, Captain."

"I expect you're hungry. You'll dine with us tonight, of course."

"Thank you, sir. I have a new recruit."

Washington turned his eyes on Jacob, who stood even straighter. "This is Private Jacob Steiner. He has come over from the Hessian force. He has quite a story to tell, Your Excellency, and I'll fill you in."

"Private Steiner, I welcome you into the Continental Army," he said and bowed his head.

"Thank you, my general," Steiner said quickly.

"You'll be interested to know that he comes highly recommended. Mr. Daniel Bradford particularly asked me to bring him."

"Ah, Mr. Bradford. How is he?"

"Still working on building cannons. I think he's about got the hang of it, Your Excellency."

"And you're a friend of Mr. Bradford's, are you, Steiner?"

"A very recent one, sir. If it had not been for his family, I would have died after I escaped from prison."

"Kind man. Fine family," Washington said.

"I'll get Steiner settled, and I'll look forward to our meal together with the staff, General Washington."

As General Washington walked away, accompanied by his staff, Layton grinned. "Well, not many privates begin their service by meeting His Excellence."

"There is something in that man," Jacob murmured.

"Yes, indeed. The troops would follow him anywhere. Come along. I'm putting you into a regiment that's lost most of their men. We're to build from the ground up. A few good officers left. I think you will have to work hard to convince them. They're a tough lot."

"Yes, Captain."

Jacob followed the officer until they came to an open field. At the edge, a group of men were sitting around smoking and chewing tobacco. They were roughly dressed, with hardly a semblance of a uniform, but one of them, obviously an officer, came over. He was a tall, rangy man with gray eyes and a hatchet face.

"Lieutenant Jones, this is a new recruit. His name is Jacob Steiner."

The slate gray eyes searched Jacob intently. Jones was a rough-looking man with a cold expression, and yet his voice was moderate as he said, "Glad to have you, Steiner. Previous service?"

"Yes, sir." Jacob hesitated and then said, "I served with the Sixth Hessians."

Although Jacob had not spoken loudly, the men who were whittling and chewing tobacco all turned instantly toward him. Lieutenant Jones did not answer for a moment, then nodded, "I'm glad to see you're on the right side at last." He exchanged glances with Captain Layton.

Layton said, "Well, I doubt if he'll need much close-order drill. He did all that with the British."

"If he can shoot, I'll take him, sir," Lieutenant Jones smiled briefly. He saluted, and after Captain Layton had returned the salute and mounted his horse to ride away, Lieutenant Jones said, "What are you doing with that horse?"

"I'll tell you what I'd like to do with him," one of the men said. "He looks fat. Let's eat him."

Laughter went around the group, and Jacob could see that despite the harsh winter, these men were fit and ready for a fight. One of the men came over and patted him. "This is Sergeant Miles Chevington, Private. He's the one who'll make your life miserable."

"Yes, sir. I'm sure the sergeant is very good at that."

A laugh went up from most of the soldiers, but one of the soldiers got to his feet. He was a hulking man with a thick, broodish face. "We don't need no baby eaters around here!"

"Now, you watch what you say, Homer!" Sergeant Chevington said. He was a keg-shaped man with broad shoulders, thick legs, and a large body. The winter did not seem to have affected him. He stared at the big soldier for a moment and then said, "This here's Homer Butler. He don't like Hessians."

"They rammed a bayonet in my little brother's back at White Plains. They didn't have to do that."

"Now, we've got to forget all that. You weren't at White Plains, were you, Steiner?"

"No, sir. I was not. I was only in part of one battle near the Delaware River, and I was captured there and spent a long time in prison camp before I escaped."

"Well, I'll make a soldier out of you. But, meanwhile, that horse—?" Sergeant Chevington said.

"He was sent by Mr. Daniel Bradford to give to his son, Micah Bradford."

"Is he the preacher?"

"Yes, I think that is right, sir. A chaplain, Mr. Bradford said."

"I still say we eat him."

Jacob saw that Homer Butler was going to be trouble. He turned to face him and said quietly, "You can do that, but as your captain will tell you, Mr. Bradford is a good friend of His Excellence. I do not think the general would like it if you ate his friend's horse."

Chevington grinned. "Like it! He'd skin you alive, Homer! Well, I guess you'd better deliver that horse, then you can get to soldiering. You see that big clump of trees over there?"

"Yes, sir."

"I reckon you'll find the chaplain over there. It's the hospital, and if he ain't there, he won't be far away. Spends most of his time there. Good as a doctor, some say."

"Yes, sir. I will deliver the horse at once."

"Come right back, and you don't have to call sergeants 'sir.' Not in this army."

"Yes, Sergeant." Not knowing the etiquette, Jacob snapped a crisp salute and a laugh went up. Chevington said, "You don't salute sergeants either."

"Is that true, Sergeant? Most sergeants in the British army impose this on their men."

"I'd like to see them try to make me salute," one small soldier said, grinning broadly.

"Never mind that," Chevington said. "Go deliver that horse and then get back here. We've got work to do."

"Yes, Sergeant."

Jacob followed the sergeant's instructions and found a cabin some thirty feet long and twenty feet deep, much larger than the other hut. He dismounted, tied the horse, and stepped up on the porch. A soldier with his leg off at the knee was sitting in a rickety chair. He gave Jacob a sharp look, and Jacob said, "I'm looking for the chaplain."

"I reckon he's right inside."

Jacob nodded and stepped inside. As in all hospitals, the odor was foul, but he ignored that. The room he entered was large, almost twenty feet square, and was filled with beds. A number of men were sitting on homemade stools or lying on cots placed around the walls. A corporal was sitting at a desk, and Jacob went over and said, "I have been sent to find Chaplain Bradford."

"Down that way. You'll find him."

Following the vague gesture to the far end of the hospital, Jacob went through a door and saw beds everywhere, but some of them were not occupied. He saw a tall man in uniform sitting on a three-legged stool talking to a soldier flat on his back. Jacob went closer but did not approach. He could hear the officer praying. He waited quietly, impressed at the man's sincerity, then the officer reached over. He got up and patted the man on the shoulder.

"I'll see you later, Thomas. Tomorrow. I'll see if I can find you some of that good venison stew."

"Thank you, sir." The voice was thready and weak. The officer hesitated one moment, looking down, and then turned.

As soon as the officer turned his face, Jacob knew he had his man. He was the exact image of Dake Bradford. Jacob knew they were twins, of course, and he stepped forward and said, "Chaplain Bradford."

"Yes. What is it?"

"I have a letter for you, sir, from your sister."

"From Rachel? How did it get here?"

Jacob hesitated. The ward was crowded, and what he had to say was actually rather private. "If you would step outside, it might be better, sir."

"Very well." Micah walked out of the hospital, nodding at the man on the porch, and then continued to walk until they were clear of the building. He turned and said, "Shall I read the letter first or have the personal message?"

"The personal message, I think, sir. My name is Jacob Steiner. The truth is, I was an escaped prisoner, a Hessian. Your sister, Rachel, found me dying. Instead of turning me in, she nursed me back to health. During that time I found myself feeling very strangely. I'm a Jew, and while I recovered, there was a man there named Caesar, who knew the Bible. To make a long story short, Chaplain"—Jacob lifted his head and smiled—"I'm a brand-new Christian. Not a very good one, I'm sure. And I'm also a brand-new American. Your father helped me find a place in the army."

"Well, that's quite a story. Steiner is your name?"

"Yes, sir."

"Let me read the letter."

Jacob stood there while Micah Bradford scanned the letter, saying nothing. Quickly Micah looked up and said, "She's asked me to look out for you."

"I would appreciate any help I could get."

"Do you have a Bible?"

"Yes, sir, I do. It was your sister's Bible. She gave it to me."

"She gave you her Bible!" Micah was astonished. "She loved that book."

"I tried to refuse it, but she would not take no for an answer. I treasure it more than anything I have."

"Well, we'll set up some time together."

"The horse is yours, your father says."

"Mine? He sent me Nellie? He loves that horse."

"He said you could use her, but I must get my things."

"Yes, of course."

The two walked back, and Jacob removed the sack he had draped over the horse's withers. "I must go back now. The sergeant said he would make a soldier of me."

"Very well. Come and see me when you get settled down. We'll have a talk, Private Steiner."

"Yes, sir. I will do that."

Micah watched as the man moved away. He watched him until he was out of sight, and then he patted Nellie on the flank. "Well, old girl, things are happening at home. It looks like my sister, Rachel, has become an evangelist. I'll have to hear more from that young lady about all of this."

⚜   ⚜   ⚜

General Washington smiled down at the stubby figure of Baron von Steuben and said, "My dear baron, we are happy to have you serving in our army. You have done marvels with the men."

"Ja. I could do better if I only had better English." Actually his speech was almost unintelligible. He spoke excellent German, of course, but it vexed him that he could not speak English well enough.

Washington put his hand on the baron's shoulder. He had become very fond of this man who had done marvelous things in teaching his men how to be soldiers. A thought came to him, and he said, "I have an idea. Last week a young man came to serve with us. His name is Jacob Steiner."

"Oh, a German!"

"A German Jew, I believe. Speaks English very well. I spoke with him myself. Why don't you let him assist you. If he has been a Hessian, he knows the drill, and if he is a German, he can speak the language."

"Then he can English *sprechen*?"

"Very well, indeed."

"Then I vill find him! Jacob Steiner, you say?"

"Yes. Put him to work, von Steuben. Use my name to get him released from his unit. Use him as long as you please."

♜ ♜ ♜

Jacob was chopping wood, as he had done every day since he arrived. He had been given the worst and most menial jobs, but he expected no better. It was the same in every army. The rawest recruit washes the dishes and chops the wood. He actually did not mind. The weather was clear and the skies were a beautiful pale blue with fleecy white clouds. It had not grown hot yet, and he had stripped off his shirt. His muscles were lean after his illness, and he welcomed the exercise.

A voice came to him speaking in German. *"Wie heißen Sie?"*

Jacob turned and saw a stubby man in the uniform of the Continental Army and the mark of a general. Instantly he snapped to attention. *"Ich heiße Jacob Steiner, mein General."*

"Ah, speak in English."

"My name is Jacob Steiner, General. I beg your pardon, sir."

"Ach, that iss gut English!" Von Steuben beamed. He came forward and looked Jacob over, noting the scars on his front side and in back. He spoke in broken English for a moment, then threw up his hands. "I can't say it in this English! Ve vill speak in German until ve get before the men."

"Before the men, sir?"

"Ja. You are now attached to me. My aide."

Jacob blinked with shock. One did not rise to be the aide of a general overnight. "I'm afraid, sir, I don't understand."

"I vill explain. Ve must drill the men. I do not speak gut English. Zo I vill speak in German, and Lieutenant Gilchrest, who speaks a little German, tries to put it into English. It iss very *shlecht*. He does the best he can, but he iss sick of me. He vill be glad to be reassigned. So, come along." He hesitated, and then said, "Lieutenant!"

"Lieutenant!" Jacob gasped.

"Ja, an aide must be an officer. The men vould not obey if he were not. Come. Ve vill begin. You vill teach me English at night, you vill cook for me, polish my boots, give my commands." Here the rosy face broke into a grin, and the small eyes twinkled. "Ve vill teach these Americans how a soldier should behave. Show me the drill."

Holding the ax instead of a musket, Jacob went through the drill, calling it out in English as von Steuben requested.

"That iss *sehr gut*. It iss almost the same as the one I have designed for this army. Come, ve must get you a uniform. You are now an officer and must look like one and sound like one."

"General, I would do anything, but I know nothing about being an officer. I've been only a private."

"You understand German and you know the drill. That iss all I require. Ja?"

"Ja, General."

Von Steuben laughed and said, "Now, we vill see what we vill see. Come, Lieutenant Steiner."

21

THE WRONG MAN

REVEREND JOSIAH GRIERSON planted his feet in the middle of
the room. He looked very much as he did in the pulpit when he intended to deliver a weighty bit of doctrine. He had a stern expression,
which occasionally was lightened by a charming smile, but now there
was no smile present. He locked his hands behind his back and looked
down at Rachel, who was seated in a red plaid chair. The reverend had
come in unexpectedly and practically forced her to invite him in. After
that he had almost dragged her into the study and shut the door behind
him. She knew he was a firm man, and now she sat quietly ready to
hear what he had to say.

"Rachel, I understand that it is usual for a young woman to refuse
a suitor once or, perhaps, even more often."

"I was not aware of that habit, Josiah."

Josiah had the feeling that this young woman was toying with him.
A man of his age was no match for a young woman with an active wit
such as Rachel Bradford, but his mind was made up to say what was
in his heart. He was a very resolute man—some might even say stubborn—and now he kept his voice down. He had a magnificent bell-like
voice that could carry for miles, so it seemed, but now he forced himself
to speak quietly. "Rachel, I've asked you to marry me before, and I understood when you said you could not give me an answer."

"But I *did* give you an answer, Josiah, and the answer was no."

Waving his hand as if to push her words away, Josiah continued to
speak for some ten minutes.

Rachel sat quietly as he enumerated the advantages that would
incur to her should she accept his hand. She heard the vague warning,
lightly veiled, that it was by no means certain that she would receive
any other offer, at least not one as favorable as that of Reverend Josiah

239

Grierson. Actually Rachel was happy that this moment had come. She was worried to death about the intentions of both Grierson and Jubal Morrison, and now she simply waited.

Finally he said, "Once and for all and I will take your answer as final. Will you marry me, yes or no?"

"No."

Reverend Grierson gaped at her. After his well-prepared speech was delivered in his best pulpit fashion, he had envisioned, and certainly hoped, that she would see his point and accept his proposal with no question.

Rachel now rose and said, "No. I am one of the last women in the world, Josiah, who could make you happy, and I'm sure you could not make me happy. We are just not meant for each other."

It took no more. The minister threw up his hands in a helpless gesture. "Well, I'll say no more about it." He dropped his hands then and reluctantly grinned. "You'll marry the pirate, I suppose."

"I can't answer that right now. Good day, Josiah. I'll be in church Sunday. You can preach on the frivolity of young women. I'm certain I need it."

🔔　　🔔　　🔔

Jubal Morrison was sitting at the tiller of the *Defiant*, staring down at a book on his lap. He heard footsteps come across the plank that led to the shore. When he looked up, his face broke out in a pleased expression. "Rachel," he said. Tossing the book down, he got up and gave her a hand as she stepped into the boat. "What a joy to see you!"

"It's always good to see you, Jubal." Rachel was wearing a blue-and-green cotton dress with a large white collar, buttons down the front of the bodice, long sleeves, and a long, full skirt, and there was a mischievous expression in her clear eyes.

"Sit down at the tiller. You can at least see what it feels like. We'll be taking her out next week. Maybe you could come along."

"Maybe I will."

Jubal stared at her. "Would you really?"

"Of course not! You don't need a woman along to take a prize."

Jubal laughed and slapped his thigh. "I suppose not. Are you looking for Sam?"

"No. I came looking for you, Jubal."

Jubal suddenly sensed something in this young woman he had not seen before. He could not identify it, and he said, "What can I do for you, Rachel?"

"I've just had a visitor—Reverend Grierson." Without pause, she said, "He came to ask me to marry him."

"You're not going to do it, are you?" Jubal asked, alarmed. He made an attractive picture as he stood there—strong and virile—but there was real anxiety in his expression.

"No, I'm not going to marry him."

For a moment Jubal was stunned. "Then you're going to marry me?"

"I came down to tell you that I cannot marry you." Rachel laughed suddenly, a delightful sound. She put out her hand and laid it flat on Jubal's chest. "I'm getting rid of all my suitors today. No more suitors, Jubal. I know you will find someone else."

Jubal stared at her. She was actually laughing, and suddenly he laughed with her. "You are *something*, Rachel Bradford, indeed you are!"

"You never really wanted to marry me," Rachel said. She smiled fondly, for she did like Jubal. "You were just practicing. I'll find you a wife much better suited than I."

Jubal found her idea attractive. "Actually," he said, "you're right. I'm not ready for marriage yet, Rachel. I'm not mature enough. And pirates can't be too careful about their mates, can they?"

"No indeed. We'll find you a lady pirate, and the two of you will seize the king's ships by the dozens. Come to supper tonight. Now that I don't have you underfoot, I'll tell you how very much I like you, Jubal. Good-bye. I'll see you at supper."

♟   ♟   ♟

Lyna did not pause at the door, and as Daniel looked up, something in her face alarmed him. He got up and went to her. "What is it, Lyna?"

"It's Grace. She's ill. I'm going to have to go to South Carolina."

"What is it? Nothing serious, I hope."

Lyna held out the letter in her hand for him to read. "It's just a note from Stephen. He says she wouldn't write to me, but he's very anxious about her."

"Well, you must go at once. I'll make the arrangements. When will you want to leave?"

"Tomorrow."

"Very well. Tomorrow it will be." He put his arms around Lyna and said gently, "These have been good days. Someday the war will be over, and we'll live in the same town maybe. Who knows?"

"Maybe," Lyna said. She was worried about Grace, but she was not at all certain that this illness was what it seemed to be.

"Will David go with you?"

"Oh yes. I'm sure he will."

The next morning the family was up early to see the pair off. Sam and Keturah had come over to the Bradford estate also to say good-bye. They all had a hearty breakfast, though Lyna ate very little. Sam was putting their luggage into the coach, and David went out to stand beside him. "Good-bye, Sam."

Sam was still embarrassed over the beating he had administered to his cousin. He turned now and bit his lower lip. "I'm sorry about that fight. I was a fool, David."

"So was I. Sometimes we're fools in different ways. Actually, your foolishness doesn't even begin to match mine. I just want to tell you that I'm proud to have you for a cousin." He put his hand out, and it was almost crushed by the strong young man's grip as he eagerly returned the gesture. "Don't break it. I've got to play cards with that hand," David laughed. He stood there for a moment after Sam released him, then said, "A word to the wise. Keturah's yours, Sam. I'm no fortune-teller, but she's a prize worth winning. She never cared for me. She's just interested because I'm different. So don't give up on her."

"Do you mean it, David?"

Looking at the brilliant blue eyes of his cousin, David laughed. "She's a woman and therefore to be won."

Sam heaved a sigh of relief. As soon as the carriage was off, he went straight to Keturah, who was watching the carriage disappear and looking rather sad. He stared at her for a moment, then said, "Don't worry. You'll miss David, but you've got me, Keturah."

The young woman stared at him in astonishment. "Sam Bradford, you are the most egotistical man I ever saw!"

"Well, I'm going to take care of you, Keturah. You don't have to worry about looking around at other men. Just look at me."

Keturah giggled. She shook her head, then pulled at his sleeve. "Come on inside. I'll feed you some more pancakes."

🔔   🔔   🔔

"I'm glad you got here, Lyna, and you, too, David." When Stephen Morrison met Lyna and David at the coach stop, his face was lined with anxiety. He said little as they drove to his home in his private carriage, but Lyna and David could tell that he was worried. As he stepped aside and ushered them into the house, he seemed to transfer his anxieties, somehow, to them. Now that Lyna was here, he would no longer have to bear the burden alone.

Lyna had said little on the way to Stephen's home. She had never been this far south and was intrigued by the palmettos that seemed to grow everywhere along the roads on the way to the plantation.

The plantation itself was a surprise. She had expected something less ornate. The main house was a large two-story building of red brick, with the front side painted white. It had a portico with six large Corinthian columns and two colonnades connecting the main house to its two wings—the kitchen and the carriage house. Two sets of six-over-six windows flanked large double doors on both levels of the home, which led out to large, roomy porches. All the other outbuildings, such as a guest house, privy, and slave cabins, were all made out of the same red brick and very well kept.

A young black woman came to take their wraps, and Stephen murmured, "This is Missy. She'll be available for anything you need."

Missy was a small young girl of approximately seventeen or eighteen wearing a starched white apron over a light gray dress. She wore a mob cap, and her smile was bright and cheerful. "I'm glad to see you," she said. "Miss Grace needs her mama."

"I suppose you'd like to go up at once," Stephen said.

"Yes, I would," Lyna nodded.

"Take Mrs. Gordon to your mistress, Missy. David, after you've visited with your sister, perhaps you'd come down and I can show you over the place."

"Yes. I'd like to see it," David replied. For some reason David had grown more and more depressed as the journey had progressed. He and his mother had spoken little of the situation, but he was aware that both of them were concerned not only about the state of Grace's health but about the state of her marriage. Now he was silent as he followed his mother and the servant upstairs. They turned at the corner of the curving staircase, and Missy led them to a room down on the right. She opened the door and stepped inside.

"Miss Grace, your mama and your brother is here," she said cheerfully.

The room into which the pair stepped was big and airy with light blue-and-green-striped wallpaper, a white ceiling, and a highly polished wood floor covered with gaily colored area rugs. There were two small windows along one wall, with dark green curtains held back by gold brocade tassels. The furniture was made of dark mahogany and covered with blue and white coverings that gave the room a feminine touch.

Lyna had time to do no more than simply glance at the room, for she had eyes only for Grace, who was sitting in a chair by the window with a multicolored blanket over her lap. She moved quickly over, and leaning down, she embraced her daughter.

Grace looked up and said, "Mother, I'm so glad you've come."

"We were worried about you, Grace," David said as he stepped forward and took a hug around his neck. He straightened up and studied her face. "How do you feel? What's wrong with you?"

"Yes," Lyna said. "We couldn't make out from Stephen's letter what the sickness was."

"Oh, I don't even like to talk about it." Grace was wearing a blue cotton dress that buttoned closely up to her neck and over it a lightweight pale gray woolen sweater. It was actually rather warm, but she seemed cold, and both Lyna and David noticed a fatigue that etched itself across her features. Grace had always been such a lively girl, and now her dark honey-colored hair was covered by a cap, and her eyes, which were of a peculiar gray-green color, had little life in them. She tried to smile, but it was a feeble effort.

"I'm glad you've come," she said again. "Sit down, both of you."

The conversation that followed was difficult, for neither David nor his mother could ask the question that was really on their minds. Finally David said, "I'll go down and let you two visit." He got up, leaned over and kissed Grace, then grinned. "You'll be better now. Mother's the best doctor I know."

As soon as David was out of the room, Grace seemed to feel some sort of relief. She had always been able to talk to her mother easily, and now she said almost eagerly, "Mother, it's so good to see you."

"Well, I was surprised to hear about your illness. When did the sickness come upon you?"

Restlessly, Grace shook her head. She had an oval face, and her brow was high under the stubborn curls that persisted in falling over it. Pushing them aside, she said wearily, "I don't know. I haven't been well since I got here."

"What does the doctor say?"

"He doesn't know what to think. He talks about tonics and things like that, but he really doesn't know what's wrong with me."

Lyna leaned forward and studied the face of this daughter of hers carefully. "What is it? Is it your stomach, or what?"

"It's everything. I'm all tied up in a knot, Mother. I can't eat. Nothing's really working right. I can't sleep." Her voice grew almost surreal, and she suddenly put her face down in her hands. "I hate to tell you, Mother, but I think I know what it is, and it's not physical."

Stunned by this confession, Lyna reached out and pulled her chair around, where she sat beside her. "What is it, Grace?" she asked quietly.

Grace lifted her eyes, and when Lyna saw tears brimming in them, she knew how bad it was. Grace had never been a woman or a child to cry. As a matter of fact, Lyna could not remember the last time she had seen tears in her daughter's eyes. She said no more but waited as Grace struggled. Finally when the words came, they were in a strained voice. It did not sound like Grace at all.

"Mother, I married the wrong man!"

And then it all came to Lyna—everything she had suspected even before they left. She sat there with her arm around Grace, who suddenly gave way and buried her face against her mother. The sobs shook her, and she whispered again, "I never should have married Stephen. Never! It's been all wrong!"

A sense of helplessness came over Lyna. Some things could be changed or fixed, but marriage was final and ultimate. Once a woman made her vows and took a man's name, it was forever, at least in the canon of the Gordons and of the Bradfords. Divorce was not an option, nor was separation. It was a bond that could never be broken this side of death. She held her daughter in her arms then, and pain went through her. She had had such high hopes, and now she realized that those hopes were dashed, that Grace had crossed a boundary and entered a world that contained nothing but unhappiness for her.

22

A Fine Soldier

MARCH, WITH ALL OF ITS WINDY GUSTS, passed slowly away. While the Continental Army drilled incessantly at Valley Forge, spurred on by Baron von Steuben, the British spent their days polishing their bayonets, cleaning their uniforms to a sparkling brightness, and preparing once more to take the field. It was a difficult time for British generals in America, for each one who had come, including Gage, Burgoyne, and now General Howe, had expected to end the ragtag revolt within a few weeks. None of them had succeeded. Although the British won battles, the Continental Army would simply fade away and reassemble at another location. Since in European wars the winner was the force that captured its enemy's capital, the generals were deceived. Their military strategy wasn't working. They had thought to hold Boston and failed. They then captured New York, but General George Washington had simply moved outward across New Jersey. Now they sat in Philadelphia, and the revolution went on. When someone told one of the political strategists in the north, "General Howe has taken Philadelphia," the surly reply was, "No. Philadelphia has captured General Howe."

The winter in Philadelphia had been pleasant enough for the officers. They could find plenty of food, had commandeered the finest homes, and entertained themselves performing dramatic skits.

But if the officers were happy, the enlisted men were not. Food was scarce and had grown more so during the winter. Nothing was sacred to the conquering British or the Germans. The inhabitants of Philadelphia, many of them staunch loyalists, had protested to General Howe that they were being treated like the enemy. Howe pretended to be upset, but he had campaigned enough to know that you cannot control a British soldier when he is set on stealing chickens or anything else that isn't tied down.

The city was ravaged, fine old houses were torn down for firewood, churches were used for stables, and the streets became unsafe for decent women to walk about.

So it went in Philadelphia, but in Boston things were much the same as they had been since the British had been driven out. After the departure of his sister and nephew, Daniel threw himself into the craft of making cannons, assisted by Dake. Sam and Jubal Morrison worked hard on training their crews. On the third day of April, they succeeded in capturing a small merchant ship loaded with hardware from England. It was not a rich find, for the ship was small, and the goods were not particularly valuable. Nevertheless, it was a victory, and Sam used part of his proceeds to buy a broach for Keturah. He had not yet gotten over the embarrassment of making her a foot warmer, while his cousin David had given her a much more feminine and welcomed gift.

Matthew continued to paint, keeping mostly to himself. After the death of Esther Denham, he had become moody and disappeared for days at a time, never revealing where he spent his time. He continued to live with Daniel and Marian, but Marian worried about him, as did his father.

Rachel was able, for a time, to breathe sighs of relief that Josiah Grierson and Jubal Morrison had given up their pursuits of her hand in marriage. Grierson was somewhat stiff, whereas Jubal was cheerful enough that Rachel enjoyed his company on his frequent visits. She even went out on one short voyage on the *Defiant* and enjoyed it immensely. They spotted no vessels that might be taken, but the fresh air and the sight of the green-gray ocean and the blue clouds overhead were refreshing.

Nevertheless, Rachel soon grew moody. This was unusual for her and she could not explain it. Sam said once, "You're getting to be as grouchy as an old crab, Rachel. What's the matter with you?"

Rachel had not answered him, for she had no answer to give. Finally Jubal got to the heart of the mystery, or at least he thought so. He had observed Rachel carefully when he was courting her and had not missed the attraction that Jacob Steiner had for her. She had said little or nothing, but Morrison was a perceptive young man. It occurred to him that Rachel's short temper and moodiness were connected to the absence of the young Hessian soldier. Being an impulsive fellow, Jubal decided to do something about it.

Sam was caulking the sides of the *Defiant* when he looked up to see

Jubal's head sticking up over the side. "Sam, you're going to have to do something about Rachel."

"What do you mean, Jubal?"

"She's getting grouchy. Haven't you noticed?"

"Sure I've noticed. I've talked to her about it, but it didn't do any good. It's not like her." Sam carefully added a piece of caulking material in a seam, picked up the hammer, and with a wedge-shaped sliver of wood, drove it in. He admired his work with satisfaction, then shook his head. "She's a pain to be around. I can tell you that. Even Father's noticed it, and she's always been his favorite."

"It's that German fellow, Steiner."

Quickly Sam looked up with astonishment. "What are you talking about, Jubal?"

"I mean she's stuck on him."

"Don't be crazy! She wouldn't have anything to do with a Hessian."

Jubal laughed, reached down, and pulled Sam's hair. "That's what you think! Women do funny things. They marry worse than Hessians."

Sam stood up and put his hands on the gunwales of the ship. "Why, he was in the enemy forces!"

"He's not anymore. He's on our side. Good-looking fellow, too, and he's got a real future ahead of him."

Sam argued vehemently for a while that no Bradford would ever marry a Hessian, but finally he began to come over to Jubal's way of thinking. "Well, I don't know what to do about it."

"I'll tell you what to do about it," Jubal said. "What you need to do is take her to see him."

"Take her to see him! How can I do that?"

"We're not going to make a trip for a while, and Phoebe hasn't seen her brother in a long time. Take the two of them and go to Valley Forge."

"Father would never let me do that."

"I'll bet he would," Jubal grinned. "Tell him you're lonesome for Micah."

"He'd see through that in a minute."

"Probably would, but I'll bet he'll let you go. Give it a try."

Sam wasted no time. That evening at the supper table, he said casually, "I miss Micah. Father, would it be all right if I would go see him for a few days?"

Immediately Phoebe looked up and cried, "Oh, could I go, too, Mr. Bradford? I haven't seen Joel in so long."

Actually Daniel had no intention of letting Sam make such a trip, but Phoebe's expression caught at him. He was very fond of the young woman and knew that she was lonely. "Well, I guess it wouldn't hurt for a few days."

"You'll have to come, too, Rachel," Sam said quickly. "You can be a chaperone."

Rachel had been eating little, but now she said eagerly, "Would that be all right, Father?"

"Of course it would. Mrs. Williams is back now and can help Marian. Go ahead and make a trip of it."

Sam winked at Rachel and said as they were leaving the table, "You know there's a chance we might see Jacob. You wouldn't mind that, would you?"

Rachel smiled happily. "I wouldn't mind a bit, Sam," she said. Then she reached over, hugged him, and gave him a kiss. Placing her lips close to his ear, she whispered, "Sometimes you show promise, Samuel Bradford—indeed you do!"

🔔   🔔   🔔

The weather had turned out to be almost perfect for the journey. Sam had commandeered a covered buggy just in case of rain or a late snow, but the small party was able to keep the top down, and all three passengers enjoyed the pleasant weather. At night they stayed in inns or homes that would take them in. Twice they camped out, which was an exciting adventure to Phoebe, who had never done anything like this.

Those nights when they camped out, Phoebe and Sam would talk until late hours beside the crackling fire, watching the sparks fly up. Rachel said little but smiled often.

Finally they crossed into Pennsylvania, and the following day they drew up in front of the camp. They were met by a guard who advanced and put his eye on them carefully. "What's your business? This is an army camp."

"I'm here to see my brother, Chaplain Micah Bradford," Sam said quickly. He saw the smile come to the man's face and added quickly, "This is my sister. Could you help us find him?"

"No problem at all. I'll go along with you."

The soldier left two fellow guards in charge and climbed up in the buggy, squeezing as close as possible to Phoebe, who was seated beside Samuel. He was a talkative fellow and gave them the news of the camp and ended by saying, "We're going to whip the lobsterbacks the next time out. You wait and see."

Guided by the talkative sentry, Sam drove the carriage until it pulled up in front of a log hut larger than most of them. "This is where the chaplain stays. This is the church. The chaplain had us build it and he lives here."

"Thank you very much, Private," Phoebe said. "Do you know Joel Bradford?"

"Why, sure I do!"

"That's my brother."

"Well, I'll wait around, and after you talk to the chaplain, I'll take you to find him."

"That would be most kind of you."

Sam hopped down from the wagon, tied the horses, then went up to the building, which was built of raw logs. It was not large and was rudely made. He called out, "Micah, are you here?"

At once he heard a voice, and then Micah appeared, his face wreathed with delight. "Sam," he said, "what are you doing here?"

Sam grinned. "I came to see if you'd been behaving yourself, and I brought Rachel and Phoebe with me."

"Wonderful! Let me go greet them." Micah went out, and for a few moments there was exchanging of news. Then Micah said, "Phoebe, I guess that you are anxious to see Joel."

"Yes, I am, Micah."

"There's a soldier here who says he'll take Phoebe to see Joel," Rachel said.

"Fine. And, Phoebe, when you find him, bring him back here. We'll fix something to eat tonight. It won't be much—"

"Yes, it will," Rachel said quickly. "Look in the back of this buggy. We brought enough food to fill even you, Micah."

"Well, bless God!" Micah exclaimed. "Look at that!" He eagerly prowled through the food that the party had brought and said, "We could ask General Washington himself to join us."

"I wish you would," Samuel said quickly. "I need to talk to him about forming a navy."

"His Excellency isn't here right now, but you can tell me about it and I'll pass it on. I'm sure he'll be glad to have your help, Sam."

Sam blurted out, "I think Rachel would like to see her soldier."

"He's not my soldier, Sam!" Rachel said with embarrassment.

"Well, you know what I mean."

"Why don't you go invite him to our feast tonight, Rachel? We have plenty for everyone."

"Are you sure?" Rachel said.

"Certainly." He walked over to the private, gave him some instructions, then returned to say, "He'll take you to find the fellows, but leave these groceries here."

The two men unloaded the food inside the church, and Micah set about locating a cook. The others left, and the soldier, whose name was John Stevens, drove them to where Joel was to be found.

"There he is!" Phoebe said, jumping out of the buggy. She ran ahead, calling out, "Joel! Joel!"

Joel Bradford heard his name called by a woman's voice. Turning, he was shocked and immensely pleased to see his sister. He ran to greet her, picked her up, and swung her around. "Phoebe!" he said. "I'm so glad to see you! How did you get here?"

"I'll tell you all about it, but we've got an invitation to supper."

"Sounds good to me. Who's with you?"

"Sam and Rachel. We'll all be there."

"Let me say hello to them."

They went over immediately and exchanged greetings, then Rachel said, "Do you know Jacob Steiner?"

She received an odd look from Private Stevens, who shrugged. "Yes. I can find him, miss."

Rachel said, "I'll meet you all back at the church. Now if you're ready, Private Stevens."

Rachel walked along with the private as he explained how he was going to win the war along with General Washington's help. It seemed like a long walk, but finally he stopped and said, "There he is. Out there drilling those men."

Rachel stood still and put her gaze on the group of soldiers out doing close-order drills. Her eyes went at once to the soldier drilling them. As she looked down the line, she said, "I don't see him."

"Don't see him? He's right there! Lieutenant Jacob Steiner."

"Lieutenant!" Rachel gasped.

Stevens shifted. "It upset a few of the fellows when that Hessian fellow came in and got made a lieutenant. But he's the only one that can speak German to please General von Steuben. He's his aide, you know, and aides got to be officers, so they made him a lieutenant. You know him pretty well, do you?"

"He's a very good friend."

Indeed, Rachel was not ready for what she was seeing. Stevens stood back and Rachel said to him, "I think I can find my way back, Private Stevens. Thank you so much." She moved forward and watched as Jacob put the men through the drill. A short, fat general was standing beside him shouting orders in German, which Jacob instantly translated into English. She could see that the men were well-trained and remembered how Dake had told her that there wasn't a man in his squad that could do a right-shoulder arms. Indeed, the rumors about this Baron von Steuben were all over the Colonies, and it was known that General Washington was putting high hopes on the baron's help.

Finally the drill ended and Jacob exchanged a few words with the general and then turned and walked away. He was walking in an oblique direction, and Rachel moved forward quickly to intercept him. When she was close enough, she looked around with embarrassment and then called out as quietly as she could, "Jacob!"

The voice reached Jacob and he straightened up and turned to see Rachel. Surprise washed over his face and then delight. He came toward her at once and reached out and took her hands. She felt it was improper in public to do so, but she could no more have rebuked him than she would have rebuked her little stepbrother Enoch. Jacob was obviously delighted to see her.

"Rachel—what are you doing here?"

"Why, I came to see my brother, of course."

"Certainly. A wonderful man," Jacob said. "I can't say enough fine things about him. He's been such a help to me."

"You're invited to dinner. We've brought a lot of food, and Micah's having it all cooked up. Sam will be there and Phoebe."

"I would be delighted." He was still holding her hands and then seemed to remember where he was. He gave a look around and saw some of the men grinning and dropped her hands abruptly. "Sorry. That was rather unthoughtful."

Rachel did not answer. "Would you like to show me around?"

"Nothing would give me greater pleasure, and I want to hear all you've been doing. Come. I will give you the grand tour."

By the time Jacob and Rachel had walked around the camp, Micah had found a willing cook to help prepare the meal. When they walked back to the church, Micah said, "Rachel, I thought I was going to get to eat this all myself."

"I've got someone here to match your appetite," Rachel said, smiling at Jacob.

The dinner was one of the most delightful that Rachel had ever known. Micah had invited Clive Gordon to join the "family reunion," also. The guest of honor was General von Steuben, who, indeed, spoke atrocious English.

He beamed at Rachel when she was introduced and said something to Jacob in German.

"What did he say, Jacob?"

"Oh, just how pleased he is to meet you."

Von Steuben roared with laughter. "That iss not what I said, but this young man iss modest indeed. He has told me all about you. I think I vill get His Excellence to give you a medal."

Rachel was charmed with von Steuben, as was almost everyone he met. He kept the table roaring with anecdotes about his life in Europe as they ate the food Rachel had brought. They had roasted chicken, warmed up beefsteak pie, slabs of thick ham, sweet potatoes and apples, green beans, cornbread, and hot black coffee.

Once von Steuben reached over and pounded Jacob on the back. "This young fellow iss a prize. He speaks perfect English, shoots like a machine, and iss the best drill master in the army. I am grateful that you saved him for me, Miss Bradford."

Rachel was embarrassed but Micah was not. "Oh, she saves everything—lame dogs, half-drowned kittens, and birds with broken wings. One Hessian wouldn't be any problem at all for my sister."

"Micah, don't talk like that!"

After the meal was over, von Steuben insisted that Jacob play. "He is the best musician in the world," the general said, waving his arms around. "Every night he plays for the men and they love it. He can play happy songs, sad songs, anything."

"What would you like to hear?"

"I will let Miss Bradford choose."

Rachel said in a quiet voice, "I would like to hear 'Rachel's Song.'"

Von Steuben's eyes lit up. "Ah, a love song for a lady. Let us hear it, my boy. Play—play!"

The crude building somehow achieved a sense of grace as Jacob Steiner drew the bow across the strings. It was not a fast song, and he skillfully made the notes linger and fill not only the building but the hearts of those who listened. When he ended, von Steuben had tears in his eyes. "Beautiful, my boy."

After Jacob had finished playing, the men sat around talking about the tactics to come. Von Steuben got into a long discussion with Sam about an invention of some sort. Jacob drew Rachel aside and the two were oblivious to all others.

"Would you like to catch a breath of air? We have a full moon tonight," Jacob said.

"Yes," Rachel said quickly. She moved outside and Jacob followed her. Indeed there was a full moon. It looked impossibly large, and the night was so clear that the craters were plainly visible. It shed beautiful silver moonbeams over the camp, and there was a quietness now, broken by the faint sounds of men's voices. Somewhere far off someone was playing on a flute, and it made a ghostly sound on the night air.

"It's beautiful here, Jacob."

"Well, at night. Rather rough in the daytime."

"Will you be here long?"

"I think not. The army's ready to fight. I do not know when. I do not think General Washington knows. He cannot lose this army, because if he loses that, the revolution is over."

"Tell me what you've been doing. I was so surprised when I found that you were a lieutenant."

Jacob laughed. "It is strange, at that. The generals must have lieutenants as their aides. That is all. I cook German food for him . . . and he likes to hear my violin. And I give the orders in English. I am no fighting officer."

"Still, I'm proud of you."

"Then I am happy."

The two stood there underneath the moonlit-drenched night and talked. Rachel was amazed at how easy it was to talk to Jacob. He told her amusing stories about his experiences, and finally she said, "Jacob, I have done something. You may not approve."

"I doubt that very much."

"I wrote to your mother. I wrote it in English and had a German lady translate it into German. I told her what had happened to you."

Jacob was silent; then he suddenly reached out and took her hands again. His voice was husky. "You are always kind," he said.

"You don't mind?"

"Mind? Certainly I don't mind. You're always the kindest person. I know I'm never surprised."

His hands were on her shoulders, and as she looked up at him, there was a luminosity in her eyes, and he was mesmerized by the beauty of her face. The moonlight softened it, and her lips were close and slightly parted. He pulled her forward, put his arms around her, and kissed her.

Rachel knew he was going to kiss her. A woman always knows such things. She savored the touch of his arms around her and did not resist.

Finally, Jacob stepped back and said, "You are a beautiful and wonderful woman."

Rachel could not reply. Her heart was full, and she knew that something in this man had touched her deeply. She did not know what to say to him. Neither of them knew what the war would bring, and in many ways they were strangers. She said quietly, "Come, we'd better go inside."

As they stepped inside the door, she saw that Micah was watching her carefully. She did not give a sign of any sort, but Micah was perceptive.

Something's going on here. I wonder if Father knows, he thought. Then he turned back and continued to listen to von Steuben's tales from his homeland.

23

A TIME TO GIVE THANKS

THE BLUE SKY OVERHEAD was scored suddenly by a flight of red-winged blackbirds. Matthew Bradford looked up quickly from the canvas in front of him. He studied the myriad of birds as they drove straight across the sky, uttering harsh cries, then suddenly wheeling as if at a given signal and turning due east.

"I wonder how they do that?" Matthew muttered. He watched them as they disappeared, then turned back to the canvas. He applied broad, bold strokes to the canvas, but his mind was not on what he was doing. He had come out to the deserted section of the plantation at dawn. Though the sun was halfway to the meridian, he had done little work. He gritted his teeth and made a slashing movement, which displeased him. Suddenly he took the brush, snapped it in two, and threw it from him. He stared at it angrily as it lay in the grass. He had paid three pounds for that particular sable brush, and now he glared at it as if somehow it were to blame for its own destruction. For a moment he did not move, then with a rash gesture he wheeled, picked up his artist's case, and began throwing the paints, brushes, cloth, and other materials inside. He slammed the case shut and fastened the leather strap. Then grasping the handle, he turned and made his way down a narrow path.

He did not notice that the first flowers of May were out. Jack-in-the-pulpits and violets with purple faces were peeping out from beneath the emerald spears of fresh spring grass, but he had no eye for them as he ordinarily would have had.

The path made a serpentine trail through the first-growth timber. Ten minutes later he emerged in an opening where a mare hitched to a buggy lifted her head and neighed at him. He ignored her for a moment, then expelled a breath and went over and stroked her silky nose. She nibbled at his hat and he laughed shortly. "Not your fault, Sally, that I can't make up my mind!" He stroked the mare for a moment, then slapped her affectionately on the neck. Slowly he moved to the buggy as if deep in thought and climbed up in it. Settling himself in the seat, he unwound the lines, held them for a moment, and, as always, when he was not busy, the problem that had plagued him for months seemed to settle over him like a dark cloud. He looked up into the sky, noting the skeins of white clouds that were beginning to gather in the south, then muttered, "It seems like a man could make up his mind. What's the matter with me?"

Suddenly Matthew looked down at his hands and stared at them. They were strong hands, but they had nothing of the Bradford look about them. Daniel Bradford and his three biological sons had hands made for strength—broad hands, muscular, able to hold and strike and grip. The hands that Matthew looked at were strong enough, perhaps, but had an aristocratic look about them. He had long, nimble fingers, the hands of an artist.

Time seemed to stop then, and Matthew lost all consciousness of sitting in a buggy out in the woods. In one of those flashes of memory, in which time is confused, he was suddenly standing in front of Sir Leo Rochester and hearing him say, "You're not Daniel Bradford's son, Matthew. You're my son!"

The memory was painful, as always, and Matthew suddenly slapped the lines on Sally's back, saying harshly, "Get up, Sally!" The mare moved forward with a jolt that threw Matthew back. He tried to blot out all that had happened since Sir Leo Rochester had revealed the secret of his birth. He had told him how Matthew's mother had been a servant and how Leo had taken her carelessly. The poor girl had run away, penniless and pregnant, and had been helped by another of Rochester's servants, Daniel Bradford. Bradford was a kind, generous man and had married the woman and had given the baby his name. Now years later, that baby had become a man, and Rochester's eyes had burned as he said in that scene that Matthew had played a thousand times in his mind, "I don't have any sons and I want one. Take my name and you will have all that is mine. Sir Matthew Rochester will be the master of a fine estate. You'll have everything you want, Matthew."

After the death of Rochester, Matthew had wavered. It had seemed a wise decision, for who would not want to have a fine estate in Virginia, property in England, and a title? But somehow the idea of giving up the name of Bradford was repugnant to him.

Now as the house came into view, Matthew had a sudden thought: *None of the Bradford men would have struggled for months over a decision like this. They would have made it on the spot.* But he also knew that the Bradford men were proud of their name. They were of one blood, while he was in some respects a stranger. True enough, Daniel had never made any difference between him, Micah, Dake, and Sam. He had shown no favoritism whatsoever. His brothers and Rachel had been as close as he would allow them to get, but once again, there was the difference in him. He was not able to get as close to people as the Bradfords. Some sort of inner resistance would not allow him to do so. He pulled the buggy up just as Caesar came out of the barn. The black man came to him at once.

"Unhitch the buggy and the mare, suh?"

"Yes, Caesar."

Grasping the mare's harness by the jaw, Caesar asked, "You hear from Miss Rachel, Mr. Matthew?"

"As a matter of fact, I did." He fumbled in his inner pocket. He had gotten a letter just the previous day and had forgotten to take it out. He looked at Caesar's eager face and asked, "Would you like to hear it?"

"If it's fittin'."

"Oh, I'm sure she wouldn't mind. As a matter of fact, she mentioned you." Unfolding the letter, he began to read:

My dear Matthew,

I promised to write from Valley Forge and give you my impressions, and I take a pen in hand to do so. I was expecting the men to look very bad, but not all of them do. Many of them have no uniforms, since only a few colonies have supplied any. The Delaware men are all well dressed, for that colony sent two wagonloads of uniforms, but other soldiers are wearing whatever they can find.

But I hasten to add, if their clothes are ragged, their spirits are fine. Food has been coming in now that spring is here, and so they have gained back the weight they had lost. They are still lean and have faces like wolves, but they are strong and fit. Micah says he has never before seen them so eager to fight.

The letter went on, describing the conditions at Valley Forge, and finally the last paragraphs read:

You would be proud of Joel. He thinks the world of you, saying over and over how he would be in prison for debt if it were not for you. He is a fine soldier, a sergeant now, and very much in love.

We are all staying in a hut that Micah commandeered for us, but we have supper together every night. Joel is there, and Jacob also. You would not know him, Matthew! He is a lieutenant now, as you know. He makes little of it, saying it's simply because he's the only one who can understand General von Steuben's German. Nevertheless, his captain says he is a fine officer, and von Steuben seems to dote on him almost like a son.

I am—

"She breaks off here and scratches out something. Blots a line," Matthew said.

"I wonder what she wanted to say that she didn't want us to know," Caesar said.

Matthew grinned. "I looked at it, and it seems like the word 'love' is in here."

"Well, that's a fine young man, Jacob Steiner."

"I believe he is," Matthew said as he folded the letter.

"Yes, suh. I'm so glad he became a follower of Jesus. I think he's going to be one of them Christians that everybody looks at."

"Well, I've got to go in now, Caesar." Turning, Matthew went into the house and up to his room. The conversation with Caesar had diverted him, and he sat in front of the window staring out, thinking of Rachel and wondering what would come of her relationship with her Hessian soldier.

But soon his mind seemed to drag him back to the difficulty he faced, and gloom descended upon him. He sat there for over an hour, and finally a sense of desperation came to him. He struck his palm with his fist, stood to his feet, and said, "I'm sick of this! Why can't I make up my mind?" He was silent for a moment, then slowly he spoke the words aloud. "I've wavered long enough. I can't go on like this the rest of my life. So, right or wrong, I'm going to do it. I'm going to take my life in my own hands and do *something*!"

🔔　　🔔　　🔔

"I've made my decision, Father."

Daniel Bradford had known the instant Matthew came into his office that he'd come to say something important. He went over to shut the door, then came back and stood before his son. "What is it, Matthew? Something about your name, I would guess."

A relief washed through Matthew. He knew his father was a discerning man, and he knew that his father wanted to make this easy for him.

"Yes, sir. It is about that. I've decided . . . to take the name of Rochester."

Daniel said quietly, "Well, of course, that would be a very fine thing. You will have a good life."

"You don't mind my putting the name Bradford aside?"

"It's just air. Just words." Daniel suddenly reached over and put his arms around Matthew. "You can call yourself anything you want to, but you'll always be my son, Matthew."

Matthew's throat began to grow thick. He blinked his eyes rapidly and muttered, "That's like you, Father, and I'll always feel that I'm your son."

Seeing that Matthew was embarrassed and seemed on the verge of weeping, Daniel slapped him on the back, saying, "Well, that's out of the way. I want you to know how very proud I am of you, son."

"I haven't served in the army like Micah or Dake."

"Well, that's the way God told them to go, but He's given you a fine gift. He's made you into an excellent artist. Now, what are your plans?"

Matthew began to speak. The fact that his father had taken this so well made him feel even worse. He felt as though he were betraying the name of Bradford. He could not deny his father's honesty and saw no animosity in him whatsoever. Still, he experienced a feeling of lostness as he left the foundry. He had one more task to do and then it was all settled.

🛡   🛡   🛡

Abigail opened the door and was unable to speak for a moment. She fixed her eyes on Matthew, who simply stood there with an odd expression on his face she could not fathom. "Come in, Matthew," she said and stepped back. When he was inside he stood uncertainly, his hat in his hand. Abigail took it and said, "Is there something wrong, Matthew?"

"Yes. I have to talk to you."

"Come into the sitting room." Turning, Abigail moved down the short hallway and turned inside the sitting room, which was a cheerful place, one that she liked best of any room in the house. "Will you sit down?" she asked.

"I . . . can't stay long," Matthew said awkwardly. He had firmly made up his mind on what to say and had practiced it on the way over, but now that he faced her, he could not find the words. Much of the pain this woman had caused him had passed away, yet not all of it. Somehow he knew that he was behaving foolishly, that people could change, and that Abigail had had a sincere change of heart. Still, there was something in him he could neither define nor explain that compelled him to carry through with his plans.

"I've decided to go away." It was not what he intended to say, and he cleared his throat nervously. "You know I've been struggling for a long time with what to do about—Leo."

The name came awkwardly to his lips. It had been Leo Rochester who had paid Abigail to make Matthew fall in love with her. It had been simple enough to Leo. Matthew could then have married Abigail, and she would have been able to influence him to take the name of Rochester. Matthew remembered how desperately in love he had been with Abigail. When she had come to him and confessed that she had been hired to make him want to marry her, the pain had been keener than anything he had ever known.

"You're going to take Leo's name, aren't you?"

"Yes. I've decided it would be best."

A silence filled the room then, and Matthew felt the need to fill it with talk. "I wanted to come tell you that you and your mother don't need to worry—about money, I mean."

"About money! Why do you say that?"

"Because I will be having a great deal of it, and I don't want you or your mother to face any hardship."

Abigail said quietly, "You don't have to do that, Matthew."

"But I want to. I know you don't have anything."

"Actually we do. Aunt Esther left everything she had to my mother and to me. So we own this house now, and there is enough money to last as long as my mother lives. As for me, I can take care of myself."

Matthew suddenly felt cheated. It had been in his mind that he could dismiss the entire business of Abigail Howland by paying her off. Now he knew it would not be that simple.

"Abigail," he said in a rush, "let me do something. I know that I've been—well, I haven't treated you right. I was so angry with you and bitter."

"You had a right to be. I treated you shamefully."

The simple admission somehow touched Matthew. He remembered how she had felt in his arms and the touch of his lips on hers. He knew that she loved him, and all he had to do was reach out and she would come. The urge came to him to do exactly that, but once again the strain he knew that he had inherited from Leo Rochester—never from Daniel Bradford!—rose up in him. Whether it was stubbornness or pride he could not tell, but now he said hastily, "I've made my mind up, Abigail. I'll be leaving right away."

"Well, this is good-bye, then."

"Well, yes. For a time."

"More than that. You'll be Sir Matthew Rochester. You'll move in different circles. I don't expect we'll be seeing each other again."

Her words hurt Matthew and jarred him. He reached out suddenly and put his arms around Abigail. "I loved you once," he murmured hoarsely. He kissed her then impetuously. The deep feelings he felt for her swept through him again, but she was standing passively in his arms. She had always responded to him before, and now he stepped back and shook his head. "I'm sorry."

"No need to be." Abigail's face was pale, and she said quietly, "Good-bye, Matthew. May the Lord give you a good life."

Matthew stood still, unable to think properly, and then he said, "If you ever need anything . . . "

"Good-bye, Matthew."

Feeling her rebuff, Matthew turned and left the house. The word was final and he knew that he had closed the door. "It's all over," he muttered. "I don't have to think about that anymore."

But he did think about it. He thought about it all day as he prepared to leave for Virginia. He thought about it as he said good-bye to everyone in the house, and he thought about it as he mounted the carriage. As he left Boston he tried to feel free. "I'm going to be Sir Matthew Rochester. I'll have everything a man wants," he said aloud. A passenger across from him stared at him curiously. Matthew pulled his gaze away and stared out the window. Somehow he knew that in turning away from the Bradford name—and from Abigail Howland—he was losing something he could never recover.

24

THE BATTLE OF MONMOUTH COURTHOUSE

ON MAY 25, 1778—three years to the day since he had arrived in Boston to oversee the demolition of George Washington's army—Sir William Howe sailed for home. Some of his critics accused him of being a poor tactician. This was an unjust accusation, for of the six major battles with Washington, he had defeated the American general each time. His movements were always slow and ponderous, sometimes even timorous; his major fault was he could not take advantage of a vulnerable foe.

"Mr." Washington, as Howe called the American general, always managed to slip away, and since Washington's army *was* the American Revolution, in effect Howe was defeated.

There was little rejoicing among the British military when Sir Henry Clinton succeeded General Howe. Howe had always been popular with the younger officers, while Clinton was a cold, withdrawn man whose career was not one to inspire loyalty.

The goal of Sir Henry Clinton was to get his army intact from Philadelphia to New York. The goal of his adversary, General George Washington, was to attack Clinton's forces and prove that the winter at Valley Forge had produced an army capable of meeting the best England had to offer. As soon as Washington heard that Clinton had abandoned Philadelphia, he immediately sent a force under the command of General Benedict Arnold to occupy the city. Then he threw all of his energies into one grand ambition—to attack Clinton's army and, if possible, annihilate it.

☙   ☙   ☙

Jacob Steiner tried to shrink himself into nothingness against the wall. He had been ordered by General von Steuben to accompany him to a staff meeting to take notes. Jacob's eyes were now fixed on the face of General George Washington, who in turn was studying his officers.

"The problem, gentlemen, is very simple," he said quietly. "We must decide whether to attack Clinton."

Immediately several of the staff officers began to speak. Jacob tried to sort them out, but they spoke too quickly. He did hear General "Mad" Anthony Wayne say loudly, "I say we hit him and hit him hard!"

General Nathaniel Greene, the tall, balding ex-Quaker and one of Washington's favorites, immediately slammed the table with his fists. "I agree with General Wayne!"

Washington listened as the talk went back and forth. His eyes went more often to General Charles Lee, who had just rejoined the army. General Lee was the one officer under Washington's command who had seen service with the British in England and knew their ways. Jacob thought he was the most obnoxious human being he had ever seen— skinny, needle-nosed, with small malicious eyes, and the most profane man Jacob had ever heard.

"Impossible!" Lee said, "We would have no hope whatsoever!"

General Greene glared at him. "I don't think I'd be in a hurry to say that, General Lee."

"You don't know the British soldiers like I do!" Lee sniffed with contempt.

Washington's face showed nothing, but he finally said, "So that is your opinion, is it, General Lee, that we must not attack?"

"What! Throw this rabble against trained English troops? Why, sir, it's impossible." He took a pinch of snuff, then shrugged. "Wait on the French. Then we will attack. They have a disciplined force."

Washington and all the patriots had hoped that the French would come in on the side of America, but so far they had not.

Finally Washington said, "Knox, what do you think?"

General Knox, the largest man in the room, blinked, then licked his lips. "I feel that an attack on Clinton might not be wise at this time."

"General Wayne?"

"Attack!"

"And you, General von Steuben?"

A volley of German and French issued from von Steuben. When finally he was through, Washington looked at Steiner, who said, "The general says, sir, that we should attack Clinton at once." Jacob wisely refrained from putting in the insulting remarks that von Steuben had laid on General Charles Lee.

The Marquis de Lafayette had said little. He rarely did in staff meetings. Now he spoke up. "If we do not attack Clinton, Your Excellency, it will look like cowardice. We must attack!"

The meeting went on for hours, with Jacob whispering in von Steuben's ear the essence of it all. Finally Washington made up his mind. Von Steuben had whispered to Jacob, "He will have to offer Lee the command, since he's the senior officer."

However, Lee, when he heard Washington say that a small force was going to be sent, said, "I want no part of it!"

Immediately Washington said, "Thank you," and began giving orders.

Finally the men stood, and Lafayette said, "When do we attack, General?"

After the meeting was over, von Steuben paced back and forth on the parade ground. Jacob kept pace with him, and finally the general said, "Did you understand what went on in there?"

"No, sir. I did not."

"General Charles Lee is a dog and I smell a traitor! I have heard that he gave information about our forces to the British while he was their captive. I do not understand why Washington listens to him! I would not trust him as far as I could throw my horse!"

"Well, General Lafayette will lead the attack. Is that not true, my General?"

"No one knows what Lee will do. He's as changeable as the wind."

�idₜ   �idₜ   �idₜ

The Battle at Monmouth Courthouse began for Jacob the next day as he stood beside General von Steuben. As von Steuben had said, Lee changed his mind and insisted that he lead the attack.

"But you refused it, General Lee."

"That was before I knew the size of the maneuver."

Washington had no choice. He turned to the Marquis de Lafayette and said, "You know the general's position with the army."

267

Lafayette was hurt by this, as everyone saw, but he bowed gracefully, saying, "You are the commander in chief, Your Excellency."

The army began moving early the next day, and Jacob stayed close to von Steuben's side. As lines moved forward, General Greene stopped by to talk to von Steuben. It was necessary for Jacob to interpret. What Greene said, in effect, was, "General Washington has ordered General Lee to attack the enemy as soon as possible. We will have to reinforce him when the battle begins."

Von Steuben gave Greene a hard look. "He vill not push the battle. He does not believe we can win."

After Jacob had interpreted this, Greene stared at von Steuben, then muttered, "He must push it! It is the only way we can win!"

What happened from that point onward would forever be a mystery to historians. Washington had enough men to do the job. What he did not know was that at the first sign of resistance, General Charles Lee simply gave up. He stopped the attack and the soldiers lost heart. General Wayne came riding up and demanded to know why the attack had been broken off. Lee replied, "Sir, you do not know British soldiers. We cannot stand against them. We shall certainly be driven back at first. We must be cautious."

It soon became evident that Charles Lee had made no plan whatsoever. Disorder soon broke out among the American army. There were marches and countermarches, but no orders came from higher up. Lee had simply withdrawn himself from the battle.

All this time General von Steuben was furious, stamping around and cursing in German and in French, but he could not find out any more than could the other generals of what Lee was doing. Finally Washington got bits of information about his troops retreating. "It cannot be!" he exclaimed, but he rode forward. He soon came to men who were obviously retreating, and he demanded loudly, "By whose orders are these troops retreating?"

"By General Lee's" was the answer.

Washington was thunderstruck. He could not believe what he was seeing. The battle was completely out of hand. He had hardly begun his journey to the front when all around men were scurrying back from the battle. They were soldiers, yet they were retreating. Everyone was retreating!

At that point George Washington knew he had made a serious mistake. For some reason he himself did not understand, he had given full command to an officer who did not believe the battle could be won. But from the point when Washington first saw the retreating soldiers, he redeemed himself from all other errors.

Riding his old English charger back and forth, he loomed up before the men and put heart into the weary soldiers. He displayed such skill that they stopped their retreat and threw themselves in a line of fire, blocking the British advance.

Jacob saw a sight shortly afterward that he had never expected to see. Washington had worked like a madman to staunch the retreat, and Jacob had been sent by von Steuben to get orders to join in the fray.

Jacob found General Washington and was approaching, when he saw Washington ride up to General Lee. Jacob was close enough to hear the conversation.

He watched as Washington, in a single movement, pulled his horse up before Lee. "What is the meaning of this, General?"

"Sir? What do you mean?" Lee seemed totally confused.

"Did you order this retreat?" He used no formality as he was accustomed and gave no ceremony. This was a Washington that Lee had never seen. Rage seemed to flow out of Washington, who contained his anger only by an effort.

"What is all this confusion, sir?"

Lee was disconcerted. "I see no confusion, sir. Besides, I'll remind you, I didn't think it proper to attack in the first place."

"If you didn't think it proper, you shouldn't have undertaken it! Go to the rear!"

At this point Washington wheeled his charger as Jacob came running up. "Sir, General von Steuben is waiting for orders."

"Have him bring all his men up. Throw them into this line right here, Lieutenant."

"Yes, Your Excellence."

Running back as fast as he could, Jacob was out of breath, and when he reached von Steuben he gasped, "The general says bring all the men up. Throw them into the line and block the British."

The light of battle came into von Steuben's eyes, and he threw himself into the attack. Jacob had difficulty staying by his side. The men moved forward in good order, and Jacob said, "Your training has paid off, my General. Look, they move like soldiers."

"As good as Hessians, eh?"

"Better," Jacob grinned.

The heat of the day soon took its toll on the British soldiers. Burdened by their heavy equipment, many had fallen out on the march from heat exhaustion.

Jacob was all over the field that day at Monmouth as he followed General von Steuben. The general was tireless, riding back and forth to encourage the men as they tried to stop the British.

It was then that von Steuben's horse was shot down by a British musket ball. Von Steuben went over his head and lay stunned. Beyond him, no more than fifty yards away, a small group of British soldiers saw the general fall. They advanced, intending, obviously, to take him captive.

Jacob saw all this in one swift glance. "Come! We will save our general!" Grabbing up a bayoneted rifle from a dead soldier, he led a bayonet charge. The British were unaccustomed to such things from the Americans. There were only about a dozen of them, and Jacob met the first one, who attempted to block his thrust. Jacob simply parried the blow and rammed the bayonet into the man's chest. He kicked the mortally wounded soldier loose, who fell to the ground clawing at his chest, then lay still. The fight swirled all around him, but then it was over as suddenly as it had begun.

Jacob ran over and lifted von Steuben to his feet. "Are you all right, my General?"

"Ja." Von Steuben had seen it all. He reached up and patted the tall young man on the shoulder with affection. "You have saved the life of an old soldier. Come now."

"It was my duty, sir."

"It was my life and I will never forget it."

🔔   🔔   🔔

General von Steuben did not forget his promise, and it was George Washington himself who, the day following the battle in a meeting of the staff, turned suddenly and asked, "General von Steuben, is this the young officer who saved your life?"

Von Steuben grinned and patted Jacob on the shoulders. "Ja, a good German boy."

"An American now." Washington's face was tense after the battle. "You did well, Lieutenant."

"Thank you, my General."

When Washington turned away, Jacob said to von Steuben, "He is a wonderful man. He won the battle almost single-handedly."

"We did not win the battle! We would have if it weren't for that coward Charles Lee! But he will no longer serve with us." Satisfaction came to von Steuben's face. "But the battle proved one thing. The army that was built at Valley Forge is good. It is a winning army, and with God's help and with His Excellency before us as our leader, we will see this country brought to birth."

25

A Doorway to Hope

DAKE MARCHED UP AND DOWN the hallway. From time to time he would stop and peer upstairs, listening as if for the sound of something very important. It was after midnight, and his pacing had started at dusk when Dr. Samuels had arrived. Dake was never known by anyone to be afraid of anything that breathed, yet now his face was pale. He pulled out a handkerchief from his inner pocket and mopped at the sweat that sprang up on his brow.

Sitting on a deacon's bench that was situated against the side of the broad hallway, Daniel Bradford studied his son with careful curiosity. Ever since Jeanne had started having her first labor pains, he had watched Dake steadily deteriorate. Keturah had sent for Daniel, and when he had arrived, she had said, "You better keep your eye on Dake. He's worse off than Jeanne."

Now as the Seth Thomas grandfather clock ticked solemnly, breaking the silence of the night, Daniel felt a gush of compassion for his son. "Come and sit down, Dake. You're not doing any good pacing back and forth like that. You're just going to wear the floor out."

"Why is it taking so long?" Dake's voice was tense, and he had to clear his throat before he could finish the sentence. Once again he looked upstairs and listened hard, but only the sound of the clock broke the silence of the hallway. Dake mopped his forehead again and then came over and slumped down on the deacon's bench, whereupon Daniel put his hand on his son's shoulder with a gesture of sympathy.

"She'll be all right. Don't worry about it."

"How can you say that? She's so . . . so fragile."

"Women are tougher than you think, son. Your mother was a very small woman, but she bore all of you. Jeanne will do the same."

His father's words did not seem to reassure Dake. He squirmed on

273

the bench for a while and gnawed on his lower lip. Finally he got up and began pacing back and forth and finally stopped to ask, "What time is it?"

"It's twelve minutes later than it was the last time you asked that question, Dake."

"It can't be! It's got to be later than that!"

"No, it's not. And it may be another four or five hours yet. Maybe longer."

"What!"

"Dake, these things aren't done like chopping a cord of wood. You always know when you're going to finish with that. So much wood to chop, so much time and you're done. But when life comes into this world, it seems time doesn't quite work as it should. I'm sure it's that way for the woman who's bearing the child."

"How can she stand it? I don't understand it. And why does it have to be this way?"

"You know your Bible better than that, Dake," Daniel said gently. "It's part of the curse that came on Adam and Eve. Eve would bear her children in sorrow just like Adam would have to wrestle with the ground with the sweat of his brow to make a living."

This theology did not seem to help Dake a great deal. He gave his father a caustic stare, then proceeded to march back and forth down the hall. Daniel noticed that his limp was somewhat less pronounced than it had been shortly after he had returned home. Once again he thought of Clive Gordon and Joel, who had saved Dake from certain death. Suddenly he said, "I've been thinking, Dake, about how Joel pulled you out of that spot you were in at Germantown."

Dake turned, stopped abruptly, and nodded. "I thought I was a goner that time, Pa," he said. "I would have been, too, if Joel hadn't come along."

"Must have been a shock for you to see him there."

"Well, I didn't know him, of course. He was dressed up like a gypsy. He was on a secret mission for the army." He sat down and seemed to be glad to talk about something to take his mind off of what was taking place upstairs. "And then when that British secret service fellow caught us, we'd have been gone for sure if Clive hadn't arrived."

The two men sat there talking for a time, and Dake was able to breathe a little bit more normally. They heard the sound of footsteps on the stairs and looked up to see Rachel coming down with a pitcher and a towel over her arm. Leaping up, Dake ran over and grabbed her roughly by the forearm. "How is she?"

Rachel looked up and grimaced. "You're breaking my arm, Dake!" She waited until he released her, then nodded. "She's doing very well."

"How much longer?"

"I don't know, and neither does she, and neither does Dr. Samuels. You'll just have to wait." With a look of compassion, she reached up and patted Dake on the shoulder. "Don't worry. She'll be fine. She's got too many people praying for her for anything to go wrong now."

Daniel had risen and came over to stand beside the two. "Rachel's right. God's promised me a grandbaby, and I'm going to have one. Now let's go into the kitchen. You can make me some coffee, Dake, and maybe find some cold biscuits or something to eat."

"Eat! I can't eat! How can I eat with a thing like this going on?"

Nevertheless, Dake turned, whirled, and half stumbled into the kitchen. Daniel shook his head. "Dake could face a tribe of wild Indians with nothing but a stick in his hand, but this thing's got him all shook up."

"Were you like this when we were born?" Rachel asked.

Daniel suddenly laughed. "Pretty much," he said, "but don't tell Dake that. I've got him convinced that I'm a pretty tough fellow." He sobered then and asked, "Is she really all right?"

Rachel hesitated. "She's having a hard time."

"It's been a hard time all the way through. But I believe that God's going to give us that baby. You know, there's something about the first grandchild. I already feel as proud of that baby as I was of any of you."

"And I'll have my first niece or nephew," Rachel said. Then she broke away, saying, "I've got to heat more water."

Daniel went into the kitchen, where he found Dake incapable of even making coffee. He made it himself and got Dake to talk about the war. Even though his son was as jumpy as a startled deer, he at least took his mind off of the unending wait. Rachel came back once, then Phoebe and Keturah, but the doctor did not come down.

"The least he could do," Dake grumbled, "is to come down and give us a report." His face was lined and his mouth drawn into a tight shape. He was a big man, strong and muscular, but there was something in him at this moment that Daniel almost did not recognize.

Finally, after what seemed like days, dawn came. Daniel went to the window and looked out. "It's daybreak," he said.

Dake was incapable of speech. He was sitting with his arms drawn up and folded against his chest, hugging himself and clenching his teeth. He did not answer, but then suddenly he lifted his head. "That's the doctor," he said abruptly and lunged to his feet. He hit the door of the kitchen, followed by Daniel, and saw Dr. Samuels as he was descending the last few steps of the stairway. Dake wanted to speak, but his throat was tight and he could not say a word. He waited, and his face had the expression of a man who had heard the leader of a firing squad say, "Ready! Aim—" and was waiting for the final command.

Dr. Samuels, a short, rotund man with a cheerful round face and rosy cheeks, reached out and struck Dake on the arm with a fist. He laughed and said, "You look like a man about ready to die, Dake. Well, you can stop worrying now. Everything's fine."

"Is she . . . all right?"

"Of course she's all right. She's only having a baby." Dr. Samuels shrugged. "She did have a hard time, though. She's a very courageous young lady." His eyes grew thoughtful and he chewed on his lower lip for a moment, then shook his head in disbelief. "Women are brave. Much braver than men," he murmured. Then he looked up at Dake and grinned. "You've got a son, Dake."

"Glory to God!" Daniel said, and then he grabbed Dake and the two big men did an awkward dance around the foyer, almost upsetting the doctor once.

"Well, I've done all I can do. You've got womenfolk here that can take care of Jeanne."

"Can we go up now?"

"Well, of course you can go up!"

Dake hit the stairs running with hardly a trace of a limp. Daniel followed. When the two men stepped inside the room, they stopped still beside Keturah. Rachel was just handing a bundle down to Jeanne. Keturah whispered, "Congratulations, Dake! You're a father!"

Dake approached the bed with trepidation, then he bent over and saw Jeanne's pale face and the skin stretched tight from the hours of dreadful pain. He wanted to cry for her and could do no more than lean over and kiss her on the cheek. "I'm glad you're all right," he said. "I've been going crazy."

Jeanne reached up with her right hand and touched his cheek. "I'll be fine," she whispered. Then she smiled a beautiful smile, despite the tension in her face. "What do you think of your son?" She reached over and drew the edge of the blanket back, and Dake's eyes went to the baby. He stared at the round red face and said nothing.

"Is he supposed to be red like that?" he finally asked.

"Why, of course he is! You just wait. He's going to be the most beautiful boy in all of America."

Dake looked at the face, and he heard his father say, "Pick him up,

Dake, and let us have a look at him."

"Can I do that, Jeanne?"

Jeanne nodded and watched as Dake picked up the baby, handling him as carefully as if he were a fragile plate. He turned to his father and Jeanne was happy then, for she saw the joy on Daniel's face as he leaned over and kissed the child.

Then Daniel stepped over to her and said, "Daughter, you've done well. What's his name?"

Jeanne looked at Dake and the two nodded. "His name is Daniel," Jeanne whispered. "He'll be Little Dan for a while."

Daniel Bradford's heart leaped with joy. "Little Dan Bradford," he said. "He's going to be an American and a man of God."

🔔   🔔   🔔

Immediately after the Battle of Monmouth Courthouse, budding historians and officers on both sides of the conflict began to evaluate what the battle had meant. The American losses amounted to sixty-nine dead, one hundred sixty-one wounded, and one hundred thirty missing. British losses, according to their reports, were sixty-five killed, one hundred sixty wounded, and sixty-four missing. However, following the battle, for weeks afterward, American burial parties counted hundreds of unburied enemy corpses in the surrounding woods. In addition to these losses, the British were faced with the loss of one hundred thirty-six British soldiers who deserted on the march from Philadelphia, as well as four hundred forty Hessians. Thousands of horses had to be put to death because there was no way to get them aboard Howe's ships.

Both sides claimed success at Monmouth, for both sides remained upon the field. Ordinarily only the victor would stay. In all probability Monmouth was a stalemate, but Washington showed an immense satisfaction at seeing his men hold their own against the best professionals of Europe. And now following the battle, as summer unfolded, the men's patriotic spirit became even more evident. The American army was now a unified force, and the patriots of the Colonies could take pride in their great leader and also in the soldiers who followed him.

One bright spot shone forth during the Battle of Monmouth. A young woman, Mary Ludwig Hayes, forever put her name in the history books of America. She obtained her fame and endeared herself to the army by rushing back and forth with pitchers of cool water for the suffering soldiers. For this day's work she earned the sobriquet of Molly Pitcher. One of the soldiers, Joseph Martin, who wrote extensively about his service in the Continental Army, reported, "While in the act of reaching for a cartridge and having one of her feet as far from the other as she could step, a cannon shot from the enemy passed directly between her legs without doing any other damage than tearing away all the lower part of her petticoat."

Molly Pitcher also, besides carrying water to fainting soldiers, served at her husband's cannon, and when he fell dead at her feet, she fired it herself. This young woman's gallantry was rewarded with a sergeant's warrant, which was small enough solace for the loss of her husband. However, it was proof of Washington's surprising tolerance in an age when most women stayed in the kitchen.

🔔 🔔 🔔

Dusk brought an oblique shadow over the land. It had been a hot July day, and Rachel had spent most of it caring for Little Dan Bradford. Jeanne had been weak from her long ordeal, and Rachel had taken over caring for the infant. She considered it a joy to help out. Dake hovered over his newborn son almost constantly until finally Rachel said with exasperation, "Dake, go do something! You're driving me crazy!"

Now the heat of the day was mitigated, and Rachel stepped out of the side door and moved along the flower beds. The musky smell of raw earth came to her, for Dake was digging a new flower bed. Now the aroma of the roses was in the air and Rachel bent over and took a deep breath, inhaling the sweet fragrance. Straightening up, she suddenly narrowed her eyes. She saw a tall figure mounted on a horse coming down the street in the falling darkness. She could not recognize the man, but she soon recognized the horse. It was the very one her father had sent to Micah. She took a sharp breath, for the man astride the mare was Jacob Steiner.

Quickly moving forward, by the time Jacob had stepped off his horse, Rachel was at his side. "Jacob, it's you!"

Jacob grinned and tied the reins to the hitching post. "Yes. It's me." He turned to her and stepped closer. "I was rewarded by the baron. He said I deserved a leave."

"Are you all right? You didn't get hurt in the battle?"

"Not a scratch. Joel's all right, too, and Micah and Clive."

Rachel noted a stiffness in Jacob that was unusual. His awkwardness was apparent and this caused Rachel to feel uneasy. "Well, come into the house," she said. "Are you hungry?"

"A little. I haven't eaten since this morning. I rode straight through. This mare is a wonder."

The two of them went into the house, where Dake suddenly appeared. He came forward at once and put out his hand. "I'm glad to see you, Jacob," he said. "We heard from Micah all about what you did in the battle."

"Wasn't as dramatic as he probably made it seem." It still embarrassed Jacob somewhat to talk about his part in the battle, but he felt warm when he saw the approval in Dake's eyes.

"Come up and see my son," Dake commanded, and grabbing Jacob by the arm, he practically hauled him upstairs.

Rachel followed and soon Jacob was admiring the beauties of the latest member of the Bradford family. He picked up the baby with such practiced ease that Rachel exclaimed, "You've held babies before!"

"I certainly have. I helped raise my sisters. This is one fine boy! Mr. and Mrs. Bradford, you are to be congratulated."

Rachel said, "I'll go down and set another place at the table." She found Keturah downstairs and told her, "Jacob is back."

"Oh, did Micah come with him?"

"No. He's all alone. We'll have to stretch the meat a little bit, or perhaps we'll have to put on another chop or two."

The two women busied themselves, and in a short time the two men came downstairs. Sam was not with them, being off with Jubal on a voyage along the coast. When they sat down, Dake said, "I guess we've all got a lot to be thankful for. Jacob, why don't you ask the blessing."

Jacob stared at him, for he had never prayed in public since he had become a Christian. He looked around the table and said, "All I've ever prayed are formal prayers out loud, but I will do my best." He bowed his head and said, "I thank you, Lord God, for this food. I thank you for the baby, and for the safety of the mother. I thank you for this house, for this family. I thank you for my Savior, Jesus Christ. Amen."

Somehow the simple blessing touched everyone at the table. Keturah shot a quick glance at Rachel and saw that her face was glowing. All throughout the meal, Keturah noticed that although Rachel said little and the men did most of the talking, there was a happiness in Rachel. She noticed also that there was a stiffness in Jacob when he spoke to Rachel. *What's the matter with him? She's the one he ought to be the gladdest to see*, she thought.

Rachel also was confused about Jacob's behavior. The talk was mostly of the future of the revolution, and afterward, Jacob rose and said, "I will be leaving now."

"Why, you can stay here with us," Dake said. "We have plenty of room." A flush came to Jacob Steiner's face, and he did not look at

Rachel. "Thank you, Dake. I have made other arrangements. I have a room in the Red Lion Inn. Thank you very much for the meal." He spoke a brief good-bye, then left the house hurriedly.

"Well, he sure was in a hurry to leave," Dake murmured. "I thought he'd stay. Does he often behave like that, Rachel?"

"I . . . don't know, Dake," Rachel said faintly. She rose and began to help Keturah clear the table. Somehow the evening had been spoiled for her. She had been anticipating a wonderful time visiting with Jacob, and now it seemed that he was stiff and unyielding. She went to bed that night unhappy and not knowing how to take the man's behavior.

🔔   🔔   🔔

The next day Rachel rose, determined to put Jacob out of her mind, which proved to be difficult. She said, "Keturah, I need to go to Father's house. Will you see to the baby and Jeanne?"

"Yes, of course. I'll take care of them."

Rachel left the house at once, and when she got to her father's house, she was greeted warmly by Daniel, who said, "How's that thumping grandson of mine?"

"Fine. Healthy and eating like a pig."

Daniel beamed with satisfaction and said, "I'll be in the study if you need me. I'm trying to get some work done here instead of down at the office. Too much going on there."

"All right, Father." Rachel left and found Marian feeling somewhat poorly. She said at once, "Phoebe and I can take care of Enoch. Why don't you lie down and rest?"

"I believe I will for an hour or so, if you don't mind."

"Why, this young man and I get along famously, don't we, Enoch?"

This was true enough, for Enoch was a happy baby. All morning long Rachel cared for him, and after she and Phoebe fixed lunch for her father and took Marian a tray, she put Enoch down and he went to sleep at once.

The afternoon went slowly. She could think of nothing but Jacob. She kept to herself, going for a long walk and visiting with old Mrs. Patterson, an elderly invalid living next door. Finally as the shadows began to grow long, she made her way back to the house. She found her father still in his study struggling with his books and was about to go upstairs and check on Enoch when a knock sounded at the door. She went at once to answer it. When she opened it, Jacob was standing there. "Why—hello, Jacob."

Jacob seemed ill at ease and without preamble said, "Is your father at home?"

"Yes. He's in his study."

"I need to speak to him." Jacob's words were clipped and short, and he seemed to be laboring under some sort of difficulty. He said no more but stood there waiting.

"Yes. I'm sure he'll want to see you." Rachel led him down the hall, opened the door, and said, "Father, Jacob is here."

"Why, come in, Jacob." Daniel closed the book and rose.

Rachel, feeling unwanted, shut the door behind her. "He could have been a little bit more polite," she muttered, very upset. Nervously she paced the floor.

Finally after ten minutes the door opened and her father said, "Rachel, will you come in, please."

Moving into the study, she saw Jacob standing as straight as a ramrod, the tension evident on his face. Rachel could not imagine what was going on, so she turned to face her father. An odd expression was on Daniel Bradford's face. Rachel could not interpret it. He stood silently for a moment and then said, "Rachel, Lieutenant Steiner has asked my permission to come calling on you."

Of all things that Rachel had expected, this was not one of them. She turned to face Jacob and studied his features. His moods had become very familiar to her, and she saw now that there was something very close to fear in him. He was not a man to be afraid, and she suddenly understood how it was. He was a foreigner without a penny except his army pay, and he had come to Daniel Bradford, who in his estimate was a wealthy man. *He's afraid of being rejected*, Rachel thought. She knew that in Jacob's country young men must obtain permission of the father, and this is what Jacob Steiner had done. "Why, certainly. I'd be happy to have you call on me."

Daniel watched the two carefully, but they had no eyes for him. *This isn't the end of this*, he thought. Then he said gently, "Why don't you two go out and take a walk?"

"Yes. I would like that," Jacob said quickly. "Would you accompany me, Miss Rachel?"

Rachel nodded and the two left the house. The darkness was falling and the heat of the day was passing away. "I'm glad it's gotten cooler," Rachel said.

"Yes. It's been very hot."

They talked inanely about the weather, walked to the end of the street, and then came back. Rachel was almost desperate. "Would you like to see the roses?" she said.

"Yes. I would like that very much." Jacob followed her to the rose garden, and she pointed out the prize roses. Finally a silence fell on them. Rachel said quietly, "It's been a long time since I found you wounded in the barn. It seems like years ago."

"I've never forgotten those days," Jacob said in a soft voice. "I never shall forget them." He moved closer and suddenly reached out and took her in his arms. Staring in her face, he found a beauty in it and was unable to find a name for the thing he saw in her. She had a sensitive and serious side, and yet there was humor in her. Her eyes mirrored a wisdom he had always admired. She was beautiful in his sight and possessed some sort of mystery with a curtain of reserve, and yet he knew that she could bring a teasing air about her. She was a complex woman, and yet he loved this girl who had such vitality and imagination. There was fire in her that made her lovely, and yet there was nothing of selfishness. "It has taken me a long time to bring myself here and talk to your father."

"It shouldn't be so difficult, Jacob," Rachel said softly.

"But I am a foreigner. I am a Jew, although a converted one, I hope. I have nothing to offer you."

"Are you asking me to marry you, Jacob?"

The abrupt question seemed to strike against Jacob Steiner. He reached out then, pulled her close, and she came to him willingly. As his lips touched hers, her heart filled with a love she had never dared dream of.

Finally he drew back and whispered, "You're a lovely woman, Rachel Bradford." He held her quietly and then suddenly stepped back but still held her hands in his. "Rachel, I am not asking you to marry me—life is too uncertain."

Rachel knew he was thinking of the battles of the war. He had seen too many men die to trust himself, and she respected him for his thoughtfulness.

"The war will be over one day."

He smiled, pulled her hands up, and kissed them. "Someday, when all this danger is over, I will return and ask for your hand in marriage."

Rachel smiled and said, "And if you do, I may say yes."

The two stood there for a moment, then suddenly joy and that spirit of playfulness that often came to Rachel swept over her. "I've lost both of my eligible suitors."

"So I have heard."

"Every young woman," she said lightly, "ought to have at least one. Come now. Let's see how romantic you can be."

He looked at her and then said, "Wait right here." He left and went to where his horse was tied and was soon back with his violin. "I have a song to play for you." He put his violin under his chin and played very softly, as softly as birds early in the morning, and yet there was a poignant sound that brought Rachel's heart up in her throat. When he had finished, he said, "That's called 'Jacob's Love Song.'"

"Oh, Jacob, it's beautiful!" She put her arms around him, kissed him, and said, "Play it again, Jacob!"

Caesar had been listening to all this. He had been working around the corner and his hearing was very good. His long-legged black-and-tan hound had come to nuzzle at him and started to whine. Caesar leaned over and put his massive hand around the muzzle of the dog. He lifted one ear and whispered into it, "Shush, dog! They is love goin' on, and I smells a weddin' in the air!"